OBLIVION

DON'T MISS THESE OTHER THRILLING STORIES IN THE WORLDS OF

HALO

Halo: Renegades
Kelly Gay

Halo: Silent Storm
Troy Denning

Halo: Bad Blood
Matt Forbeck

Halo: Legacy of Onyx
Matt Forbeck

Halo: Retribution
Troy Denning

Halo: Envoy
Tobias S. Buckell

Halo: Smoke and Shadow
Kelly Gay

*Halo: Fractures: Extraordinary Tales
from the Halo Canon* (anthology)

Halo: Shadow of Intent
Joseph Staten

Halo: Last Light
Troy Denning

Halo: Saint's Testimony
Frank O'Connor

Halo: Hunters in the Dark
Peter David

Halo: New Blood
Matt Forbeck

Halo: Broken Circle
John Shirley

THE KILO-FIVE TRILOGY
Karen Traviss

Halo: Glasslands

Halo: The Thursday War

Halo: Mortal Dictata

THE FORERUNNER SAGA
Greg Bear

Halo: Cryptum

Halo: Primordium

Halo: Silentium

*Halo: Evolutions: Essential Tales of
the Halo Universe* (anthology)

Halo: The Cole Protocol
Tobias S. Buckell

Halo: Contact Harvest
Joseph Staten

Halo: Ghosts of Onyx
Eric Nylund

Halo: First Strike
Eric Nylund

Halo: The Flood
William C. Dietz

Halo: The Fall of Reach
Eric Nylund

HALO

OBLIVION

TROY DENNING

BASED ON THE BESTSELLING VIDEO GAME FOR XBOX®

GALLERY BOOKS

New York | London | Toronto | Sydney | New Delhi

Gallery Books
An Imprint of Simon & Schuster, LLC
1230 Avenue of the Americas
New York, NY 10020

First Gallery Books trade paperback edition April 2020

GALLERY BOOKS and colophon are registered trademarks of
Simon & Schuster, LLC

For information about special discounts for bulk purchases,
please contact Simon & Schuster Special Sales at 1-866-506-1949
or business@simonandschuster.com.

The Simon & Schuster Speakers Bureau can bring authors
to your live event. For more information or to book an event,
contact the Simon & Schuster Speakers Bureau at 1-866-248-3049
or visit our website at www.simonspeakers.com.

Manufactured in the United States of America

10   9   8   7

Library of Congress Cataloging-in-Publication Data is available.

ISBN 978-1-9821-1476-3
ISBN 978-1-9821-4203-2 (pbk)
ISBN 978-1-9821-1477-0 (ebook)

HISTORIAN'S NOTE

On April 15, 2526, more than a year after the loss of the planet Harvest to the Covenant during first contact, humanity struck back with Operation: SILENT STORM. Invading enemy space for the first time, a combined force of Spartans and ODST Space Assault Troopers attacked a supply world on the outer fringes of the hegemony, leveling two alien cities, eliminating an orbital shipyard, and decimating an enemy fleet. Now, just six weeks later, the Covenant is bringing its full might to bear. Human colonies are falling two and three a week, and new invasion routes are opening faster than the Office of Naval Intelligence can identify them. Like all of the Spartans, Blue Team is rushing from one disaster to another, desperately attempting to stem a brutal tide of violence that even the United Nations Space Command's top brass is beginning to believe cannot be stopped. . . .

OBLIVION

CHAPTER 1

The Covenant armor emerged from the cloud-draped jungle on the opposite rim of the gorge, an unending line of sleek forms gliding up the muddy road on cushions of nothingness. Still five kilometers distant, the gun carriages appeared the size of fingertips, with a pair of tiny plasma cannons sitting atop smooth, sagittate hulls so purple they nearly vanished into the surrounding gloom. Interspersed among the gun carriages were more than a hundred armored personnel carriers and the articulated cylinders of three CBVs—combat bridging vehicles—enveloped in the faint shimmer of heavy-duty energy shielding.

A CBV could launch a telescoping span across a kilometer-wide chasm in less than a minute, so blowing the Nasim Bridge was not going to stop the enemy advance. The aliens would still cross the

Samalat Gorge in force, and the Fifth Ghost Battalion would have to stop a hundred armored vehicles with little more than hand grenades and shoulder-fired rockets.

Impossible.

The Fifth Ghost Battalion was down to quarter strength, just two-hundred-and-eighty soldiers. They were low on food, medicine, and ammunition, and they had come straight from a two-day battle, marching thirty hours nonstop because they were the Militia of Mesra's sole remaining battalion and *someone* had to delay the enemy advance. The UNSC's 24th Marine Engineering Brigade needed time to demolish a huge xenotime mine in the next valley—not just collapse the underground workings, but pack the passages with enough nukes to render the ore body utterly useless.

The only thing John-117 knew about xenotime was that it yielded ytterbium and erbium, lanthanide elements essential to the manufacture of ultra-efficient lasers and small-scale fusion reactors. Apparently, *that* made denying it to the Covenant important enough to risk Blue Team in support of a simple delaying action.

But Mesra also had huge deposits of other lanthanide ores—many associated with ancient cave systems that had formed millennia before humans arrived—and it happened to be one of the few worlds that had been spared planetary plasma bombardment when the Covenant attacked. From that, the intelligence analysts of Battle Group X-Ray had inferred that the aliens wanted to capture Mesra's mining facilities intact, and Admiral Preston Cole had asked the Militia of Mesra to forgo evacuation in support of UNSC denial efforts. To a soldier, the Mesranis had responded by vowing not to leave their home until they had killed every alien who set foot on it.

Even by Spartan standards, the oath was over the top, but the Mesranis were doing their best to make good on their word. During eight days of pitched battle, they had sacrificed brigade after brigade to prevent the Covenant from capturing *any* mine intact. Now the Militia of Mesra was down to a single understrength battalion protecting the planet's most remote mine—and John was glad he and Blue Team had arrived in time to help.

Especially when the Mesranis were making their last stand just to buy a little time for the rest of humanity.

John eased back from the cliff edge, down behind the rocky crest that overlooked the gorge. Most of the Mesranis lay on the reverse slope, trying to catch an hour of sleep in hastily dug belly scrapes. The rest of Blue Team—Fred-104, Kelly-087, and Linda-058—were humping equipment in from the makeshift landing zone on a tailings dam, and they were probably ascending the back side of the slope by now.

At least, he *hoped* they were. This battle was going to start sooner than expected, and they still had a lot of digging to do. He descended the slope a dozen meters so he wouldn't disturb the sleeping Mesranis, then crab-walked across the mist-swaddled slope toward the Fifth Battalion command post.

The tangled undergrowth in this part of the jungle was blanketed by a buildup of gossamer web so deep and thick it was impossible to see the terrain beneath. The stuff wasn't strong enough to impede movement, but it *did* conceal a lot of sunken ground and fallen logs—tripping hazards that could turn a solid tactical plan into a disaster. He would have to keep that in mind.

He reached the command post, an open-topped bunker dug into the reverse slope. An arm-length arachnid crouched atop the dirt wall opposite him, lurking in the gossamer ground web and keeping watch on the soldiers in the pit below. With pincers the size of combat knives and eight dorsal eyes set above eight furry legs, the creature looked more dangerous than it was. As long as no one stuck an unarmored hand or boot into a hatching crèche, the arachnids were supposed to be pretty harmless, and the Mesranis usually tried to leave the things undisturbed.

In the bottom of the bunker, a dozen Mesrani aides were working comm sets and adjusting tactical arrays. Four officers stood at a portable field table with slumped shoulders and uneven balance, studying a bank of video displays linked to remote observation cameras. As combat-control technology went, the system was primitive and cumbersome, but it had the advantage of not requiring a satellite feed or drone link—a major benefit in an environment where the enemy dominated both air and orbit.

John picked an open spot, then jumped down into the bunker. Most everyone glanced in his direction—when a Spartan in four-hundred-and-fifty kilograms of Mjolnir power armor dropped two meters into a two-meter-deep hole, even soldiers asleep on their feet felt him land—then turned their attention back to their tasks. But the commanding major, a slender woman in a full helmet and muddy jungle-pattern uniform, allowed her gaze to linger.

"You are the support I was promised?"

"Yes, ma'am." Through the major's transparent eye shield, John could see a narrow nose, high cheeks, and black brows over eyes sunken with exhaustion. She had a wide mouth with thin lips savaged by chewing and dehydration. He raised his hand in salute. "Master Chief John-117, at your service."

She touched her fingertips to her helmet in a gesture that seemed more greeting than salute. "Your surname is a number, one hundred seventeen?"

"Ma'am, it'll be simpler if you call me John or Master Chief." He was not at liberty to explain the designation protocols used in the top-secret SPARTAN-II super-soldier program, so he tried to change the subject by dipping his faceplate toward the long squiggle of unrecognizable characters on the major's name tape. "I apologize, Major. I don't know how to pronounce your name."

"Bah'd de Gaya y Elazia de los Karim." She lowered her hand, and the corners of her eyes wrinkled in amusement. "It will be simpler if you call me Bah'd."

John snapped his hand down. "Yes, ma'am."

"Bah'd."

"Yes, ma'am." John winced as soon as he spoke. He and Blue Team had been fighting alongside the Mesranis for six days, but he still found their egalitarian militia so odd that he had trouble remembering to address the officers by their first names. "Apologies, ma'am I mean, *Bah'd.*"

"Better."

Bah'd looked out the back of the bunker and down the ridge toward the xenotime mine, where the chunky silhouettes of three huge figures were pushing through the mossy undergrowth. They were moving slowly, dragging sledges stacked high with crates of ammunition and explosives, as well as six big M68 Gauss cannons scavenged from destroyed Warthog LRVs. Like John, all three Spartans wore power armor, though the MJOLNIR program was still so new that as part of the COBALT field-testing project, each of their suits bore modifications that made them look like different-colored variations on a theme.

"I had hoped there would be more of you," Bah'd said. "It is going to be close, this battle."

"Not that close," John replied. "We'll stop them."

"With six Gauss cannons?" Bah'd shook her helmet and did not bother to ask about UNSC air support. Between the low cloud ceiling and the Covenant's air superiority, a Sparrowhawk would not have lasted two minutes over the battlefield. "I do not think you have fought many armor columns, John. Your Gauss cannons will fire only a few rounds before they are taken out by those Wraiths."

"Wraith" was the common human nickname for the big gun carriages that dominated the Covenant column. John had counted fifty Wraiths in the column before leaving his observation post. He and Blue Team had destroyed at least twice that number since inserting on Mesra, but he didn't bother to tell Bah'd. She wouldn't have believed him.

"We'll use fire-and-move tactics," John said. "Two bursts, and we're gone. Reposition and repeat."

"On foot?" Bah'd asked. At more than a hundred kilograms apiece, M68s were unwieldy weapons for dismounted combat. "How is that possible?"

"That would take too long to explain." Again, John was dodging. Few people had the necessary security clearance to be briefed on the SPARTAN program. And, even had Bah'd been one of them, the last thing John wanted to do was recount how he and his fellow Blue Team members had been conscripted at age six and put into a top-secret project to develop bioengineered super-soldiers. "But we can do it. Trust me."

Bah'd ran her gaze over his power-armored form again, appraising him from his angular helmet down to his lug-soled sabbatons. John was glad that his face remained hidden behind a gold reflective faceplate. The biological augmentations that he had endured as he entered adolescence had increased his height to more than two meters and his mass to almost a hundred-and-thirty kilograms. But he was still only fifteen years old, with a youthful face that tended to undermine the confidence of seasoned commanders like Bah'd.

Finally Bah'd nodded. "Very well, John. I will trust you." She turned back to her weary officers and motioned him to join them. "It seems I have no choice."

John stepped to her side and waited while she introduced the commanders leading the remnants of the battalion's three companies.

There were two men and a woman, all identified by first name only, all haggard and sunken-eyed from many straight days of combat and movement. None of Bah'd's officers looked older than twenty-three or -four, and only one wore the double bars of a captain on his collar tips. The other two were still lieutenants—a sign they had been reassigned in the field to take the place of a fallen superior.

"As you can see, the enemy approach is cautious." Bah'd pointed to the leftmost video display, where a swarm of chest-high, mask-wearing bipeds were pushing through the mist ahead of a slow-moving armored personnel carrier. The UNSC had nicknamed the short bipeds "Grunts," and they were just one of five different species of Covenant aliens that John had fought so far.

"We assume that the Covenant expect us to hit them several kilometers below the Nasim Bridge," Bah'd continued, "then force them to fight for every meter of ground. And, had we the strength, that is exactly what we would do."

As she spoke, a plume of fire erupted at one corner of the screen, hurling pieces of an unlucky Grunt two meters into the air. Immediately the APC's cannon turret swung around and began to cut through the nearby undergrowth, triggering a half dozen antipersonnel mines and filling the mist with pillars of flame. The Grunts panicked and dived for cover, two of them landing on mines that sent them riding fiery geysers straight back into the air. Then more plasma bolts began to pour in from the left side of the display as several vehicles offscreen opened fire.

"The aliens have reached our first field of antipersonnel mines, five kilometers from the bridge," Bah'd explained. "There are three more small fields between there and the two-kilometer mark, all laid in the undergrowth alongside the road."

"To encourage the Covenant to stay on the road," John surmised. "And then?"

"A kilometer of antivehicle mines," answered the man with the captain's bars—Bah'd had introduced him as Aurello. "Planted under the roadbed and on its far side."

"Why not the near side?" John asked. "Short on mines?"

Aurello's eyes remained blank for nearly five seconds before he finally seemed to realize he had been asked a question.

"We have plenty of mines, thanks to your 24th Marine Engineering Brigade," he said, "but not very much time. If we encourage the aliens to travel close to the gorge, there is hope some vehicles may slip over the side."

"We have learned to seize every advantage we can," Bah'd added. "The last kilometer before the bridge is heavily mined, and there are supplemental explosives alongside the gorge. With luck, the rim will collapse when their combat bridging vehicles attempt to launch their spans."

"Luck works best when you're prepared," John said. It was something that Franklin Mendez, the Spartans' senior drill instructor, had been fond of saying back on Reach. "And you definitely seem prepared."

The corners of Bah'd's eyes wrinkled again, and she and Aurello exchanged glances. John didn't understand what they found so funny, but he didn't take offense. The entire battalion would probably die in the next few hours, so he was glad to brighten their day in any way he could.

John turned to the middle display screen, which showed a relief map of the anticipated battlefield, and asked, "Where do you want us?"

"Perhaps we should tell you what we have planned," Bah'd replied. "Then we will discuss it."

"Discuss it?"

John glanced at the chronometer on the heads-up display inside his helmet. In response, the Mjolnir's onboard computer—linked to his mind via a neural lace implanted at the base of his skull—immediately displayed an ETA for the enemy column. That was how the lace worked, reacting to his thoughts even before they grew conscious. It made John feel like there was a ghost living inside his head. But it was the neural interface that allowed him to manipulate a half ton of power armor as effortlessly as his own body—and to process a raging torrent of tactical data without drowning in irrelevant detail. Without the lace, he would have died a dozen times during the last six weeks alone.

"With all due respect, Bah'd, I'm not sure we have time for discussions. The first Wraiths will reach the Nasim Bridge in"—John checked the ETA on his HUD—"seventy-eight minutes. My team and I have firing lanes to clear and emplacements to dig."

"Then why do you waste time questioning my wishes?" Bah'd's tone switched from sharp to gentle: "This is how we do things in the Militia of Mesra—together."

"Yes, ma'am," John said. "My apologies, ma'am."

Bah'd rolled her eyes at his reflexive deference, then turned to her female lieutenant. "Hiyat, will you share our thinking?"

Hiyat was a tall woman with coffee-colored skin and tired amber eyes that nevertheless sparkled with amusement.

"Yes, ma'am." She shot John a look of contrition—then added, "Of course, ma'am."

Everyone laughed too hard, and John found himself a bit unsettled by their forced humor in the face of certain death. Altered mental states were a symptom of combat fatigue, especially in exhausted soldiers who were using too many stim-packs in an effort to maintain alertness. Still, John forced a scratchy chuckle through his helmet's external voicemitter. It never hurt to be a good sport.

Hiyat took a step back, then traced her finger along a jungle road as it left the Nasim Bridge and ran along the near side of the gorge.

After a kilometer, it made a sharp hairpin swing around the end of Sarpesi Ridge and proceeded back toward the command post before turning off toward the xenotime mine, three kilometers away. Along its entire length, the road was the only level ground on the map.

"As you see," Hiyat said, "the Ytterbium Road runs beneath our position for over two kilometers, from the Nasim Bridge until it turns toward the Doukala Xenotime Works. The road is mined with Lotus antitank charges the entire length."

"So the enemy's progress will be slow, and they'll be exposed to attack the whole time."

John was eyeing the rugged terrain on the back side of Sarpesi Ridge, noting how difficult it would be for the Wraiths to leave the road without plummeting into the sheer-walled valley below. He reached over Hiyat's head and touched the screen where the road snaked along the notch-shaped walls of a precipitous ravine marked the Kharsis Flume.

"Have you thought about adding supplemental explosives above this flume?"

Hiyat craned her neck, her eyes running along John's arm as though she had just realized how tall he was. When her gaze reached his fingertip, her eyes drifted back to his faceplate.

"We have already done so," she said. "And that is why our highest priority will be to eliminate their combat bridging vehicles."

"If we can destroy the CBVs," Aurello explained, "the Wraiths will be forced to stop when we blow the Kharsis Flume. The Covenant will have no choice but to dismount and attack the Doukala on foot. Your Marine Engineering Brigade should be able to hold them off long enough to finish its work."

John didn't ask why it would fall to the engineering brigade to hold off the foot attack. The Samalat Gorge yawned a kilometer wide at the Nasim Bridge. That was more than twice the effective range of the battalion's man-portable rocket launchers, so the Mesranis would have to engage on *this* side of the gorge. At such close ranges—less than two hundred meters in most places—the battle would be brisk and bloody. Even if the plan worked perfectly, there wouldn't be any Ghosts *left* by the time the Covenant dismounted.

John turned to Bah'd. "What if Blue Team could stop the CBVs on the far side of the gorge?"

"*Can* you?"

"Our M68 Gauss cannons have an effective range of eight kilometers," John said. "The gorge is a fraction of that. Our problem will be the enemy's air superiority."

"That we can help with," Hiyat said. She touched her fingers to the screen, then made a pinching motion. The map scale contracted to include the mountainous terrain surrounding both ends of the Nasim Bridge. "Our battalion has placed twelve antiaircraft batteries on these mountains, just below the cloud ceiling. Our missiles will be striking from *above* the enemy's ground-attack craft."

"Nice." The missile batteries wouldn't take out all of the Covenant attack craft, of course. But given the mountainous terrain and low clouds, the unusual attack angle would be a real distraction for enemy pilots—and *that* would be enough advantage for Blue Team to succeed. "Blue Team can take out the CBVs before they cross the gorge."

"You are certain?" Bah'd asked.

"As certain as I *can* be in a situation like this." John was beginning to think the Ghosts might not need to live up to their name. If their provisions for blowing the Nasim Bridge were as thorough as the rest of their preparations, the battalion could probably buy the 24th Engineering Brigade enough time to destroy the Doukala mine and *still* survive to evacuate. He touched a finger to the screen again. "When the Covenant reaches the far bridgehead, they'll start by having a platoon of Drones fly underneath the decking to disarm your demolition charges."

The Drones were another type of alien in the enemy ranks, an insectile species with wings. Most Covenant brigades included a light company of a hundred Drones to serve as scouts.

"We have decoys," Bah'd said. "And tamper traps. The bridge will blow when we are ready for it."

"Good," John said. "Then you should wait until the first Wraiths are almost across. If the column is under way when the bridge blows, the disarray will buy us some extra targeting time."

The third commander, the lieutenant who had not yet spoken, stepped forward. John couldn't recall the lieutenant's name, so the Mjolnir's onboard computer displayed JAKOME on the HUD.

"I do not understand, John." Jakome was a square-faced man with sunken eyes and a broad nose. "If we destroy the bridge so early, and you eliminate the combat bridging vehicles before they deploy, how will we attack the rest of the column?"

"We won't need to," John said. Clearly, Jakome's thought process had been slowed by sleep deprivation. "The column will be stranded on the far side of the gorge, and the Doukala mine will be safe."

"But the aliens will be out of range," Jakome said.

"And the Doukala mine will be safe," John repeated. "By the time the enemy can organize another attack, the 24th will have turned the entire mine into radioactive slag."

"So you hope," Aurello said. "But if we give the aliens time to think, they will find another way to seize the mine."

"There *is* no other way," John said. "With the bridge out, they would have to launch a large-scale air assault. Even the Covenant can't mount that kind of operation on short notice—not through heavy cloud cover into jungle mountains."

"You have no idea what the Covenant can do," Aurello said. "If the last six weeks have taught the UNSC anything, surely it has taught you *that*."

Aurello was more right than he knew. Seven weeks earlier, John and three teams of Spartans had joined the 21st ODST Space Assault Battalion on Operation: SILENT STORM, a top-secret, high-risk raid into Covenant space. Their objective had been to hit the aliens hard and buy time for humanity to develop countermeasures against Covenant technology. The operation had destroyed two enemy cities, an orbital fleet-support ring, and eight capital ships.

Even so, success hadn't changed much of anything. Less than two weeks later, the Covenant had returned with more fleets than the UNSC could track, and Blue Team found itself deploying to Circinius IV to rescue the surviving cadets of the Corbulo Academy of Military Science. John managed to get three of the students off the planet alive, and even that was doing well in comparison to how the fight was going elsewhere. The invasion became an onslaught. Every day, the alien enemy destroyed another human outpost, and another UNSC convoy vanished without a trace. Worlds fell two and three a week, and new incursion routes opened faster than the Office of Naval Intelligence could identify them. Unable to consolidate battlefield intelligence before it became inactionable, FLEETCOM had stopped trying to coordinate core strategy and granted operational autonomy to each battle group. It was a bad way to run a war, but it was the best humanity could do.

While it lasted.

After a moment, John said, "We may not know all of the enemy's capabilities, but we *do* know basic field tactics—and the most basic tactic of all is 'don't waste your soldiers.'"

"Which is what will happen if we give the aliens time to regroup." Aurello glanced at Jakome and Hiyat, who both nodded vigorously, then said, "We must keep the pressure on, and take our vengeance now. Here."

"Vengeance?" John had to be missing something. The Mesranis were disciplined soldiers, and disciplined soldiers did not launch suicide attacks out of spite. "What does vengeance have to do with anything?"

"The Nasim Bridge is a chokepoint," Jakome said. "And the Ytterbium Road is a gauntlet. Our rockets will fall on their heads like rain."

"Like . . . rain." John repeated. He knew from his combat psychology training back on Reach that too much combat stress could sometimes result in mindless, murderous rages. But such episodes were heat-of-the-moment events that erupted without warning—not carefully prepared actions like the commanders were suggesting now. He turned to Bah'd. "What kind of combat stimulants are you using?"

"Stimulants?" Bah'd narrowed her eyes. "Be careful what you imply, John."

"Major, I never imply." John was puzzled by Bah'd's testy reaction. Stim-packs were standard issue for UNSC special operations troops—who often had to fight for days at a time without sleep—but they were easy to overuse in the heat of a long battle. "Your commanders are focus-locked on a pointless goal. That's a classic sign of stim-pack overload."

Bah'd's voice turned icy. "The Mesrani do not use stim-packs, John."

"You don't?" John glanced at the company commanders, not sure he believed her. After more than three days of combat and hard marching with no sleep, it seemed impossible they could still be even this functional without help. "You're sure?"

"*Very* sure, John." Bah'd's resentment certainly sounded sincere. "We would never debase ourselves with such poison."

John saw the eyes of her subordinates harden with indignation. But if they didn't use stim-packs, there was even more reason to worry. The human brain needed sleep to flush out the toxins that accumulated during periods of wakeful activity, and John knew that going even twenty-four hours without rest could lead to concentration and memory problems. After forty-eight hours, the brain started to shut down for microsleeps, which lasted anywhere from half a second to half a minute—all followed by short periods of confusion and disorientation that could prove disastrous in a combat situation. By seventy-two hours, the brain's toxin load grew so acute that severe lapses in concentration, motivation, and memory were inevitable—and hallucinatory episodes were common.

The only way to counteract the effects of sleep deprivation was to temporarily increase the signal-carrying capacity of the brain's synapses. That was how stim-packs worked—and why they were sometimes necessary in combat. If there were natural methods for accomplishing the same thing, John had never heard of them.

After a moment, he said, "My apologies—I didn't mean to offend anyone. The UNSC has a more, uh, pragmatic view of battlefield enhancements."

"Which is but one of the reasons the Children of Mesra were forced to seek a world of their own." Bah'd turned to her subordinate commanders. "And why we *will* have vengeance on the aliens who have come to take it from us."

"Just not *here*." John's tone was firm, but technically he was making a request. Bah'd and the others not only outranked him, they were part of a different army that didn't even report to the same chain of command. "We need to keep our eye on the objective. The enemy is a far superior force, and it doesn't make sense to give them a free shot at the Doukala mine."

Bah'd remained silent for so long that John thought she had fallen into an open-eyed sleep; then she finally said, "We share the same objective, John—deny Mesra's xenotime to the Covenant. But the Mesranis have another objective too—kill the aliens who invaded our world."

"You'll kill a lot more of them by fighting smart," John said. "Your battalion could evacuate with the 24th, get some rest, and take on the Covenant on a hundred other worlds."

"*If* everything goes right . . . and the enemy remains trapped on the far side of the gorge."

Bah'd looked back to the leftmost display screen, which showed the enemy armor column as it continued to advance toward the Nasim Bridge. The Covenant commander had adjusted his marching order to deal with the minefields, and now the column was being led by single-seat RAVs—rapid assault vehicles that looked like motorcycles with front wings and no wheels. Squads of Drone scouts were flying alongside the column, passing safely over the mined undergrowth on small flickering wings that seemed barely large enough to keep their multisegmented bodies aloft. John's HUD showed sixty-seven minutes before the enemy column reached the far bridgehead.

Without turning from the screen, Bah'd asked, "Tell me, John-117, how many battles have you seen?"

"More than a few." The number was classified, of course, but John needed Bah'd to understand that when he made a recommendation, he was speaking with the voice of experience. "Way more than a few, actually. I can't even tell you the number."

"So, more than my five." Bah'd continued to watch the display screen. "And in how many of *your* battles did everything go as planned?"

"Not a one," John admitted. "Usually we were happy if the first three minutes went as planned."

Bah'd nodded. "That has been my experience too." She turned to face her subordinates. "So here is what I suggest."

The exhausted commanders drew themselves up straight, the way soldiers everywhere did when receiving orders, and John realized the discussion phase of their meeting was at an end.

"I would like John and his team to open fire on the first combat bridging vehicle as soon as their Gauss cannons have a good chance of destroying it. That will force the aliens to rush forward in order to seize the Nasim Bridge."

Hiyat raised her brow, and Aurello and Jakome just looked confused. Maybe it was the lack of sleep, because John realized what was coming next . . . and he didn't like it.

"You're going to set an ambush on the far side of the gorge?" he asked. "And blow the bridge *before* the enemy crosses?"

"Exactly," Bah'd said. "That is the *last* place the Covenant will expect us. They will be trapped in the minefield, with no advance possible and with our rockets pounding their turrets."

Aurello and Jakome broke into broad grins, and Hiyat began to nod enthusiastically. Even John had to admit that her solution gave everyone what they wanted. The Mesranis would keep the pressure on and kill a lot of alien invaders, and the Covenant would have almost no chance of capturing the Doukala mine. The only part John didn't like was the part where two-hundred-and-eighty good soldiers died in a suicide attack—even if they *had* named themselves the Ghost Battalion.

"It will work," John said. "But you're putting yourselves in the trap with the enemy, and there's no need for it—not if you destroy the bridge from this side of the gorge."

"You worry for us, John?" Bah'd's eyes wrinkled at the corners again. "How kind."

Bah'd turned back to the display screens, where geysers of flame and dirt were engulfing the single-seat RAVs as they led the alien column into a minefield, and fell silent. Her stooped shoulders and tucked chin suggested she had slipped into another microsleep. In a UNSC unit, that kind of acute sleep-deprivation would have been reason enough to challenge her judgment, perhaps even temporarily relieve her of command. But John had no authority over anyone in the Mesrani Militia—least of all Bah'd—and he had already come close to alienating her with his stim-pack query. So, he could not risk losing her cooperation—not if he wanted to protect the Doukala mine.

Bah'd's head jerked as she returned to wakefulness.

"I'm not being kind, Bah'd." John was careful to speak softly, knowing that the Mjolnir's voicemitter would add an extra measure of assertiveness to his words. "The Fifth is a good battalion, and it doesn't need to die today."

"Perhaps not." Bah'd's voice dropped to a whisper, and she turned back to John with steel in her eyes. "But the *aliens* do."

CHAPTER 2

The enemy Wraiths advanced through the depleted minefield two abreast, their purple hulls floating on cushions of intangible force as they brushed past the smoking hulks of demolished rapid assault vehicles. They kept their plasma cannons trained on the jungle-covered slope above the road, though that was only because the weapons lacked the range to return fire across the kilometer-wide Samalat Gorge to Sarpesi Ridge. With only a kilometer to the bridgehead, the vehicle commanders would be plenty worried about long-range flank attacks, and they would be ready with half a dozen responses.

John-117 just wished he knew which tactics they would choose: run-and-gun or stand-and-return? Area suppression or radar-assisted counterfire? Independent targeting or coordinated fire? Each tactic created different hazards and opportunities and required unique preparations, and that was one of the most difficult things about fighting the Covenant—they didn't think like humans, so it was hard to anticipate their choices.

John was still looking for hints when a head-size lizard-thing dropped out of the jungle canopy and spread a pair of leathery wings . . . then fanned its tail and landed at the tip of his Gauss cannon. He did not have a proper mount for the weapon, so he and the rest of Blue Team were lying in their belly scrapes, using the dirt piled in front of them as makeshift barrel supports—and now the creature was blocking his view, both naturally and through the aiming reticle in his heads-up display.

But he did not dare shoo it away. Covenant spotters would be searching Sarpesi Ridge for emplacements and firing lanes, and a startled reptile taking flight would draw their eyes straight to his position.

"Blue Leader's line of sight temporarily blocked." John spoke over TEAMCOM, a secure channel available only to his three fellow Spartans on Blue Team. The enemy signals-intelligence unit would probably detect the transmission, but by now Fifth Battalion's own electronic warfare squad was blasting a hundred thousand decoy transmissions per second. The chance that John's message would be decrypted, or even traced to its source, was almost nil. "Keep me posted."

"The first combat bridging vehicle has already entered Blue Four's LOS." Blue Four was Linda-058, who had been placed at the far end of the firing line because she was the best sniper in the entire SPARTAN-II program. "It's shielded by four Wraiths."

They had expected this. That was why Blue Team had taken positions an extra half-kilometer away, high atop Sarpesi Ridge where they would be able to fire over the large Wraiths and hit the

CBVs from above. Still, the tactic made John nervous. The targeting software in their Mjolnir would calculate trajectory and adjust the minute-of-angle in their HUD sights to reflect Mesra's dense atmosphere and above-normal gravity. But even with an onboard computer doing the math, down-angle shots at long range were tricky, and if their first shots missed, there would be no time to recalculate.

After a moment, John asked, "Can we still get the angle?"

"Affirmative," Linda said.

"Good," John said. The lizard-thing was still perched on the end of his Gauss cannon, its neck frills half-flared as it stared up the camouflaged barrel toward him. His helmet and armor were swaddled in the same gossamer filament that covered the jungle floor, but the faceplate remained exposed. He suspected the creature was mesmerized by its own reflection. "Everyone else check off as the target enters your LOS."

"Blue Two, target acquired," said Fred-104, John's dry witted second-in-command. "Last chance for the Mesranis to wise up and fall back."

"Not going to happen," John said.

Despite his protests, Bah'd had slipped most of the battalion across the gorge while the Covenant armor was still kilometers away. The Mesranis had done a good job of hiding their redeployment by concealing their movement behind the bridge's side barriers and waiting for land mine detonations, which left the enemy column temporarily blinded by smoke. But Fifth Battalion was going to be trapped on the far side of the gorge whether or not Blue Team destroyed the CBVs, and the knowledge that so many Mesranis were going to perish in a pointless battle troubled all four of the Spartans.

"You are sure?" Linda asked.

"I'm sure," John said. "Their commanders are afraid this plan will backfire if they don't keep the pressure on."

"And you bought that?" asked Kelly-087, who was rarely slow to speak her mind. "They're just crazy to kill aliens."

"That too," John said. "Especially the crazy part."

He had gone along with Bah'd's plan because it protected the xenotime mine while assuring the cooperation of her subordinates, and that had been the safe play. He could have insisted on his own plan, arguing that Bah'd and her commanders were too sleep-deprived to make sound tactical decisions. And maybe he should have. But that would have meant risking Fifth Battalion's cooperation and endangering the mission, and the mission came first.

The mission *always* came first.

"Blue Three, target acquired," Kelly announced.

"Acknowledged."

Still perched on the end of John's Gauss cannon, the lizard-thing hissed at its own reflection and continued to block his line of sight. John was about the same distance from Kelly as she was from Fred, and it had taken less than ten seconds for the target to enter Kelly's LOS after it had been acquired by Fred. It would not be long before Blue Team was ready to open fire.

The thought had barely formed before the Mjolnir's onboard computer initiated a six-second countdown on his HUD display. At three seconds, John activated his voicemitter.

"Move it, bud."

The creature spread its wings as though to take flight—then opened its beak and charged up the two-meter cannon barrel. With the targeting relay no longer obscured, the aiming reticle turned red, and John knew he had *something* in the M68's sights. He just didn't know what because the lizard-thing now blocked even more of his view. He raised his bracing hand to bat it aside—and saw a yellow gob shooting from its gullet.

John turned his head, taking the hit on the side of his helmet, and ribbons of mucus sprayed across the left half of his faceplate. The creature clunked against his helmet and began to peck and scratch; then he had it in his grasp.

He crushed it one-handed—not out of malice, but because he couldn't risk it taking flight and drawing attention to his location— then dropped its body beside him and took a swipe at his faceplate. No luck. With the left side of his faceplate smeared yellow, he had to turn his helmet to get a clear view of the enemy column. His aiming reticle was set on a Wraith, which was floating along beside the bulbous operators' cabin at the front of the combat bridging vehicle. Behind the first Wraith followed three more, in close formation and doing their best to screen the articulated cylinders that contained the CBV's bridging equipment.

Nice try.

John increased his faceplate image magnification. The beaklike snouts of four Jackals—a tall, vaguely avian species that the Spartans had tangled with before— grew visible inside the operators' cabin. He raised the nose of his Gauss cannon, resting the aiming reticle at the forward edge of the bubble-shaped observation canopy.

"Blue Leader, target acquired," John said. "Initiate."

Three status lights winked green inside John's HUD; then Linda said, "Blue Four engaging."

The CBV's energy shield shimmered violently as Linda's first burst hit home. Kelly added her fire to Linda's, and the shielding dissolved in a spray of overload sparks.

By then the Wraiths were slowing to a halt and swinging their noses toward Sarpesi Ridge. Their only weapons capable of returning fire across the kilometer-wide Samalat Gorge were their plasma mortars, and those were mounted on fixed bases that required the vehicle to face its target.

Linda and Kelly each hit the CBV with a second burst, riddling the operators' cabin with star-shaped holes and coating the remnants of the shattered canopy in Jackal blood.

A volley of white mortar shells arced away from the four Wraiths closest to the CBV. Too slow. Kelly and Linda were running for their next position before the rounds reached their zenith. John and Fred opened fire, each targeting the operators' cabin. Flames and smoke started to billow out through the shattered canopy, so they ran their second bursts down the cargo cylinder.

The bridging vehicle veered sharply toward the gorge, but John had no intention of hanging around to see what happened. Scooping up the Gauss cannon in both arms, he launched himself from his scrape like a sprinter out of the blocks. There was no anti-infantry attack quite as horrifying as a plasma strike, which unleashed such a searing blast that anything inside the impact zone was flash-incinerated, while anything nearby by was merely knocked down and immolated. John had seen direct hits reduce concrete bunkers to swirling clouds of white-hot dust and near-misses leave men standing on smoking pegs of charred bone.

He angled across the slope toward his next position. With the lizard mucus obscuring half his faceplate, he had a choice: watch how the Covenant was responding to his attack, or turn his faceplate away from the enemy and focus on where he was running.

He chose running.

He had taken barely five steps when the jungle went white with plasma flash. A concussion wave hit him from behind, and the temperature spiked inside his Mjolnir. He kept his feet and continued to run, bouncing off the rubbery stalk of a giant sponge tree he barely glimpsed. He spun and kept going, knees pumping high to avoid tripping over deadfalls, eyes locked on the HUD waypoint directing him to his next scrape.

All three status lights in his HUD showed yellow. The rest of the team was still on the move, racing for their next positions. Had any-one been pinned down or KIA, their light would have shown red.

John switched to the Fifth Battalion comm channel. "First bridg-ing vehicle down; disabled but destruction uncertain."

"I can confirm destruction." Bah'd sounded troubled. "It went into the gorge—pushing two Wraiths ahead of it."

"And that's not a good thing?"

"Of course it is."

He waited for Bah'd to elaborate. The jungle flashed brighter as the alien fire intensified. Sponge trees and giant club mosses began to top-ple under the relentless concussion waves, and Linda's and Kelly's status lights changed to green. John outran the artillery blanket and began to breathe easier—then hit an outcropping obscured by the lizard mucus and nearly dropped the Gauss cannon. Still Bah'd did not speak.

"Major, it's not too late to fall back," John said. The waypoint arrow finally sank to the bottom of his HUD, and he looked down to see the two-meter hollow he had scraped into the slope earlier. "If you're having second thoughts, you still have time—"

"Stop that, John. We are not having second thoughts."

"Then why do you sound worried?" John asked. He dropped to his knees and propped the cannon barrel on the dirt pile he had left to serve as a weapon support. "What's the problem?"

"The same as always," Bah'd said. "The Covenant is not doing what we expected."

John had already cleared a firing lane to the road, so even look-ing out only half his faceplate, he could see that at least five Wraiths had interrupted their advance to launch an artillery strike. That was expected. With Samalat Gorge between the column and the Spar-tans, there was no simply no way the Wraiths could advance and fire simultaneously. When he still didn't see the cause of Bah'd's con-cern, he again tried to wipe the lizard mucus from his faceplate.

He only succeeded in smearing it around some more. He gave up and magnified the image he *could* actually see—and thought he understood the reason for Bah'd's alarm.

Instead of continuing forward as expected to secure the bridgehead—where Fifth Battalion was waiting in ambush—the single-seat assault vehicles had stopped with the Wraiths and were tucking in behind the big gun carriages. And the Grunt foot soldiers in turn were tucking in behind the RAVs, crouching on their knees and covering their heads as though expecting shrapnel to start raining from the sky at any moment.

"Am I seeing what I think I am?" John asked. Blue Team was about five hundred meters down-gorge from Fifth Battalion's position overlooking the Nasim Bridge, observing from deep cover, so he didn't have the kind of situational overview that Bah'd would. "I have Wraiths standing up for an artillery duel."

"Not a duel," Bah'd said. "The entire column has stopped. They are preparing to barrage."

"To barrage?" John echoed. Artillery barrages were more effective at disrupting infantry units than actually destroying them, so they were typically employed to break up an enemy assault or support a friendly one. But with Samalat Gorge in the way, the only infantry assault possible would be airborne—and that was *still* unlikely, given the short notice and low cloud ceiling. "That seems like a stretch."

"We can see dozens of combat support vehicles coming forward," Bah'd said. Combat support vehicles were armored transports capable of carrying anything from personnel to ammunition and explosives to medical supplies—including the liquefied carrier gas used to recharge plasma weapons. "What do *you* think they are hauling?"

"Good point," John said. "Alert your antiaircraft batteries. Have them give priority to transport craft."

"I have done that already." Bah'd hesitated, then said, "But what are we missing, John? You said yourself the Covenant wouldn't launch an airborne assault in these conditions."

"Maybe I was wrong," John said, though he realized as he spoke that he couldn't be. Were the aliens capable of launching a full-scale airborne assault, they would bypass Sarpesi Ridge entirely and drop directly on the Doukala Xenotime Works. "But let's be ready for anything."

The artillery blanket continued to intensify and creep across the jungle slope toward John, flooding the right side of his faceplate with blinding strobe light. The plasma rounds were the least of his concerns. The Mjolnir armor he and his Spartans wore would protect them from anything short of a direct hit. Besides, once the Covenant had flattened the jungle, Blue Team wouldn't have to wait for the bridging vehicles to enter a predetermined firing zone. The four Spartans would be able to look down the entire length of the gorge and attack as soon as the remaining two CBVs came into range.

John switched to TEAMCOM. "Anyone see the next target?"

The status lights inside his HUD all blinked red.

"Then hold all fire," John said. "They must be trying to get us to give our positions away."

"Well, *that*'s a relief." Fred's tone was dry, as it always was when he cracked wise. "I thought they might be trying to kill us."

"Keep making those dreadful jokes, and they won't need to," Kelly replied. "Your sense of humor could drive a lady to violence."

"Let's can the chatter," John said. Normally he didn't mind a little humor—it helped the team relax, and a relaxed team was an efficient team. But for the next few minutes, he needed the channel kept clear for injury reports and combat coordination. "Nobody really wants to die laughing."

"Ha-ha," Linda said, then: *"Incoming!"*

Then a terrible thunder was upon them, shaking the jungle and bursting through the canopy in globules of white-hot plasma. Chunks of scorched fungi caps showered the slope, and streamers of burning moss snaked through the air. Most soldiers were trained to cover their heads and stay flat under artillery bombardment, but Spartans weren't most soldiers.

John kept his head up, cocking it to one side so he could watch for strike patterns through the clear half of his faceplate. Soil and flame jetted skyward in solid curtains, sponge trees and club mosses erupted into pillars of fire, concussion waves pounded his armor like forge hammers, and still the booming grew more ferocious. The ground quaked and the undergrowth vanished in winks of blinding heat-flash, the air growing so thick with smoke and mud it was hard to see the vase-shaped brilliance of fresh impacts. His onboard computer would keep monitoring his visuals, using millisecond-long spikes of light intensity to plot plasma strikes and infer the enemy barrage plan.

Linda's status light changed from green to yellow; then her voice, almost lost to the roar of the barrage, came over TEAMCOM: "Moving!"

John knew her computer had projected a hit on her position and was now guiding her to a safer location. Still, his gut clenched. Plasma rounds incinerated everything within a twenty-meter radius of the strike, with an even larger secondary damage ring. The concussion wave alone increased the mortality risk of a maneuvering infantry soldier tenfold. Linda would be okay in her Mjolnir armor unless she happened to run directly under an incoming strike—but in a barrage this heavy, the chances of that happening were high. Close to fifty percent, according to his onboard computer.

John kept one eye on his HUD, waiting for Linda's status light to return to green. But he was also careful to keep his faceplate turned into the bombardment so his onboard computer could continue monitoring the strike patterns. Sooner or later the plasma mortars would start running low on carrier gas, which meant the crews would need to resupply from the combat support vehicles. When that happened, the intensity of the barrage would diminish, and Blue Team would have a chance to locate its next target.

John glanced back toward the enemy column, but the smoke and debris remained too thick to see whether the combat support vehicles were moving into position behind the Wraiths . . . *behind the Wraiths*, where he had seen the Grunts and rapid assault vehicles taking cover earlier. Was the enemy really going to resupply over its own infantry and RAVs?

John switched back to the Fifth Battalion channel. "Bah'd, are those RAVs still taking cover behind the Wraiths?"

"They are," she said. Even with his helmet speakers set directly next to his ears, the major's voice was barely audible over the constant booming of the barrage. "The Covenant must have worse field intelligence than we do. They seem to believe we have some ability to offer counterbattery fire."

John had no idea what the aliens believed—and it was probably a mistake to guess. "What about those combat support vehicles?" he asked. "Where are they?"

"Pulling onto the far edge of the road, behind the RAVs." Bah'd fell silent. John began to fear the enemy was jamming their comms; then she finally asked, "How are they going to reload the Wraiths from *behind* the RAVs?"

"Good question," John said. Linda's status light returned to green, and he felt his gut untangle. She had reached a new position—presumably one that her onboard computer projected would be safe from a direct hit. "Stand by."

Before Bah'd could acknowledge, Linda's voice came over TEAMCOM. "New position in strike crater, twenty-seven meters from—" The thunderclap of a nearby hit sounded over the channel, and John's heart climbed into his throat until Linda's voice grew audible again. "—have LOS to second bridging vehicle."

"What are you using?" Fred asked. "X-ray vision?"

"Negative." Linda's tone grew sharp. "What is wrong with you? The X-ray sniper scope does not even exist."

"Yet."

"Focus, people," John said. The Spartans' childhood training had inoculated them against the paralyzing effects of heavy bombardment—but no one was totally immune to that much psychological stress. Fred and Linda's banter was just their way of relieving the nerve-grating tension of being shelled. "Under fire, remember?"

"Difficult to forget, Blue Leader." Linda took a breath, then said, "I observed the bridging vehicle as I was changing positions. Visibility is fair at head height."

"Good catch. Everyone, take a look," John said, rising. "Carefully."

Standing in the middle of a plasma barrage was dangerous even for Spartans, but it was worth the risk. If they could bring enough Gauss cannons to bear on the target, the barrage itself would mask their attack and allow Blue Team to destroy a second CBV without giving its position away.

"Linda, share your targeting coordinates."

A waypoint arrow appeared on John's HUD, fluttering around the inside of his half-obscured faceplate as he was buffeted by concussion waves from all sides. But visibility *was* much better at head height. The curtains of flying mud were almost nonexistent, and the smoke had thinned to a gauzy gray haze. Most of the slope below had been defoliated by the alien bombardment, so even through one side of his helmet, he could see all the way down to the Samalat Gorge. But when he looked in the direction of the waypoint, his view remained blocked by a corner of jungle that had not yet been flattened.

"Blue Leader, negative LOS," he reported.

"Blue Two, target acquired," Fred said. "Just the front half, but that's enough."

"Blue Three, negative LOS," Kelly said. "It would take only a small move to correct that."

"Hold position for now." John staggered as another nearby strike nearly knocked him off his feet. "And back into your belly scrapes."

Before dropping into his own scrape, John turned to examine the road on the far rim of the gorge. The line of Wraiths was barely visible through the smoke haze, a ghostly fringe of tiny purple arrowheads lobbing pinpoints of brilliance at Sarpesi Ridge. He increased his magnification and saw that the RAVs were still tucked in behind the Wraiths, and the Grunts were still cowering behind the RAVs.

Fifty combat support vehicles were pulling up on the far side of the road behind the Grunts, floating on air and resembling giant barrel-bodied beetles with bulbous heads. They *had* to be carrying the liquefied carrier gas the Wraiths would soon need to recharge their mortars. But there was no sign of any conveyor apparatus or filler nozzle anywhere on their exteriors, and the only attention the Grunts paid them was to move away.

John didn't know what the enemy commander was thinking, and he didn't like that. While the Covenant had tremendous superiority in fleet and weapons technology, so far their ground troops had proven no match for elite human units like Force Recon or Orbital Drop Shock Troopers. But if they were starting to field leaders capable of anticipating UNSC tactics—and then turning those tactics to the Covenant's advantage—the UNSC was in danger of losing the only edge it *did* have.

Once the support vehicles had come to a stop, the RAV drivers spun their vehicles toward the bridge and began to move off. John thought for a moment—hoped, really—that they might be making way for transfer operations. But when the Grunts simply crowded closer to the Wraiths without making any effort to prepare, he realized he was wishing in vain.

"Bah'd, be ready," John transmitted. "The RAVs are moving on the bridgehead."

"I can see that, John." Bah'd's tone was a little impatient. "We *are* ready."

"Sorry, ma'am," John said, though he wasn't really. Given the exhaustion levels of Bah'd and her officers, it was only wise to state the obvious. "I just wanted to be sure you were seeing them."

"We *see*, John," Bah'd said. "Our view is better than yours."

As she spoke, the combat support vehicles began to drop their struts and settle to the ground. Their cargo compartments began to spread apart like clamshells, each half folding outward along its length. In the bottom of each compartment lay a quivering mass of chitin that John did not recognize as a mass of kneeling figures until it shifted and began to rise, becoming a group of tall beings with segmented bodies and two sets of elongated wings. Their heart-shaped heads were dominated by luminous eyes and heavy mandibles, and each one's cephalothorax and thorax was set above a mammal-like pelvis, with a long abdomen dangling down behind, resembling a fat ovoid tail.

Drones.

John counted twenty to a compartment, all armed with plasma rifles and not much else, and there were fifty support vehicles lined up behind the Wraiths. That was a thousand Drones. He had never heard of such a large formation before—or of them riding into battle hidden inside armored transports.

Now he understood the barrage.

"Prepare for air cavalry," John said over TEAMCOM. "Battalion strength and coming hard!"

CHAPTER 3

Still standing in the swirling smoke, still rocked by the searing concussion of nearby mortar strikes, John watched the combat support vehicles across the gorge rushing to unload. As the cargo compartment doors continued to spread open, hundreds of Drones clambered out onto the descending halves, trying to find room to fan their wings and prepare for flight.

"Bah'd, you're seeing this . . . right?" John asked over the Fifth Battalion command channel. There was no way she could miss it, but in her exhausted state, she might have trouble recognizing what it meant—and what she had to do. "The Covenant is preparing to launch air cavalry. You need to—"

"Do you think I am blind?" Bah'd's tone was gentle but annoyed. "Or an idiot?"

"Neither, ma'am." John resisted the temptation to point out that her decision to redeploy across the bridge had left the Doukala Xenotime Works open to a long-shot air assault. "I just think you're very tired."

"Your concern is noted," Bah'd said. "And stop calling me 'ma'am.' I am not your auntie."

She switched to a different channel, and an instant later, rocket trails began to stream down out of the jungle above the Nasim Bridge.

The three combat support vehicles nearest the attack erupted into pillars of flame, but the rest of the column was beyond Fifth Battalion's range. The Drones continued to creep out onto the spreading halves of their cargo compartments, fanning their wings and fiddling with something on their thighs and shoulders.

John increased his image magnification to maximum and saw that the Drones were making adjustments to little horseshoe-shaped pods affixed to their exoskeletons. Over the past few days, Blue Team had traded a lot of fire with Drones wearing such devices and had been close enough on a few occasions to establish that they didn't seem to contain any spare equipment—not even ration packs or spare gas cartridges.

John thought the pods probably provided extra buoyancy, because Drones wearing them appeared more mobile than those without. But that was just a theory. Confirmation would have to wait until they could capture a few of the devices and deliver them to the science jockeys in ONI's new Beta-3 Division, which had been established to analyze and replicate Covenant technology.

Whatever the pods' purpose, it seemed clear the Drones were preparing to take flight. Their most likely objective was to protect the column's bridging vehicles by taking out Blue Team's Gauss cannons. That would be the obvious move—but the alien commander had already proven sly. He might very well be sending his air cavalry to seize the Doukala mine before it could be demolished.

John opened a UNSC command channel.

"Brigade Tactical." He was using the call sign for the 24th Marine Engineering Brigade headquarters, located just a few kilometers away at the Doukala's crushing mill. "This is Blue Leader."

The reply came almost instantly. "Blue Leader, Brigade Actual." Brigade Actual was Brigadier General Artur Pahlavi, commander of the 24th. Clearly, headquarters was more than a little concerned about the situation at the Nasim Bridge. "Go ahead."

"Possible incoming air cavalry."

"Through *these* clouds?" Pahlavi asked. "Did you take a head wound, Spartan?"

"Negative," John said. "The enemy is *already* below the cloud cciling, launching from ground transport. Drones with plasma rifles, estimated strength one thousand."

"What . . . ? A *thousand*?"

"Affirmative."

As they spoke, volleys of Anaconda missiles began to descend on the Covenant column, streaking down from the antiaircraft batteries hidden on the surrounding hilltops. The Anaconda launchers could only depress so far, and surface-to-air targeting sensors were easily confused by ground clutter. A lot of the missiles strayed into the hillside or disappeared into the gorge, and a few locked onto the heavier sensor profiles of Wraiths and dropped down their mortar tubes. The resulting explosions were not spectacular—carrier gas was pretty harmless until an electric arc stripped it of electrons—but John did see the cannon turrets blown off five of the big gun carriages.

"How soon?"

John didn't know how fast the Drones could fly, or exactly how far it was from the Samalat Gorge to the Doukala Xenotime Works by air, but his onboard computer did. It displayed an estimate on his HUD.

"ETA between five and ten minutes, sir."

"What about the Wraiths?" Pahlavi asked. "How long before they're in our laps?"

"Uncertain," John said. The barraging Wraiths would need to replenish their carrier gas before launching another major attack. But a good tactician would have held half of the fifty Wraiths in reserve to exploit a successful attack. And the Covenant commander had already proven a very good tactician who would be sending the reserve forward as soon as the bridgehead was secured. "About twenty minutes, maybe twice that. *If* we don't stop them first."

As the missile volleys continued, the Anacondas began to find the correct targets. Dozens of support vehicles burst into flames, and clusters of burning Drones leaped from the cargo compartments and dropped to the ground, still fanning the smoking tatters of their wings.

"Sir, you can make that Drone strength closer to eight hundred," John said. "The Mesranis scored some hits."

"Good for them," the general said. "But it's the Wraiths that worry me."

"I understand, sir."

"You need to stop those Wraiths, Master Chief," the general said. "If you don't, the Doukala is theirs."

"I'll keep you informed." It was the military way of saying he'd do his best. "I need to get back to the fight, sir."

"You do that," the general said. "And stop those Wraiths. Out."

Fifth Battalion had taken advantage of the Anaconda volleys to press its attack, rustling through the undergrowth alongside the road as they continued to pour flanking fire on the Drones. Through the dense foliage, John couldn't see how many of the human soldiers were advancing. A careful tactician would have sent a single company to press the attack, while an aggressive commander would have sent two. Given Bah'd's sleep deprivation, he wouldn't have been surprised to learn that she had sent all three—and was leading the attack herself.

The Covenant RAVs were racing to meet them, spitting plasma bolts and flipping through the air one after the other as they triggered Lotus antitank mines. Then the closest Wraiths got involved, not even interrupting their mortar barrage as cannon turrets spun around. They began to chew the jungle down with direct fire, and the Mesrani rocket attacks quickly diminished to almost nothing. It was obvious that Fifth Battalion was never going to disrupt the Drone assault. They were in the wrong position to do anything but die.

John spoke again over TEAMCOM. "Blue Two and Four, take out the CBVs."

The team's status lights remained dark for just an instant as they absorbed what John was asking. With only two Gauss cannons attacking, Fred and Linda would need to fire at least four bursts apiece to take down each CBV's shields and destroy it. Even under cover of a barrage, that would give the enemy time to locate them and return fire.

But the best way to stop the Wraiths from reaching the Doukala mine was to prevent them from crossing Samalat Gorge—and to do that, Blue Team had to take out the bridging vehicles.

"Shall I relocate and assist?" Kelly asked.

"Negative," John said. "You're with me."

"Doing what?"

"Drawing fire," John said. "We'll knock down some Drones. That should pull the Wraiths' attention away from Fred and Linda."

John stepped into a tangle of fallen sponge trees and, still standing, rested the barrel of his Gauss cannon on a horizontal stalk. It wasn't the steadiest firing support he had ever used, but he didn't need pinpoint accuracy. The Wraiths' cannon turrets had already broken up Fifth Battalion's flanking attack, and now the Drones were leaping into the air and forming themselves into a battle line that hung above the road in a long, undulating ribbon. As long as John fired in the general direction of the Drones, he was *going* to draw a reaction.

"Blue Leader ready," John said.

Before announcing her own readiness, Linda asked, "Fred, two-burst alternating fire?"

"Why not?" Fred replied. Alternating fire wouldn't put a target down as rapidly as simultaneous fire, but it would make the Gauss cannons harder to locate and counterattack. "Might as well make the fun last."

"You have a strange idea of fun," Linda said. "Lock and drop?"

"Affirmative."

Gauss cannons were too awkward to fire with real accuracy from a standing position, so Fred and Linda would have to rise above the smoke, mark the target on their HUD, then drop back to their bellies and brace the M68s on the preconstructed barrel supports in front of their scrapes. The software in their Mjolnir's onboard computers would automatically adjust the HUD marker to account for their movement. But they would still be firing at the target manually, through blinding smoke. There was every chance they would need six or seven bursts to destroy the target.

Fred's status light changed to green, as did Kelly's and Linda's.

The Drones were already sweeping forward over the Wraiths, so John set his targeting reticle on the middle of the line.

"Engage."

He pressed the Gauss cannon's trigger, activating a magnetic induction motor that accelerated the weapon's steel projectiles to hypersonic velocity in little more than two meters of barrel length. The result was an earsplitting sonic boom, coupled with a stream of blue friction flashes that seemed to cross the gorge almost before the trigger reached the back of its guard.

The first Drones erupted into sprays of chitin and bug juice, and John ran the rest of the burst down the battle line, knocking out a dozen more before he reset the trigger and ran the second burst in the opposite direction. By then the Wraiths were pivoting toward him, preparing to concentrate fire on his position.

John cradled the Gauss cannon in both arms and sprinted toward Kelly's position. Normally he preferred to avoid clustering. But with one side of his faceplate still covered in lizard mucus, he had to run toward Kelly if he wanted to keep an eye on the enemy.

The Drones were already starting over the gorge, taking as many casualties from their own plasma mortars as they were from Kelly's M68. John knew better than to think the friendly fire would do much to diminish the barrage. The Covenant had proved many times that they valued the lives of their own soldiers less than the deaths of their enemies, and barrages were only effective as long as they were sustained.

A flash of heat and light enveloped him as a volley of plasma rounds detonated on his previous position. John found himself stumbling through the smoke as one blast wave after another pushed him across the slope. It took a half dozen steps, tripping over fallen club mosses and hidden tree stalks, before he finally managed to catch his balance again and take shelter behind a rocky outcropping.

A second burst of blue dashes shot across the gorge from Kelly's position, and the hail of mortar rounds shifted away from John toward her. He clambered atop the outcropping to lie prone above the smoke, braced the cannon barrel against the rock, and opened fire again.

The Drones were halfway across the gorge. Even from five hundred meters, John could see their thoraxes and abdomens burst apart as each of his rounds hit. With the cannon barrel resting atop a stable support, he was able to move the aiming reticle from alien to alien with a precision that left the air clouded with flying chitin.

John took satisfaction in his efficiency, but he knew it would not break the Drone attack. At best, he and Kelly might eliminate half the battle line before it passed overhead and out of range, and that would still leave four hundred Drones to swarm the Doukala. The real goal remained the same: to draw fire away from Fred and Kelly, so *they* could eliminate the last two CBVs.

John checked the team's status lights and saw that Fred's and Linda's had changed to amber—in good shape, but still working on the next bridging vehicle. He fired his second burst, then grabbed the Gauss cannon and leaped off the front of the outcropping down into the smoke. He hated to abandon such a great firing position, but not as much as he'd hate being there when the plasma rounds arrived.

Kelly's status light was green, indicating that she was in a new firing position and ready to attack. John turned in the direction opposite to where he had run last time and started across the slope, back toward the Nasim Bridge. He wouldn't be able to keep an eye on the Drones' advance, but continuing to move toward Kelly would be too predictable and could put them in overlap proximity.

Again the air erupted into heat and swirling smoke and concussion waves as mortar rounds rained down on the outcropping behind John. He stumbled across a glassy crater—his last position, after it had been hit by a plasma strike—and found a splintered sponge tree that had somehow remained standing. He propped his cannon barrel into a notch formed by a split in the stalk, then looked out over the gorge.

The Drones were coming up from the gorge now, a long undulating bank of dark figures skimming through the smoke on fast-beating wings, their crooked arms holding plasma rifles beneath their elongated bodies, their heart-shaped heads swiveling side to side in search of targets. John opened up with his M68, tearing a twenty-meter hole in their battle line as his fire reduced a dozen Drones to a rain of chitinous shards.

A wall of plasma bolts swept back in John's direction, but his position near the top of the ridge put him a hundred meters above his foes, and it was no easier to fire accurately uphill than it was downhill. Most of the Drone fire went over his head, and the closest he came to taking damage was a few pieces of charred sponge tree raining down on his shoulders.

John stayed behind the disintegrating tree and fired another burst, opening the gap in their line to fifty meters. The Drones continued up the slope in their original formation and on course, over the far end of Sarpesi Ridge toward the Doukala.

Instead of trying to suppress John's fire by detaching a swarm to meet him, they were offering instead a devastating flank attack. Trying to hold his attention.

Never take the bait.

Leaving the Gauss cannon to drop at the base of the sponge tree, John grabbed the BR55 battle rifle off the magnetic mount on the back of his Mjolnir and spun toward his blind side.

He saw nothing. There were no Drones sliding into view as his mucus-covered faceplate swung back toward the ridge crest, only the blue dashes of Kelly's cannon rounds streaming through smoke, chewing through the close end of the enemy battle line. The Drones weren't turning to meet her either.

John didn't like it.

But it was still time to move. He needed to abandon his position before the next mortar rounds arrived. Rather than continuing back toward Kelly, into the enemy's next strike zone, he turned toward the ridge crest.

"Blue Three, cease fire," John said over TEAMCOM. "Abandon the M68 and meet me on the reverse slope."

Kelly's status light winked green.

John raced for the ridge top, pushed along by the concussion of the first mortar rounds falling on his last position. He wasn't worried about abandoning the two Gauss cannons because Blue Team had two spares stowed in the Fifth Battalion's original command bunker above the Nasim Bridge . . . near the far end of the Drones' battle line.

And if the Drones were between Blue Team and the command bunker, then they were also between Blue Team and the demolition boxes that controlled the charges on the Nasim Bridge and in the Kharsis Flume.

Maybe the enemy commander wasn't launching a long-shot air cavalry assault on the Doukala mine. Maybe he was trying to find the command bunker—and therefore save the bridge.

John switched to the Fifth Battalion comm channel. "Ghost Leader," he said, using Bah'd's call sign, "the Drones are advancing on the Sarpesi Ridge command bunker. Repeat, advancing on—"

"There's no need to repeat yourself, John," Bah'd said. "We can see that."

John waited. The next order Bah'd needed to give was painfully obvious. He didn't want to be the one to say it . . . but when Bah'd remained silent, he realized he might need to.

"Major, it's time to blow the bridge." John crested the ridge and saw that the barrage was hitting the reverse slope even harder than the front. He could not find five square meters that had not been cratered by a plasma strike. "You need to give the order."

"I have been trying." Bah'd's curtness had less to do with John's suggestion than with the roar of combat he heard in the background—at least, he hoped so. "Their comms are dead."

"Understood," John said. Fifth Battalion had left two squads at the command bunker to guard and operate the demolition boxes. Looking at the sea of craters below him, it was not hard to imagine what had happened to them. "What about backup boxes?"

"Yes, of course." Bah'd was starting to huff as though she were wounded—or winded. "We have backups for both demolition targets. We're trying to reach the bridge box now."

John turned toward the front side of Sarpesi Ridge and dropped to a knee. The artillery fire had finally ceased, but even if that hadn't been the case, he was above the smoke and flying debris, and he had a clear view all the way to the gorge.

A company of Mesrani soldiers was about a third of the way across the Nasim Bridge, racing back toward Sarpesi Ridge on foot. The other two companies—what remained of them—were cowering in the tangle of cannon-cleared jungle beyond, pouring a fast-dwindling rain of rockets down on a line of Wraiths pushing toward the bridgehead through a junkyard of mine-savaged RAVs.

The race was on, and John wasn't betting on the Mesranis to win. He would have to check the demolition boxes in the original command bunker and hope they were still usable or repairable. He didn't want to consider the possibility they had been completely destroyed, but he had to.

"What about the Kharsis Flume?" John asked. "Where's the backup box for that site?"

"A hundred meters above the road," Bah'd replied. "Follow the wires."

"Acknowledged," John said. Backup boxes were always connected to the detonators by wire, to safeguard against the detonation signal being jammed. "And good luck."

Kelly's identifier symbol appeared on the motion tracker on John's HUD, and he turned his helmet hard to the left so he could see her out of the clear side of his faceplate. Her green Mjolnir was spattered with mud and soot from close calls with mortar rounds, and her full-bubble faceplate was streaked with white strands of ground filament. John made a mental note to add some sort of cleaning solvent to their combat kits.

"Oh, *that*'s lovely," Kelly said over TEAMCOM. She dropped prone five meters down the ridge from John, then pointed her battle rifle toward the bridge. The leading Wraiths were already approaching the bridgehead, their cannon turrets spraying plasma bolts into the fleeing Mesranis. "What are they thinking?"

"Probably the same thing I am." John had the onboard computer set a waypoint for the command bunker, then stood and started across the reverse slope. "I should have stopped Fifth Battalion from redeploying across the bridge."

"I hardly see how you could have." Kelly rose and followed. She was careful to stay out of overlap range, in case a Drone spotted them and called in a mortar strike. "You're not Fifth Battalion's commander. You're not even in the same military."

"I should have tried."

He had gone along with Bah'd's compromise because it gave everyone what they wanted, but the battlefield was no place for accommodation. It wasted lives and put missions at risk.

John stayed high enough on the slope to poke his head up every few steps and peer over the crest. The barrage had flattened the jungle and cratered the road clear to the far end of Sarpesi Ridge, where the Ytterbium Road made the hairpin turn and started back toward the Kharsis Flume. Now that the Wraiths had stopped firing, hundreds of Drones were blanketing the slope, fluttering from one strike crater to another as they searched for hidden enemies.

Or something else.

"They're looking for the demolition boxes," John said over TEAMCOM. A good tactician—which the enemy commander clearly was—would be trying to confirm that the boxes had been destroyed in the barrage. "The Covenant wants the bridge intact."

"They don't have a chance." Kelly paused, then asked, "Do they?"

John risked poking his head up high enough to see the bridge. The lead Wraith was halfway across the span, with two more following thirty meters apart. They were followed close behind by a full company of Jackal-piloted RAVs, but the rest of the column was waiting on the far side of the gorge, ready to pour across once the opposite bridgehead was secured.

At least a hundred Mesranis lay scattered across the decking in pieces, cut to shreds by the lead Wraith's cannon turrets. John magnified the image and searched the faces of the dead until he found Bali'd's, her helmet caved in and much of her chin blown away by a plasma bolt. He took a long look, committing to memory an image he never wanted to forget. This was what came of compromising on tactics. This is what came of surrendering to consensus.

Finally John dropped back down beneath the ridge crest.

"Yeah, they have a chance." He continued across the crater-pocked slope at a run. "Maybe better than ours. It depends on what we find at the command bunker."

"You must be joking," Kelly said. "Look at this mess. The only thing we'll find there is charred bones."

"Still need to check," John said.

With the first Wraith already halfway across the bridge, trying to reach the backup box at the near end of the bridge was out of the question. They would have to fight their way past hundreds of Drones, and even if they made it—well, Mjolnir was no match for sustained fire from plasma cannons.

Fred's and Linda's status lights changed to green inside John's HUD. He didn't bother to ask for a status update. They had destroyed the second bridging vehicle and would be searching for the third. Once they had destroyed it, they would report and request a new assignment. That was how Spartans operated.

Efficiently.

John was still fifty meters from the command bunker—or, rather, what remained of the bunker—when Drones began to pour over the ridge crest ahead in a dark, buzzing wave.

"Oh, bloody hell." As Kelly spoke, the wave of chitin and wings became a tide, and the tide became a tsunami. "We'll never fight through *that*."

"We'll grab the boxes on the run."

"John, there *aren't* any boxes," Kelly said. "The bunker took a direct hit. From a plasma strike. There's nothing there."

A Drone spotted John and began to pour white bolts in his direction. He returned fire and dropped the shooter, but by then dozens more were swinging their weapons in his direction.

John was still twenty-five meters from the bunker and could already see that its walls had been turned to glass. He didn't need to check out the bottom to know that it was the same. And a dozen Drones were already in the crater, with more pouring in every second.

John pulled a fragmentation grenade off its magnetic mount, then thumbed the priming switch and said, "Let's assume you're right."

He tossed the grenade into the crater and turned downslope toward the Kharsis Flume. Spartans didn't give up—but they didn't commit suicide either.

Plasma bolts began to flash past on all sides, his armor pinging and sizzling as many of them glanced off. He checked his motion sensor and saw Kelly's identifier symbol moving into position twenty meters below him and to his right, then swung in her direction.

Dodging and leaping as he descended the slope, John opened the UNSC command channel again. "Brigade Tactical," he said. "Blue Leader."

"Blue Leader, Brigade Actual." It was General Pahlavi again. "Go ahead."

"Be advised, air cavalry assault not imminent," John said. "Drone force engaged Sarpesi Ridge."

"What about those Wraiths?"

Kelly's helmet and rifle barrel popped above the glassy rim of a strike crater. Stars of white light began to blaze from the muzzle, tracer rounds streaking past so close to John's helmet that they made him wince.

At least, he thought it was the tracer rounds. It might have been the prospect of what he needed to tell the general.

"They're coming across, sir." The plasma fire diminished as Kelly dropped Drones and forced the survivors to dive for cover. "We couldn't blow the bridge."

"God*damn* it, Master Chief! What happened?"

"I'm kind of busy right now, sir. Can I explain in the debriefing?" John reached the crater where Kelly lay covering him, then set a new waypoint and angled down toward the Kharsis Flume. If he could find the backup box, he could still stop the column. "We have one more chance."

A new voice, crisp and female, sounded over the channel. "*What chance, Spartan?*"

John was so surprised by this that he forgot the mucus on his faceplate and stepped into a crater and went down. The voice belonged to Captain Amalea Petrov, who commanded the *Night Watch*, the *Razor*-class prowler that had been serving as Blue Team's mobile base since the Covenant onslaught began six weeks ago. Technically, she was John's superior and mission commander only when the Spartans were aboard her ship—but she had been pushing those boundaries almost since the day Blue Team had been berthed aboard the *Night Watch*.

John clambered to the rim of the crater and opened fire with his battle rifle, covering Kelly as she raced down across the slope toward him.

"Ma'am." John continued to speak over the command channel, firing as he talked, dropping three Drones in as many shots. "I was under the impression that in hostile space, prowlers needed to maintain comm silence to avoid betraying their position."

"So was I." General Pahlavi's voice was gravelly and ominous. "Especially when they're breaking into someone else's channel."

"My apologies, General." Petrov did not sound even slightly apologetic. "Not my choice."

"Then whose choice was it?" the general demanded.

"Admiral Cole's." Petrov's smirk was almost audible. "We're on the way down."

"What?!"

John wasn't sure whether he or the general had barked the question, and it really didn't matter. Kelly jumped into the crater beside him, then ejected her empty magazine and slipped a fresh one into the receiver.

"You heard me," Petrov said. "We're extracting Blue Team."

"What?!" This time, John *did* know it was his own voice. Kelly climbed up beside him and opened fire, and John slid back into the bottom of the crater and reloaded. "We're in the middle of a *battle*, ma'am."

"I'm aware," Petrov said. "But this is big, Master Chief. Blue Team needs to be ready to extract when I arrive. That's straight from Admiral Cole."

John sighed. "When?"

"You have fourteen minutes," Petrov said. A navpoint to the LZ appeared on his HUD, nine hundred meters back toward Fred and Linda. "And don't be late. This will be a hot extraction."

She had barely clicked off before General Pahlavi demanded, "What about those Wraiths?"

John was already climbing out of the crater he'd stepped into. "I'll keep you informed, sir."

A long burst sounded behind him as Kelly continued to lay covering fire. She asked, "John, what are—"

"You heard the lady," John said. "We have fourteen minutes."

John was angling down the slope with the obstructed part of his faceplate on his uphill side, so every few steps he had to swing his head around to check on the Drones above him. Twice in fifty meters he had to bring his battle rifle up to drop a handful of speedsters, but the swarm still seemed more focused on their search for the demolition boxes than on pursuing Spartans, and Kelly's covering fire was more than adequate to keep him protected.

But Fred's and Linda's status lights had switched back to amber and were staying that way. Either they had not been able to target the third bridging vehicle, or they were having trouble destroying it.

John switched to TEAMCOM. "Blue Two, status?"

"They're holding the target back," Fred reported. "No shot."

Of course. The aliens wouldn't risk their last CBV if the bridge was already captured. The Covenant commander was too good for that.

John dropped into a crater less than two hundred meters above the Kharsis Flume. The slope below him had not been as heavily shelled as the higher parts of Sarpesi Ridge, and through the sponge trees he could see only short glimpses of the Ytterbium Road as it bent inward to snake along the walls of the steep gully.

So far, he saw no sign of Covenant aliens working to locate mines or disarm explosive charges, but it wouldn't be long. By now the first Wraiths and their RAV escorts would be rounding the hairpin at the end of Sarpesi Ridge, and as soon as they saw the Flume, they would recognize the danger it posed to their advance.

John looked back up the slope and began to lay covering fire for Kelly. "Blue Two, Blue Four—abandon assignment," he ordered. "Rendezvous at extraction point asap."

"Are you certain?" Linda asked. "When you take out the Flume, they will bring the CBV forward—"

"We don't know how soon," John said. Spartans never gave up. "And you are *going* to be aboard the *Night Watch* in fourteen minutes. Abandon assignment."

"Copy," Linda said. "We'll be waiting."

"Good." Kelly dropped into the crater next to John and changed magazines. "We may need the cover."

A sharp *boom* sounded on the road below, and John glanced back to see an RAV tumbling into the air atop a pillar of dirt and flame. Then he heard a second *boom* and saw another RAV rising on a column of fire, then a third and a fourth, each a dozen meters nearer the Kharsis Flume than the last.

"Out of time." John put a fresh magazine into his battle rifle, then turned downslope and clambered out of the crater. "Keep the bugs off my back."

"Of course," Kelly said. "But if they still have a CBV, what's the—"

The jungle below began to smoke and fall, then the cannon bolts grew obvious, chewing through tree stalks and club mosses, raising head-high curtains of mud and filament, spraying shards of demolition box and broken wire in five directions, clearing the slope all the way down to where the first Wraith was snaking around the Kharsis Flume, spitting plasma up into the jungle as it crept forward along the Ytterbium Road.

"Inbound Wraiths!" John was opening the UNSC command channel even as he turned and dived back into the crater. "We couldn't stop them, General. I'm sorry. We just couldn't."

CHAPTER 4

1558 hours, June 5, 2526 (military calendar)
Sarpesi Ridge, Samalat Gorge
Karpos Mountain Range, Planet Mesra, Qusdar System

The plasma bolts kept coming, slashing through the moss curtains and walls of fronds at a steadily flattening angle, raising jets of smoke and mud all around, pinging off John's Mjolnir in an ever-deepening scale that suggested shell failure was growing likely. Fred and Linda had already checked in at the LZ, but he and Kelly were still three hundred meters out and at least four minutes late, and if the *Night Watch* was gone, the two of them were done.

Maybe they shouldn't have ducked back into the jungle after all. It had seemed like a good idea at the time, stumbling across the crater-pocked terrain on the reverse slope of Sarpesi Ridge with a hundred Drones gaining on them by the second. The dense undergrowth had slowed their pursuers and offered some concealment, but now . . . now John wondered if they hadn't just been delaying the inevitable.

Kelly was sprinting a dozen paces ahead, far enough away to be sure they wouldn't be taken out by a single burst, but her lead should have been more than that. She was the fastest runner among the Spartans, and she could have been *at* the extraction point by now.

"Blue Three, move out," John said. "Confirm Commander Petrov is holding for us."

"She's holding. You know she is."

"Confirm that," John ordered. "If the *Night Watch* isn't there, we need to divert and catch a ride with the combat engineers."

It took a couple of heartbeats for Kelly to answer. "Affirmative," she said. "But I know what you're doing."

"Giving you an order." John wasn't trying to be a hero—he knew that dead heroes made poor leaders—but he also knew that good leaders never spent a soldier's life needlessly. "Move on and tell me what you find."

Kelly began to accelerate, her armor quickly vanishing into the undergrowth as she pulled away. John took his last grenade off its mount. The blast would knock down a handful of Drones, at best. But it would disorient dozens more, and with the extraction point only two hundred meters ahead, that might buy him the time he needed. He thumbed the priming slider and tossed it over his shoulder, and the clear side of his faceplate flashed white—much too soon.

His helmet snapped sideways, one ear and one cheek and one side of his jaw scalding hot, as if boiling water had been poured down his face. He sprang away as plasma bolts came in bursts, dodging toward his mucus-blinded side, hitting something hard and bouncing back in the other direction.

He went with it and spun, bringing up his BR55 one-handed, spraying rounds into the dark mass of Drones skimming across the frond-tops behind him. The first two dropped, and then there was a fireball in their midst, spattering his faceplate with grenade shrapnel and bug juice, and the concussion wave toppled him over backward—until a titanium gauntlet caught the collar of his outer shell.

"Will you stop clowning around?" It was Fred. "We have places to be."

As Fred pulled John back to his feet, the jungle to both sides of them erupted into small-arms fire—and it wasn't just a couple of Spartans firing battle rifles. It was the thunder of an entire platoon's worth of fully automatic weapons, mostly MA5B bullpups, but also a few M739 squad automatic weapons and even a couple of M247 general-purpose machine guns mounted on portable stands.

It was done in two seconds. The Drone swarm simply dropped to the ground in pieces and chunks, and an odd silence fell over the area, broken only by the distant rumble of the first mortar rounds falling on the Doukala mine.

John checked his motion tracker and saw a line of FRIEND designators stretching into the jungle to both sides of him. He made a visual check and found four squads of marines in full assault armor rising from concealed positions.

Kelly stepped to John's side. "Confirming that Petrov is holding for us." She turned her faceplate toward his. "Imagine that."

"There was never any doubt," Fred said. He tipped his helmet toward the extraction point behind him. "She's eager to see you. *Really* eager."

"Thanks for the heads-up," John said, turning. "Let's not keep her waiting."

Linda dropped out of a sponge tree and fell in beside Fred. Together they led Blue Team onto a path of recently trampled ground that angled down the slope toward a gurgling ravine, where a makeshift landing zone had been blasted out of the jungle. The bed of the ravine was too narrow for the broad beam of a *Razor*-class prowler, so the *Night Watch* was sitting astride the little stream in the bottom, her struts resting atop downed tree stalks and club mosses on the steep banks. The vessel's nose was pointed downstream in the general direction of the Doukala, with the stern upstream toward the arriving Spartans.

In the mouth of the open drop bay stood a slender woman in black battle dress, flanked by a pair of crewmen manning sling-mounted M247H heavy machine guns. As soon as she saw the Spartans emerging from the jungle, she jabbed a finger at John, then spun on her heel and stalked toward the back of the bay.

"Prepare for incoming," Linda said over her shoulder. "Will you need backup?"

"Thanks, but I'll survive . . . I think."

John followed Fred and Linda into the drop bay, then returned his battle rifle to its magmount and started across the deck toward Lieutenant Commander Amalca Petrov. She had a worry-lined face with ice-colored eyes set over a button nose and a fine chin, all framed by chin-length, copper-red hair. But there was nothing delicate about her scowl, which only seemed to deepen as John approached.

He stopped a pace away and raised his hand in salute. Despite the current status of his faceplate, he did not remove his helmet. Petrov was well aware of his true age, but there was no use reminding her. Like most officers, she tended to take his opinions and recommendations more seriously when she was not speaking to a fifteen-year-old face.

Petrov snapped a return salute. "I told you fourteen minutes, Spartan. Not eighteen." She glanced at her chronometer, then added, "Not *nineteen*."

"We couldn't complete the mission in fourteen minutes, ma'am." John lowered his hand, finishing his salute, but did not apologize. When Blue Team was on the ground, he was in command of the mission, not Petrov—and apologizing to her for doing his job would only encourage her to keep blurring the lines. "We needed nineteen."

"And *did* you?"

"Did we what, ma'am?"

"*Complete your mission*, Master Chief. Did you stop the Wraith column?"

"No, ma'am."

The admission shook John more than he expected—not because the mission had failed, but because of the *reason* it had failed. Humanity's one advantage over the Covenant—its superior infantry and better ground tactics—appeared to be slipping away.

The aliens had been just as good on tactical as John—perhaps even better. They had masked their intentions and attacked with the element of surprise. Even more alarming, they had taken advantage of a single mistake—Fifth Battalion's redeployment across the Nasim Bridge—to carry the battle. If the enemy's other ground commanders proved to be even half as good, humanity was in even more trouble than FLEETCOM thought.

"Master Chief?"

Petrov's tone was sharp, and John realized he had missed a question. Between today's plasma cyclone at Sarpesi Ridge and yesterday's squall on the Bogadlan Plain, he and Blue Team had been fighting for twenty-two hours straight. Pretty soon, *he* was going to be the one suffering from sleep deprivation.

"Are you *injured*, I said?" Petrov demanded. "Or just ignoring me?"

"Neither." John's motion tracker began to fill up with FRIEND designators as the marine platoon began to pack the drop bay. "Analyzing."

"Analyzing?" Petrov's eyes narrowed, and she turned toward the access hatch that led forward into the *Night Watch*. "We'll continue this discussion on the flight deck, Spartan."

"Yes, ma'am." As John started through the hatch after her, he activated TEAMCOM and spoke privately to his Spartans. "Head to the support cabin and get the maintenance team started on your Mjolnir. Whatever she's fired up about, we'd better be ready."

Their status lights winked green, and John followed Petrov. There were several places where they could have spoken privately, so John was not sure why she was taking him to the flight deck. But he *did* know she had a reason. Petrov was a cunning tactician who planned every move for maximum effect. It often made John wary of her, but he was trying to keep an open mind. Recently he had learned the hard way that officers who were more interested in being friends than leaders were the ones who really bore watching.

Petrov stepped through the open hatch onto a hushed flight deck manned by a full crew. The pilot and copilot sat in a dropped cockpit down in front. The communications officer and navigator were behind them, facing bulkhead-mounted instrument panels, with the sensor operator and weapons controller adjacent.

After a quick "carry on" to keep the flight crew focused on their jobs, Petrov dropped into the commander's chair at the back of the compartment and began to punch buttons set into the control pad on the arm. A tactical display of the surrounding terrain appeared below a holopad affixed overhead just forward of her chair. It showed the ravine walls as rolling blankets of luminous green, the sky above as a narrow wedge capped by gauzy white clouds two hundred meters up.

She pushed a finger into the near edge of the holograph, where a line of tiny *W*s—Wraith symbols—was passing by the ravine mouth.

"You put my crew and my prowler at risk, Master Chief," she said. "You also did the same for yourselves and First Platoon. And it was for *nothing*."

"It was my call," John said. "We had to try."

"Even if it costs the lives of everyone aboard?" Petrov asked. "Because it very well may."

John stepped closer and leaned across the commander's chair, turning his helmet so that he could study the tactical holo out of the clear side of his faceplate. The only hostiles he saw were the Wraiths, and they seemed entirely unaware of the prowler hiding four kilometers up the ravine.

Finally he said, "I don't see the threat. The aliens don't even know we're here."

"You're looking at the wrong aliens."

Petrov entered another command into her control pad, and the ceiling of white clouds in the holograph became a gauzy floor. The display wedge flared upward, all the way into space, where a steady stream of enemy Seraphs—each designated by a red *S*—was drifting past in low orbit.

But it was the designators at the *bottom* of the wedge that alarmed John. The aliens had deployed a lot of Banshee interceptors over the battlefield, and there were at least twenty circling just above the cloud floor, more or less above Sarpesi Ridge and the Doukala Xenotime Works.

Petrov looked toward the blond woman at the sensor station. "How many now, Ensign Gombaz?"

"I make it three squadrons of Banshees," Gombaz replied. "And probably one squadron of Seraphs. It's hard to tell, because our sensor window is pretty limited down here, and the Seraphs keep moving in and out as they change orbits to stay above us."

"Any sign of the mothership?"

"No, ma'am," Gombaz said. "But it's there. Those fighters are coming from somewhere."

"Very well. Keep me posted." Petrov turned to John. "Those

fighters weren't here four minutes ago. We should have been gone before they arrived—*not* hiding out on the ground, hoping for a chance to escape."

"We had a mission to complete."

"Wrong. You had a mission you *couldn't* complete." Petrov shook her head, then spoke in a gentler tone. "Look, I know Spartans never quit—I *get* that. But you need to temper your determination with perspective, John. Sometimes your pride isn't worth what you're risking."

"It wasn't about pride, ma'am," John said. "It was about denying a huge xenotime deposit to the Covenant."

"If you say so," Petrov said. "But we don't even know what the aliens *do* with xenotime. And a Spartan is worth a dozen xenotime mines—in equipment and training costs alone."

"It's pretty hard to fight a war without taking risks."

"It's even harder to win a war without balancing risks against reward." Petrov exhaled hard, then asked, "John, do you think Admiral Cole would have ordered me to pull Blue Team out of the middle of a mission if this wasn't something bigger than a xenotime mine? A *lot* bigger?"

Before John could answer, the communications officer turned toward Petrov and said, "Excuse me, Commander."

Petrov raised a finger, signaling John to wait, then nodded to the officer. "Proceed, Lieutenant Heuse."

"Comms traffic indicates the 24th is launching a mass evacuation, twelve minutes from now."

"*Twelve minutes?*" Petrov repeated. "Why so long?"

"The 24th is a full engineering brigade, ma'am," John said. "It takes time to recover and load five thousand soldiers."

Petrov shot John another scowl, but before she could rebuke him for injecting himself into the conversation, Heuse shook his head.

"That's not the delay," he said. "They found another of those weird tunnel networks beneath the ore body. The engineers think they can use it to collapse the Mesrani workings—*and* take out a bunch of Covenant armor. Shall I make contact and suggest they abandon that plan?"

Petrov thought for a moment, then shook her head. "Negative, Lieutenant. We don't want the 24th to know we're still here."

"We *don't*?" John was not eager to draw another of Petrov's withering gazes, but he couldn't contain his surprise. "How are we going to coordinate?"

Heuse gave him a sad look, then turned back to his instruments.

Petrov just appeared annoyed. "We're a prowler, Master Chief. We don't *do* coordination."

"Yes, ma'am." John had worked with a lot of prowler commanders over the last few months. They all shared two traits: they were exceptionally competent and exceptionally sneaky. But Petrov was in a class of her own. "You're going to hide behind the evacuation."

Petrov nodded. Reluctantly.

"Ma'am . . ."

John couldn't quite find the words. The engineering transports were barely combat vessels, slow and lumbering, with thin armor and not much weaponry. They might survive the Banshees without the *Night Watch* escorting them. But once they reached orbit, they would be easy pickings for the Seraphs . . . and completely defenseless against the starfighters' mothership.

"Is that ethical?"

Petrov's expression went blank. "It's *effective*," she said. "At the moment, that's all that matters."

She entered a command on her control pad, and the tactical holograph was replaced by a two-dimensional video showing a disk swaddled in a pall of brown clouds. It took John a moment to recognize the world as Netherop, an uninhabited greenhouse planet that he had actually orbited during a failed attempt to capture a Covenant combat vessel. It was in the same sector as Mesra, only a couple of short slipspace transits away—and well inside the nebulous frontier where UNSC "wolf pack" task forces were stalking Covenant transit routes, jumping lone vessels and harassing supply convoys in an effort to blunt the enemy onslaught.

As the video continued, the orange streaks of seven errant missiles flashed into the image. They skipped across Netherop's pearl-colored mesosphere, then abruptly lost velocity and sank into the planet's brown atmosphere. Behind them came the long-necked disk of a Covenant light frigate—or what the UNSC would classify as such, at least. Its dovetail stern was flaring with missile impacts, and there was a notch at one corner that suggested it had been taking damage for some time.

The steely voice of Vice Admiral Preston J. Cole rang from the overhead speaker. "This video was taken above Netherop at 2100 hours, June third, from the bridge of the *Kayenta.*"

Less than two days old, John realized.

"The *Kayenta* is the leader of Task Force Pantea," Petrov explained. There was no need to add that it was a *Halberd*-class destroyer without a marine complement. All of the UNSC wolf packs operating out of Battle Group X-Ray were composed of *Halberd*-class destroyers without marine complements. "She's accompanied by the *Chaco, Cibola, Mesa Verde,* and *Rio Grande.*"

John did not ask what had happened to the other half of the task force. The service expectancy of destroyers on wolf-pack duty was measured in weeks.

Cole's voice continued in the vid: "We've designated the Covenant frigate *Lucky Break.* Her shields and primary weapons were knocked out in the wolf pack's initial MAC volley, and Captain Greyveld had the good sense to recognize an opportunity when he saw one."

As Cole spoke, the slender, arrowhead profiles of a pair of *Halberd*-class destroyers slid into view behind the alien frigate, still chewing pieces off her stern with volleys of Archer missiles. The *Lucky Break* responded by swinging hard to port, trying to bring her flank around so she could deliver a broadside with a line of still-functioning pulse lasers.

It was a terrible mistake. The lasers chewed a few divots into her pursuers' thick-armored bows, but the opposite rim of the frigate's disk-shaped hull dipped into the mesosphere sideways, then flared red as the friction slowly began to drag the vessel out of orbit. For a few minutes, it looked as though the *Lucky Break* would be able to bring her long nose around and recover; then the nose dipped too, and she began a long, smoky descent into Netherop's brown clouds.

The vid switched to a close-up of Admiral Cole's gray-haired head. His face was slender and furrowed with deep worry lines.

"The *Chaco* sent its Pelicans down to take a look," he said. "Only one of them made it back, but it had a vid of the other one taking fire from the *Lucky Break*'s pulse lasers."

Cole paused so long that John started to wonder if the vid had gotten stuck. When the admiral finally continued, it was with a light in his eyes that made him look ten years younger.

"I don't need to tell you what that means, Amalea, so I'll get straight to the point. Section Three has already dispatched an ONI salvage ship to recover the *Lucky Break*, but its security company doesn't have the expertise or equipment to board a manned Covenant frigate—much less secure it before someone activates the self-destruct charge."

John exhaled slowly, then said, "So . . . we're going to Netherop."

Petrov paused the vid. "You don't sound very excited about it," she said. "In fact, it sounds like you'd rather stay here on Mesra."

"With all due respect, ma'am, it's never smart to get excited about bait."

"Too convenient?"

"I don't trust coincidence," John said. "Netherop is where we made our first attempt to capture a Covenant vessel, so the enemy knows we're watching it. And it's close to Mesra, where they've had repeated contact with a team of Spartans."

Petrov cocked her brow. "And you think they'd be willing to sacrifice an entire frigate to kill four Spartans?"

"Kill—or capture." John turned his helmet so that he could see her whole face. "You're the one who just said each of us is worth a dozen xenotime mines."

"I can see *that* was a mistake," Petrov said. "I'd better learn to keep my mouth shut, or your head won't fit inside your big helmet."

John was glad she couldn't see him smile behind his faceplate. "Is that a joke, ma'am?"

"Let's hope so." Petrov paused, then asked, "The special unit?"

John quietly sighed. During the recent operation that had culminated in the strike on the Covenant depot world, the Spartans had repeatedly engaged well-trained warriors in dark-red armor. After a time, John had begun to believe the enemy had created a special Spartan-hunting unit. A month ago, he had made the mistake of mentioning his suspicion to Dr. Catherine Halsey, who was the creator, chief scientist, and administrative overseer of the SPARTAN-II program.

Two parts scientist and one part mother hen, Dr. Halsey had immediately distributed a list of precautions and procedures she wanted implemented whenever her Spartans were in a combat theater. John had been noticing hints of disbelief and mockery in the attitudes of some tradition-bound officers ever since.

"Too early to suggest it's a special unit, ma'am," John said. "Let's wait until we see some red armor."

"That wasn't a dig at you, John."

Petrov touched her control pad again. The vid began to move forward at triple speed, Cole's face contorting in swift, comical expressions as his message continued.

"The admiral is saying that Task Force Pantea will stay on station near Netherop to provide fleet support and delay any Covenant efforts to recover the *Lucky Break*," Petrov summarized. "But they can't be expected to hold for long. We have to move fast—which is why your backup will be a regular marine platoon instead of a space-assault ODST unit. The Black Dagger survivors have been dispersed to train other units, and Admiral Cole doesn't have anyone to send."

"Wouldn't make a difference either way," John said. "It's a trap."

"Probably. You're certainly not the only one who thinks that."

Petrov clicked the vid again, and Cole's face was replaced by that of a middle-aged woman with a slender nose, blue almond-shaped eyes, and dark collar-length hair.

"John, this is a trap." Dr. Halsey's voice was steady but brittle. "I want you to go anyway."

John glanced over at Petrov, who simply shrugged and said, "She's your . . . well, whatever she is to you Spartans."

"A little hard to describe, ma'am," John said. "I'm not sure we know ourselves."

Halsey continued, "We're losing this war because we don't understand even the *basic* parameters of Covenant technology. And right now, the enemy is offering us a fully functional vessel, packed to the beams with that technology—technology that will give us the knowledge we need to develop effective countermeasures."

"That's a lot of bait," Petrov said. "You might even say overkill."

"They know we'll suspect a trap," John said. "They have to make it worth the gamble."

Halsey's message continued: "John, you know how important the starholo was to us."

She was referring to an enemy navigation instrument that Task Force Yama had recovered from a downed corvette during SILENT STORM. Halsey had used it to find a depot world just inside Covenant space, and it had been that discovery that led to the successful raid with the 21st ODST Space Assault Battalion. Their victory had come at a high price, though. John had lost a valuable mentor in Colonel Marmon Crowther and learned an important lesson about respecting the ability and selflessness of nonaugmented soldiers.

"The *Lucky Break* is a thousand times more important," Halsey continued. "If you can take the frigate from them whole, it gives humanity a fighting chance. Safe travels, John."

Halsey's image winked out. Petrov deactivated the overhead projection pads, then leaned on the arm of her chair and looked up at John.

"What do you think?" she asked. "Can you do it?"

"I wasn't aware I had a choice, ma'am."

"You don't," Petrov said. "But I like knowing that you're committed."

John rocked his helmet forward. "I'm committed."

"Good." Petrov checked the chronometer on the display built into the arm of her chair, then nodded aft. "Report to the support cabin and get your equipment in order."

"Yes, ma'am."

John started toward the hatch.

"And, John? Make sure your people are strapped in. It's going to be a rough ride out of here."

CHAPTER 5

Ninth Age of Reclamation
41st Cycle, 144 Units (Covenant Battle Calendar)
Flotilla of Unsung Piety, Intrusion Corvette *Quiet Faith*
Supersynchronous Orbit, Planet N'ba, Eryya System

From so far away, N'ba was but a russet smudge hanging in the unbounded darkness, the arriving vessel a point of brilliance approaching the brown planet ever more slowly. Nizat 'Kvarosee had been watching from the *Quiet Faith*'s cramped observation blister for only three hundred breaths, and already he ached from hip to ankle. He did not shift his weight or attempt to fold his legs beneath himself more naturally. His discomfort was a consequence of his fall from glory, and he would not affront the gods by trying to deny it.

A polite mandible-rattle sounded behind him. Nizat turned his head and found his young steward stepping into the drop-decked vestibule between the pilots' station and the observation blister. A typical Sangheili male, Tam 'Lakosee was an imposing figure with an arrow-shaped head, small eyes, and a mouth rimmed by four mandibles lined with short, curved fangs. He was armored in a light shipboard duty harness—basically a nanolaminate tabard that left bare his sinewy arms and huge legs. Like all Sangheili, including Nizat himself, he had elongated tarsi that gave him a springy, digitigrade gait.

'Lakosee stopped a pace from the blister. There was a time, just five cycles ago, when the steward would have stopped *three* paces away. But that had been aboard Nizat's flagship, the *Pious Rampage,* where a fleetmaster enjoyed an entire suite of compartments dedicated to his personal use. Aboard an intrusion corvette such as the *Quiet Faith,* there was no room for such formalities—an indignity that Nizat welcomed as an element of his humble devotion.

"You have news?"

'Lakosee touched his four fingertips to his brow. "The readers believe the vessel to be human," he said. "It is using deuterium fusion drives and has enough mass to be a salvage ship."

"Atmosphere-capable?"

"The readers cannot confirm it from this distance," 'Lakosee said. "But the ship's mass puts it in the midrange of human direct-lift transports, and it has ten drives."

"Ten?"

During Nizat's first invasion of infidel space, his spies had observed emergency evacuations executed by humanity's very largest direct-lift transports—and those vessels carried only six drives. Ten drives was unheard of on a midsize transport.

"Then it *is* atmosphere-capable," Nizat said. "It is designed to lift itself and a companion. There can be no other explanation for having so much power on such a vessel. How many patrol craft has it launched?"

"Twelve." 'Lakosee did not trouble to ask how Nizat knew the vessel had launched patrol craft. The humans had proven themselves capable foes when they raided Zhoist and destroyed the Ring of Mighty Abundance, and capable foes did not launch perilous missions without reconnoitering. "They are inspecting the moons and checking the libration points."

"Good," Nizat said. "It would worry me if they were not looking for a trap. It would mean they have already confirmed it and are trying to trick *us*."

Still, it did not *feel* good. Save for the *Steadfast Strike*—the baitship on the planet's surface—all of the vessels in the Flotilla of Unsung Piety were intrusion corvettes with stealth capabilities. But Covenant masking technology was only about eighty percent effective with optimal maintenance. And for a flotilla such as his own—a rogue operation with no access to regular supply chains or reconditioning support—it was impossible to achieve optimal maintenance. Nizat suspected that most of the intrusion corvettes in his ten-vessel flotilla would be seventy-percent likely to remain undetected, and two might be closer to fifty percent.

Nizat ticked his mandibles together, resigning himself to a long, uneasy wait. The human patrol craft would need at least one full rotation of the planet to complete their searches, and he knew he would remain in the observation blister the entire time, unable to leave until he saw whether the gods favored his plan, unable even to eat or drink until he was certain his intrusion corvettes remained undiscovered.

It would not be the first time Nizat had stood vigil in an observation blister.

After the disaster at Zhoist, the High Prophets had summoned Nizat to the Holy City of High Charity to explain his defeat, and for that entire journey he stood alone in his observation blister aboard the *Pious Rampage*, taking no sustenance and gazing out on the light-less splendor of slipspace, reflecting on his failed war against the humans and wondering how he had allowed a species so weak to better him . . . doubting his faith and searching for the flicker of corruption that had led him astray.

He found nothing. Not once had he recoiled from the terrible tasks set before him. World after world he had showered with the cleansing fire of plasma bombardment, burning bone and boiling stone and melting ground to glass. A hundred thousand refugee ships he had stopped, breaching their hulls and leaving their passen-gers to float frozen in the suffocating vastness of space. An untold number of prisoners he had given over to his mind melters and mer-ciless Jiralhanae interrogation squads, and not once had he balked at the fierce cruelty he was inflicting on beings whose only depravity was being born one of the contemptibles.

Always, he had ignored the darkness growing between his hearts. Always, he had done as the High Prophets commanded, certain that in obeying them he was honoring the Great Journey, that he would one day join the ancient Forerunners in divine transcendence.

Yet despite all of his accomplishments, he had proven unworthy. Not only had the humans decimated his Fleet of Inexorable Obed-ience, they had obliterated the Ring of Mighty Abundance and demolished the megacarrier *Hammer of Faith* in her construction docks . . . and they had hellbombed two of the Ten Cities of Edifica-tion, sacred places once inhabited by the Forerunners themselves. It was inconceivable.

And even as the *Pious Rampage* reverted to normal space after a hundred units in slipspace, Nizat still understood nothing of his shortcomings . . . only that he had failed the gods and himself, that he had crossed onto the Path of Oblivion and could not find his way off.

Then the *Pious Rampage* brought her nose around, and he saw his destination hanging against the darkness.

An immense space station with a vast, brown-red dome spread over a long glittering stalk of semirigid docking berths, High Charity was both the Covenant's most sacred city and the seat of its imperial government. Though its existence remained forever secret to the unworthy, it was home to billions, beings from every world in the Covenant hegemony. It was the core of a holy manufacturing complex of boundless capacity, home port to the greatest navy in the galaxy, and a maze of soul-stirring wonder for every species privileged to wander its ways.

Tethered to the stalk beneath the dome were thousands of capital ships—a hundred the size of the *Pious Rampage*, and twenty even larger. In his hundred years of service to the Covenant navy, Nizat had never seen such a gathering of vessels in one place, and he could tell by the tiny lights of the tender ships swarming around them that they were making ready to depart . . . and soon.

Nizat continued to study the armada as the *Pious Rampage* approached its berth near the top of the stalk, and he soon realized the vessels were clustered into twenty groups surrounding the twenty largest ships, each group a fleet twice the size of the one he had been given to eliminate the human scourge. The High Prophets were taking no chances this time. They were determined to expunge the human pestilence from the galaxy.

And they would fail.

Nizat knew that as certainly as he knew he had two hearts, for when he looked upon the unprecedented gathering of might, he saw the source of his own defeat. Humanity would never be crushed by force alone. It was like trying to smash a *jellusuj*. When the club struck, the creature flew apart and the pieces slithered away in all directions—only to return a cycle later, each larva more voracious than its progenitor.

Nizat stepped out of the observation blister and turned toward the interior of his suite. *Now* he understood his failure—and it was his duty to make the High Prophets understand as well.

A short time later, Nizat arrived with ten loyal escorts at the entrance to the Sanctum of the Hierarchs. He had donned his blue shipboard armor, absent his helmet and weapons, because it was his right to die in his armor, and he knew what was coming.

He would present himself to the High Prophets and hear their condemnations. When an opportunity presented itself, he would explain his mistakes and suggest ways for other fleetmasters to avoid similar miscalculations. If he did well, the High Prophets would take his words to heart, and he would be returned to the Path of Divine Transcendence. If he did poorly, they would thank him for his service and send him back to the *Pious Rampage* to await reassignment, and he would languish on the Path of Oblivion.

Either way, the Silent Shadow would strike soon after his dismissal. It could be ten breaths or ten cycles, depending on the honor they felt he deserved. But they *would* come for him.

Once Nizat and his escorts had stopped at the entrance, the exterior honor guard—twenty Sangheili armored in red-and-yellow harness—brought their fork-bladed energy staves to full upright. Their commander, a tall blademaster in a gilded gold harness, dipped his oblong helmet in greeting.

"Fleetmaster 'Kvarosee, welcome." He stepped to Nizat's side and glanced behind him to make certain no weapons were carried on his back. "The Hierarchs are most desirous to give you an audience."

"I am not surprised."

Nizat turned to present his escorts, most of whom were shipmasters

armored in full shipboard harness. Unlike Nizat, they were also hel-
meted and armed, with their belt carriers openly bearing energy
swords and plasma rifles. All ten were ceremonial volunteers who
had offered to serve as Nizat's bodyguard. Once the Silent Shadow attacked, all would perish, of course, but he would never have insulted
their courage by refusing their service.

As was customary, seven of Nizat's escorts also carried small stone
boxes, each fashioned from the native stone of a different world. An
eighth guard—his steward, Tam 'Lakosee—held an even smaller,
translucent box fashioned from the finest Subanese aragonite.

Nizat waved a hand toward his escorts. "I have brought some
decoration for the Shard Chamber."

"How prescient." The blademaster's voice was intimate but re-
spectful. Nizat wondered if they had met on his previous visit, when
he had been given command of the Fleet of Inexorable Obedience,
but there was no way to know. The honor guards who protected the
High Prophets seldom revealed their identities. "The Shard Chamber is where the High Ones await."

The trophy boxes were hardly prescient. The Hierarchs always
received their military commanders in the Shard Chamber, which
was decorated with slabs of lechatelierite—heat-fused silica—that
had been retrieved from worlds cleansed by Covenant plasma bombardment. It would have been a sacrilege for any fleetmaster to enter
the chamber without a fragment from each of the worlds he had
purged since his last visit.

Nizat's bodyguard could not be permitted beyond the Sanctum
doors—even were they to surrender their weapons and helmets. The
blademaster motioned seven of his subordinates to come forward,
then shifted his attention back to the escorts.

"You must open them."

Each of the escorts did as instructed, displaying glassy slabs of fused silica sparkling in colors ranging from alabaster-white to bronze-brown. The honor guards looked beneath the fragments to be certain there was nothing hidden there, then closed and took the boxes.

The blademaster turned to 'Lakosee. "You too. Open."

"Not that one," Nizat said. "It is for the Beacon Keeper."

The blademaster tilted his helmet to one side, perhaps only now understanding why Nizat had been summoned back to High Charity, then tipped it forward in acknowledgment.

"Nizat 'Kvarosee has always enjoyed a reputation for piety and clairvoyance." The blademaster turned toward the Sanctum and opened the reinforced doors with a wave, then gestured for Nizat to join him. "Allow me the honor of walking at your side."

The route to the Shard Chamber was a simple one that Nizat recalled from his first visit, just a long walk down a vaulted corridor so immense that the hard-light walls seemed to rise from the horizon of a distant green sea. After a hundred paces, they turned left into a vast hall whose floor, walls, and ceiling were faced with sheets of polished lechatelierite.

A ring of three hundred honor guards stood watch in the middle of the room, half facing outward toward the glimmering walls, half facing inward toward a trio of frail figures floating in grandiloquent antigravity thrones.

Nizat always found it ironic that San'Shyuum were such infirm beings. Their bodies were so withered they could barely stand, their long serpentine necks ready for the wringing. Yet there the High Prophets sat, their small, elongated heads almost lost beneath crowns and shoulder mantles so massive it was difficult to tell where the finery ended and the throne began, the unlikely, enfeebled rulers of an interstellar empire that was the greatest known since the holy Forerunners ascended to godhood.

When Nizat and the blademaster reached the circle of honor guards, the blademaster stopped in the gap that had been left open to allow them to pass. Nizat continued forward without awaiting permission. He knew as well as the Hierarchs that they had already ordered the Silent Shadow to retire him, and he wanted to make clear he did not fear his sentence.

The blademaster, who seemed to understand and perhaps even approve of Nizat's unspoken statement, waited until Nizat was halfway to the crescent of thrones, then announced, "Your Most High Graces, Fleetmaster Nizat 'Kvarosee presents himself."

"So we see," said the San'Shyuum seated in the middle of the crescent. The High Prophet of Mercy, he was oldest of the trio, with tufts of white hair protruding from his brows and a long wattle beneath his chin. His papery skin was so pale it seemed translucent. "Welcome, Fleetmaster."

Nizat stopped a short five paces from the thrones and looked briefly to the floor as he touched his brow.

"I am honored by your summons." He turned and extended a hand toward the box-bearing honor guards behind him. "I bring keepsakes from our victories."

The San'Shyuum to Mercy's right leaned forward in his chair. The Prophet of Regret, he was the youngest of the three, with umber skin, large nostrils, and only a hint of wattle beneath his chin.

"But do you bring us *Spartans*?" Without awaiting Nizat's reply, Regret turned to his fellow Hierarchs. "The demons must suffer for the desecrations at Zhoist. The Priests of Pain will make them wail for a hundred cycles before letting them die."

"It would be a mistake to focus too heavily on the Spartan demons, Most High." This was the revelation that had come to Nizat earlier—that the humans fought with their hearts and their minds far more effectively than they did with their fleets and their weapons.

"The Spartans are but the tip of the infidel spear. To stop the humans from affixing another point, we must break the shaft."

Regret's complexion deepened to angry bronze. "Mind your tongue. High Prophets do not *make* mistakes."

"So I have been instructed," Nizat replied. If he was going to die soon—and he *was*, given the immensity of his failure at Zhoist—he was resolved to make his death worthwhile by speaking truth to those who most needed to hear it. "And that is why I am certain you are wise enough to strike at the fountain of humanity's strength, rather than the spray."

Regret's lips began to writhe, but the Prophet of Truth, who sat to Mercy's left, spoke first.

"Daring will serve you better in battle than here, Fleetmaster." Commonly viewed as the most influential of the Hierarchs by those few who had appeared before the trio, Truth was somewhere between the ages of Regret and Mercy, with pinkish skin and tiny nostrils almost hidden beneath a wide nasal fold. "But this 'fountain of strength' you speak of . . . what form does it take?"

"None, Most High Grace," Nizat said. "It is like the Silent Shadow, ever present and seldom seen. The humans call it *Oh-nee*."

"Oh-nee?" Truth asked.

"Their abbreviation for what is known as the Office of Naval Intelligence," Nizat explained. "I learned this from Tel 'Szatulai, the First Blade who once led the Bloodstars against the Spartan scourge. He described ONI as the crèche of human cunning. It was ONI that masterminded the raid against Zhoist, and ONI that created the Spartans and built their battle armor."

"He knew this *how*?" asked Mercy. He glanced at his fellow Hierarchs. "It seems so . . . informed."

"Prisoner interrogations, Most High, and some demon-armor schematics taken from the infidels." Nizat did not dare explain that the schematics had actually been given to 'Szatulai by a band of human traitors hoping to form an alliance with the Covenant. The High Prophets would not look favorably on even *speaking* with such contemptibles, especially at this very moment. "Much of this information has been confirmed by later events, and none has been contradicted. There is every reason to believe it is all accurate."

Mercy tipped forward in his throne. "Where are these demon-armor schematics now? Have you delivered them to the Minister of Infidels?"

"I fear that was not possible." As Nizat spoke, Mercy tipped his throne back into its normal position, seemingly more relieved than disappointed. "I know only what the First Blade reported. His flagship was tethered to the Ring of Mighty Abundance when it fell, and I assume the schematics burned up with the *Sacred Whisper* in Zhoist's atmosphere."

"That is probably for the best," Mercy said, again glancing to his fellow Hierarchs. "Who knows what manner of blasphemies there may have been in such a document?"

The other two prophets dipped their enormous crowns in agreement—and Nizat was barely able to hide his surprise. Whatever blasphemies the schematics *might* have harbored, they had certainly contained important intelligence that would have helped the Minister of Infidels comprehend the thinking and capabilities of the humans. Their loss was as great a tragedy as the destruction of the *Hammer of Faith*—perhaps even as significant as the fall of the Ring of Mighty Abundance.

But it was not Nizat's place to contemplate the priorities of the High Prophets—only to guide them onto the Path of Victory. He gathered his courage, then pressed ahead with what he expected to be his final recommendation as an officer of the Covenant navy.

"Most High Graces, as I approached High Charity today in the

Pious Rampage, I could not help but notice the mighty armada you are preparing to send against the humans."

"It *is* a most impressive force," Regret said. "The largest the galaxy has ever seen."

Nizat chose to ignore Regret's sacrilege in claiming supremacy over the fleets of the Forerunners. Surely the Hierarch had misspoken, for no High Prophet would intentionally claim such a thing.

"It is certainly the largest fleet group *I* have ever seen," Nizat said carefully. "And it will not be enough."

Regret's eyes bulged out so far Nizat thought they might roll down his cheeks. *"What?"*

"You cannot crush water in your hand," Nizat said. "You must stop it at its source."

Truth raised a thin finger to forestall another outburst from Regret, then leaned forward in his throne. "You are talking about this ONI again?"

"Indeed, Most High," Nizat said. "ONI is the fountain of their cleverness and ingenuity. If you wish to eradicate humanity, you must first eliminate ONI. Otherwise the humans will keep slipping through your fingers, only to return later with even more hellbombs and stealth vessels, more Spartans in more kinds of demon armor, and more weapons, all of them more terrible than the Ministry of Discovery can imagine."

"A disturbing prospect indeed," Mercy said. He barely looked at Nizat as he spoke, instead keeping his gaze fixed on the floor between them. "We have started this thing, and now we cannot fail. If we—"

"We *cannot* fail because the gods are with us," Truth said, deliberately cutting off Mercy. He turned to Nizat. "But we would be fools to assume our enemies will never challenge us. How many fleets will we need?"

"To destroy ONI?"

"That *is* your recommendation, is it not?"

"It is, Most High." Nizat was astonished at the progress he was making. After his experiences with the Minor Minister of Artifact Survey—the young San'Shyuum who had been assigned to Nizat's fleet to sanctify the cleansing of infidel planets—he had not expected the Hierarchs to listen so well. "But I cannot say how many fleets will be needed until ONI is found."

"You see?" Regret shot a hand toward Nizat. "He is gulling us."

Truth continued to watch Nizat. "I trust that is not the case, Fleetmaster."

"I have no illusions on that score, Most High. I am here only to serve."

"As I thought," Truth said. "Then where do we look for this ONI?"

Nizat spread his hands. "Everywhere and nowhere," he said. "In the spirits that haunt the battlefields. I cannot say."

"Until we give you another fleet, no doubt." Regret raised a tridactyl hand and jabbed a crooked finger at Nizat with each word he spoke. "You are trying to save your command with this nonsense, and it is not going to work."

Nizat paused before answering, reminding himself that such a response was to be expected. The Hierarchs had summoned him to their sanctum not because they hoped to learn from his mistakes, but because they wanted someone to blame.

And the blame was certainly Nizat's to carry. He had entered the war against the humans as brash and overbold as the Hierarchs themselves, and for that mistake, ONI had taken from him everything he was. All that remained now was the duty to share the hard lessons the humans had taught him—and to help other fleetmasters avoid the same fate.

Finally he said, "I am trying to save nothing but the war, Most High. There are a hundred fleetmasters more capable of destroying ONI than I."

"But none who have fought them so directly." Truth was looking at Regret as he spoke. "Experience is not to be dismissed lightly."

"Nor is losing a fleet, an orbital abundance ring, and two sacred cities!" Regret said. "Some experiences should not be repeated."

"Which is why we must consider our options carefully," Truth said. He shifted his throne forward, then stared at Nizat. "But if we cannot *find* ONI, we cannot destroy it. Would I be mistaken to think you have thought of a way, Fleetmaster?"

Nizat dipped his mandibles. "High Prophets are never mistaken, Most High." He hesitated, knowing that what he was about to propose was a sacrilege . . . and the only way to find the ONI nerve center. "I *have* thought of a way, but it is not something that should be considered."

"Is that not for *us* to judge, Fleetmaster?" Truth's tone was growing impatient. "Speak your thoughts and plainly. No harm will come to you because of what you say."

"As you command." Nizat took a breath, then said, "We could use Luminal Beacons."

All three Hierarchs reacted in the same way—by dropping their jaws and staring at him with wide, bulging eyes. Luminal Beacons were among the rarest and most sacred of all Covenant instruments, utilizing Forerunner technology that even the Ministry of Discovery barely understood and could not replicate.

From what Nizat had been told, the tiny Beacons relied on quantum-dot processing machines and integrated sensors to track their own location through gravity-wave analysis and temporal distortion. Of course, many forms of navigation equipment could perform the same task through more understandable methods. What made

Luminal Beacons so special was that they used another Forerunner technology, something called quantum entanglement, to instantly relay their locations to reception units held in the Beacon Keeper's Vault in High Charity.

Regret was the first Hierarch to overcome his shock. "I see now why the gods have turned from you," he said. "You are more depraved than any human. At least they do not understand their blasphemy."

"The gods did not destroy my fleet, Most High." He turned toward Truth, the Hierarch who had urged him to speak freely, then continued, "ONI did—with but a handful of their Spartan demons."

"Fortune may have favored the demons once," Regret said. "But it will not favor them every time. Not every fleetmaster is as inept as you."

"Nor as experienced." Mercy was looking to Regret as he spoke. "With experience comes wisdom, and a wise commander will avoid battles that a daring one would lose."

Regret gasped. "You would do this? You would place a sacred Beacon in the hands of humans . . . when just three remain?"

Actually, just two usable Beacons remained, but Nizat had no intention of revealing that to the Prophets. In all the Forerunner ruins ever searched, only four Luminal Beacons had ever been found. Considered holy relics, they were entrusted solely to fleets entering unexplored territory, to be used for a single purpose: to announce the discovery of one of the legendary Sacred Rings required to begin the Great Journey.

One Beacon—the fabled Lost Beacon—had gone missing more than five thousand cycles earlier, when the fleet it was aboard vanished. When Nizat was given the Fleet of Inexorable Obedience, he had been entrusted with two of the remaining three Beacons—an honor that reflected the importance of his mission. Before sending him to eradicate humanity, the Hierarchs had confided to him that they had good reason to believe the secret to finding the Sacred Rings lay in human space. They had carefully avoided revealing the nature of that reason—and he had dared not ask—but it was why they had taken the unusual step of entrusting him with two of the sacred Beacons. And to his ever-enduring shame, one of Nizat's Beacons had been destroyed when the *Almighty Persuasion* was obliterated by a human hellbomb during the raid on Zhoist.

That left only two Luminal Beacons available: the one that remained in the Beacon Keeper's Vault on the Terrace of Illumination, and the one that Tam 'Lakosee was now holding in the aragonite box outside the Sanctum of the Hierarchs.

The Beacon that Nizat would use to find ONI.

When Regret's question continued to hang, Nizat saw that Mercy was looking to him, expecting him to answer the objection.

"Forgive me, Most High," Nizat said, addressing Regret. "But you would not be placing the Beacons in human hands. You would be using them to eradicate humanity."

"Which is the very task the gods have set before us," Mercy said, speaking more to Truth than Regret. "Can there be any doubt the gods would look favorably on this use? In all honesty, I would not be surprised if it were their will, the very reason they put the Beacons into our hands."

Truth stared at Mercy for a few breaths, then finally said, "Who can say what the gods will?" Without awaiting a reply, he turned to Nizat. "I will allow this, but the Beacons must be returned to the Keeper immediately afterward. It would be an unimaginable sacrilege to leave them in human hands."

"That would never happen, Your Grace," Nizat said. The unthinkable was about to occur, he realized. The Hierarchs were going to call off the Silent Shadow and assign him another command. "The Beacons will show us the way to ONI's heart, ONI will fall, and the Beacons will then be back in our hands. The humans will never even know they exist."

"I hope that is so . . . for your sake." Mercy turned to Truth and tipped his crown forward. "Perhaps you are right. Perhaps this ONI is the reason we were given the Luminal Beacons."

A rattle of disgust sounded deep in Regret's throat, and he sank back in his throne. "This is a mistake."

"High Prophets do not make mistakes," Truth replied. He turned to Nizat. "Tell us your plan."

"It is not complicated," Nizat said. "ONI is eager to capture our technology to learn more about it. At least once already, they have sent a team of demons to attempt a ship capture. And there is reason to believe they used a captured *kelguid* to find Zhoist."

"How did they come by that?" Mercy asked, worried again. A *kelguid* was used to map and navigate common slipspace routes. "Could they use it to find High Charity?"

"They downed an intrusion corvette on a moon of Borodan," Nizat said, answering Mercy's first question. "There was time for them to search the wreckage and recover the device before we arrived to cleanse the site."

"But what of High Charity?" Mercy asked again.

"They would have to know what High Charity is," Nizat said. "And a *kelguid* is merely a star chart. There are as many names on it as there are stars, and humans cannot read any of them."

"And yet, ONI found Zhoist." Mercy glanced at Truth, then Regret. "Perhaps it is time to relocate High Charity."

Nizat was not surprised to see the other Hierarchs immediately incline their heads in agreement. If there was anything the San'Shyuum valued more than the Covenant's mobile capital world, it was their own safety.

"Whatever you use to bait this trap," Regret said, "I hope it is less dangerous to us than a *kelguid*."

"But it must be something tempting," Truth said. "If we are

going to risk a Luminal Beacon, we must be certain ONI will take it back to their innovation temple."

"There are a great many possibilities," Nizat said. "And Luminal Beacons are rather small. I am certain we can hide one inside some device that will tempt ONI without endangering us."

He was glad to see that the Hierarchs grasped his plan. In all likelihood, and as he had promised the San'Shyuum, the Luminal Beacon would never even be detected by the humans. The relic would simply reveal the location of the bait to which it was attached—and, he hoped, that would be somewhere inside ONI's primary innovation temple, as Truth had noted.

"Would ONI be tempted by a Spike of Obeisance?" Mercy asked. "Or an Omnitab? No great harm would follow from allowing the humans to capture either one."

"Because the humans already have their own communication nodes and processing devices," Nizat said. "Were we to hide a Luminal Beacon inside either device, we could not be certain they would find it so valuable they would feel compelled to take it to their innovation temple. We need to choose something they do not have, something of such compelling interest that ONI cannot resist it."

"You have suggestions?" asked Truth.

"There are two good possibilities, High One. The infidels have no antigravity devices or energy barriers. It is a matter of deciding which device will be more tempting—and also complicated enough to disguise the Beacon's presence."

"Why not use both devices and be sure?" Truth asked. "You have two Beacons, do you not?"

Nizat hesitated. After the destruction of the *Almighty Persuasion*, of course, he now had just one Beacon. It would be a terrible blasphemy to lie to a High Prophet—especially one trying to support him—but to admit the truth was to forsake all hope of destroying

ONI and earning redemption. Were the Hierarchs to learn that he had already lost one of the Beacons entrusted to him, they would reject out of hand his plan to risk the other.

When Nizat did not answer quickly, Truth craned his neck in impatience. "Well?"

"An excellent idea, Most High," Nizat said. "I was merely wondering whether there could be any drawbacks. But now that I have considered—"

"Wait." Mercy tipped his throne so far toward Nizat that he appeared on the verge of falling out. "You are not answering the Prophet of Truth's question."

"A wise observation," Regret said. He also tipped his throne forward. "You *do* have both Beacons we entrusted to you, do you not?"

Nizat silently cursed his luck, which now appeared to have run out. He might have been able to dupe Mercy with a steady lie, but never Regret. He had made an enemy of Regret with his initial boldness, and now that Regret's suspicions had been raised, he would demand confirmation of whatever Nizat claimed.

"I did have two Beacons, Most High," Nizat said. "But I only need one to lay the trap."

"But we gave you *two*," Regret said, still at the edge of his throne. "Are you telling us . . . that you *lost* one?"

"No, I did not lose it, Your Grace. The Beacon was aboard the *Almighty Persuasion* when it was destroyed on Zhoist." Nizat paused. "I still have the other."

"I see." Regret's tone grew mocking. "You have allowed one Beacon to be destroyed and are asking us to risk another, in some wild scheme to eliminate an enemy we cannot even see. Perhaps you would like us to send for the Lost Beacon, so you can obliterate that one as well?"

"Most High, respectfully, we both know that is not possible."

After the fleet carrying the Lost Beacon had vanished, the Beacon Keeper had activated the receiver unit to track it. The Beacon was currently deep in the core of the galaxy, where the gravity tides and star density were too severe for even the sturdiest Covenant vessel to venture. "But I thank you for the offer."

Regret's eyes grew narrow and angry. "Well, at least there is some limit to your audacity." He turned to Mercy. "I leave it to you, but the risk of losing all of our sacred Beacons to this incompetent fool seems much too high to me."

Nizat felt a coldness seeping into his veins. Mercy's gaze had not left his face since he'd confirmed the loss of the Beacon, and he could feel his dream of redemption slipping from his grasp on the oil of Regret's tongue. Nizat would be remembered—if at all—as an inept commander who'd had his fleet bested by a flotilla of marauders so primitive they could barely navigate slipspace.

Worse, the Hierarchs were about to make the same terrible mistake as Nizat. They were going to place all of their faith in the multitude of their ships and the power of their weapons, and they were going to measure their success by the billions they killed. But for every billion annihilated, ONI would send a thousand demons or their space-assault troopers to mine convoy routes and destroy provisioning depots, to demolish maintenance docks and poison stores. And the more fleets the Hierarchs sent, the more support facilities ONI would destroy, the more logistics hubs it would sabotage. The humans would suffer vast losses, but their numbers were even greater. In the end, it would be the Covenant's might that perished— spent not in battle, but devoured by maintenance failures and starvation and disease and a simple lack of supply.

Finally, Mercy tore his gaze from Nizat and turned toward Truth. "Perhaps we should have paid more attention to the missives from the Minor Minister of Artifact Survey," he said. "He *did* say that the Fleet of Inexorable Obedience would have been lost at Borodan, save for his own recommendations."

"The Minor Minister *did* deliver some sage advice on other matters," Nizat said.

It took an effort of will to offer even *that* much flattery without gnashing his own tongue to ribbons. The Minor Minister of Artifact Survey had been the most self-serving magistrate Nizat had ever suffered. In fact, Survey had proven such an irritant and political opportunist that Tam 'Lakosee had finally beheaded the ceremonial magistrate just to silence his ceaseless prattling. Concealing the murder was one of the darkest things Nizat had ever done—and the absolute easiest.

"But had I followed the Minor Minister's advice on fleet tactics," Nizat continued, "the Fleet of Inexorable Obedience would have been destroyed by an escort corvette at E'gini."

"I have no doubt," Truth said. He glanced from Nizat to his fellow Hierarchs, then back again. "But, with only two Luminal Beacons remaining, we dare not risk your plan."

"We would be endangering the Great Journey itself," Mercy added. "You must see that."

"Absolutely."

What Nizat saw, though, was that Regret had stolen from him any hope of returning to the Path of Honor, that the Hierarch had condemned him to walk the Path of Oblivion, and now he would never be called to join the Forerunners in divine transcendence. He saw that in persuading Mercy and Truth to change their minds, Regret was destroying not only Nizat, but all of the fleets the Hierarchs sent against humanity. Most of all, Nizat saw that it had fallen to him to destroy ONI—that unless he found a way, the Covenant would never eradicate the humans, and the Great Journey itself would be placed in peril.

Nizat stole a final glance at Regret's smirking face, then bent forward at the waist and touched his fingers to his brow. "If the High Prophets have no further questions . . ."

"We have heard enough, Fleetmaster." Regret flicked his three fingers in dismissal. "Return to your ship and await reassignment."

Nizat's "reassignment" would, of course, be delivered by a warrior of the Silent Shadow . . . a now-inevitable fate that he would never see coming.

"As you wish, Most High," Nizat said.

"And return the remaining Beacon to the Keeper," Regret said. "Do so at your first opportunity."

"As you wish," Nizat said. "It will be done before I return to the *Pious Rampage*."

"You brought it with you?" Truth seemed surprised for only a breath, then said, "Of course you did. A good fleetmaster is always clear about his situation."

Why the blademaster had chosen to accompany Nizat and his escorts was impossible to know. Perhaps he was merely ensuring that Nizat delivered the Luminal Beacon to the Keeper's Vault, or perhaps he hoped to ward off the Silent Shadow's attack until Nizat had left High Charity. Either way, it was an unfortunate choice. The blademaster had treated Nizat with more dignity than circumstance warranted, and repaying such kindness in the manner Nizat intended was a dark necessity he would rue the rest of his life.

Short as that might be.

Located in a seldom-visited corner of the Terrace of Illumination, the Beacon Keeper's Vault stood alone in the heart of the Four-Spoked Bridge of Patience. It was a celadon dome sculpted to resemble the tidal swell of the Ut'hua Moonsea as it was dragged across the Flats of Forever by the immense gravity of the gas planet Thua. The entrance to the structure was at the bottom, hidden inside the curl of a wave fashioned so eloquently that it actually appeared to be breaking against the broad balcony that ringed the dome. The blademaster stopped there, in front of two honor guards who flanked the entry portal, and faced Nizat.

"You can give the Beacon to the door guards." He gestured to the guard standing to his right. "They will see that it's delivered to the Keeper."

"As you wish."

Nizat took an instant to glance at the two guards, gauging the distance from the blademaster to the closest one, and from him to the next, and wondering if he had any chance at all. What was the saying from his youth? *Anyone can kill a blademaster, as long as he does it on the first stroke. . . .* He inclined his head to the blademaster.

"You have been most kind in the honor you have shown a defeated fleetmaster." Nizat touched his fingers to his brow. It was an unprecedented sign of respect, as he was still far superior in rank to the blademaster. But given what he intended, it was a gesture he felt compelled to offer. "I am grateful."

"The only dishonor is surrender." The blademaster touched his own fingers to the brow of his helmet, then lowered his hand to his chest, a gesture of fondness that made Nizat wonder if he could go through with what he intended. "You did not surrender. I would have been proud to die in your fleet."

"Thank you, Blademaster," Nizat said. "I would have been proud to have you in my service."

Fearing he would lose his resolve if he faced the blademaster any longer, Nizat turned to his steward and extended his arms. Instead of taking the Beacon box, however, he reached down and drew the energy sword from the carrier on 'Lakosee's hip.

Behind Nizat, the farthest portal guard shouted, "Blademaster, beware—"

It was too late. Nizat was already spinning, activating the blade and driving it through the blademaster's throat while the portal guard was still shouting. The blademaster collapsed, dead before he knew he had been betrayed, and Nizat deactivated the sword to keep it from being ripped from his grasp by the falling body.

Still moving forward, he reactivated it and sprang toward the nearest guard, who was distracted by his shouting companion. The guard went down even more easily than the blademaster, the energy blade catching him in the back of the neck and cleanly lopping off his head.

But the farthest portal guard had stopped shouting and was moving in, the head of his energy stave leveled at Nizat's unprotected face.

Nizat pivoted hard. The forked blade shot past so close he felt the heat on his eyes, and he brought the energy sword up in a back-handed slash. The blade severed the stave halfway up the shaft. Nizat rolled his wrist around to strike at the guard's neck, but the guard was spinning into him, lifting him by the throat and slamming him against the wall of the Keeper's Vault.

Nizat's blade struck nothing, his wrist blocked when it hit the guard's neck just below the helmet. The guard slammed his helmet forward, almost driving the visor into Nizat's eyes before Nizat managed to turn his head aside. He saw the guard's hand drop toward the sword carrier on his belt, and he tried to bring his blade down into his attacker's back. His wrist remained blocked and the angle was wrong. He brought his knee up, slamming it between the guard's legs . . . to no effect.

Then the odor of melting armor and scorched flesh filled the air as Nizat's escorts sent a volley of plasma bolts into the guard's backplate. His enemy's knees buckled and he collapsed forward, pinning Nizat against the wall.

Nizat knew better than to assume the guard had been killed. He deactivated his sword, then drew his hand back, pressed the emitter slots to the guard's neck, and reactivated the blade. A muffled gurgle sounded inside the guard's helmet; then he crumpled at Nizat's feet.

Nizat then stepped over the corpse and deactivated the energy sword, offering it back to 'Lakosee.

The steward was too stunned to accept. He had dropped the Beacon box and, like the rest of Nizat's escorts, was holding his plasma rifle and staring at the dead honor guards in shock.

He finally looked up. "Fleetmaster, I . . . what have we done?"

"I will explain later." Nizat hung 'Lakosee's energy sword back on its carrier. "For now, we must hide these bodies. Bring them into the Keeper's Vault."

"I don't understand," 'Lakosee said, making no move to obey. "Were they Silent Shadow?"

In his desperation to spur 'Lakosee and the others into action, Nizat was tempted to lie and explain the truth later. But once a commander lost the trust of a subordinate, it could never be won back—and if he hoped to destroy ONI, he would need the trust of *all* his shipmasters. He retrieved the box from 'Lakosee's feet, then straightened and looked into his steward's visor.

"They were devoted warriors who died for a worthy cause—just as you swore to do for me." He shifted his gaze, looking over 'Lakosee's shoulder toward the shipmasters who had volunteered to serve as his escorts. "Will you honor your promise and trust me to explain later? Or shall we wait here until the rest of the honor guard discovers what we have done?"

'Lakosee turned to the escorts behind him. "Bring the bodies into the vault," he said. "Whatever the fleetmaster is doing, it is the will of the gods. I have served under him long enough to be certain of that."

Even now, though Nizat's gaze remained fixed on the brown clouds swirling across N'ba, his thoughts lingered on High Charity, where he and his escorts had stormed the Beacon Keeper's Vault to find the ancient San'Shyuum asleep in his gravity chair. After rousing him and forcing him to open the coffers where the last Beacon and the reception units were stowed, Nizat had ordered the Keeper bound and secured inside a coffer to prevent him from sounding the alarm too soon.

It had been one Nizat's escorts, Yey 'Mootasee, who objected, pointing out that the wonders of the Beacon Keeper's Vault were a mystery to them. There was only one way to be sure the old fellow did not sound the alarm and prevent them from departing on their holy mission.

The others had agreed, and together the nine shipmasters and Tam 'Lakosee had plunged their energy swords into the breast of the ancient San'Shyuum.

After that, there could be no question of their commitment to the holy mission Nizat had set before them, and he actually viewed them as his disciples. He could but hope his skill was equal to their devotion.

Nizat's thoughts were dragged back into the present by an urgent mandible-rattle behind him.

"Forgive my insistence." 'Lakosee was no more than a pace behind Nizat, speaking from the observation blister's entry vestibule.

"But this needs immediate attention. The *Divine Whisper* is tracking an infidel dropship. It will be out of striking range soon."

The *Divine Whisper* was the intrusion corvette now under Yey 'Mootasee's command. "What type of ship?"

"One of their dropships," 'Lakosee reported. "We haven't found the mothership."

"Then one of their stealth vessels," Nizat said.

The last time he had faced human stealth vessels, they had been carrying Spartans and Black Dagger space-assault troopers—and they had decimated his fleet at Zhoist.

"Fleetmaster?" 'Lakosee asked. "We have little time."

"If the dropship is carrying demons, the infidel salvage ship may have a true chance of capturing the *Steadfast Strike*." And that was the last thing Nizat wanted. His plan was to let a party of humans board the frigate and find the two items containing the Luminal Beacons, then use a cadre of Fleet Rangers to drive them off. Once the infidels were at a safe distance, the *Steadfast Strike* would self-destruct to reinforce the ruse—and to forestall any possibility of being captured in a second boarding attempt. "Our Fleet Rangers are no match for a company of Spartans. The demons would slay them and take control of the vessel."

"Did we not anticipate this possibility?" 'Lakosee asked. "There is still time to send the Guarding Spear."

"Launch it," Nizat said. "And find that stealth ship. Spartans are like *mulegs*. Where you see one, there may be a hundred."

CHAPTER 6

0450 hours, June 7, 2526 (military calendar)
UNSC *Razor*-class Prowler *Night Watch*
Low Polar Orbit, Planet Netherop, Ephyra System

After two days in slipspace, John-117 stood on Amalea Petrov's flight deck, watching the distant speck of a D75-TC/r reconnaissance boat vanish into the pearly glow of Netherop's mesosphere. A standard Pelican dropship equipped with a special scouting package, the boat had been launched as soon as the *Night Watch* entered orbit, and John was not happy about it.

Before sending out recon missions, prowlers usually spent anywhere from ten to twelve hours in orbit, hiding in the twilight darkness of a planet's terminator zone while they made passive observations and searched for enemy vessels. This time, Lieutenant Commander Petrov had launched the mission immediately after establishing orbit—essentially bypassing the scouting window by using the Pelican and its three-person crew to draw fire.

John knew she was just trying to speed the operation along. The longer it took for his unit to insert on Netherop and reach the Covenant frigate, the less likely they were to capture the downed ship intact. But a *Razor*-class prowler carried only two Pelicans in its hangar bay, and the boarding force would need both of them to reach the planet's surface in a single drop.

"Mark three minutes," the navigation officer reported. He was floating in his seat behind the copilot, his arms moving with fluid grace in the zero-g environment. "Fifteen seconds to tropopause."

John began to relax. The Pelican would be much safer after dropping through the tropopause, where it would be hidden from view beneath Netherop's thick pall of clouds—and even partially shielded from sensor sweeps by the electrostatic energy generated in the planet's churning atmosphere. And if it actually succeeded in confirming the target's location and gathering some intelligence on defensive preparations, the risk Petrov was taking might even prove justified.

"Commander," the sensor operator said, "I have targeting radiation in a superior trailing orbit, twenty-thousand-kilometer range."

Petrov tapped the control pad on her chair arm. "All hands, brace brace brace!"

John took hold of a recessed grab bar in the bulkhead and pushed his boots down onto the deck, creating a two-plane contact zone that would keep him moving along with the ship if it was suddenly jarred by an enemy attack. Nobody had actually said the *Night Watch* was being targeted, but space battles were quick. By the time the target was identified, the first attacks would be under way.

"Ensign Gombaz, have you—"

A blinding-bright line slashed past in the distance, angling down from high in the terminator zone into the mesosphere on the daylight side of the planet.

"They're firing on the reconnaissance mission," Gombaz reported. The line streaked onward almost too fast for the eye to follow, the far end flaring into an area-strike cone. "Their firing resolution will be good."

"Very well." Petrov's voice quavered—there could be no question of a Pelican surviving even a glancing strike from a ship-mounted plasma cannon. "Do we have a fix on the attacking vessel?"

"Temporarily. It may have—" Gombaz paused, then said, "Contact lost with the Pelican, ma'am."

"Thank you, Ensign." Petrov's tone was impatient. "Now, what about the *attacking* vessel?"

"Gone again," Gombaz said. "It may have stealth capabilities."

"I can find and lock it if we go active *now*," the weapons controller said. "We might be able to take it out—"

"Negative. Maintain covert status." Petrov looked to John. She was strapped only loosely into her chair, and the act of turning her head rotated her entire body. "Thoughts, Master Chief?"

"It's the right call at this point." John hated that the Pelican crew was dead because Petrov hadn't taken the time for a passive sweep, but no good ever came of criticizing a prowler captain on her own flight deck. "Even if we nail *that* vessel, we don't know how many others might be lurking out there."

"Because we didn't take ten hours to make passive sweeps?"

"I didn't say that, Commander."

"Sure you did," Petrov said. "And maybe you're right. But that still doesn't make the *Lucky Break* bait . . . or this a trap."

"A trap seems like the simplest explanation, ma'am."

"It seems like *one* explanation," Petrov countered. "Another is that a Covenant stealth ship slipped past Task Force Pantea, and now it's trying to protect the downed frigate until a battle fleet arrives to recover it."

"That's possible, I guess."

"More than possible. It's the only explanation for jumping the Pelican before entry." Petrov paused, locking her gaze on John's faceplate, then said, "*Think*, John. If the enemy is setting a trap to kill Spartans, why spring it *before* they know where the Spartans are?"

She had a point. Attacking the Pelican prior to its insertion run suggested the aliens were trying to prevent it from reaching the downed frigate—not that they had a special forces cohort waiting for it on the surface, hoping to ambush the presumed occupants.

"Okay, maybe they're *not* trying to ambush Spartans," John said. He released the bulkhead grab bar and began to float free again. "Maybe they're after something else."

"A salvage ship and a few scientists?" Petrov asked. "Because so far, that's all they've allowed to reach the surface."

"I don't know," John admitted. Covenant technology was so superior that risking the capture of an intact frigate to snatch a few human scientists made no sense. But the situation still smelled off to him—he just didn't trust the coincidences. "And *that*'s the problem. We have no idea how the Covenant thinks, because we don't know their capabilities."

"Isn't that what we're here to change, Spartan?"

"Yes, ma'am," John said. "But if we want to capture the *Lucky Break*, we have to use sound tactics. That's the only thing we have going for us."

Petrov studied him a moment, then asked, "What are you afraid of, John?"

"Mission failure," John said at once. If she was trying to put him off-balance with the question, it was a mistake. "The Mesranis improvised at Sarpesi Ridge, and the xenotime mine fell to the Covenant. Now Blue Force will insert onto a hostile environment at half strength—"

"Because I lost a Pelican," Petrov finished. Even packed tight, a Pelican dropship had a maximum capacity of just twenty soldiers. And Blue Force—the name they had selected for the combined unit of Blue Team and First Platoon—had a total strength of thirty-five. "Is that what you're thinking, Spartan?"

"The slash-g can't make two runs," John said. The slash-g was shorthand for the D75-TC/g Pelican, with a ground-support package consisting of two wing-mounted miniguns and a pair of belly-mounted cannon turrets. "Even if we *can* get by without the air cover."

Petrov did not bother arguing the point. Dropships rarely survived two runs, because by the time they unloaded, climbed back into orbit, and reloaded, the enemy interceptors were on station and waiting for them.

"I see," Petrov said. "After a year of prowler school and three years of command, do you think I might have thought of that before I launched the recon mission?"

"Did you?"

Petrov rolled her eyes into the tops of their sockets. "Move Blue Force into the drop bay, Master Chief. Full-pressure dress and safety slings—we may be going in hot."

"We're inserting aboard the *Night Watch*?" John was just starting to realize how committed Petrov was to capturing the *Lucky Break*—and how far ahead of him she was thinking. She had launched the recon mission for the sole purpose of ascertaining whether a dropship would get jumped. Now that it had, she felt safe in assuming the Covenant was actually trying to keep boarding forces away from the downed frigate, rather than using it to lay an ambush.

"I hope you have a backup extraction plan," John said. Given the stakes, the only real quarrel he had with Petrov's gambit was her keeping him in the dark—that, and what was clearly the casual sacrifice of a slash-r Pelican crew. "A lot of things can go wrong down there."

Petrov looked back to her status display. "*Now*, Master Chief," she said. "We may not know how the Covenant thinks, but we do know they're not stupid. Let's assume they're already looking for the *Night Watch*."

"Yes, ma'am."

John relayed the order over the prowler intercom, then went aft to join Blue Force in the drop bay. First Platoon was already in full EVA battle dress—basically torso armor over seven-layer vacuum suits, with enclosed CH252 helmets and airtight gloves and boots. Lieutenant Cacyuk was lining them up by squad, making sure they were securely webbed into their quick-release stability slings, and that their eight-point arresting straps were secured to the recessed D-rings in the deck and overhead. A short, black-haired woman who would barely stand as high as John's breastbone in a gravity environment, Sesi Cacyuk had a round face with flat, broad cheeks and honey-colored eyes. When she saw John working his way aft, she pushed away from the wide-eyed private she had been coaching in safe sling-rigging and floated over to intercept him.

"What's the plan, Master Chief?"

"There isn't one yet. Commander Petrov is just trying to get us to the target before the enemy can stop us. After that, I suspect the plan will be to move fast and hit hard."

Cacyuk furrowed her brow. "Will that work?"

"Of course, ma'am," John said. "We'll *make* it work."

"Very well, Master Chief." Cacyuk looked reassured, if not quite confident. "Let me know what you need from First Platoon."

"I will," John said. Cacyuk was ten years older than John and, as a commissioned officer, technically his superior. But nobody had any illusions about who would be leading the mission once they were on the ground. Admiral Cole's orders had made it clear that First Platoon would be supporting the Spartans, and that meant John was in charge. "Thank you, Lieutenant."

John pulled himself aft toward the jump hatch, where the rest of Blue Team was waiting. A safety sling did not exist that would hold four-hundred-and-fifty kilograms of Mjolnir-armored Spartan when a *Razor*-class prowler began to evade enemy fire, so Blue Team would simply kneel on the deck, holding on to a set of recessed tie-down bars designed to secure a Warthog LRV. Their force-multiplied grasps were stronger than the nylon arresting straps holding the marines in place; if anyone broke free and started to tumble around the drop bay, it would not be a Spartan.

An alert chime sounded, and a female voice came over the prowler intercom. "All hands, ready for combat insertion. Repeat: ready for combat insertion."

She clicked off, and a gentle pulse shook the drop bay as a set of hangar doors opened on the deck above. The overhead gave a soft rumble as the prowler's last Pelican ignited its hybrid fusion drives and departed. John and Petrov had not discussed the matter, but since Blue Force was inserting aboard the *Night Watch*, he knew the D75-TC/g would be carrying only its three-person crew—a solid hint that Petrov did not expect it to survive insertion. A heartbeat later, John's center-of-mass rose as the prowler decelerated and dropped out of orbit.

Linda-058 tipped her helmet back, looking up and aft in the presumed direction of the departed Pelican, and spoke over TEAM-COM. "It is too early." She turned her goggle-eyed faceplate back to John. "She is launching a decoy?"

"That's my guess," John said. "It's how she used the first one."

"Then we have no close air support." Linda shook her helmet from side to side. "I hope this commander knows what she is doing."

"She knows." John paused. He had told Lieutenant Cacyuk what he *knew* about Petrov's intentions, just not how he felt about them. But his own team deserved more. If he was worried, they should know. "She just hasn't told me. I think the commander is improvising."

"That's a relief," Fred instantly said. "I was worried she might have something in mind."

"Plans can be overrated," Kelly said. "Especially when there's no time to develop one."

John turned toward her and cocked his helmet. "You're not worried about striking blind like this?"

"Oh, I'm worried . . . one might even say troubled. But what's the alternative? Wait for *more* Covenant ships to arrive?"

"Good point," John said. As the leader not only of Blue Team but of the entire Spartan force, he had been admonished many times never to unnecessarily risk one of his subordinates. With only thirty-three Spartans in the entire UNSC, they were irreplaceable assets who took a decade to train and cost as much as a destroyer to equip. "But striking blind is the kind of thing that can get a whole team killed."

"And it's worth the gamble," Kelly said. "If ever there was a time to risk everything, it's now."

John dipped his helmet to acknowledge the point. Capturing the *Lucky Break* was the kind of mission that could make the difference between losing the war in a year or holding out to win it in ten. But he needed to be sure everyone was thinking the same thing. If part of the team was in total-commitment mode and part of it was trying to preserve assets . . . well, that could be a disaster. He turned to Fred.

Normally John would have turned up his palms to indicate he was asking for an opinion. But with the *Night Watch* beginning to buck and shake on its steep insertion, he needed both hands on the tie-down bars to keep himself on the deck. Instead, he flashed a green status LED inside Fred's helmet.

"What? We're taking votes now?" Fred asked. "I'm not sure that was the Mesrani Militia's best idea."

"Not a vote," John said. "I just want to know your thinking."

"I don't think Commander Crazy cares about my thinking." Fred glanced toward the overhead, then shrugged. "But she's not wrong. If we don't move fast, we might not be able to move at all."

John turned to Linda next, but before he could flash the status LED, she said, "If I *had* different thoughts, I would tell them to you."

"Understood. Just so we're clear," John said. "And the Commander Crazy stuff? Let's keep that between us."

A trio of status LEDs winked green, then John's arms jerked hard to starboard as the *Night Watch* made a sharp course correction. A chorus of grunts and a few cries of surprise rose from the marines hanging in their webs behind him. He had barely drifted back to center when the deck rose up beneath him so hard his Mjolnir's knee cops rang like bells.

"Evasive action," Kelly said, over her external voicemitter. "That's never a good sign."

"Would have been better off in drop pods," Fred said. "At least we'd have been smaller targets."

"Our fault." Cacyuk's emitter-filtered voice came from behind Kelly. John glanced over his shoulder and saw that the lieutenant was at the far end of the first row of marines, hanging in her safety sling with only her eyes and cheeks showing through the faceplate of her pressure mask. "First Platoon's not pod-rated. We're regular assault."

"It wouldn't have made a difference," John said. Cacyuk's explanation was a reminder of both the mission's improvised nature and the relative inexperience of her unit. Instead of the elite ODST units that Spartans usually worked with, First Platoon was just a bunch of regular soldiers—well trained in the basics, but probably inexperienced and certainly unfamiliar with special tactics. "It's hard to make a pinpoint drop through a high-energy atmosphere like Netherop's. Hit just one vortex, and we'd spend the entire mission trying to find each other."

John's arms strained as the *Night Watch* slipped sideways, then he went weightless again as she dived hard. He wanted to comm the flight deck and ask about their situation, but there were few moves more boneheaded than distracting a flight crew while it was in the middle of saving a ship.

John slammed down on his flank and found himself struggling to hold the recessed tie-downs he was using as anchors. The sound of retching and vomiting arose behind him, and as his own inner ears began to protest, he realized the prowler had entered a violent gyre. It was going to be fun trying to shoot straight if they found themselves disembarked into a hot LZ.

The thunk and ping of impacting fuel rod rounds and plasma bolts began to echo through the hull of the *Night Watch*. She answered the attacks with four chugging autocannons, and the interior of the drop bay began to sound like the inside of a thunderstorm. John slid across the deck and rolled onto the opposite flank as the prowler reversed her roll, and more retching sounded behind him.

The thunking and pinging grew even steadier and louder as the enemy closed. The chugging of the prowler's autocannons dwindled from constant to rhythmic as one of the turrets went down. Petrov's voice sounded in John's helmet speakers, coming over the ship's intercom channel:

"Prepare for running dump. Two minutes to LZ."

Two minutes was about twenty-five hundred kilometers at full insertion speed. But the *Night Watch* could not just open the jump hatch and expect Blue Force to leap out and survive. The prowler would have to decelerate hard—and that meant it would need to reverse orientation so it could use its fusion drives. There was no need to tell Blue Team what to do. They were already swinging around, bracing their feet against the jump hatch and tightening their grasp on the tie-down bars. Now they were facing Lieutenant Cacyuk and her platoon, who were hanging in their safety slings like bugs in a spiderweb, their eyes showing round and bright behind their pressure-mask faceplates.

They were probably scared because they'd never inserted under fighter attack. John knew they'd do fine once they got their boots on the ground. Marines always did.

"If you've lifted your mask to vomit, check your pressure seal," John said. As long as their chins were back in their chin-cups, the seals would automatically be good. But checking the seals gave them something to think about other than getting shot down. "We might be jumping into smoke or fumes, and you don't want that inside your mask."

To a soldier, the marines covered their outlet valves and began to exhale into their masks.

Then the entire *Night Watch* shuddered beneath the launch of her Archer missiles. The Covenant strikes fell silent as her pursuers either broke off or were destroyed. A couple of moments later, after the debris had been given a chance to clear, the rumble of firing fusion drives shook the bay.

The prowler lurched as if she had backed into a stone wall, and John felt his legs taking four thousand kilograms of weight under the vessel's nine-g deceleration. The marines bulged toward him in their safety slings, their eyes bugging and their skin pouching toward their faceplates, their gear pulling little cones into their pressure suits.

Petrov's voice came over the intercom again. "One minute to LZ." Translation: about 750 kilometers. "We have another Banshee squadron coming in, but the *Wheatley* is putting up her Baselards to cover your drop."

The marines' faces were too g-stretched to show fear, but with the rumble of the fusion drives filling the jump bay and word that their prowler would soon be under attack again, John knew they would be anxious. Terrified, maybe. He opened a Blue Force comm channel and began to speak to them over their helmet speakers.

"Ten seconds before drop, the pilot will double our deceleration. You'll feel like your heart is pulling out of your chest. Some of you may black out. But the Banshees will overshoot us and be dozens of kilometers away when we exit the vessel."

John paused, making sure they were all listening to him instead of all of the enemy fire starting to reverberate through the hull again.

"Three seconds before the jump hatch opens, the pilot will cut the fusion drives and spin us around. The prowler will be moving forward at approximately fifty kilometers per hour, and the drop bay will be facing away from the direction of travel. You'll take your primary weapon in one hand and hold your free hand over your safety-sling quick-release."

Most of First Platoon probably knew this last part as well as John did—"running disembarks" were a standard skill in every marine's basic training. But he doubted many of them had ever done it in full combat conditions, under enemy attack, after a stomach-churning insertion run. He hoped a few words of reminder might help them focus.

"When the jump hatch opens, a drag ramp will extend from the rear of the drop bay. You marines in the first row will quick-release out of your safety slings and follow the Spartans down the drag ramp.

You'll jump off the bottom edge at a full sprint, then keep running until your feet touch the ground and your momentum knocks—"

A tremendous bang sounded somewhere forward, and John saw dozens of bulging eyeballs strain to look toward the sound.

"Pay attention! There's nothing you can do about anything up there." All eyes returned to John. "Each row of marines will quick-release as soon as the row ahead—"

Another bang, this one louder and sharper. Followed instantly by three *booms*, each deeper than the last. The tie-down bars vibrated in John's hands. The fusion drives rumbled louder, and the prowler decelerated even harder, doubling and then tripling the force against John's legs. Arresting straps began to pop, marines screaming freely into their masks.

John wondered what their chances were of making the LZ. His onboard computer did not even try to develop an estimate, instead putting a simple countdown on his HUD: 27 SECONDS, 99 KILO-METERS TO LZ.

A male voice came over the prowler's intercom channel, straining against the g-force: *"Brace . . . bra . . . ce . . . br . . . a . . . ce!"*

"How in the . . . hell do . . . we . . . brace . . . ev . . . en . . . moooore?" Fred asked.

The countdown on John's HUD read 24 SECONDS, 94 KILOMETERS TO LZ.

The fusion drives fell silent, leaving only the sound of chugging autocannons and pinging plasma strikes to fill the bay. The marines sagged back into their safety slings, and the weight on John's legs returned to almost normal and shifted toward his side as the *Night Watch* reversed orientation.

He and the other Spartans tried to swing their legs around so they were facing the jump hatch again, but the prowler responded slowly. She seemed to be sliding sideways through the air, bucking and shuddering beneath each cannon round, occasionally dipping into a bank. She was losing altitude so fast that John's knees left the deck and he was stuck hanging in the air, facing port.

The LZ countdown reached 14 seconds, 73 kilometers.

One second later, a deafening clang echoed through the compartment. The starboard bulkhead folded inward, spraying rivets and shards of titanium ship armor across the bay like shrapnel, puncturing pressure suits and slashing safety slings. Half a dozen marines slammed into the overhead shrieking and spurting blood, secured by only their upper arresting straps.

Then the prowler's nose swung about and came up, bringing John and the Spartans the rest of the way around, planting their toes and knees firmly on the deck.

Petrov's voice came over the intercom. "Impact!"

She was a few seconds early. John lay pinned against the deck, reminding himself to breathe, listening to marines yell, watching Covenant rounds punch through the jump hatch in front of him. He kept expecting Fred to crack wise—maybe *hoping* for some smart remark to break the tension—but all the Spartans remained quiet, their attention fixed on the fuel rod rounds striking half a meter from their faceplates.

And finally . . . impact.

The deck bucked hard, launching everyone toward the overhead. John felt the Mjolnir's reactive circuits lock his gauntlets around the tie-downs, and the prowler slowed beneath him. The fuel rod strikes came to an abrupt end—the enemy fighters overflying their quarry. John saw the marines slamming backward in their safety slings, the grunts and cries almost loud enough to drown out the screech of tearing hull.

A ring of little smoke plumes billowed around the jump hatch, someone on the flight deck—probably Petrov, if she was still alive—blowing the emergency bolts. And the hatch tumbled away in two halves, revealing a brown and yellow blur . . . desert terrain . . . flashing past behind the *Night Watch*.

John yelled, "Go go go!"

He launched himself forward, sprinting out of the bay's dim light into Netherop's bright amber haze.

The countdown on his HUD read 8 SECONDS, 60 KILOMETERS TO LZ.

CHAPTER 7

0512 hours, June 7, 2526 (military calendar)
UNSC *Razor*-class Prowler *Night Watch*
Crash Site, Planet Netherop, Ephyra System

The buttons on Amalea Petrov's commpad had never felt so small. She'd drilled the Catastrophic Event Self-Destruct Self-Initiation Override a hundred times, and not once had she failed to complete the task in less than the allotted forty-five seconds. But now that it counted, now that her prowler had gone down and she was kneeling in front of the engineering station with the self-destruction system security cover unlocked and pushed aside, *now* her fingers were too damn big to depress the correct keys and enter the proper codes.

Amalea exhaled slowly, then held her wrist-worn commpad close to the system command port. A message appeared on the system display: ENTER IDENTIFICATION CODE.

This time she tried a different approach. Instead of carefully entering each character, as she had on her first three attempts, Amalea tapped the pad quickly and naturally, as if sending a hurried message to one of her subordinates.

AMALEA 78^&9 PETROV TANGO VICTOT FOCTROT.

There were at least two typos in the code, but that was common for her messages, and the *Night Watch*'s AI seemed to recognize her natural pattern.

COMMAND?

SYNC PETROV COMMPAD NIGHT WATCH SELF-DESTRUCT CONTROL.

The display went blank—a security feature designed to make unauthorized users think they would soon be the target of a ship-wide security sweep. She waited, knowing it would be ten seconds before the next message came, and that any attempt to rush the procedure now would only result in starting over. It was a precaution that she doubted anyone who had ever actually been forced to abandon ship would have designed into the system. But she recognized its wisdom. If there wasn't ten seconds to spare, the last thing a captain should be doing was taking control of her prowler's self-destruct routines.

And maybe Amalea was making a mistake even *with* the extra ten seconds. She didn't think the Covenant commander had actually been outsmarting her so far. After all, he—Amalea *assumed* it was a he, because the ONI intelligence briefings she had read indicated that the dead aliens recovered from battlefields were over ninety percent male—had taken the bait when she launched the slash-r recon Pelican as soon as the *Night Watch* entered orbit. And the subsequent launch of the slash-s close air support Pelican had caught him so flat-footed that she had come within sixty kilometers of dropping Blue Force right on top of his downed frigate. But the alien *had* surprised her with the number of fighter craft he had available. She had expected the second Pelican, the D75 TC/s, to draw off the last of his fighters so she could insert Blue Force unmolested.

Instead, he had hit her with two more waves. There were more Covenant stealth vessels in the area than she'd anticipated. Had she spent the standard ten or twelve hours making passive observations, Amalea might well have realized that. But as Covenant ships continued to arrive to defend the downed frigate, Blue Force would probably have lost all hope of capturing the vessel intact. It had been a tough choice, and even knowing it had cost her the *Night Watch*, she believed she had made the right one.

Still, it *did* trouble her that the Master Chief hadn't seemed to support her. In all of their previous interactions, John-117 had always struck her as aggressive to a fault, so she had expected him to greet her boldness with enthusiasm. Now she didn't know what to make of his concern. Did he really think she was taking too many risks? Or did he just resent her attempts to leaven the Spartans' prowess with some cold calculation?

The system display returned to life with a new message: AUTHORIZATION CODE?

Amalea began to tap her commpad again: FLEET ^DMIR^L PETROV.

Her chosen code phrase was more than vanity; it was a reminder of what Amalea was striving for, an exhortation to stay focused and execute her plan.

The next step in that plan was making sure Blue Force captured the *Lucky Break*. If Amalea could seize the alien frigate, she would be responsible for the greatest coup of the war so far. Admirals Stanforth and Cole would not be able to help seeing what she had done with Blue Team—how she had elevated it to its full potential—and they would want the same for all of their Spartan teams.

And if Amalea could hone the fighting edge of all Spartan teams as she was doing for Blue Team, there would be no limit. FLEETCOM would entrust her with the development of other projects crucial to surviving the war—projects so sensitive she would only hear of them when she was placed in charge of them—and she would begin her sure and steady climb into the UNSC's highest levels of command.

All Amalea had to do was capture one helpless frigate.

After a three-second delay, Amalea's commpad chirped, and a new message appeared on the systems display above the command port:

CATASTROPHIC EVENT SELF-DESTRUCT SELF-INITIATION OVERRIDE SUCCESSFUL.

CONTROL OF NIGHT WATCH FURY MEDIUM FUSION SELF-DESTRUCT DEVICE RESIDES WITH LIEUTENANT COMMANDER PETROV.

IN EVENT OF COMMANDER PETROV'S DEATH OR LOSS OF CONTACT, SELF-DESTRUCT INITIATION WILL RETURN TO NIGHT WATCH.

CONFIRM?

Amalea tapped AFFIRMATIVE.

The system display went blank. She slid the security cover closed, then pressed her thumb to the biometric lock. A triple chirp assured her that should anyone attempt to access the self-destruct system cabinet, she would be notified. She stood, then checked the chronometer on her commpad. It had been over two minutes since the *Night Watch*'s pilot and copilot had made their incredible dead-stick landing, skipping the prowler up a narrow mountain bench in a display of skill and grace under pressure that had made her glad she always insisted on a rigorous training regimen.

But her bungled attempts to engage the override had cost her. By now, the enemy fighter craft would be returning to orbit the crash site—and that meant she would have to chance being strafed as she left the *Night Watch*. It wasn't the thought of getting hit that frightened her, not really. What troubled Amalea was that now *she* had become the prowler's self-destruct initiation trigger.

If she died, the Fury would detonate, initiating a thermonuclear explosion that would incinerate everything close by. The theory was that if a prowler needed to self-destruct, it was likely to be surrounded by hostile vessels, and there was no use passing up an opportunity to attack an enemy ship at close range. Again, it was not a feature that any prowler commander would have designed into the self-destruct system . . . but it *did* have a certain ruthlessness that Amalea admired.

In this case, however, that might be counterproductive. If she were to die, so would Blue Team—and that would mean complete mission failure.

Amalea turned aft and started for the drop bay—only to see John emerging from the life support section. He carried a hundred-liter storage tank under each arm, and he had a purifying filter attached to a hard point on the back of his armor. He immediately spun in her direction, and for an instant she thought he was about to hurl one of the tanks up the passageway at her.

"Commander?" John's posture relaxed when he realized it was her, and he stepped out of the hatchway to allow the rest of Blue Team to pass. They were also carrying storage tanks under their arms. "What are you still doing aboard?"

"It's my ship, so you first." Amalea started toward John. "Why are you stripping the water tanks?"

"Ma'am, it's hot outside. I mean, *really* hot."

"Ah," she said. "Good thinking."

John cocked his helmet at her as though trying to figure out what she had come back for. "What about you, Commander? The first officer said all surviving crewmembers had been evacuated."

"I'm not really a crew*member*, John." Amalea saw no reason to hide what she had been doing—in fact, there was a good case for making sure he knew. "And I needed to override the prowler's self-destruct initiation trigger."

"Oh yeah." John's helmet returned to vertical. "The Fury."

"I thought you might understand." A Fury Medium Fusion Destructive Device yielded close to a megaton—which meant that, on a planet with an atmosphere, the crater alone would be sixty meters deep and four hundred meters across. The heat flash would incinerate everything within two kilometers, and the conflagration zone would extend several times that distance. "And, Master Chief?"

"Yes, ma'am?"

"You *really* need to keep me alive when we exit the prowler," Amalea said. "Can you do that?"

"Of course, Commander." John looked down the passageway, and the rest of Blue Team stopped and made a space for her in the center of the group. "Just stay in the middle, and everyone will be fine."

CHAPTER 8

0715 hours, June 7, 2526 (military calendar)
Near *Night Watch* crash site
Mountains of Despair, Planet Netherop, Ephyra System

A shapeless wad of hot sun, shining down through a blanket of low brown clouds onto a ribbon of dusty benchland. The benchland clinging to an arid slope so steep that the dust avalanches down in powdery gray fans. On the uphill side, the mountains loom skyward in an unending wall, their summits so high they vanish into the low brown clouds. On the downhill side, the slope drops over a line of cliffs into a searing mirage-filled basin, the basin so deep the floor vanishes beneath a shimmering blue sea of refracted light.

The *Night Watch* could have gone down in worse places, John knew. But it sure hadn't gone down in a good place.

The survivors had hiked eight kilometers in two hours, more or less toward their intended landing zone near the *Lucky Break*—the downed Covenant frigate that John and Petrov and the rest of Blue Force still intended to capture.

Actually, *intended* might have been too strong a word for some of the marines in First Platoon. A lot of them were sweating profusely and doubled over with heat cramps, weak and staggering and dizzy. But they were still walking, and if they survived the fifty-kilometer hike to the *Lucky Break,* John had no doubt they would fight.

It was the hike that was going to be the problem for most of them. So far, the aliens had not bothered to strafe the column. Petrov claimed it was likely because the Covenant commander was low on Banshees and didn't want to risk losing any to small-arms fire. And maybe there was something to that. Linda had already taken down two observation craft with her SRS99 sniper rifle, and they hadn't seen another one for more than an hour.

John had a simpler theory.

The alien reconnaissance pilots had seen that the *Night Watch* survivors were dying in the heat, and the Covenant commander was just waiting them out. After all, there was no use risking Banshees and wasting ammunition when a deadly environment would do the killing instead. And any targets that *did* survive were going to be a lot easier to kill after a lengthy walk in the scorching heat.

That's what John would have done, were the situation reversed. Wait the enemy out.

"What about in here?" Commander Petrov pointed into a big, steep-walled gulch cut into the mountainside above the bench. Dressed in her blue flight utilities, she had been traveling next to John since they departed the crash site, doing an impressive job of keeping pace despite Netherop's high gravity. "It looks big enough to hold everyone."

John stopped to examine the gulch. It was filled with masses of orange leafless plants that looked like chest-high candelabra, but the leeward rim was overhung by a cornice of wind-packed dust that would break free when the blast wave hit.

"No good." John pointed at the cornice. "Look. That has to be a few thousand tons up there. We Spartans would probably survive, if we weren't swept away. But a lot of First Platoon would be crushed, and anyone without a self-contained air supply would suffocate."

Petrov blanched, then looked down the bench in the direction they were coming from. A line of marines and prowler crew was strung out for half a kilometer behind them, carrying the wounded and dragging water tanks uphill, already staggering in the gravity and forty-five-degree-Celsius heat. Lacking any environmental control in their emergency pressure suits, the marines had removed their masks and pulled their tops down around their hips, and the prowler crew had unbuttoned their utilities to their waists. But the air was warmer than their body temperatures, so the only cooling effect came from their own sweat, evaporating into the arid air.

"Well, we need to find cover soon," Petrov said. "If we keep pushing this hard, it won't matter how far away we are when I detonate. Everyone will be dead of heatstroke."

John knew better than to suggest calling in a rescue mission courtesy of the *Phyllis Wheatley*—yet. Petrov had barely managed to assume remote control of the prowler's self-destruct device—and Blue Team to pull the water tanks out of the reclamation system—before half a dozen Covenant fighters had returned and begun to circle overhead, ready to strafe anyone who tried to approach the vessel. Another ten had quickly arrived and descended to the crash site, precluding all hope of asking for help from the *Wheatley*.

John had a high opinion of ONI pilots, but the recovery ship carried only two Pelicans and twelve Baselards. The Baselards were space interceptors first and air-superiority fighters second, which made them too clumsy in atmospheric combat to prevail against a superior Banshee force. Until Petrov detonated the Fury and sanitized the crash site, the *Night Watch* survivors were on their own, and the only thing they could do was keep moving until they were far enough away to safely activate the self-destruct charge.

And when the charge was a one-megaton Fury tactical nuclear device, that was quite a distance.

"I mean it, John," Petrov said. "We may need to take the chance, before we start losing people to heatstroke."

"I know, ma'am."

"And it's not just our people I'm thinking about." Petrov glanced back toward the crash site, then leaned in and looked up into John's faceplate. Her face was flushed and dry, a sign that she herself was starting to succumb to the elements. "It's been over two hours since we abandoned ship. Do you know what that means? It means the Covenant has been aboard my prowler for two hours."

"I know, ma'am."

John's HUD showed exactly one-hundred-twenty-seven minutes since the *Night Watch* had gone down. But without a satellite network to provide global positioning coordinates, their distance from the crash site was a dead-reckoning estimate from the Mjolnir's onboard computer, based solely on the length of John's stride and the number of steps he had taken.

8.56 KILOMETERS.

The Fury Medium Fusion Destructive Device used as a self-destruct charge aboard UNSC prowlers was a "clean" bomb that didn't release much radiation. At their current distance, the ship's complement would be relatively safe from gamma rays, neutron bombardment, and fallout. And eight kilometers was just beyond the conflagration zone. As long as everyone was behind good cover, they would avoid third-degree burns.

It was the shockwaves that posed the problem. They wouldn't be strong enough to cause direct injury to anyone lying in even a shallow depression. But they *would* uproot plants and hurl small stones, as well as trigger dust-slides.

John looked up the gulch again. If they climbed high enough, the mouth would serve as a baffle to divert the shockwave, and a few grenades would probably bring the cornice down before Petrov detonated the self-destruct charge. But the chute ran straight up the mountainside into the low brown clouds, two steep kilometers at a minimum, all of it lined by other wind-packed cornices and filled with dust. When the Fury vaporized the *Night Watch*, the whole mountainside would let loose and avalanche down on them.

"I can't let my ship be the first prowler the Covenant captures," Petrov said. She might have been suffering the early symptoms of heatstroke, but she was still very, very focused. "Even if it means taking our chances in the open."

"I know, ma'am." Stealth technology was the one area of space warfare where humanity wasn't hopelessly outclassed, so allowing a prowler to fall into enemy hands would be as much a disaster for the UNSC as capturing a Covenant capital ship would be a boon. "But it won't come to that."

"I don't see how you can promise that, John. It's not in your power to prevent. They're already on board my ship."

Petrov continued to look down the bench, gazing over the heads of her crew and the marines toward the *Night Watch*'s crash site. Even magnified through John's faceplate, the prowler was visible only as a tiny delta-shaped shadow, surrounded by the barely visible dots of more than a dozen Banshees. All of the craft were blurry, and they seemed to be floating dozens of meters above the ground.

John knew it was an illusion—a superior mirage, caused by light being refracted as it passed through hot air above cooler ground.

But that did not keep him from feeling uneasy. The Covenant employed all kinds of technology the UNSC had never seen before, and he could not help worrying that the aliens might be using some kind of powerful anti-gravity device to float the disabled prowler up into orbit.

John opened TEAMCOM. "Blue Four, is that prowler rising any higher off the ground?"

"Negative." Linda was two kilometers down the bench, using her sniper optics to keep tabs on the aliens' progress. "I am measuring the angle of refraction. The *Night Watch* remains on the ground, even if it does not appear so."

"Any sign of surveillance craft hanging around?" Even if the Covenant couldn't take the entire prowler, they might try taking measurements and recording images. "Or of a comm tower being erected?"

"I would have *told* you." Linda sounded exasperated. *"Immediately."*

"How about movement back and forth?" John asked. Even if the Covenant wasn't trying to retrieve images and specifications, they would at least be attempting to snag as many instruments and engineering systems as possible. "Any signs they're gathering equipment?"

"Unable to determine. The heat shimmer prevents my optics from resolving to that scale." Linda paused, then added, "But, John, it has been two hours."

"So I keep being told." John let his gaze drop to the column of overheated marines and ship's crew. Even if the aliens weren't ready to start ferrying the prowler's equipment back to their mothership— and after all this time, they *had* to be—the Spartans were the only ones in climate-controlled power armor. And that meant they were the only ones who could keep hiking. "Okay. Break off observation and rejoin the column. Blue Three?"

Kelly's status light winked green to confirm she was listening.

"Give all your explosive ordnance to Blue Two, then find a good observation post and take over the watch." Kelly and Fred were about half a kilometer ahead of John, looking for a good place to shelter from the self-destruct charge. "Let me and Commander Petrov know the instant you see any Covenant craft departing the crash site."

"Affirmative," Kelly said.

"Blue Two?"

"Let me guess," Fred said. "The cornices?"

Blue Team could be like that. They had been training together since childhood. At times it seemed like they were somehow plugged into each other's brains through their neural implants and onboard computers.

"Can you do it?" John asked.

"I think I can handle it." There was a note of sarcasm in Fred's tone. "As long as they don't fight back."

"How long?" John asked.

Fred was quiet a moment, then finally said, "Depends on what I find in the clouds, I guess."

It took sixteen minutes for Fred to traverse to the gulch and climb up to the low brown clouds. He might have been faster, except that he was carrying two extra tube sets for his M41 rocket launcher, and enough grenades to fill a Brute's helmet. In Netherop's high gravity, the extra weight made it harder to be sure of his footing on the dusty slope.

The strange vegetation—what there was of it—didn't help. He quickly learned to avoid any area near those orange candelabra trees, since they were showing only their crowns, and the rest of their habit was hidden beneath the powdery surface, a tangled mass of rubbery twigs that trapped a foot or leg as efficiently as it did any dust. And where the slabs of red shale protruded to form a ridge of solid footing, he first had to fight his way through a chest-high tangle of carnivorous bushes he quickly dubbed "paddle plants."

The paddle plants tended to mass along the windward edges of the shale outcroppings. They had big, gray-green pads covered in a curly white fuzz full of tiny trapped insects . . . or at least, what *looked* like insects. The creatures were about half the size of a fingernail, but they had smooth blue skin, three emerald eyes, and five legs. And they were currently being eaten whole by scaly, thumb-sized grubs, each attached to the bottom of one of the pads by a throbbing umbilical.

Nice place, this Netherop.

Before climbing into the clouds to locate the head of the gulch, Fred glanced down its length to be sure everyone was clear of the mouth. He could see an almost unbroken cornice of wind-packed dust hanging over his side of the chute, sometimes extending halfway across. At the bottom, the gulch sank into a depression and entered a large, diamond-shaped cavern that ran all the way under the bench and opened into empty air on the other side. The sides were asymmetric, and the bottom was buried in dust. But, save for a few shell-shaped spall pits, the face was as smooth as concrete, and the top edges were as straight as anything a combat engineer would build.

It was hardly the way a human would design a giant culvert. But it obviously wasn't the way nature would design one either.

Fred spoke over TEAMCOM. "What would you say if I told you that you're on some sort of forgotten highway?"

"I'd say hurry up with those cornices," John said. "Kelly thinks the Covenant might be loading their Seraphs."

"Or it could be mirage ghosts dancing in the heat shimmer," Kelly said. "It's hard to tell exactly *what* I'm watching."

"You are watching something," Linda said. "I also see dark shapes moving between the *Night Watch* and the closest Seraph."

"On it," Fred said. Taking care to stay well back from the edge of the gulch so he didn't prematurely collapse a cornice, he started up a shale outcropping into the low brown clouds. "There's a culvert at the bottom of the gulch. It might make a good bunker, if you can dig down into it after I drop the cornices."

"A *culvert?*"

John didn't sound as surprised as he might have. Blue Team had spent the slipspace jump from Mesra preparing for their mission and studying what the UNSC knew about Netherop—which wasn't much. The *Military Survey of Uninhabited Planets* listed Netherop as uninhabited, marginally survivable, of minimal strategic value, with no exploitable resources. The assessor's notes added that the hostile environment had cut the survey mission short. The notes ended with the recommendation that a properly equipped expedition should return to continue the investigation. But a classified ONI addendum listed the planet as possibly abandoned—a nebulous designation that could suggest the survey had found anything from an old Colonial habitability probe to the presence of terrain features that could have been artificially constructed.

Fred could guess what had happened next: the survey had been electronically added to the *MSUP* by some clerk who'd read no further than "minimal strategic value, no exploitable resources," and the assessor's recommendation had remained unread until the *first* time Blue Team was dispatched to Netherop, in an attempt to snatch a Covenant survey vessel out of orbit.

And by then, there had been other things for the UNSC to worry about.

"A culvert?" John repeated. "Fred, you're sure?"

"I'm sure it'll make a good bunker." Fred was well into the cloud layer now, surrounded by a greasy brown fog that seemed to coat his faceplate like oil. "Take a look. You'll see."

"If you say so," John said. "Just hurry. If anything tries to leave the crash site, Commander Petrov won't wait to detonate the Fury."

"Understood," Fred said.

And he *did* understand—the UNSC didn't want the Covenant to learn the secrets of their prowler technology any more than the Covenant wanted the UNSC to learn the secrets of their energy shields and plasma weapons. So no aliens could be permitted to leave the crash site alive—not a single one, even if it meant everyone who had been aboard the *Night Watch* had to die.

A hundred meters into the clouds, the gulch finally narrowed to a couple of meters. It ended at the base of a shale outcropping, which continued straight up the mountain and vanished into the brown clouds about two hundred meters above. As usual, the windward side of the outcropping was covered in a tangle of paddle plants, and a few paces above the head of the gulch, a three-meter swath had been smashed through the strange foliage.

Something large had pushed through the tangle and clambered over the outcropping, but Fred didn't have a lot of time to contemplate what kind of giant fauna might be crawling around Netherop's mountains. He climbed around the windward side of the plants, where he found two sets of circular hoofprints running parallel to each other, about two meters apart and leading into the broken swath. All the prints had a split down the center, like the hoof of a goat, but they were too uniform in size and shape to have been made by more than one animal. Or, really, any kind of animal. Nature just didn't make feet that perfectly round.

But there was no time to puzzle over that now. He entered the ruined swath and traversed back toward the gulch, trying to position himself directly above it. As he moved, he saw that the paddles had been broken off at the stem. The ground was littered with those scaly grubs, all squashed flat and ripped free of their umbilicals. In the dust, he noticed dozens of tracks that looked an awful lot like the footprints of a human child—as unlikely as that seemed. But a lot of animals made tracks that could look somewhat human—bears, for example.

He just didn't think there were any bears on Netherop.

Fred came to the spot he had been trying to reach, directly above the gulch, and saw that a wide cornice of dust extended over the top of the gulch. Had he attempted to jump across, it would probably have collapsed under his weight and dropped him into the chute, and he would have wasted the next few minutes trying to stop his slide and climb back to where he was now.

Fred grabbed a grenade and opened a general channel. "All clear on the Forgotten Highway?"

"Forgotten Highway?" Petrov asked.

"You're standing on it," Fred said. "I keep telling you—"

"All clear," Petrov said. "Do it already."

"This could take a few tries," Fred said. "Stay away from the culvert until I give the word."

"If we can," Petrov said. "Just do it."

"Yes, ma'am." Fred thumbed the arming slider. "Fire in the hole!"

He tossed the grenade down onto the cornice, then watched it sink through the dust and vanish. A second later, it dropped out the bottom side and started to roll down the gulch . . . then detonated with a sharp bang and an orange flash.

A section of cornice disintegrated into a powdery cloud and plumed ten meters skyward, and a downslope segment broke free and dropped into the gulch. After that, all Fred could see was a billowing fog of dust, but the muffled rumble rolling up the chute suggested that at least *something* was avalanching down toward the culvert.

He grabbed the M41 off his back mounts and fired the first rocket through the dust, aiming for a point about two hundred meters down the gulch and toward the windward side. The detonation was louder and deeper than the grenade, but there was so much dust in the air now that the fireball was barely an orange glow.

Still, that muffled rumbling grew louder, and he knew the avalanche was growing. He fired the second rocket at a point he hoped was four hundred meters down the gulch, and this time, he did not even see the flare.

"Good job," John said over TEAMCOM. "There's a wall of dust about five hundred meters high over the gulch. Is that all of it?"

"Your guess is as good as mine." Fred detached the used tubes from the M41 and reached for a reload. "I can't see anything."

"Then I suggest you start firing blind," Kelly said. "I have figures leaving the *Night Watch*. Quite a few figures, actually."

"I think the avalanche has attracted their attention," Linda said. "They are spreading out . . . and stopping."

"Maybe trying to figure out what they're seeing," Fred said. "Same as you are."

"Maybe," John said. "And pretty soon, someone's going to hop in a Banshee to come check on us."

He did not need to spell out what would follow. Even if the Covenant didn't send a flight of Banshees to strafe them, Petrov could not afford to take chances. As soon as the first alien craft left the *Night Watch* crash site, she would detonate the Fury.

"I've got this." Fred locked the reload tubes in place. He would have a better view of the cornices from the leeward side of the gulch, so he began to clamber across the shale outcropping, following the same path the mysterious creature—or *creatures*—had taken. "I'll keep putting rockets into the cornice as I come down the mountain. Let me know when Commander Crazy decides to detonate."

"Affirmative," John said. "And, Fred, take it easy with that nickname. If the commander hears you using it—"

"I know," Fred said. "Sorry. The truth hurts—usually the one telling it."

As he crested the outcropping, he noticed a ghostly, spiderlike silhouette standing two hundred meters distant. Swaddled in the brown fog, it was an almost illusory figure that he might not have believed was real, had he not spotted a trail of parallel, split-hoofed tracks leading across the slope straight toward it. He magnified the image, but between the dust and the oily film clouding his faceplate, it did not help much.

All he could tell was that it was probably half again the size of a Warthog LRV, and it had five pairs of cursorial legs spaced evenly around a bulbous body with a flattened dorsal area. The legs on the uphill side were folded upward almost in two, so that its feet were planted on the slope at almost the same level as its belly. On the downhill side, the legs extended straight out from its flank and dropped to the ground at a ninety-degree angle, so that the body was supported more or less evenly. There appeared to be a pair of round spheres on the top of the body, which might have been forward-facing ears, but could have been very large external eyes—or very small heads.

"What the hell . . . ?"

"If that question's for me," John said, "I have no idea. How are those cornices looking?"

Seeming to sense it was being watched, the spider-thing scurried forward with astonishing speed, then dropped out of sight behind a fold in the terrain. Whatever it was, Fred hoped it would have the sense to hunker down and hold on tight—at least until after the *Night Watch* was incinerated. He turned and began to bound down the slope alongside the gulch.

"Not sure yet," he said. "Working on it."

He dropped out of the clouds and found himself traveling alongside the dust curtain billowing out of the gulch. There was no hope of seeing through it to the other side, especially as the chute widened again. But as he descended, the growl of the avalanche began to fade and the curtain seemed to grow less dense and high. After five hundred meters, he stopped and blind-fired a rocket into the far side of the gulch.

The dust curtain billowed even higher and thicker than before, and the sound of the avalanche rose to a rumble again. Fred raced another two hundred meters down the mountainside and fired again, though the dust was already so thick and the noise so loud he couldn't tell whether he was having any effect.

He changed barrels again and continued down the mountainside. By the next time he fired, the sound of the avalanche had receded and the dust curtain had thinned so much that he was catching glimpses of a rocky face on the opposite side of the gulch. When the detonation didn't launch any more dust into the air or heighten the sound of the avalanche, he bounded down the slope another few hundred meters and tried again.

The dust curtain continued to thin, and the sound of the avalanche faded entirely. He was less than a kilometer from the Forgotten Highway, and at the bottom of the gulch, he even thought he could see a flattened diamond of blue light where the culvert opened out onto the mirage basin.

He unlocked the M41's empty tubes and switched to the general comm channel. "I think the gulch is clear," he said. "Look for the culvert at the bottom."

"Well done, Spartan," Petrov said. "Now, take cover. You have twenty seconds."

Fred looked toward the culvert. Before he had quite realized what he was trying to figure out, his onboard computer activated his rangefinder, and the distance to the culvert appeared on his HUD.

709 METERS.

Even Spartans weren't that fast. "Crap."

"Quickly, Fred," Kelly said over TEAMCOM. "Commander Crazy is serious. We're out of time."

"Why? What's happening?"

Fred knew the answer before he finished asking the question. The Covenant had to be launching something from the crash site. He tossed the empty missile tubes aside and turned to see what they were putting up—and instead found his eye drawn to a distant pair of figures sprawled atop the next outcropping, perhaps five hundred meters away, their legs and arms splayed across the slope, the tiny dots of their heads protruding just above the crest as they studied the activity at the crash site.

He magnified the image and could see a little more—enough to tell that they resembled human children, with small frames, gaunt builds, and unruly hair. They wore rough clothing that might have been woven from raw plant fibers, and they had some sort of black-soled sandals strapped to their feet. Behind them, at the bottom of the outcropping, stood one of the strange spider-creatures Fred had glimpsed earlier—maybe even the same one.

Fred switched to the general comm channel. "Wait, there are—"

"Can't wait," Petrov said. "Those Banshees are lifting off."

Fred looked toward the *Night Watch* and saw the violet splinters of three impulse drives snaking through the heat shimmer above the tiny prowler floating on the blue mirage. Petrov was right—she couldn't wait, but those kids (if that's what they really were) on the next outcropping didn't know what was coming or how to protect themselves from it. Fred cupped his hands around his voicemitter and began to yell. Even if they could speak the language, there was little chance of making himself understood at such a distance. But if he could attract their attention, maybe he could wave them down—

The tiny prowler became a marble of blinding radiance, and the marble swelled into an immense white burst of eye-stabbing brilliance. The small figures scrambled to their feet, and Fred saw a wall of gray dust rolling up before them, boiling across the mountainside to swallow them both. Then he felt the heat sinking through his Mjolnir, the blast wave hurling him into the gulch, and he saw the dust coming, and his faceplate darkened, and then he saw nothing at all.

CHAPTER 9

0758 hours, June 7, 2526 (military calendar)
Blue Force Bunker, Big Surprise Culvert
Forgotten Highway, Planet Netherop, Ephyra System

The shockwave arrived in a blast of dust that threatened to tear John's hands and boots free of the spall pits he was using as finger- and toeholds. Above him, at the entrance to the cave—okay, maybe it *was* a culvert—the ghostly figures of a half dozen soldiers broke free and tumbled into the V-shaped trough at the center of the diamond-shaped passage, then began a short, steep slide toward John and his two Spartan companions.

John dug his fingers and feet into the spall pits even harder. "Get ready," he said over TEAMCOM.

Two status LEDs—Kelly's and Linda's—flashed green. Fred's remained dark, but that was better than red. Dark just signaled CONDITION UNKNOWN. Red would mean he was in trouble, or dead.

As the ghostly figures drew near, they loomed larger and became four cursing marines and two screaming crewmen, all kicking and clawing at the culvert's steeply pitched floor, trying in vain to brake their slide. John stopped one marine when her boots came to a rest on his shoulders, then managed to latch onto a crewman even when the man bounced over John's outstretched arm.

"Caught two," he reported over TEAMCOM.

"I have only one," Linda said.

"No worries." Kelly's voice was strained. "I have the other three—though I wish they would quit fidgeting."

John activated his voicemitter. "Everyone, hold still!"

He glanced over his shoulder and saw Kelly next to him, straddling the central trough with three dusty marines half-sitting and half-standing on her shoulders. Linda was on her far side, using her elbow to pin down a female crewmember who had nearly slid under her arm. Had Linda not trapped the woman in place, she would have slid another fifty meters down the culvert, then plunged out the opening and dropped half a kilometer to the floor of the mirage basin.

"Anyone hurt?" John asked. When no one said yes, he looked up the culvert. The floor was steep but climbable, and the entrance was only twenty meters above. "Then let's move out. Kelly, your bunch first."

"You heard him," Kelly said. "Quickly now, or I'll toss you down the chute myself."

The first marine was already climbing, wisely wiping the dust out of the spall pits before using them as handholds. Once it grew clear she wasn't likely to slide down on top of them, the rest followed, and it was not long before John was scrambling out into the gulch behind Linda and Kelly.

The first thing he did was contact Fred over TEAMCOM. "Blue Two, status?"

"Be there soon," Fred said. His status LED blinked yellow. "Still bleeding off pressure."

"You're in lockdown?" Kelly asked.

"Oh yeah," Fred said. To protect a Mjolnir-wearer from impact trauma, the onboard computer automatically pressurized the armor's hydrostatic gel layer when subjected to high-g levels. "That's what happens when you take a Fury shockwave in the chest."

John turned to look up the mountain, but the dust was still too thick in the air to see more than a dozen meters. "Why didn't you take cover?"

"No time," Fred said. His voice began to sound a little less strained. "I was trying to tell you—I think there are kids out here."

"Kids?" John said. He glanced over at Kelly, who merely turned her palms out to indicate she had no idea what Fred was talking about. "As in children? Here on *Netherop*?"

"That's what *I* thought," Fred said. "But I *saw* them. Small figures. Two of them. They were riding some sort of spider machine."

John crooked a finger for Kelly to accompany him, but pointed Linda toward Petrov and Cacyuk. He wanted a Spartan with the two officers to keep them apprised of the situation and to press for his own recommendations if the situation grew complicated. "Where are you now, Fred?"

"I know what you're thinking," Fred said. "And I know what I saw. They were only a half kilometer away."

"Not what I asked."

Fred sighed. "About four hundred meters above you," he said. "I got blown into the gulch."

"Do you remember hitting your head?" Kelly asked.

"I remember hitting a lot of things."

"Stay where you are," John said. "We're coming to you."

"That's not necessary."

"But it *is* an order," John said. "We need to have a look at you."

John and Kelly started up the gulch. After kicking through the dust for close to a minute, they finally spotted Fred a hundred meters ahead, a gray silhouette standing atop a slab of boulder with his hands on his hips.

"Do I look dizzy to you?" he demanded.

"No, but you *sound* bonkers," Kelly said. "Even more than usual."

Fred jumped off the boulder and started down the gulch to meet them. "Permission to walk?"

Before John could reply, Petrov's voice sounded inside his helmet. "We don't have much time, Master Chief." Clearly, Linda had told her about Fred's request to investigate—though maybe she had been a little less forthcoming about the team's concern over his mental state. "The *Wheatley*'s Pelicans are on the way."

"Thank you, ma'am," John said. With the *Night Watch*'s crash site sanitized, now was the best time for the *Wheatley* to send aid—before the Covenant had a chance to send any more fighter craft down to jump them. "I think he might have been confused by a mirage. He actually appears steady."

"It wasn't a mirage," Fred said. "I was only half a kilometer away."

"That may be far enough on Netherop," Linda said. They were all speaking on the general comm channel now. "In this heat, with an atmosphere this thick, who can know how light bends?"

"They weren't shimmering." Fred abruptly changed direction, turning toward the leeward side of the gulch. "Whoever they were, they were probably killed and swept away, but their spider machine could still be there. It was down behind a ridge, and it probably had a secure grip."

"Their spider machine held on?" John looked toward Kelly, who only spread her hands and adjusted her angle of ascent. "Fred . . . listen to yourself."

"It sounds crazy, I know. Netherop is supposed to be uninhabited." Fred reached the gulch wall and began to scramble up through the bank of fresh dust carried in by the shockwave. "But that's a culvert down there, and that highway we've been hiking? *Someone* built that stuff."

"Not kids on spider machines—at least, not *human* kids," John said. By tradition, human expansion into the Outer Colonies wasn't even considered to have begun until the settling of Alluvion in 2412, and a hundred-and-fourteen years was barely enough time to discover a far-flung world like Netherop—much less civilize it, build a highway across it, and then *forget* about it. "The timing doesn't work. That highway would have had to be built in the last hundred years—and it looks a lot older than that. I'm not even sure it *is* a highway."

"So maybe what might be kids and the spider machines aren't connected to the culvert and the highway," Fred said. He reached the rim of the gulch and turned to face John. "But what does it hurt to have a look?"

John fell silent and continued to climb. He could not actually think of a good reason *not* to look—as long as they were at the landing zone when the Pelicans arrived to pick them up.

"Okay, five minutes," he said. "But be careful. Whatever you saw could be some sort of Covenant trick. And if we don't find anything—"

"Give me ten minutes," Fred said. "There's no telling how far the shockwave—"

"*Four minutes,*" Petrov announced. "Our transport will be here in five, and we are *not* going to make them wait. Clear?"

"Yes, ma'am," Fred said. "Very clear."

John reached the rim of the gulch and knew instantly they weren't going to find anything. The entire mountainside had been swept bare, either by the shockwave itself or by the massive dust-slides that had followed. As far as the eye could see, there was just one reddish-brown ridge of shale layered atop another, their crests all parallel and all running vertically up into the low brown clouds, broken only in the far distance by the black gouges of gulches similar to the one out of which they had climbed.

The *Night Watch*'s crash site was just a divot in the distant mirage, a tiny blue depression floating a finger's width above what appeared to be ground. The prowler itself was only a memory, the alien fighter swarm just scattered atoms.

John's view of the blast crater was momentarily blocked as Fred raced past, descending the mountainside toward the rocky bench—or the Forgotten Highway, as Fred insisted on calling it.

"Fred!" John started after him. "We didn't find anything—"

"I still have three and a half minutes." Fred pointed toward the massive dust banks that had accumulated on Fred's highway as the avalanches spilled down from the mountainsides. "Maybe something got buried."

Now John *knew* Fred wasn't thinking straight. Even had there been anyone—or *anything*—standing on the mountainside when the Fury detonated, the chances of finding them buried somewhere in all that dust was almost nil. Especially in less than four minutes.

But it would take longer than that to convince Fred he was wasting his time, so John simply waved Kelly along and started down the slope. Fred adjusted his angle of descent so that he reached the highway at the base of a high ridge, about five hundred meters back down the highway from the culvert. He stopped and looked up the mountainside first, no doubt using his faceplate magnification to search for any sign of the kids or the spider machine he believed he had seen earlier.

John and Kelly caught up to him a few seconds later, and scanned the slope for more than a minute. John saw nothing that looked like evidence of Fred's phantasm—only bare stone and a few stems and roots that he twice mistook for human limbs.

Finally John asked, "See anything?"

"Not yet," Fred said. "Let's try the highway."

They turned around and peered down into a pile of dust so massive it hid the highway almost completely, sloping down toward the mirage basin at the same angle as the mountainside, but easily discernible because of its powdery texture. Along the far edge of the roadbed—assuming that's what it was—lay several dozen dust-covered lumps with the long, layered shapes of shale boulders. John saw nothing that looked human or arachnid, or even like a piece of either.

A timer appeared on his HUD: 94 SECONDS—his onboard computer answering the unformed query in his mind about how much longer they had to placate Fred.

Fred stepped off the mountainside and sank over his head into dust, then continued to search in a blind grid, sliding his boots along the roadbed for approximately a meter, then turning left and continuing for another meter before turning left again.

"You coming?" Fred asked over TEAMCOM.

John turned to Kelly, who cocked her helmet and said, "You must be mad."

"Let's just give it a try." John used his motion detector and the furrow of sinking dust to locate Fred's grid, then jumped into the dust bank a meter to the right. He was plunged instantly into gray darkness as the dust swallowed him. "It'll be easier than arguing with him."

Kelly dropped into the dust a meter to John's right, and they began to shuffle through the powder, using their motion trackers to coordinate and avoid covering the same ground. Their Mjolnir had a self-contained air supply, so breathing wasn't a problem, and the dust was not as deep on the far side of the road. When their boots touched something they couldn't identify by feel, they picked it up and crossed toward the basin until their helmets were above the surface, then wiped their faceplates clear and looked at what they had.

John found four oblong rocks that he briefly thought could have been heads or feet, and two half-meter lengths of root that might have been limbs. But when his HUD timer reached zero, nobody had found anything to indicate that Fred had seen what he believed he had. John waded out to the shallow side of the dust pile and turned toward the grid of furrows Fred had created.

"Time's up."

"And we have a mission to complete." Fred sighed into his helmet comm, then emerged holding a rock in one hand and a dusty chunk of paddle plant in the other. He shook his helmet and tossed both items into the mirage basin. "But, damn it, I know what I saw."

"Nobody's saying you don't," John said. Kelly emerged empty-handed, and they turned toward the culvert where First Platoon and the *Night Watch* crew were waiting. "But the Pelicans will be here in less than a minute, and this isn't part of the mission."

"I know, I know." Fred took one last look up the mountainside, then stepped closer to the edge of the roadbed, where the dust lay little more than ankle-deep.

A distant *boom* echoed over the mirage basin, and John looked up to see an orange ball blossoming inside the brown overcast. The ball stretched into a plume and dropped out of the clouds, becoming a small, wedge-shaped fleck trailing a long ribbon of red flame. He magnified the image—and identified the fleck as a burning Pelican.

A flight of four Banshee fighters appeared on the Pelican's tail, still pouring plasma bolts into her stern as she plummeted into the mirage basin—until four smoke trails dropped out of the clouds behind the alien fighters and streaked into *their* tails. All four Banshees flashed white and broke into sprays of metallic confetti, while below them the burning Pelican plunged through the sea of refracted light and spread across the basin floor in a fiery disk.

Petrov's voice came over the common channel. "John, get back here! When that last Pelican lands—"

"We'll be there," John said. All three Spartans were already racing toward the culvert at a full sprint. "No worries."

But John wasn't so sure the second Pelican would make it. The clouds ahead were now so full of plasma attacks and missile strikes that it looked as though a lightning storm were sweeping in instead of a transport mission. And a steady rain of flaming fighter craft—both alien Banshees and UNSC Baselards—was dropping out of the brown sky.

"Where do all these Covenant fighters keep coming from?" Linda asked over TEAMCOM. "It cannot be from a few stealth corvettes."

"Must be a *lot* of stealth corvettes," Fred said. "The Banshees are coming in waves. Maybe they're launching as fast as they enter—"

"Later," John said. They were assuming the Covenant thought the same way humans did, and that was the kind of mistake that got people killed—he had at least learned *that* much on Mesra. "Let's survive this bunch first and worry about the rest later."

As John spoke, the remaining Pelican dropped out of the clouds with a flight of four Banshee fighters chewing pieces off its tail. A pair of the *Wheatley*'s Baselards followed close behind, spraying the aliens with cannon fire. One Banshee trailed smoke and spiraled out of control; then two more swooped down from the clouds and fell in behind the Baselards and poured plasma bolts up their thrust nozzles.

The Baselards were done, and their pilots knew it. One began to smoke and the other lost thrust, and both launched their Archer missiles in a desperate attempt to save the Pelican.

Everything seemed to explode at once, the Banshees and the Pelican and the Baselards, all erupting into a single fire-cloud that poured a steady rain of flame-drops and fluttering metal down into the mirage basin.

Then only two Banshees remained, the pair that had swooped down out of the clouds to attack the Baselards. They leveled out a few hundred meters above the basin floor and cruised along, silhouetted against the refracted light, their cruciform shapes shimmering in the rising heat. John thought for a moment they might do the sensible thing and head for home after a costly victory.

But that was not Covenant strategy.

The two Banshees pulled their noses up and began to circle toward the mountains, preparing to begin a strafing run straight down the highway. John grabbed his BR55 off its magnetic mount, then spun around and dropped to a knee. "Linda—"

"Yes, I see them."

A pair of dark stars appeared in the nose of the lead Banshee as Linda opened fire with her powerful SRS99 sniper rifle. The craft began to wobble, then dropped its nose and plunged into the mirage and tumbled across the basin floor in a flaming pinwheel of blue and white.

By then the last Banshee was above the highway, its plasma bolts already stitching a line of flying rock-chips into the mountainside as it swung around to begin its strafing run. John set the sights of his battle rifle just above its dome and opened fire on full automatic, not trying to hit the Banshee so much as put a wall of bullets into the air in front of it. With Fred and Kelly kneeling beside him doing the same thing, it would have been impossible for any low-flying craft to avoid taking hits. A dozen rounds sparked off the nose and perhaps half that many actually penetrated. A line of dust-geysers began to advance up the road as the Banshee continued to close on them.

John ejected his empty magazine and reached for another, then heard the sonic crack of two sniper rounds passing just above his head. Something dark spurted out the top of the Banshee's dome; then it rolled toward the mountainside and plowed into the deepest part of the dust bank.

The crash raised a gray fan of dust twenty meters high before there came the muted crumpling of metal, followed by a muffled *boom* so powerful John felt it in the soles of his boots. The air went hazy and dark with dust, and a moment later, something metallic clanged off John's shoulder pauldron.

"Heads up!"

He looked up, searching the swirling murk above for the swelling shadow of something he might need to dodge.

But none of the debris from the Banshee was all that large or dangerous. Anything heavy enough to damage his Mjolnir was too heavy to reach him, and anything light didn't carry enough momentum. He spent a couple of seconds listening to the clangs fade to pings, then finally reached down and grabbed the object that had struck his shoulder pauldron and planted itself at his feet. It looked like some sort of strut, but not of a design he had ever seen before. He tucked it into his armpit and tried to check on First Platoon and the prowler crew. The dust haze was so thick that anyone more than a couple of meters away looked like a ghost, and anything more than ten meters away was simply not visible.

When the chance presented itself, Blue Team was going to need to do some serious maintenance on both their armor and their weapons.

"Status," John said over TEAMCOM.

All three status LEDs flashed green inside his helmet; then Fred stepped to John's side and took the strut from his armpit.

"Where did you find this?"

"It fell on me," John said.

The strut was about a meter long, with a dull gray finish, a busted ball joint at one end, and a round metal pad at the other. The pad was about the size of John's palm, with a hinged split down the center that allowed the two halves to flex outward or inward.

"Why?"

"I can't believe your luck!" Fred was starting to sound crazy again. "Do you know what this *is*?"

"A Banshee landing strut?"

Fred made a horizontal slicing motion with his free hand to indicate that John was dead wrong. *"Proof,"* he said. "It's a spider leg!"

"Oh no, please," Kelly said. "Not that again."

"You'll see." Fred tried to attach it to the magnetic mount on the back of his Mjolnir and failed—apparently the strut had no ferrous metal—then simply clutched it tight and started toward the Banshee crash. "There are nine more, just like this one."

John caught him by the arm. "You're forgetting something."

He tipped his helmet up the highway, where, fifty meters away, Commander Petrov was standing above the cliffside end of the culvert, her hands on her hips and her chin resting on her chest as she stared down at the smoke plumes rising from the basin floor. Behind her, the rest of the ship's complement sat waiting in the dust, most of the prowler crew looking at the ground between their feet, the marines watching her back with vacant gazes.

"Oh yeah." Fred tucked the spider leg under the strap of the load-carrying harness he used to haul extra equipment. "The heat casualties."

"You mean our backup force," Kelly said.

Fred glanced out at the shimmering mirage basin. "On this hell-world, I don't think there's a difference."

"Just try to be positive." John started forward, angling toward Petrov. "And not a word about this spider machine. Half the unit is probably dazed with heatstroke, and I don't want you confusing them any more than they already are."

"Acknowledged," Fred said. "But what are you going to do when they *see* one?"

"Don't worry. They won't," John said.

As they drew near Commander Petrov, he noticed that Linda was already moving from one overheated marine to another, making sure they were drinking and encouraging them to use their weapons and shirts to create makeshift shade-shelters. John signaled Fred and Kelly to help her, then stepped to Petrov's side and activated his voicemitter.

"I don't see any new casualties," he said. Petrov continued to stare at the smoke plumes for a moment, then finally turned to look at him. Her face was drier and more flushed than before, and her furrowed brow suggested she had a bad headache. "Ma'am, when was the last time you had a drink?"

"Are you trying to change the subject, Master Chief?"

"I wasn't aware there was one."

"Casualties," Petrov reminded him. She turned back to the smoke columns rising out of the mirage basin. "How far is it to the target?"

"The *Lucky Break*?" John asked. When she nodded, he checked the waypoint that appeared on his HUD. "Fifty-one kilometers, as the crow flies."

Petrov snorted. "You think a crow could survive in this place?"

"I wouldn't know, ma'am," John said. "I've never seen one."

Petrov turned back to him. "No, I suppose you haven't." Her tone was gentle. "Trust me, no crow could survive here . . . and neither can we."

John began to wonder if he should reconsider keeping Fred quiet about his talk of phantom children and their spider machine. It was beginning to seem like Petrov was confused enough to believe him, and thinking that there were a bunch of kids wandering around might give her a more optimistic attitude about their chances of survival.

"We'll make it," John said. "We have plenty of water and a reclamation tool."

"Which you can leave with us," Petrov said. "I believe you have your own reclamation systems, correct?"

"Ma'am?"

Petrov pursed her lips. "I believe your Mjolnir is self-contained," she said. "If I understand your file correctly, you can survive indefinitely in almost any environment."

"That's correct." John began to have a bad feeling about where Petrov was headed with this conversation. "But if you think we're going to leave your crew and First Platoon behind—"

"Don't be daft, Master Chief. *Of course* you're going to leave us behind. It's the only way you have any chance of completing the mission."

"No offense, ma'am," John said, "but we're on the ground now. So that's not your decision—and even if it were, I'm not sure you're thinking clearly."

"More clearly than *you*, apparently." She looked up the highway. "How fast can four Spartans travel fifty kilometers on foot?"

"It depends on the terrain—"

"Stop dodging," Petrov said. "Your file says you can average twenty kilometers an hour over long distances. That means you can reach the *Lucky Break* in two and a half hours if the terrain is good, double that if it isn't."

"I wouldn't count on the terrain being good," John said.

"If it's not good for you, it will be terrible for us," Petrov said. "And marines march at an average of five kilometers an hour in good conditions. What will their rate be in this heat? Dragging water tanks, casualties, and probably half my crew? Two kilometers an hour? *One*?"

John looked away. Given the necessity of going slowly and stopping frequently to keep cool, they would be doing well to average one per hour.

"Blue Team can reach the *Lucky Break* in a few hours," Petrov said. "It will take the rest of us a couple of days—*if* we can make it the whole way—and nothing you can do here will change any of that. Even Spartans can't carry thirty people on their backs."

John swung his faceplate back toward Petrov. She was starting to make sense . . . damn it.

"There must be something we can do to increase your odds."

"Complete your mission," Petrov said. "Capture the damn frigate and get back to us as fast as you can, with *whatever* you can. That has to be better than hanging around to watch us die."

"Okay, then," John said. "I see your point. I may not like it—"

"You think *I* do?" Petrov asked. "You should find the *Wheatley* at the original LZ, keeping an eye on the *Lucky Break* from five kilometers out. Enlist the security team, if you think it will increase your odds."

"I'll consider it, ma'am," John said. "Will they accept my—"

"They'll do anything you ask of them," Petrov said. "And if they won't, *make* them."

"I understand."

"Do you? Make sure of it." Petrov put a hand on his back and pushed him toward the rest of the company, where Blue Team was still busy handing out canteens and constructing shade-shelters. "Take that ship, Master Chief—and do it in the next ten hours. You can't have any longer than that."

CHAPTER 10

1041 hours, June 7, 2526 (military calendar)
Serpentine Canyon, Forgotten Highway
Mountains of Despair, Planet Netherop, Ephyra System

Blue Team had no choice. The Forgotten Highway had more bends in it than a Klein bottle, but it led generally in the right direction, and loping along its smooth surface was faster than scrambling through hundreds of deep ravines. Still, John's HUD showed they had actually covered forty-seven kilometers on the ground, yet advanced only twenty-three kilometers toward the *Lucky Break*. That was a bad ratio. They had been traveling two hours already, and it meant they had at least three more hours of hard running ahead.

Assuming the ratio didn't swing any further against them.

The highway climbed away from the mirage basin and entered a narrow gorge. To one side of the road, the canyon plunged hundreds of meters to a shimmering blue ribbon that was probably just a mirage. To the other side, a craggy face of banded gneiss rose a similar distance before crowning beneath a dingy canopy of clouds.

Kelly was on-point three hundred meters ahead of John, her small image rippling in the heat. As she led the team deeper into the gorge, the endless dust-drifts gave way to overflow mounds spilling out of tributary ravines. The overflow mounds grew ever smaller, until the road was covered by only wind-packed dust, and even that soon thinned into nothingness and exposed a bed of triangular paving blocks—the final proof, had they needed any, that the Forgotten Highway was an apt name.

The blocks were the color of bleached bone, cupped with wear and spalled by heat and age.

Blue Team ran deeper into the gorge. On most other planets, a canyon would be shady and cool. Here, the temperature climbed steadily. Kelly soon blurred into invisibility. John began to doubt First Platoon and the prowler crew would make it through this without any protection. The dark walls were a natural energy sink, collecting and holding heat like bricks in a kiln. When darkness fell, they would radiate it back into the canyon, and John doubted the road would grow noticeably cooler until late into the night.

Whenever that might come.

He looked up between the canyon rims, searching the crooked belt of brown sky for the white patch of Netherop's sun. It had barely moved all morning. For all John knew, daylight on Netherop could last twenty hours.

A message from his onboard computer appeared on the HUD: SOLAR TRACKING INDICATES DAYLIGHT AT THIS LATITUDE LASTS 23 HOURS, 5 MINUTES.

John felt his breath grow labored and realized he was clenching his jaw. Their circadian rhythms were going to be massively disrupted. Was *everything* on Netherop incredibly hostile to human life?

"Who *does* this?"

Fred was four hundred meters behind John, bringing up the rear of the formation, so his voice came over TEAMCOM.

"You must be specific," Linda said. "Who does *what*?"

"Who builds a highway halfway up a cliff face?" Fred said. "Either it should run along the bottom of the canyon, or it should go up on the rim. Why cut it into the side of a cliff—especially in hard stone like this?"

"You keep expecting aliens to think like humans," John said.

"What makes you think it was built by aliens?"

"That's rather obvious, isn't it?" Kelly replied. "No human would build a road halfway up the cliff."

Fred groaned, and they continued to run. The canyon bends grew sharper and more frequent, the tributary ravines narrower and steeper. The temperature continued to climb, and visibility decreased even more. John had the team reduce its spacing to two hundred meters so they could maintain visual contact, then a hundred and fifty.

After fifteen more minutes, Kelly's status LED flashed red twice, the signal to stop while she checked something out. Everyone flashed green to acknowledge. John protected his back by moving close to the cliff face, then dropped to a knee and scanned the winding belt of sky for incoming Banshees. A month ago, a twisting gorge would have been the last place he expected to be strafed. But the Covenant did not face the same technical limitations as the UNSC, as had been evident on Mesra.

"You may not believe this," Kelly said, "but I think someone dropped range markers on the road."

"When it comes to the Covenant, I'll believe anything," John said. Despite the gorge's narrow confines, it was hardly an ideal place for an ambush. The sheer walls left no place for attackers to hide except up on the rim, where their firing angles would be both awkward and at long range. And with all the curves in the road, their targets would be within a few steps of hard cover. "What are you looking at?"

"Rock spatters," Kelly said. "Scattered along the road ahead."

"You find it surprising that rocks fall from cliffs?" Linda asked.

"I do when they're a different *color* of rock," Kelly replied. "And a different kind. The cliffs are brown, granular, and very hard. The rock I'm looking at is black and dusty, and there are a lot of chunks with shell-shaped fracture marks. I think it might be coal."

John moved as far away from the cliff face as he could without stepping off the highway, then craned his neck back. The light refraction wasn't as pronounced when he looked skyward, because the air temperature directly overhead was not much different from where he was standing, and he had a decent view of the top of the canyon.

From what he could tell, Kelly had stopped at the beginning of a sharp curve, where the canyon turned to the right and continued for a couple of hundred meters before bending back in the opposite direction. If it went true to form, it would return an equal distance, completing one of the oxbow meanders that were forcing Blue Team to travel two or three kilometers along the road for every kilometer it advanced toward the target.

John magnified the image. There was some shimmer near the rim itself, where the rock was holding heat from Netherop's sun, but he could see well enough to tell that the rim had a clean edge. There were no ragged borders or knobby bulges to suggest that the canyon's gneiss was overlaid by a coal seam—or any other kind of stone.

Which meant those black chunks were inexplicable.

The last thing John wanted to do was interrupt their march to investigate a bunch of rocks lying on a roadbed that probably hadn't been used in millennia. But if the rocks hadn't come from the cliff, that made their presence a mystery—and in hostile territory, what couldn't be explained couldn't be ignored.

"We'd better check it out," John said. "Linda, come forward and cover the canyon rim above those rocks. If it's an ambush, you might see their heads pop up when they realize it didn't work."

Linda's LED flashed green.

"Fred—"

"Already moving," Fred replied. "I'll go three ravines back."

"Affirmative," John said. "Kelly and I will come up the second."

Fred's and Kelly's LEDs flashed green.

Everyone knew what to do. When sneaking up on an ambush, it was never smart to take the first obvious approach. A skilled foe would have sentries watching for a flank attack, so it was best to advance from an unexpected direction.

John and Linda passed each other without exchanging so much as a helmet nod. If the enemy was lying in wait, and if that enemy could see them, the less time given for them to adjust, the better.

John ran a kilometer to the second ravine back and began to climb. The gneiss was good stone, solid and unbroken, but the ravine itself was steep and very narrow, rising to the canyon rim at more than a sixty percent grade. He pushed his hands and boots against opposite sides and scrambled up it chimney-style, using counterpressure to avoid the tedious process of searching out tiny finger- and toeholds.

By the time he reached the rim, he was breathing heavily, and the Mjolnir's environmental control system was working hard to keep him cool. John curled his fingers over the top and braced both boots against the opposite wall, then carefully raised his helmet to take a look. What he found was heat shimmer so dense he saw only green vase shapes, presumably foliage, dancing atop black undulating stone.

"Blue Two, status?"

"Advancing toward your ravine," Fred said. "Nothing's shot me yet."

John looked over his shoulder and saw a blocky, slate-blue figure thirty meters away, pushing through the presumed foliage, the visual distortion at ground level so severe that nothing substantial could be perceived.

The figure seemed to be hunched down to about two-thirds of Fred's normal height, which put his helmet at the same level as the top of the vase shapes. Presumably, that was high enough to clear the worst of the refraction. John crawled out of the ravine, then pulled the BR55 off his back and slowly rose to a high crouch. The heat shimmer diminished enough for him to see that the vase shapes were indeed some sort of plant.

Maybe.

The triangular leaves had no stems. Instead, they grew directly out of the ground in tight, concentric rings that were so perfectly formed it made John wonder if they were crystalline growths rather than plants. But the center of each leaf was puffy, and the edges had little hooked barbs that did not seem very mineral-like.

A FRIEND marker appeared on John's motion tracker as Fred came up behind him. John looked down into the ravine and spotted Kelly a hundred meters below, climbing fast. He saw no good reason for the Covenant to launch an ambush from up here on the plateau, but neither did he see a source for the dark rock-splatters she had reported. They still had to spend the time and investigate.

"Blue Two, advance parallel to the canyon rim at a hundred meters," John said. "I'll advance at fifty. Kelly will take rear guard, staying low and out of sight."

A trio of LEDs flashed green—despite being down in the canyon, Linda was also acknowledging the transmission—and John set off across the plateau. The crystalline plants had a flaring habit that left only about a half meter between their crowns. Whenever John brushed against a leaf, it would break off, and the wound oozed green sap. The leaf would shatter, then the shards would rise on tiny gossamer wings that made him wonder whether the bushes were plant, animal, or mineral—or somehow all three.

He advanced fifty meters at a time in a high crouch, then rose to his full height for a quick look around before dropping back into the brush and continuing forward. After nine hundred meters, he spotted a line of broken crystal plants crossing his path at an angle. He signaled Fred and Kelly to stop, then remained in a high crouch, keeping watch for a full five minutes in case there was an alien close by, trying to lure him into an ambush.

Finally, when he saw no sign of trouble, he spoke over TEAM-COM. "There's some sort of trail ten meters ahead of my position. I'm going to check it out."

He received a trio of green flashes, then slowly rose and examined the area more closely. The rim of the canyon was fifty meters to his left, just starting a gentle rightward curve as it followed the oxbow where Kelly had spotted the rock spatters on the road. He knew Fred was fifty meters to his right, hidden too well to be spotted even when John knew exactly where to look. He didn't even bother to check behind him. Kelly was back there somewhere, keeping watch over both him and Fred, but she would be even better hidden than Fred.

John dropped back into a crouch, then advanced to the line of broken crystal plants. It was actually more of a furrow, with a quarter-meter-wide swath of leaf stumps leading from the interior of the plateau toward the suspicious oxbow—or perhaps it led away from the oxbow. There was really no way to tell which direction their mysterious traveler had been going.

A few meters down-trail—which meant toward the canyon in John's mind—an entire crystal plant had been crushed. He went over and found a round, hand-size impression in the leaf stumps. There seemed to be a raised ridge down the center, perhaps where there had been a split in the pad.

John examined the ground in each direction. Whatever had crushed the plant would have picked up a lot of green sap. So if he could find a smear or two, he could track which way the thing had been traveling.

He discovered nothing for three meters in either direction. Either it had a very long stride, or the sap didn't smear.

Both seemed pretty unlikely.

John rose to his full height again, intending to see if he could spot the source of the trail.

Instead, he found a second trail, about four meters away and running parallel to the first. *Exactly* parallel, as if it had been made by a second leg. Whatever had left the evidence was a lot bigger than John had realized. He dropped back into a crouch.

"Blue Two, you still have that strut?"

"You mean the spider leg?"

"I mean get over here," John said. "I need you to look at something."

John spent the next couple of minutes searching down-trail for more tracks. He found another print in a dust-filled hollow, but it was as round as the first one. There was no way to tell which direction it was pointing, and there was no green sap left behind.

Fred emerged from the brush, strut in hand, and knelt next to the print. He displayed the bottom of the pad, showing it to be a perfect match in size and shape, then looked up.

"How about that. Still think I was seeing things back there?"

"I'm not sure *what* you saw." John squatted and took the strut, trying to determine whether there was a way to tell which direction the track was pointing, then asked, "Could it have been some sort of Covenant all-terrain vehicle?"

"Sure," Fred said. "Except I think it was carrying *kids*, not aliens."

"You could tell that from five hundred meters?" John asked. "It couldn't have been Grunts?"

"No. It didn't look like they were wearing breathing masks. Or methane tanks."

"What about some other kind of alien? Maybe Covenant, but one we don't even know about?"

Fred considered that, then finally said, "I'm going to go with kids."

"So you could see their faces?"

"It was more their body shape and proportions. They looked human. Maybe a meter and a half tall. Skinny arms and legs, small hands and feet. No fur, no wings." Fred rose to a high crouch and started down-trail toward the canyon. "You know . . . *kids*."

"That just doesn't make sense," John said, falling in beside him. "Netherop is uninhabited. Where would a couple of human kids come from?"

"I don't know," Fred said. "Where did *we* come from?"

"You think a prowler dropped them off? Two kids and their spider wagon?" John slapped the strut into Fred's belly armor. "I don't think so. They're aliens. That means we need to be on guard."

Linda's status LED flashed red, and by the time they had dropped to a squat, her voice was coming over TEAMCOM.

"I have movement on the rim," she reported. "At least twenty figures . . . and, Blue Leader?"

John flashed a green status light, telling her to continue.

"I believe I'm going to give this one to Fred. They *do* resemble kids," Linda said. "I think they are human."

John rose to his full height and looked down-trail toward the canyon. It ran straight to the canyon rim, which was only a hundred meters distant, and he saw nothing at the end of the trail except the shimmering brown ribbon of a reflection mirage.

"There."

Fred pointed toward the end of the oxbow, where an oval-bodied machine was rising out of the brush. And it *did* look like a spider— one with six small torsos protruding above its back. John could tell that they wore loose-fitting cloaks and swaddled their faces in scarves. He magnified the image and immediately realized Fred had been right all along. They had stringy blond hair and delicate brows over blue eyes, but it was their expressions that convinced him— anger and fear, alarm and determination, all mixed together and all very human.

After a moment, John realized the children were looking back at him, so he raised his free hand and waved.

Only the pilot did not duck down inside their machine. A moment later, two kids popped back up, holding what looked like a sickle-shaped dish antenna. They dropped the support pole into a notch on the back edge of the passenger compartment and swung it toward John and Fred. John thought it might be some sort of communications device, but then the spider machine began to scurry off across the plain, its ten legs moving so fast he could barely see them.

"Wait!" Fred waved both arms above his head. "Hold on!"

Three more spider machines rose out of the brush, their sickle-shaped antennae already affixed and pointing toward him and John, and they quickly turned to race after the first one.

Fred started after them. "We just want to—"

Twenty meters ahead of him, crystal plants began to shatter and burst into short-lived towers of flame. John had no idea what the antennae were shooting at them. He caught Fred by the arm and pulled him back.

"Stand down," he said. "They think you're chasing them."

"I kinda am," Fred said. He turned to John. "Don't you want to know who they are? And what they're doing here?"

"Sure," John said. The spider machines were still running and still making crystal plants burst into flame, and now there was a thin curtain of white smoke rising in front of the two Spartans. "But maybe giving chase isn't the best way to introduce ourselves."

Fred stared through the smoke at the rapidly diminishing ovals of the spider machines, then said, "You're right. It might be better to wait for them to come to us."

"Maybe." John started down the trail toward the canyon rim. "That depends on what they were planning."

Fred fell in beside him, but Kelly remained behind them in hiding. John left her there. Until he had evidence to the contrary, he would continue to treat the kids as a potential threat.

"You think they wanted to ambush us?" Fred asked.

"It crossed my mind."

"Why would they do that?"

"Good question."

They reached the canyon rim. John peered over the edge, but he could not locate Linda in the heat haze. He waved anyway.

"Go another fifty meters," Linda said over TEAMCOM. "They seemed to be spread along the sharpest part of the bend."

"Acknowledged."

John led the way toward the end of the oxbow and quickly began to see black, head-size rocks lined up along the rim. He stepped on the first one, crushing it beneath his weight and confirming that it was exactly what it looked like—coal. More puzzled than ever, he knelt and peered into the canyon again.

On the ribbon of highway three hundred meters below, a handful of dark dots shifted back and forth in the rippling light—almost certainly the range markers Kelly had identified earlier.

He sat back on his heels and looked up at Fred. "They were definitely planning to hit us."

"Yeah." Fred picked up a chunk of coal and crushed it in his power-armored grasp. "What'd we ever do to—"

"On your six!" Kelly warned over TEAMCOM. "Spider machine coming fast!"

John dived past Fred's legs, and Fred leaped over his back, and they both went into a forward roll and came up ten meters apart, their battle rifles cocked and ready to fire.

A spider machine was crashing through the crystal plants at a full charge, a young girl leaning over the pilot's controls with her blond hair flying behind her. A pair of boys stood beside her, braced in the front corners of the passenger compartment, working together as they swung their antenna weapon toward Fred.

A line of crystal plants leading toward Fred shattered and burst into flame, then a cage of lightning crackled over his armor. His FRIEND symbol vanished from John's motion tracker, and he went down as stiff as a steel beam.

John opened fire, putting a long burst through the dish of the weapon. It flashed white and began to spark, and the flaming crystal plants around Fred subsided into a smolder. Then the dish exploded, spraying shrapnel over the entire vehicle. One of the boys screamed and thrust a bloody hand toward the sky, then fell back into the passenger compartment and disappeared.

The pilot pushed her control orb in John's direction, and the spider machine banked toward him, folding its legs low on his side and pushing off with the legs on Fred's side. It was a meter in front of John almost before he could react, its round nose rising up to block his firing angle and protect the pilot.

He threw himself onto his back, intending to let the spider charge over him, but the thing stopped dead above him. The legs folded upward, and the belly dropped.

"Blue Leader?" Kelly's tone was almost panicked. "Are—"

"Under it." John rolled toward the legs, then felt the thing's under-carriage land on his shoulder—and stopped short. "Stuck."

He had no idea how heavy the spider machine was, but it wasn't all that much larger than a Warthog, and he had been pinned under a couple of those before without having his Mjolnir crushed. He pushed off with his lower arm and felt the thing rock . . . then it lifted its legs off the ground, and his arm collapsed beneath him as its weight dropped.

"Stuck harder," he said. "Help."

"Have patience."

A string of pings echoed through the spider as Kelly fired a burst into its back end. Muffled voices, panicked and young, echoed down through the hull. John tried again to dislodge himself, this time by rolling off his side, but it was no good. The thing had lowered its entire weight onto him, so even if he managed to roll onto his belly, it would simply drop down on top of him.

The bang of a detonating grenade sounded somewhere out in front of the machine. The results were visible to John only through the top edge of his faceplate, a small curtain of dust and plant shards dropping to the ground. But it was clear that the grenade had been intended only as a warning, having landed too far away to cause any damage to either passengers or vehicle. There were more pings from the rear of the machine, then a muffled clunk as something landed on the floor of the passenger compartment.

"Kelly, you didn't—"

"*Of course* I did," Kelly said. "But it's not armed."

The girl and her two boys were already leaping out of the ma-chine on John's side of the passenger compartment. The girl's hair was matted with blood—it could only be a result of the dish weapon's unexpected eruption—and one of the boys landed awkwardly and went down when his knee bent sideways. He cried out, and his two companions circled back and grabbed him under the arms.

The second boy could only use one hand, because the other had an antenna shard through it. The girl had a jagged shrapnel wound in her scalp, and when she glanced back toward John, her face was covered in blood. But at least all three were alive—and John was pretty sure that was better than what they had intended for him and Fred.

The trio glanced toward the rear of their machine, then hobbled into the brush as Kelly raced up with her MA5B assault rifle in hand. She eyed them long enough to be sure they were no longer a threat, then returned her weapon to its mount and grabbed the spider thing where its legs entered the body. She managed to lift it high enough for John to roll onto his belly.

As he scrambled from beneath it, Fred's FRIEND symbol reappeared on his motion tracker.

"Blue Two, status," John said.

Fred's status LED flashed amber. "In the middle of a hard reboot, but it looks like all systems are coming back online."

John rose, keeping a careful eye on the departing kids. They had mostly vanished into the crystal plants, but were leaving enough of a blood trail that it would be a simple matter to track them down.

"Any injuries?"

"No, my armor went into lockdown when everything started to short-circuit. They must have hit me with some kind of electromagnetic blast." Fred paused a moment, then added, "My onboard says it was a microwave burst."

"Microwave?" John had never heard of such a weapon; microwave kilns and microwave cauterizing wands, sure. But a microwave gun? That was a new one. He signaled Kelly to catch the kids, then

returned to the spider machine and rose onto his toes so he could look into the riding compartment. "None of this makes any sense."

The back third of the compartment was divided into a trio of low coal bins, which were separated from each other by a pair of narrow corridors. A meter aft of the coal bins, a soot-filled pipe rose about ten centimeters above a cabinet set into the surrounding deck. Even to John, who had never been a passionate student of mechanical engineering, it seemed obvious that the cabinet contained a coal-fired engine.

But there was no smoke rising from the pipe, nor were any fumes shooting out of the bullet holes that Kelly's rounds had opened on the interior side of the engine cabinet. Whatever the spider machine had been using for power when the kids charged, it wasn't a coal-fired engine.

Forward of the coal bins, the passenger area was filled with coarsely woven baskets filled with foodstuffs—tear-shaped leaf paddles, curly orange stems, long snaky roots—and water bladders made from what seemed to be animal stomachs. On the floor between the baskets, John could see the seams of pull-up access panels, while the meter-high walls that encircled the compartment were divided by a line of pullout drawers. At the front rose the spider machine's controls, a thick glass column that ended in a transparent orb larger around than John's helmet.

"It's like a band of hunter-gatherers built a luxury ATV," Fred said. He was across from John, peering into the compartment from the other side. "Before they invented wheels."

"Like I said." John spotted Kelly's unarmed grenade lying on the floor next to a basket of water bladders and hoisted himself up to retrieve it. "It doesn't make sense."

"I could use some help with these children," Kelly said, still speaking over TEAMCOM. "Unless you'd rather I just shoot them?"

"Negative," John said. He didn't think Kelly was serious, but better to be safe. She was not the most patient of Spartans. "I want to talk to them."

"You're not the only one," Fred said. "They have a *lot* of explaining to do."

John flashed a green status light to show that he agreed, but he was actually less interested in what the kids were doing on Netherop than he was in their spider machines. If he could find a way to strike a bargain with them, he might be able to send some of them back to retrieve Petrov and the rest of Blue Force. Or, at the very least, to force these three to give him and the other Spartans a ride.

John and Fred followed Kelly's trail for fifty meters before they saw her crouching next to a broken crystal plant. The kids had stopped about ten meters ahead of her, and the girl was standing behind her companions, whirling a loaded stone-sling over her head. The blood was streaming down over one eye, and she kept wiping it away with a dirt-crusted robe sleeve. With the lower half of her face still hidden behind a loosely wrapped scarf, it was hard to tell her age. But judging by their size, neither she nor her companions could be much over ten years old.

John began to pull his weapons and grenades off their mounts and lay them on the stone at Fred's feet.

"I'll catch the girl," he said over TEAMCOM. "Kelly, you take the standing boy. We'll leave the one on the ground for now."

A loud *clang* sounded inside his helmet as it was struck by a fast-moving stone. He looked back toward the kids and saw the blond girl, eyes wide with fear, folding another stone into the pocket of her sling. The boy with the wounded hand stepped forward and hurled a rock with his good hand. The noise was not as loud.

"They're fierce," Fred said. "I'll give them that."

"They're idiots." Kelly began to lay her own weapons at Fred's feet. "Sooner or later, I *will* grow tired of having my helmet rung."

"Let's start by disarming them," John said. "It might be easier to figure out what's going on here if we don't kill them."

Another stone sailed from the girl's sling and bounced off Kelly's breastplate.

"I wouldn't be too sure," she said. "But I see no harm in trying."

John turned his palms out, then spread his arms and began to circle toward the kids' left flank.

"Blue Four," he said over TEAMCOM, "advance to the next access point, then climb out of the canyon and take overwatch. There are still four spider machines out there, and I don't want them coming back to protect their friends with those microwave blasters."

Linda's LED flashed green.

Kelly mirrored John's gesture and circled toward the children's right flank. The girl slung another rock at her, and the boy threw a stone at John, and the kid on the ground immediately raised his hands, handing another rock to each.

"Now," John said.

He and Kelly dashed in, grabbing the kids by their throwing arms. John lifted the girl off the ground and quickly retreated a half dozen steps, far enough to encourage a sense of separation yet let her see that her friends were not being harmed.

"Let me go, scab!" She swung a foot up, kicking the inside of his elbow so hard he heard a toe pop. "I'll cook you good!"

Not releasing her, John activated his voicemitter. "I can understand you."

She stopped struggling, then studied him out of narrowed eyes. "Why wouldn't you? I have a tongue."

John looked across at Kelly, who was holding the boy at arm's length and ignoring him.

"Don't ask me," she said over TEAMCOM. "I'm no good with children."

John turned back to the girl, trying to decide what he should ask. While he had been trained in five different interrogation techniques, they all assumed at least some knowledge about the enemy. In this case, he wasn't even sure the prisoners *were* an enemy . . . but the first step was always to establish control.

John reached up with his free hand and pulled the scarf away from the girl's face. With sunken cheeks and a face so gaunt it was almost skeletal, she looked so malnourished that he could not even begin to guess her age. She could have been eight . . . or eighteen.

"What's your name?"

"Lena," she answered. "And you're called . . . ?"

John thought for a moment. The girl and her companions were behaving like enemies, but there wasn't any reason they needed to be—at least, not that he could see. And he wasn't about to use any coercion techniques on a child, hostile or not. Nor was there time for domination and control. So that left rapport-building and deal-making.

"John," he said. "I'm called John."

"John?" Lena pronounced it *Yon*. "Your name is *John*?"

"Affirmative."

"If you say so."

"I do, because it is," John said, coming to the realization that she didn't believe him. "Why wouldn't my name be John?"

Lena looked away. "No reason."

"No," John said. "Tell me."

"Well . . ." Lena gave him a cagey smile. "John is a strange name for an alien, yes?"

Fred snorted, and Kelly groaned.

"We're not aliens," John said.

Lena looked away, and the boy hanging from Kelly's grasp said, "You *have* to be aliens."

"Why?"

"Look at you," he said. "People are never that tall."

"Some people are," Fred said.

"No way," the boy said. "And nobody can run that fast—not for that long."

"And people can't wear heavy metal suits," said the other boy. "Not without getting cooked."

"What if I told you that we can run fast *because* of the metal suits?" John asked. "And that we don't get cooked because the suits keep us cool?"

The boy snorted and said, "I wouldn't believe you. We're not stupid."

John turned to Fred, then said, "Show them."

Fred turned his faceplate toward the boy with the injured knee. "If you throw a rock at me, I'm going to crush your head like an egg."

"What's an egg?"

"It breaks easy—and then gooey stuff runs out. No tricks, okay?"

Fred reached up with both hands, then slipped his fingers under the helmet's chin guard and ran them around to the back, separating the systems-sock from the inner layers beneath the rest of the suit. All three kids went wide-eyed, as though expecting something horrible to be revealed when the helmet came off. Once Fred reached the back of his neck, he used both hands to disconnect the neural interface, then carefully rocked the helmet forward and pulled it away like a mask.

The face he revealed was slender and strong-featured, with black brows above blue-green eyes, a blade-thin nose, high cheeks, and a broad mouth over a square chin. He still had the wrinkle-free brow and smooth face of a fifteen-year-old adolescent, but everything else about him—especially his rugged features and penetrating gaze—hinted at the hardened soldier he already was.

John looked back to Lena. "What do you think?" he asked. "Human enough?"

"I'm . . . I'm not sure *what* to think." She looked from Fred back to John. "Are *all* of the people from your world so big?"

"Not all of us," John said. He lowered Lena until her feet were back on the ground. "Can we talk now? No fighting? No running?"

Lena nodded. "I think we don't have any choice. If we fight, your friend will break our heads until the gooey stuff comes out." She glanced toward the boy with the knee injury. "And if we run, we leave Arne to be cooked."

"You should run anyway," Arne said. "There's no reason to let them cook us all."

"We're not going to cook anyone." John was beginning to wonder if *cook* was more than the local slang for *kill*. "We don't even want to hurt you."

"Then why are you chasing us?" Lena asked.

"We're not chasing you," John said.

"And yet . . ." Lena spread her arms, a gesture that encompassed everyone in the area. "Here we are."

"Because you were trying to ambush us." John motioned Kelly to release the third kid, then asked him, "What's your name?"

"Why should I tell you?"

"So I know what to call you." John was beginning to think he should have tried a coercion technique—establishing rapport was proving more difficult than expected. He pointed at his own companions. "He's Fred, she's Kelly."

Lena's gaze swung toward Kelly. "You're a girl?"

"A woman, but yeah." Kelly looked to the third kid. "And John asked your name."

"I heard him."

Lena sighed. "Oskar, if they wanted to cook us, we'd be dead now."

Oskar glared at her. "*Think*, Lena. They want us all. The whole camp."

Kelly spoke over TEAMCOM. "This is going nowhere fast, and we have a mission to complete. We need to get back on the trail."

The heads of all three children snapped toward Fred's open helmet, but they looked more surprised than alarmed. John hoped that meant they had only been able to hear Kelly's voice, not understand what she was actually saying.

Unable to respond over TEAMCOM without drawing more attention to Fred's helmet, John spread his fingers and made a small, horizontal waving motion—a signal to be patient. Oskar was a little antagonistic, but he was making progress with Lena, and that meant he had a pretty good chance of striking a bargain to help the rest of Blue Force.

Or at least get Blue Team to the target faster.

John turned to Oskar. "You're wrong about wanting to . . . cook you," he said. "We don't want to cook any of you—but if I were in your position, I'd be thinking the same thing."

Oskar smirked in Lena's direction. "You see?"

Lena rolled her eyes and looked away.

"So let's make a deal here." As John spoke, he motioned for Fred to put his helmet back on. "We'll patch you up and put you back in your riding spider—"

"What's a spider?" Arne asked.

"Your people carrier," John said. He pointed toward the spider machine. "The thing you were riding."

"We call them mountain runners," Lena said. "I've seen spiders in learning pictures, but they didn't look big enough to ride."

"I'm sure they didn't," John said. He had a thousand questions about these kids and why they were on a supposedly uninhabited world and didn't know what eggs or spiders were, but he also had a mission to complete—and time was running out. He returned his focus to Oskar. "We'll fix you up and return you to your mountain runner. Then we'll continue on our way, you rejoin your parents—"

"Our *parents*?" Oskar burst out. He turned to Lena. "You see?"

Lena went pale and nodded.

"I don't understand," John said.

He truly didn't. Like all Spartans, he had been taken from his own parents when he was six—a highly classified fact that usually elicited shock and disbelief from anyone being briefed on it for the first time. They always seemed to think he should feel angry and resentful about what had been done to him, but he didn't, because he had been conscripted into a top-secret development program that had turned him into the bioengineered super-soldier that he was today. But he had a few vague, pleasant memories of his parents, and most of the people he knew who had been raised by parents seemed to have very fond memories of them.

"Don't you *want* to go back to your parents?"

Lena's eyes lit with understanding. "John, you're offering to kill us. Our parents are dead."

"Dead?" He looked from Lena back to Oskar. "All of them?"

"Yes, *all* of them," Oskar said.

"What happened to them?" Kelly asked.

"They died," Arne replied. "They starved or fell sick, or got hurt or too thirsty or too hot. Take your pick. Something always happens."

"Always?" Kelly said. "Surely, that's an exaggeration."

Arne and Oskar just looked at each other.

"*None* of you have parents?" John asked. He didn't see any indication that they were lying—he just couldn't believe what they were telling him. "Really?"

"I remember mine," Lena said. "My mother, at least. I think she had green eyes."

"You don't actually know?" Fred asked.

"I was young," she said. "I had just learned to walk."

"Okay, I'm starting to get the picture," John said. "Parents die young on Netherop. So who takes care of you?"

"We're not babies," Oskar said.

"I mean when you *are* babies," John asked. "Before you learn to walk."

Lena looked at him as though he were crazy.

"Somebody has to do it," John said. "No one is born walking."

"Of course not . . . but what an odd question." Lena made a circling motion with her finger, taking in herself and the two boys. "We all do . . . the whole camp."

Oskar scowled and leaned forward. "Why are you so interested in our babies, John?"

"I'm not, really," John said. "It's just . . . different. And I'm sorry about mentioning your parents. I didn't mean we were going to send you to join your ancestors, only that you would be free to go—as long as we all agree to leave each other alone."

"Why should we trust you?" Oskar asked.

"Because the gooey stuff is still inside your head," Lena said. "And *I* am ready to crack your egg."

John smiled inside his helmet. "That's the gist of it." He picked up one of the rocks they had bounced off his armor earlier. "You try to ambush us again, and . . ."

He closed his fist and crushed the stone.

Oskar's eyes grew round. "That seems fair," he said. "As long as you stop chasing us."

"We were never chasing you." John pulled a med-kit out of a load-carrier compartment, then dropped to his knees and pointed toward Oskar's wounded hand. "Now, let me see what I can do about that shrapnel. It looks painful."

Oskar shot a furtive glance toward Lena, who caught it and pointed him toward John.

"Go," she ordered. "It has to be better than a mudpack."

Oskar came over and presented a hand he was lucky to still have. The antenna shard was about five centimeters wide, and it had pushed clear through his hand. John examined the shard, then grabbed the thin part on the back of the hand and snapped it off.

Oskar howled in pain and tried to pull away. John held tight and reached around under the palm with his free hand, then drew the shard free. Oskar howled again, but did not try to withdraw his hand this time. John turned it over and examined the wound. There was a wide hole through the center of the palm, and through the blood, he could see that many of the bones had been shattered so badly that the middle two fingers were hanging only by flesh and muscle. It would take more than John's first-aid skills to make it usable again, but he could ease the pain and help prevent it from getting infected. He pulled the biofoam out of his med-kit.

"So, how long have you been on Netherop?" he asked.

"That's a dumb question," Oskar said.

"Don't be nasty, Oskar." Lena was facing away from Oskar, her head tilted back while Kelly cut the blood-matted hair away from her scalp wound. "He could crush your head, and I wouldn't care."

Oskar sighed, then said, "Our whole lives. What's it to you?"

John began to squeeze the biofoam into Oskar's wound. He wasn't particularly careful about avoiding shattered bones.

"Then you must know the area pretty well," he said.

"We know what we need to," Oskar said. "And what we need *not* to know. There are plenty of places we just can't go."

"I imagine," John said. He continued to work the biofoam nozzle back and forth, packing the wound with what would serve as a temporary plug until Oskar received proper medical attention. "Have you seen the wreck yet?"

"What wreck?"

There was a confused note in Oskar's tone that made John realize he had phrased his question poorly. There had been lots of wrecks in the area lately, starting with the *Night Watch*, the *Wheatley*'s Pelicans and fighter complement, and a bunch of Covenant craft.

"The big frigate," John clarified.

"What's a frigate?"

John sighed. "Never mind." He finished up with the biofoam, then said, "You're a tough guy, Oskar. That has to hurt."

"It's starting to," Oskar said. "But at first, I didn't even notice it until I saw the blood."

"Bad wounds are like that," John said. "The nerve shock lets you keep going for a few minutes. But when that wears off . . . well, don't do anything where you need to stay conscious. The pain will knock you out."

"Then you have been wounded before?"

"Once or twice," John said. "But I was never more than a few hours from the infirmary, so I didn't suffer the way you're going to."

Fred's voice sounded inside John's helmet. "I see what you're doing," he said. "Clever . . . and kind of cruel."

"No choice," John answered, also over TEAMCOM. "We have a target to capture—and these kids have a mountain runner that can get us there. See if you can win your kids over too."

Fred's and Kelly's status LEDs winked green, and they each began to talk about how bad their patients' wounds were.

John returned his focus to Oskar. "How long will it take you to reach an infirmary?"

"What's an infirmary?"

"A medical center," John said. He was only pretending to think

Oskar would have access to modern medicine. Mountain runners aside, there was nothing about these kids that suggested they came from a civilization advanced enough to have anything but primitive treatments. "You know, where they'll do the surgery to fix your hand."

"What's surgery?"

John sank back on his heels. "You don't have an infirmary, do you?"

"I don't think so," Oskar said. "Is that bad?"

"It *wouldn't* be, if you were coming with us." John pulled a bandage from his med-kit and began to wrap it around Oskar's hand. "But since you're not . . . well, you probably won't be able to use your hand anymore."

"No?" Oskar's face went pale. "So then . . . what if I did? Come with you?"

"Then one of our surgeons could fix your hand," John said.

"And Arne's knee," Fred said. He was holding Arne's leg in both hands, and Arne was leaning back on his elbows, his eyes rolled back in pain. "I have it back in the socket, but there's bound to be a lot of ligament damage. If he's ever going to walk right again, he'll definitely need surgery."

John looked across at Lena, who had just had her hair cut away from the shrapnel wound and was having biofoam sprayed into the laceration.

"Doesn't your colony have *any* kind of doctor?"

"Colony?" Lena replied. "Why would anyone build a colony on *this* place?"

"We've been asking ourselves the same question since—" Fred broke off, no doubt deciding it might not be wise to mention the two riders who'd vanished in the *Night Watch* shockwave. "Since we first noticed you."

"They wouldn't have built a colony here." Kelly's tone was suddenly sympathetic. "You're not here by choice."

"No way," Arne said. "We're castoffs."

"You mean castaways?" John asked. "Your ship crashed here?"

"He means 'Castoffs,'" Lena said. "That's what we call ourselves."

"Our ship did not *crash* here," Oskar explained. "Our ancestors were pirates. They were *marooned* here."

They all fell silent while the Spartans digested this. John activated TEAMCOM so Linda would be looped in on whatever followed—not because he thought it would be a threat to Blue Team, but because he wanted her to hear it firsthand. Planetary marooning was a gross violation of the Uniform Code of Military Justice, a practice so inhumane that the Colonial Administration Authority prohibited its inclusion as a punishment in any Planetary Penal Code and would imprison anyone involved in doing it. And to maroon someone on a place like Netherop? John could not even imagine that kind of cruelty.

Finally he asked, "Your ancestors were marooned here on Netherop? Somebody left them here with no way off?"

"That is how it has been explained to us." Lena shrugged. "Our ancestors preyed on the cargo ships supplying the colonies. I am sure when someone caught them and put them here, everyone expected them to die in the misery they deserved."

"But they *didn't* die," Kelly said. "They managed to survive . . . and have children?"

Lena nodded. "Because they found the Cave Cities," she said. "There was no food, but they had water."

"And there were tools." John looked back toward the spider machine. "Like your mountain runners?"

"A few tools," Arne said. "Most came from our ancestors. The other things . . . well, even when someone can dig it out and figure out what it did, it usually doesn't work."

"Understandable," Fred said. "The Cave Cities have to be, what, ten thousand years old? A hundred thousand?"

Lena cocked her head and looked at him. "What's a year?"

"It's . . ." John stopped, realizing that he didn't know how to answer. It was obvious these "Castoffs" knew some terminology and drew a blank on other things. His onboard computer displayed a not-so-helpful message on his HUD: NETHEROP COMPLETES ONE SOLAR REVOLUTION EVERY 2.4 STANDARD YEARS.

But what would that mean to Lena and her companions? If Netherop had anything like a year, it would be measured in terms of seasons or changes in light—and Blue Team had not been on the planet long enough make any meaningful observations about either.

Finally John said, "I'll explain later." He switched to TEAM-COM. "Blue Four, are you following all this?"

"Affirmative," Linda said. "It makes me want to shoot someone—a lot of someones."

"Me too," John said. "But whoever did this probably died fifty years ago. Are you on the rim yet?"

"Affirmative."

"What are the rest of the Castoffs doing?"

"They are still running, and it does not look as though they are coming back," Linda said. "But I am observing one problem."

"Go ahead."

"They are following the same bearing we are," Linda said. "I think perhaps they are trying to beat us to the *Lucky Break*."

CHAPTER 11

Ninth Age of Reclamation
41ˢᵗ Cycle, 150 Units (Covenant Battle Calendar)
Flotilla of Unsung Piety, Intrusion Corvette *Quiet Faith*
Supersynchronous Orbit, Planet N'ba, Eryya System

Nizat 'Kvarosee forced himself to stand motionless near the back of the bridge, his fingers steepled in front of him to keep his hands from fidgeting, his gaze fixed on the overhead to be sure his eyes did not lock on a tracking station or communications console. He would have liked to pace the deck, but such actions from a commander did not inspire confidence.

Nizat's plan to sniff out the infidels' Office of Naval Intelligence could not have been simpler. First, he would allow an ONI boarding party to storm the *Steadfast Strike* and capture the anti-gravity harness and personal shield in which the two Luminal Beacons were hidden. Then he would repel the assault and, once the humans were a short distance away, detonate the frigate's self-destruct charge to make it appear the crew was truly trying to protect Covenant technology. After that, it would be an easy matter of waiting until the ONI knowledge priests took the captured technology back to their discovery temple.

But the mere presence of the demon Spartans changed everything. The chance of them appearing in such a remote location should have been almost zero. In fact, that was why he had chosen N'ba for his plan.

And yet, here they were.

An unanticipated test of his worthiness. If the demons were allowed to reach the *Steadfast Strike*, there would be no controlling the situation. They might be able to deactivate the self-destruct charges and capture the vessel intact—and even Nizat did not believe ONI's destruction to be worth the risk of allowing the humans to reverse-engineer a fully equipped Covenant frigate. But if he could thwart them and capture one—alive or dead, it did not matter—perhaps he could turn their presence to his favor.

Was it possible that they had been sent to him by the gods themselves? It seemed too much to ask, and yet . . . capturing a Spartan was the one victory that might convince the Hierarchs of his truth—of the danger their ONI creators posed to the Covenant and its Great Journey—and return him to the Path of Honor.

Tam 'Lakosee spun away from the surface monitoring console and came aft. At first Nizat thought his young steward was bringing word that the demons had been located again, but that hope was crushed when 'Lakosee paused at the listening station. Had the news been good, there would have been no need to ask for more information. Nizat continued to study the overhead until 'Lakosee left the communications station, then finally lowered his gaze as the steward arrived.

"You have something to report?" Nizat was careful to keep the frustration from his voice. After all, it was not 'Lakosee who had allowed the demons to slip away. "Proceed."

"One of the Wasals has started to detect personal communication signals."

Wasals were small surveillance craft normally used to find hostile vessels in multibody orbital systems. They were poorly suited to hunting enemy foot soldiers on a planetary surface, but they were what Nizat had, so they were what was dispatched.

"I regret to report that the signals are too feeble to locate," 'Lakosee continued. "We know little more than before."

"Yet, a little more *is* more," Nizat said. "What have we learned?"

"The signal could have come from anywhere between the main body of survivors and ten thousand units short of the *Steadfast Strike*. If we ignore our assumptions about the enemy's destination, the signals could even be coming from down in the flatlands or the far side of the mountains."

"I see." Nizat was no expert in human transmission modes, but he had heard terms such as *multipath propagation*, *frequency jumping*, *terrain diffraction*, and *ionospheric reflection* often enough to know how difficult it could be to locate a source inside a planetary atmosphere—especially when the signal creators were taking measures to keep themselves hidden. "How long before the Wasals narrow that down?"

'Lakosee hesitated. "The gods may take pity on us and give us a signal they can triangulate. But if that has not happened yet . . ."

"It would be folly to count on it," Nizat finished.

"Your wisdom is boundless, Fleetmaster." 'Lakosee dipped his head, then gave a tentative mandible clack and said, "Perhaps it is time to send in a close-reconnaissance mission."

"Send it *where*?" Nizat asked. "Did you not say the signal could be coming from anywhere?"

"I did," 'Lakosee said. "I mean to suggest we reconnoiter the entire route."

It was an obvious step, one that any commander with an adequate supply of fighter craft would readily employ. But the Flotilla of Unsung Piety did not have an adequate supply of anything here. And after the losses it had already taken trying to stop the Spartans from interfering with Nizat's plan, it was especially short of fighter craft.

Still, 'Lakosee would learn nothing if Nizat dismissed the suggestion out of hand. Better to let him see its weaknesses for himself. And there *was*, after all, a small possibility that 'Lakosee himself had developed a workable plan.

"Tell me what you are thinking," Nizat said.

'Lakosee once again dipped his head and gave another subtle clack. "It would be my honor, Fleetmaster. I suggest we start with a strafing run on the main body of survivors."

"Why waste the carrier gas?" Nizat asked. "N'ba and its heat will kill them soon enough."

"Because an attack will tell us whether the demons remain with them," 'Lakosee said. "If they are there, they will defend the column and reveal themselves."

"By destroying our craft, as they did last time?"

"We might lose a fighter or two," 'Lakosee admitted. "But then we would know where to find the demons."

"And *they* would know we are coming," Nizat said. "Which means our ground forces would require close air support to prevail. How many more craft would we lose?"

"A few, most likely," 'Lakosee said. "But is it not better to lose a few fighters than to allow the demons a chance to capture the *Steadfast Strike*?"

"Perhaps, had the flotilla not lost so many ships already," Nizat said. "But the infidels have taken half our fighter complement now. If they take more, we will lack the support craft we need to continue the crusade."

'Lakosee glanced away, thinking. "Then it would be unwise to risk a low reconnaissance run along the rest of the route."

"Perhaps so." Nizat was pleased to see his steward coming to terms with their situation. When a rogue flotilla ran low on support craft, it could not send for more. "We would be most likely to find the Spartans when they downed our reconnaissance craft. And they would *know* they'd been found, then prepare a defense requiring us to put *more* of our forces at risk."

"So we must find the demons without betraying that we have done so," 'Lakosee said. "And we must kill them before they realize they are under attack."

"That would be ideal."

"Then why look for them at all?" 'Lakosee asked. "We know where they are going."

"You wish to intercept them at the *Steadfast Strike* itself?"

"It seems the surest way to accomplish our mission," 'Lakosee said. "We cannot risk our air support, but the demons have none to risk. So we prepare a defensive position and force them to attack."

"What if they win?"

"They *will*." 'Lakosee opened his mandibles in predatory delight. "We would set our defenses a safe distance from the *Steadfast Strike*, then allow a small force of the infidels' standard infantry to slip through the perimeter and board the vessel . . . *before* the Spartans."

"This small force would be the ones to recover the harness and the shield containing the Luminal Beacons?"

"Indeed," 'Lakosee said. "Once their assault has been repelled and they have been driven to a safe distance, we allow the demons to break through and board the ship."

"Then we use the humans' favorite trick against them, and destroy the *Steadfast Strike* with the demons aboard?"

"It seems a good way to safeguard such sacred knowledge," 'Lakosee said. "No Spartan—especially a dead one—can steal what has already been destroyed."

"A cunning plan," Nizat said, truly impressed. "But you assume the standard infantry will be the first to reach the frigate. We can hope to arrange that, but it is folly to believe we can control what the Spartans do. What if they anticipate our plan? Or if we cannot delay them long enough?"

"The *Steadfast Strike* can still launch," 'Lakosee said. "If the demons approach before we are ready, it can simply leave."

"True enough."

Nizat looked away, signaling his desire to think. Unless he was willing to sacrifice more fighter craft, there was little he could do to stop the demons before they reached the *Steadfast Strike* anyway. Better to use his bane's strength against them, which might blind the demons to their danger, and lure them into 'Lakosee's trap.

Nizat clacked his mandibles in satisfaction. "The first stage must look convincing," he said, turning back to 'Lakosee. "You will concentrate the great majority of your defenses against the Spartans, as though they are the only enemy you have."

'Lakosee's head rose in surprise. "*Me*, Fleetmaster?"

"It is your idea, so it will be your . . . command."

As Nizat spoke, the *Quiet Faith*'s broad-bodied shipmaster, Qoo 'Weyodosee, suddenly left his station and rushed forward to the communications console. He tipped his blocky head to one side and listened for a moment, then pivoted to face the rear of the bridge. His stubby mandibles were parted in shock, his eyes round with alarm.

Motioning 'Lakosee to follow, Nizat went to 'Weyodosee. "There is trouble?"

'Weyodosee tipped his head back in confirmation, then turned to the communications adept. "Play the avowal."

The adept began to tickle the glider switches on his console, and a coldness settled between Nizat's hearts. An avowal was a formal declaration of intent—usually issued as divine justification just prior to a subject's imminent execution.

After a breath, a soft and wispy voice spoke gently. *"Agony is the consequence of betrayal, and the Fleet of Swift Justice will deliver it."*

Nizat turned immediately toward the tactical hologram at the back of the bridge, where an image of the N'ba planetary system floated above a projection pad surrounded by ten instrument lecterns. At the five lecterns arrayed around the planet's night side, the readers were busy tapping and sliding their crystal display screens, enhancing the display with the images of Covenant ships—five destroyers and frigates so far, but also a cruiser and an assault carrier. The Fleet of Swift Justice had already arrived . . . and it was not there for the infidels.

'Weyodosee came to Nizat's side. "If our flotilla breaks orbit now, it will survive." He spoke quietly, so the readers would not overhear. "The Fleet of Swift Justice emerged from slipspace on vector to insert into our orbit, but intrusion corvettes are not easy to catch. Most of our ships should escape."

"If you believe that, you do not understand the Silent Shadow."

Nizat stepped to the partition rail that separated the tactical planning salon from the rest of the bridge and began to study the human destroyers that had been keeping watch over N'ba since "downing" the *Steadfast Strike*. The humans had been slipping more vessels into their flotilla as quickly as the vessels could travel here, and now there were eleven destroyers supported by two small cruisers. A force of that size was hardly sufficient to destroy the Fleet of Swift Justice—but it *was* large enough to make it pay attention.

'Weyodosee seemed unable to move his gaze away from the arriving fleet. Swift Justice had grown to ten vessels now—five destroyers and three frigates, plus the cruiser and the assault carrier.

"Fleetmaster, we must act soon," 'Weyodosee said. "Every second we delay reduces our chance of escape."

"Being driven before an onrushing enemy like a *gortoa* to the slaughter is *not* acting," Nizat said. "It is reacting—and that places us at the mercy of the Silent Shadow."

'Weyodosee's gaze remained fixed on the Fleet of Swift Justice. The destroyers and frigates were spreading out to screen the two larger ships, and it would not be long before they began to launch reconnaissance patrols to pinpoint the locations of the Flotilla of Unsung Piety's intrusion corvettes.

Normally.

Nizat studied the tactical holograph a little longer, then pointed at the arriving fleet. "It is not by chance that the Fleet of Swift Justice emerged from slipspace on the side of N'ba opposite the human flotilla."

"Of course not," 'Weyodosee said. "They are using the humans to limit our options and slow our escape."

"And that is why we must act quickly?" Nizat asked. In his fear, 'Weyodosee was growing insubordinate, but in a rogue flotilla, no fleetmaster could afford to harshly discipline the commander of his flagship. Persuasion and education were safer options. He glanced toward 'Lakosee and was glad to see his steward's eyes narrow in thought. "So they don't close off all hope of escaping around the far side of the planet?"

"Yes." 'Weyodosee spoke the word as though he were talking to an inexperienced hatchling. "If we allow that, they will push us into the humans. We can certainly destroy such a small flotilla, but it will take time—"

"And the Fleet of Swift Justice will arrive to crush us from behind," 'Lakosee said. "It will be a classic boot-on-the-stone attack."

'Weyodosee clacked his mandibles in agreement. "You see?" His focus remained on Nizat. "Even your steward sees the danger."

"I suspect he sees the trap as well." Nizat turned his gaze on 'Lakosee. "Is that correct?"

"It *does* seem that the Fleet of Swift Justice has left us with only one option." 'Lakosee looked to 'Weyodosee. "And the fleetmaster has a saying for such situations."

'Weyodosee trilled his throat in irritation. "It is a trap?"

"Essentially," 'Lakosee said. "But what he says is: 'When the enemy leaves you one option, take another.' "

"Well enough when there *is* another option," 'Weyodosee said. "But the only options I see are either death now or death later, and I prefer later."

"And abandon our quest?" Nizat looked away in negation. "That is not an option."

"It is our only hope," 'Weyodosee said. "How can we destroy ONI if we are dead?"

"We will not die," Nizat said. "Not if we take the third option."

"There *is* no third option."

"Of course there is," Nizat said. "Begin an insertion run."

'Weyodosee cocked his head, watching Nizat out of one eye. "Perhaps the fleetmaster has forgotten we are in an intrusion corvette? When we fire our engines to break orbit—"

"The humans will detect our presence and assume we are attempting to aid the *Steadfast Strike*." 'Lakosee's voice crackled with enthusiasm. "They will move to intercept us, and when we break off, *they* will be the ones between us and the Fleet of Swift Justice."

'Weyodosee closed his mandibles tight and fell silent, then finally dropped his gaze to the deck.

"I offer my apologies. The fleetmaster has forgotten nothing." His tone was chagrined. "You wish the order relayed to the entire flotilla?"

"You are most perceptive," Nizat said. "I leave the timing of the gravity-whip maneuver to you, but you must bring the *Quiet Faith* in low, with the rest of the flotilla behind it."

"As you command." 'Weyodosee started to turn away, then thought better of it. "I hesitate to question the fleetmaster again, but the *Quiet Faith* will perform better if I understand the purpose of this maneuver."

"I have no doubt," Nizat said. "The lower the *Quiet Faith* dips, the more likely two drop pods are to go unnoticed."

"Drop pods?" 'Lakosee asked. "Who are we dropping?"

"You and myself," Nizat said. "Who else?"

'Lakosee rocked his head forward, studying Nizat out of the upper parts of his eyes. "Why would *you* drop onto N'ba?"

"Because the Fleet of Swift Justice changes everything," Nizat said. "The humans will never hold it off long enough for the demons to reach the *Steadfast Strike*."

'Lakosee continued to look confused. "What are we to do about that? Offer them transport offworld?"

"Not exactly." Nizat turned aft toward his stateroom, where he had his energy sword and a full suit of combat armor. "But if we can no longer wait for the humans to attack *our* ship—"

"Yes, I see. Then we will attack theirs." 'Lakosee fell in behind Nizat. "And take the Luminal Beacons to *them*."

CHAPTER 12

1146 hours, June 7, 2526 (military calendar)
Crystal Bush Plateau
Mountains of Despair, Planet Netherop, Ephyra System

John-117's heads-up display showed nineteen kilometers to target when the spiderlike mountain runner gave its first little lurch. He had no idea who had built the thing, but it had probably been the same beings who constructed the Forgotten Highway and lived in the Cave Cities that Lena had mentioned earlier, and they had been accomplished engineers. The odd craft was humming and clicking over the stony terrain of the vast, crystal bush–covered plateau with a gait so smooth it felt like the machine was gliding. So John paid the hitch no attention and continued to focus on the task at hand—as did everyone on Blue Team.

Fred was driving, Linda was standing watch, and Kelly was playing doctor, making sure the two Castoff boys weren't suffering any complications from the polypseudomorphine they had been given to dull their pain. John was leaning back against the curved wall of the passenger compartment, studying his HUD and planning logistics.

Assuming his onboard computer's dead-reckoning navigation was accurate, the mountain runner had traveled fifteen kilometers across the plateau in the last half hour. They seemed to be moving straight toward the *Lucky Break*, so the Covenant ship would probably come into view within the next thirty minutes. Presumably, they would find the rest of the Castoffs nearby, either a few kilometers away at the *Wheatley*, or watching the *Lucky Break* and planning their approach.

At least, John *hoped* the Castoffs would be watching and planning. He couldn't know how the stranded alien crew would react to a bunch of young humans just riding up to ask for a lift, but he was relatively certain the outcome would not be what they hoped for.

In any case, once Blue Team caught up to the rest of the Castoffs, there would be five mountain runners available—enough to send back for First Platoon and the rest of the *Night Watch*'s complement. Holding the attack until the runners returned would mean delaying the assault an extra four hours, so the final decision would depend on what the *Wheatley*'s captain could tell John about Covenant fleet disposition in the Polona sector—and whether there seemed to be many assets moving toward Netherop's inbound slipspace routes—but he was inclined to wait. Another twenty or thirty soldiers could be the difference between taking the frigate intact and getting blown up during a prolonged boarding action.

The runner gave another little lurch. The sensation was almost imperceptible, but it was enough to make John look from his HUD toward the pilot's station at the front of the passenger compartment.

"You must be really tough," Lena said. The Castoff girl was sitting next to John, with her back against the nearest coal bin. "Because you're a terrible captain."

John turned his faceplate toward her. Rather than waste water washing the blood out of her hair, Lena had insisted that Kelly cut it away, and now she had a shaved patch over her brow, with a crusty brown ridge of biofoam running up the center. She looked even more gaunt and sunken-eyed than before, but tough . . . maybe even ODST tough.

"I'm not a captain," John said.

"No wonder." Lena glanced around the interior of the passenger compartment, allowing her gaze to linger on the other Spartans. "Who would elect you, when you make everyone else work while you sleep?"

"What makes you think I'm sleeping?"

"You haven't moved since those fireballs came down."

"Haven't had a reason to."

Twenty minutes earlier, two trails of flame had burned through the cloud cover and descended in the direction of the *Lucky Break*. John and the other Spartans had agreed over TEAMCOM that the fireballs were probably Covenant drop pods delivering weapons or supplies, but John hadn't shared that theory with their companions. He was still trying to decide whether the three Castoffs were prisoners, allies, or recruits—and until he did, he intended to be careful about what intelligence he shared.

"I think you were napping," Lena said. "What else would you be doing, sitting there so still?"

"Thinking."

"Then thinking must be really hard for you, if you can't even move when you do it." Lena watched him carefully, as though trying to read his faceplate's expression. "What are you thinking about, John?"

"About what happens next," John said. "And about why you lied about your friends trying to reach the ships."

"Who says they *are*?"

John tapped the side of his helmet. "Logical deduction," he said. "They're headed straight for them."

Lena shrugged and looked away. "We're moving camp, and the Old Way goes where it goes."

"They're not *on* the Old Way," John said. He wasn't entirely sure how the Castoffs knew the location of the *Lucky Break*, but Kelly had suggested a theory via TEAMCOM that matched the apparent timing. After seeing it go down, the Castoffs had sent scouts to investigate and learned that a spaceship had landed. The scouts had reported back, and the entire camp had moved out to make contact. "They're cutting straight across this plateau, and every time Linda spots them, they're headed for the ships."

"If you say so," Lena said. "I have no way of knowing that."

"So the Castoffs *don't* want to be rescued?" John spread his hands. "If you want to stay on Netherop, that's fine by me. Less thinking."

Lena glanced at Arne and Oskar, who lay half-conscious and stretched along the deck beside her, then said, "That's up to the captains. They're not here."

"Because they left you behind," John said. "And went on to the ships without you."

"What were they supposed to do?" Lena scowled. "Come back and get *everyone* killed?"

"So they *are* trying to reach the ships." John did not bother responding to Lena's question. She and her companions were still alive, and after their attacks on him and Fred, that was proof enough of Blue Team's friendly intentions. "Why lie about that? Why not just say so?"

Lena gave him a sidelong look. "Aren't *you* trying to reach the ships?"

John dipped his helmet in affirmation. "That's pretty clear."

"Are you going to tell me why?"

"I can't," John said. "Our mission is classified."

Lena furrowed her brow. "What does that mean?"

"It means we can't tell you," Kelly said. "It's a secret."

"So. We have secrets too."

"Yes, but it's no secret you want a ride off this planet," John said. "And we'll give it to you. All you have to do is ask."

Lena looked more suspicious than she did interested, but before she could reply, the runner lurched a third time and began to slow. John turned back toward the pilot's station and saw Fred's helmet tipped forward over the control globe. The sphere was pulsing yellow, and his hands were gliding over the surface as he tried to regain control.

"What's wrong?" John asked over TEAMCOM.

"If I knew, we wouldn't be slowing down," Fred replied. "I think it just got tired."

The runner continued to decelerate, and Kelly and Linda both spoke at the same time. *"Fuel."*

John turned to Lena. "Are we running out of fuel?"

She hooked a thumb at the heaped coal bins behind her. "Does it look like we're running out of fuel?"

"Then why is the runner stopping?"

"Because we're out of power." She pointed at the access panels in the deck. "The batteries need to be charged."

"Can we do that and keep traveling?"

Lena rose without replying and went aft between two coal bins. She shot a wary glance at the bullet holes in the back wall of the passenger compartment, then stretched over the back deck and opened the cabinet in front of the sooty pipe. Once the doors had clanged aside, she pulled herself up so she could see into the engine area.

"Not anymore," she said. "You broke the steamer."

John peered over her shoulder and saw a sealed tank with half a dozen bullet holes in it. About twice the size of his helmet, it had tubes curving out of the top toward a pair of generators on either side, and it sat atop a grimy firebox fed by a flap-covered feeder chute. A pressure boiler with holes in it wasn't going to charge anything.

John had no idea why an engineer capable of building a coal-fired engine wouldn't use it for direct power, rather than adding an intermediary step and using it to charge the batteries of an electric vehicle. But the mountain runners had been built by an extinct alien species, and as was evident in humanity's all-out war with the Covenant, aliens had their own logic.

"Is there a way to patch the boiler?" John asked.

Lena twisted around and looked up at him as though he were crazy. "You can't bandage a steamer, John. The pressure is too much."

John nodded. "I thought you might say that."

He retreated into the passenger compartment and began to look around at the cabinet doors and floor panels. Blue Team had performed a quick inspection of the cargo areas before setting off, and he didn't recall seeing anything that looked like a welding torch or spare engine parts. But he wasn't entirely willing to accept Lena's assertion that there was no way to repair the boiler either. As much as she wanted her friends to receive medical attention, Lena continued to be secretive about the intentions of the other Castoffs. Maybe it was just good operational security, but John could not help thinking she didn't want Blue Team anywhere near when the rest of the band reached the two ships.

He looked back toward Lena. "You know, every hour it takes for Oskar and Arne to reach help reduces their chances of—"

John stopped when an emergency alert dinged inside his helmet.

"Of what?" Lena asked. "There's no trade to make, John. Even if you leave them behind, that steamer can't be fixed."

John barely heard her. He was listening to an alarmed message over the emergency channel.

"*All UNSC.* Phyllis Wheatley *reporting imminent attack, Netherop surface, five kilometers from recovery target.*" The *Wheatley* voice was mature and gravelly, so probably a senior officer—or even the captain himself. "*We are on a rocky plateau with Covenant boarding party approaching on foot, approximate distance three kilometers, approximate strength one or two hundred, heavy weapons and support vehicles, ETA uncertain but under thirty minutes. Tactical sensors show fighter canopy overhead. Please advise available support. Over.*"

"*Task Force Pantea inbound with ten squadrons Nandao fighters,*" replied a crisp voice. "*ETA close orbit twenty minutes.*"

"*Twenty minutes, acknowledged. Wait reply.*"

"*Negative wait,*" Pantea said. "*Message continues. Enemy stealth vessels inbound, strength eight minimum, planetary insertion imminent though uncertain, probable source of enemy fighter canopy.*"

"*Eight stealth vessels, acknowledged,*" Wheatley replied. "*Imminent planetary insertion possible. Acknowledged.*"

"*Report continues.*"

"*There's more?*" Wheatley gasped.

"*Sorry,*" Pantea replied. "*Full enemy task force also inbound, destroyers and frigates escorting a cruiser and assault carrier. ETA orbital insertion twenty minutes.*"

"*Confirm ETA twenty minutes Pantea and enemy task force?*"

"*Affirmative,*" Pantea replied. "*We'll try to insert into a lower orbit and hold off the task force, but no guarantees. It will be close.*"

"*Acknowledged. Can you provide ground forces?*"

"*Negative ground forces,*" Pantea replied. "*We're a wolf pack. No marines. Over.*"

"Negative ground forces acknowledged. Wait reply."

The runner lurched and slowed again, then slowed some more and lurched to a stop.

Lena, who remained unaware of the exchange John was listening to inside his helmet, came forward and stood in front of him.

"Did you mean what you said—"

John raised a finger, signaling her to wait.

She continued anyway. "—about giving us a ride off the planet?"

John ignored her. He hated to break comm silence by replying over the emergency channel—broadband transmissions were a good way to alert the enemy to one's location—but the *Wheatley* needed to know help was on the way.

"Blue Team inbound with four Spartans," John said. "ETA thirty to forty minutes. Over."

"Forty would be too late," Wheatley said. *"Once the enemy crosses the canyon, we have to scuttle our ship. We don't have the personnel to defend it."*

"Acknowledged. Do what you have to." Even at a full sprint, it would take Blue Team at least twenty minutes to reach the *Wheatley*—and across unfamiliar terrain, it could easily take them twice as long. "And be advised, there are three vehicles of young castaways ahead of us."

"Confirm: castaways?" Pantea and *Wheatley* made the request almost simultaneously; then *Wheatley* added, "Human *castaways? On Netherop?"*

"Affirmative. Human castaways." As John spoke, the rest of Blue Team stood and turned their eyes to the sky, keeping watch for any enemy fighters drawn by their comm signal. "Estimate their strength at twenty, fleeing our location in . . . well, in spider machines."

"Continue," Wheatley said.

"Descendants of marooned pirates," John said. "Hostile approach possible."

"You mean likely," Fred said over TEAMCOM. "Those kids think we're aliens, remember?"

"Correction," John said, still speaking over the emergency channel. "Hostile approach likely."

"Acknowledged. Young hostile pirates in spider machines. Sure, why not?" The *Wheatley* man sighed, then asked, *"How about armaments?"*

"Microwave-beam weapons mounted on the spider machines," John said. "Otherwise . . . slingshots and rocks."

"Slingshots and . . . rocks. Okay, acknowledged." *Wheatley* sounded more surprised by the primitive tools than by the mention of an entirely new class of weapons. At this point, they were probably beyond surprise. *"Anything else?"*

"Negative," John said. "We'll be there as soon as possible."

"Acknowledged . . . and appreciated," *Wheatley* said. *"Captain Dkani advises: Unless there is a crewman waving you in, board with caution. Utmost caution."*

"Wilco," John said. Dkani's unspoken message was clear—if he had to abandon the *Wheatley*, he was going to leave it booby-trapped. "Out."

John waited a couple of seconds for any last messages from the *Wheatley* or Task Force Pantea, then closed the channel and turned to his companions. All three were scanning different thirds of the horizon, looking for inbound fighter craft. They did not bother to search above thirty degrees, as high-angle strafing runs were both ineffective and more dangerous to the attacking craft than to the target.

Still, Covenant.

Before collecting his equipment, John took a moment to crane his neck and look up at the sky overhead—and felt something thunk his hip armor. He glanced down to see Lena holding a lump of coal and pulling back to hit him again.

He activated his voicemitter. "I wouldn't."

"About time." Lena lowered her hand, then looked up and asked, "Did you pull a wire loose or something? I asked you a question."

"There have been some developments," John said.

"That's hard to miss." Lena spread her arms, her palms turned upward. "We stopped."

"It's a bad time to stop," John said.

"Not my fault." Lena pointed a hand toward Kelly. "*She*'s the one who shot up the steamer."

"That doesn't matter," John said. "Unless you can get this thing going again—"

"Do you have a spare steamer somewhere?"

"Not exactly."

"Then I can't get it going again."

"Then you need to keep quiet." John switched to TEAMCOM so Lena could not hear his orders. "Fred, you're lead. Linda, move out with me. Kelly, you're skywatch. Find a safe place to—"

"Hello?" Lena hit him with the coal again. "I'm talking to you!"

John looked down, then switched back to his voicemitter. "Stop."

"Are you serious about helping us get off Netherop or not?"

"Getting unserious fast." He continued to speak over his voicemitter. "Kelly, you're skywatch—"

"And babysitter," she said, also over her voicemitter. "Why me? I hate kids."

"*That*'s why." John wasn't being entirely honest. As the fastest runner on the team, Kelly was simply the best choice to secure Lena and her two companions. Once she found a safe place to stash them, she would have the best chance of being able to catch up to the rest of the team. "You'll shoot if they don't obey orders."

Lena's eyes went wide. "She wouldn't."

"There's a shrapnel wound in your head that suggests otherwise." Kelly looked down at Lena. "But try me if you like."

Lena shook her head. "That's okay."

"I'm glad we finally understand each other," John said. "Now, keep quiet for ten seconds." He switched back to TEAMCOM. "Your first priority is to watch for fighter craft. I don't want any dropping in behind us."

"I *know* what skywatch is," Kelly said, also over TEAMCOM.

"I said first priority. You'll also have to find a safe place to stow our allies."

"*Allies* is a bit much, don't you think?"

Kelly tipped her helmet toward Lena, who was looking back and forth between the two Spartans as though she was actually trying to read lips through their reflective faceplates.

"Maybe," John said. "But they're not our prisoners either."

"I suppose not. If they were prisoners, I could just shoot them."

"Something like that," John said. "So just hide them and make sure they know how to avoid air attacks . . . and you'd better destroy the mountain runner too."

"The air attack, I understand. But why destroy the runner? It's already disabled."

"As far as we know. But Lena is holding out on us. If that thing *can* be repaired, I don't want her sneaking back after you stash them."

"Understood." Kelly turned to Lena, then switched to her voice-mitter and pointed at the collection of water bladders and foodstuffs piled on the deck. "Unload enough food and water to keep you for a week."

"What's a week?"

Kelly let her chin drop. "Never mind." She knelt on the deck and began to move supplies off the battery access panels. "Unload as much food and water as you can."

"Why?"

"Because it's an order," John said. He retrieved his BR55 and his M7 submachine gun from the deck where he had been sitting earlier. "And you know what happens if you don't obey orders."

Lena grew pale, then began to pile the water bladders on the side deck. Fred jumped out of the front of the runner and set off across the plateau, with his BR55 battle rifle in hand and his rocket launcher and two extra sets of tubes on his magmounts. John secured the M7 and two extra tube sets for the M41 to his own mounts, then checked to see if Linda was ready.

She carried an MA5C assault rifle with an underslung M301 grenade launcher in hand, with plenty of ammunition and her SRS99 sniper rifle clamped to her magmounts. Linda was always ready.

For anything.

John nodded, and she jumped out of the runner and followed a hundred meters behind Fred. The spacing was greater than normal, but they would be moving at near-vehicle speeds without concern for stealth or their own safety. The extra distance would give them more reaction time if Fred stumbled into an ambush, and it would prevent a single air strike from taking out the entire patrol.

As John gathered himself to leap out of the runner, Lena said, "They won't trust you, but that doesn't mean you have to kill them."

John paused with his foot on the bow of the runner. "Kill who?"

"Samson and Roselle," she said. "The captains. They just want to get the camp off Netherop."

"Then we all want the same thing," John said.

"You're a terrible liar, John. You want something else."

"I want a lot of things," John said. "Getting your camp off Netherop is one of them . . . and it might help if you can tell me how to make Samson and Roselle trust us."

"Why would I do that?" Lena asked. "*I* don't even trust you."

John turned up the palm of his free hand. "Your choice, then."

He jumped off the runner and started across the plateau, sprinting the first twenty seconds until he had closed to a hundred meters behind Linda. Even had he not been able to see her armor shimmering in the heat ahead, he could have followed the trail of broken stems she was cutting through the crystal bushes. Realizing that he was in a straight line behind her, he moved fifty meters to the right of her path.

He spoke over TEAMCOM. "Blue Two and Four, let's stagger our line. After all the emergency comms, the enemy fighters have to know where we are."

"You're clear so far," Kelly said. "And if they were coming, they would come quickly—before we have time to vanish again."

"That's how *we* would do it." John wasn't worried about giving away their position as they talked. They were still within a kilometer of the disabled runner, so the enemy would already have a pretty good idea of their location from the conversation over the emergency channel. "But the Covenant might have more confidence in its remote tracking technology."

"You think they hope to jump us later with surprise?" Linda asked.

"I don't know," John said. "They could be studying us, or just playing with us. The only thing we know about how aliens think is that it's not the same way we do."

"None of this makes any sense," Fred said. "And it doesn't matter whether you think like an alien or a human. Why are they attacking the *Wheatley* at all?"

"It couldn't be because their own vessel is disabled and they want to leave," Kelly said.

"Can't be," Fred said. "If that was all, they'd just wait. The Covenant has a big fleet coming in, and Pantea can't hold it off for long."

"I *did* say 'couldn't be.'"

"Perhaps they don't know about the Covenant fleet," Linda said. "If their vessel is disabled, perhaps their communications are out too."

"That could explain the drop pods," John said. "Someone bringing a message."

"And what did the message say?" Fred asked. " 'Help is coming, so go hijack that human salvage ship?' "

"No," Linda said. "That makes no sense."

"Kinda my point."

"But it could be they worry about *us*," Linda said. "They know we want their frigate, and they think we will try for it when we see their fleet arriving. So they attack our salvage ship to stop us?"

"A preemptive strike," John said. That didn't make a lot of tactical sense, as it was always much easier to defend a target than assault one. But there he was, trying to force human logic onto alien minds again. "That's as good as an explanation as any, I guess."

"Maybe not any," Fred said. "Don't forget about the Castoffs."

"What about them?" John asked.

"They're at least ten minutes ahead of us," Fred said. "Maybe even twenty, since their runners weren't damaged. The Covenant sentries have probably spotted them by now."

"So?" Linda asked. "Why would a bunch of children make the aliens attack?"

"Think about how the Castoffs are mounted," Fred said. "Maybe the aliens are afraid of spiders."

Kelly groaned. "Seriously? Better check your suit temperature, mate. I think your brain is boiling."

"You have a better explanation?"

"Nobody does. Because they're *aliens*." John hated to admit it, but Fred's explanation was as likely to be right as Linda's. "And there's no use locating ourselves for them while we argue. Let's go to Silent Mode Charlie."

Silent Mode Charlie was a communications protocol that disallowed casual transmissions, even over TEAMCOM. It was probably over-kill, since TEAMCOM's low signal-strength and random frequency-hopping made it almost impossible to triangulate. But given how little the UNSC knew about alien capabilities, there was no sense taking chances. Besides, given a half hour of quiet time, someone might think of an explanation that actually made some sense.

At least, John hoped someone would, because the closer they came to the *Lucky Break*, the more he realized that they had no idea what the Covenant was really doing here on Netherop.

CHAPTER 13

The makeshift drag sleds had cut two long paths leading straight to the shadowed gully where Kelly intended to stash the three Castoffs, but there was nothing to be done about it. Even Spartans could not haul three wounded children and a hundred kilos of food and water across three kilometers of crystal bushes without leaving a trail. She didn't think it would be a liability though. The children were far from helpless, and the closest thing to a predator she had seen on Netherop was those little grubs on the paddle plants. And she was not at all certain the grubs were actually animals.

She checked the time on her HUD again. Twenty-one minutes had passed since she had parted ways with John and the rest of Blue Team. They should be reaching the *Wheatley* soon—if they were not there already. Within the next ten minutes, the Covenant force from the *Lucky Break* would also arrive, and the opening salvos of the battle would be fired.

So the Castoffs would have to take their chances. Kelly had gotten them into the shade, with plenty of nourishment, and that would have to do. Her mates on Blue Team needed her now.

She turned back toward the center of the gully. Arne and Oskar were sitting in the shade, next to a lean-to fashioned from the battery panels she had used to transport the children and their supplies into the gully. Lena was crawling in and out of the shelter, moving the water bladders and food baskets under cover. Kelly crossed the bottom of the rocky gully, then knelt in front of the lean-to entrance and began to pass the stores to Lena.

"Don't leave the area for at least three—" Kelly stopped, realizing that the length of her day was probably very different from Lena's. "How *do* you measure time here?"

"What difference does it make?" Lena took a basket of tubers from Kelly and pushed it into the back of the shelter. "You're not coming back anyway."

"We will if we can," Kelly said. "And even if we lose the battle and can't because of that, there is a platoon of marines following along behind us."

Lena looked confused, but did not ask what a marine or a platoon was.

"Marine battle dress isn't equipped with a temperature-regulating skinsuit like our Mjolnir . . ."

Lena looked even more confused.

Kelly kept going. ". . . so it could take them three or four—" She almost said *days*, then caught herself and said, "A fair while to arrive. But I'll transmit these coordinates to their lieutenant, and they'll rendezvous with you here."

Lena's expression was blank.

"How much of what I just explained did you actually under-stand?" Kelly asked.

"You're going to leave us here," Lena said. "Even if you don't make it back, there are more of you coming. Wearing dresses or something."

"Battle dress. It's a uniform combined with armor, just not like *our* armor. The important thing is, they'll need to know where to find you. If you don't stay here, they won't be able to."

"Why would we want them to?"

"Because they'll get you off the planet. And you want that, right?" Kelly had to fight to keep from shaking her helmet; these silly, endless questions were the kind of thing that could turn her *I don't like children* act into more than an act.

"It doesn't mean we want your marines to do it," Lena said.

"It won't happen any other way," Kelly said. "If you don't extract with us, it has to be with the marines."

Lena's gaze shifted away; then she grabbed a pair of water blad-ders and quickly turned toward the interior of the shelter. "Maybe."

It wasn't a resigned reply, as in: *Maybe that would be okay*. It was more confident, as in: *Maybe it doesn't have to be your marines.*

Kelly was silent for a moment, wondering if Lena thought the Castoffs might be able to strike a bargain with the Covenant. Cer-tainly she wouldn't be the first human foolish enough to believe such a thing.

And then Kelly remembered who the Castoffs' ancestors had been.

"You must be mad," she said. "You've never even been aboard a spaceship. How do you expect to *steal* one?"

Lena whirled around with fire in her eyes. "We know what to do."

"No, you really don't. And even if you did, you'd never be able to fly it. Why won't you accept our help?"

"Because that's the oldest con in the bag," Lena said. " 'We're the UNSC, and we're here to help.' "

Kelly rolled her eyes back and looked into the top of her helmet. "Oh, *now* I get it. Your ancestors weren't just pirates, were they? They were Separatists."

"So what if they were?" Lena said. "You still want to help?"

"Actually, yes," Kelly said. "No matter what their crimes—"

"Wanting to live free is no crime."

"Certainly not," Kelly said. "I was referring to the piracy part—"

"Hey, Bowl-face Lady?" Arne's voice was behind her, still mumbly and slow. Kelly had administered some stimulants to counteract the sedative effects of polypseudomorphine, but they were still kicking in. "What's that thing?"

Kelly didn't turn to look—that ruse truly *was* the oldest trick in the book.

"Lena, you can't be held responsible for your ancestors' crimes," she said. "You weren't even born when those offenses were committed."

"Whoa." Oskar was sounding as addle-headed as Arne. "How is that fork-thing even flying?"

Fork-thing . . . ?

Kelly felt her stomach sink. She turned to find both Oskar and Arne pointing into the sky, where an elongated vessel with sharp, angular lines was slipping down out of the brown clouds. Still dozens of kilometers out, it was just large enough for her to see three forward-mounted troop bays sticking out like the prongs on a trident. A Covenant dropship, similar to the Spirit the UNSC had encountered many times before, but this one was equipped with a little more vehicle-carrying capacity and an extra troop bay.

A sort of Super Spirit, Kelly decided—though the longer she looked at it, the more the troop bays looked stubbier than on the two-pronged variety. So maybe it was an entirely different kind of craft, or just a variation designed to carry an extra vehicle and not really all that "super" then. She would leave the formal designation to Section Three. Between the three prongs, a blanket of blue force shimmered over two arch-shaped vehicles. Kelly suspected they were Umbras—fast, lightly armed surface transports used to ferry troops into battle.

As the dropship drew nearer, Kelly saw that its approach path would carry it over the disabled mountain runner that she and her young companions had left behind. She didn't think the Covenant pilot would notice it—or at least, she hoped not. Kelly had seen a few Spirits up close, and she didn't recall their basic design having any lenses or viewing ports on the underside. She hoped the same would be true of their three-pronged cousin, and the vehicles hanging between the prongs would help block the pilot's view of the ground. But there could be up to fifteen troops in each transport prong, and it only made sense that *they* would have some ability to anticipate what awaited below when the hull folded outward to let them disembark.

Kelly grabbed the two battery-cover panels they had used to build the lean-to, then tossed them to the other side of the gully, where they would not be visible from the dropship's approach angle.

"So . . . that's *not* one of yours?" Lena asked.

"Does it look like I'm trying to wave it down?" Kelly grabbed the two boys under their arms and carried them across the gully. "It's an alien dropship."

"You mean, like *real* aliens?" Oskar asked. "Not just you giants in armored space suits?"

"I mean the kind of aliens you don't want to meet," Kelly said. "The kind that will fry you without a second thought."

"Is that why you wear the weird armor?" Arne asked. "So you can pass for an alien?"

"I *can't* pass for an alien," Kelly said. "I don't look anything like one."

She deposited the boys at the bottom of the gully wall—"Stay here"—then crept to the top and pushed her helmet far enough above the rim to see. The dropship had grown to the size of her hand and was now crossing the drag-path she had left through the crystal brush. It was hard to tell whether it was passing over the middle of the path or the far end, where the disabled mountain runner lay. But if one of the aliens was able to look downward, they would definitely see evidence of her group's passage.

Kelly should probably have randomized her trail, so that the path looked like something a wild animal might have left. But that took time, and her number-one priority had been catching up to the rest of Blue Team.

"Maybe you shouldn't have blasted our runner apart," Lena said, crawling up beside her. "All that smoke was like a *here we are* signal."

"There wasn't that much smoke," Kelly said. "And it lasted about thirty seconds."

"Thirty seconds is plenty of time to pick a route and a destination mark," Lena said. "I could pick ten in thirty seconds."

"It wasn't the smoke," Kelly said. "How would they have seen it through the clouds?"

Of course, there were a lot of ways another Covenant vessel might have detected the blast—infrared imaging or cloud-penetrating radar, for instance. But the *Wheatley*'s emergency transmission had come even before the runner was incapacitated, so if anything had drawn the dropship to Kelly's general location, it would have been the broadband comm messages being passed back and forth among John and everyone else.

What Kelly didn't understand was why it had taken the aliens more than twenty minutes to arrive. If its mothership had been that far out of position, any decent commander would have sent a reconnaissance flight to check out the situation before going to the trouble—and risk—of a troop insertion.

Any decent *UNSC* commander, actually. The Covenant had a different way of thinking, as John kept pointing out. Better to avoid assumptions and observe carefully, then build one's plans based on what the aliens were actually doing—rather than what one thought they should be doing.

Kelly waited another five seconds for more dropships to descend out of the clouds. When that didn't happen, she decided she could not be watching a full assault. The aliens were either inserting a special forces unit or a reconnaissance patrol—and her bet was on special forces. During one of the Spartans' earlier operations, it had grown increasingly apparent that the enemy had created a dedicated cadre to hunt them down, which was why John had warned them—repeatedly—that the downing of the *Lucky Break* could be an elaborate ploy to lure a group of Spartans into a trap.

And from what she was seeing now, it appeared John was right.

As the dropship continued its descent, Kelly realized the pilot was trying to insert covertly. He was coming in slow to avoid a sonic boom, and he was maintaining a steep, steady course that minimized time-of-visibility, but made his craft easy prey for ground-based missile systems. Clearly the aliens believed they were landing unobserved. And that was the kind of mistake that could be used to turn a mission into a disaster.

Rather than betraying her own presence by breaking comm silence, Kelly had her onboard computer project the dropship's probable landing zone. She was only a little surprised to discover that the site was less than a kilometer away, just beyond the gully where she and the Castoffs were now hiding. But it made sense. She had strayed only a little distance off the rest of Blue Team's course to the

Wheatley, and if the Covenant intended to attack Blue Team from behind, they would naturally try to follow the same path.

Kelly retreated back into the gully bottom, then gathered Lena and the boys in front of her and pointed in the general direction of the landing zone.

"In a few minutes, you're going to hear some battle sounds from that direction. But you need to stay here."

"No way," Lena said. "What if they hurt you?"

"They won't." Kelly took her M6D sidearm off its thigh mount. "But take this and some water, and find a good place to hide. Someplace where you can watch your stores without being seen."

Lena's gaze was locked on the sidearm. "What's that for?"

"Nothing, I hope," Kelly said. "But if anything other than me or another human comes up that gully, you might need it."

Lena's eyes grew round. "To do what?"

Kelly tapped the muzzle. "The bullets come out of this end. So never point it at anything you don't want to kill." She showed Lena how the safety and trigger worked, then said, "If you need to use it, wait until the enemy is almost close enough to touch you. Then point the bullet end at your target, hold tight with both hands, and keep squeezing the trigger until they drop. Got it?"

"What's not to get?" Lena asked. "Rocks work the same way."

"Not quite."

"Sure they do," Lena said. "You just keep banging until they die."

"I see your point, but this is better than a rock. It punches through armor." Kelly glanced toward the landing zone and saw the dropship still approaching the gully, about five hundred meters off the ground and gently descending. She needed to get moving. "Whatever happens, stay close to this spot. Somebody *will* come for you, even if it's not me—"

"Why wouldn't it be you?" Oskar asked.

"Because she might get killed," Arne said. "Pay attention."

"Oh." Oskar frowned. "So if she gets killed, who gets her stuff?"

"Forget about my stuff." Kelly was about ready to kill Oskar herself. "If something happens to me, it blows up."

"Really?" Arne said. "That's pretty selfish."

"Live with it." Kelly handed the M6D to Lena. "I have to go. What are *you* going to do?"

"Stay here. Hide." Lena turned the sidearm away from the gathering. "Don't point this at anything I don't want to kill."

"I'm glad we finally understand each other."

Kelly pulled the MA5B off her back magmount and loaded the underslung M301 grenade launcher, then started down the gully at a sprint. The dropship was still three hundred meters off the ground, with the pilot's compartment hidden behind its bulk. The two Umbras were secured just beneath the craft, between the three transport prongs.

The propulsion plates beneath the Umbras remained dark and inactive, so it appeared the Covenant did not intend to risk damaging equipment and personnel in one of their dump-and-run drops. That meant the dropship would lower the vehicles to the ground, then wait for the drivers to climb into their seats and bring the propulsion systems online. Once both vehicles had moved a short distance away, the transport prongs would open, the troops would disembark, and the craft would withdraw to its mothership as fast as possible.

And that was when Kelly needed to strike—after the heavily armored dropship and its big plasma cannon were gone. If she'd had Blue Team's M41 rocket launcher, she would have waited until the two Umbras were fully loaded and then tried to take out both vehicles and the troops aboard them. Quick and efficient.

But all Kelly had was an MA5B assault rifle with an underslung M301 and two satchels of grenades—one filled with 40mm rounds for the M301 and one filled with hand-thrown M9s. That meant she needed to attack after the dropship had withdrawn, but before the ground troops were safely protected inside their Umbras.

On her second magmount, Kelly also carried an M45E tactical shotgun, which she truly hoped she wouldn't have to use. The odds would be very much against her in close-quarters combat facing so many Covenant special forces troops.

The dropship crossed the gully and sank out of sight. As she ran, Kelly prepared an emergency channel transmission, warning Blue Team that an enemy platoon—possibly special forces—was moving up behind them, and outlining her intentions. She had her onboard computer provide dead-reckoning course bearings from both the destroyed runner and her anticipated ambush site back to where she had left Lena and the two boys. What Kelly did *not* share was her suspicion that John had been right all along, that the Covenant had been using the downed frigate as bait from the get-go. That was speculation, and such a thing could be its own kind of trap.

Kelly reached the area where the dropship had crossed the gully and crawled up to the rim. She could see the craft two hundred meters ahead, a long band of dark metal hovering fifteen meters off the ground. Beneath it, the first Umbra was already rocking on its propulsion pads. The driver and accompanying gunner—both Elites in dark armor—were visible in their cockpits atop the arched vehicle, running equipment checks in preparation for pulling forward so they could embark Covenant troops.

And that deployment would be quick. The carrier pod beneath each Umbra had a capacity of twenty soldiers—ten on each side of a passenger bay split vertically down the center—but the dropship carried only ten aliens in each of its stubby transport bays, for a total of thirty. And that meant there would be no time spent jockeying for stations or packing in equipment. The soldiers would simply debark the dropship and walk a dozen meters to one of the Umbras, where they would ascend loading ramps that folded out on either side of the carrier pods, secure their equipment, and buckle into their transport stations. Then the loading ramps would close, and the Umbras would depart to attack John and the rest of Blue Team.

Kelly slipped over the rim and began a high-crawl forward. The only watch the aliens had posted so far was the driver and the gunner atop the first Umbra, and they appeared more concerned with preparations than watching for an attack. Kelly would have liked to move quickly, but she had to be cautious, taking care to keep well below the crowns of the crystal bushes and to remain as far from their stems as possible. It was a frustrating and slow process, but after a few minutes she reached a circle of empty ground where the crystal bushes had been destroyed by the dropship's arrival.

Kelly stopped a meter back from the clearing edge, which would help keep her hidden while providing a full view of the target zone. The dropship was about fifty meters away, hovering at a forty-five-degree angle to her direction of travel. The second Umbra was already floating on its own propulsion pads and would soon move forward to join its companion vehicle. That would put the two Umbras about ninety meters from where Kelly now was—well within range of her weapons, but a little beyond their zone of maximum lethality. And if she wanted to spoil the trap they were laying for her friends, she needed to be lethal.

Kelly dropped to her stomach and began to belly-crawl backward, veering away from her original path. She would circle around to the front of the landing zone, where she could approach to within fifty meters of the Umbras and use her grenade launcher to take out the gunner stations. Then she would switch to her assault rifle and kill the pilots. That would force the rest of the Covenant troops to dismount and pursue her on foot, which would allow Kelly to use her speed to good advantage and, if all went well, pick them off at her leisure. But she would have to be sure the aliens didn't regroup and circle back to the Umbras—

A FRIEND symbol appeared on Kelly's motion tracker, coming from the direction of the gully along the same path she had taken. Kelly cursed into her helmet. It could only be one of the Castoffs— Kelly had designated all three as friendlies after destroying the mountain runner. She rolled onto her back and swung her legs around, so her assault rifle was pointed toward the new arrival. Motion trackers rarely misidentified a contact. But Spartans *had* been known to make the rare mistake in applying the friendly designation in the first place.

Lena appeared a few breaths later, belly-crawling along the same path Kelly had followed. When the girl started past without realizing she was being watched, Kelly reduced the volume of her voice-mitter to almost silent, then gave a very soft hiss.

Lena reversed course without even taking the time to look toward the sound, and a moment later the barrel of Kelly's M6D began to slide past the stems of a crystal bush.

"Don't you dare." Kelly's words were so quiet that even she could barely hear them. "The aliens will cook you . . . and I'll leave them to it."

The M6D went flat against the ground, and Lena's face slowly came into view above it, her blue eyes as big and round as coins.

"Wow," she whispered. "You're *good*."

Kelly raised a finger to her faceplate, then motioned Lena forward. The girl was only a few meters distant, so if the loaned pistol barrel started to swing in the wrong direction, Kelly thought she would be able to disarm the Castoff before she fired. Still, Kelly found herself wondering what the hell she had been thinking in the first place, trusting an orphan girl to follow orders. Lena had probably never even heard the phrase *unit discipline*.

As soon as Lena was within arm's reach, Kelly snatched the pistol away and returned it to her thigh mount. "What are you doing here?" she demanded, keeping her voice barely above a whisper. "I gave you an order."

Lena shrugged. "What are you gonna do?" She glanced toward the dropship. "Bullet me?"

"Too noisy." Kelly menacingly splayed her free hand. "Now, are you going to explain yourself? Or do I crush your head like an egg and go about my business?"

"What's to explain?" Lena asked. "Arne and Oskar talked it over with me, and we decided John would never believe us if we let you get killed."

"What wouldn't he believe?" Kelly asked. "It's not *your* responsibility to protect me."

"Maybe not," Lena said. "That doesn't mean John would be okay with us letting it happen."

"That makes no sense," Kelly said. "John wouldn't hold you responsible for anything that happens to me."

Lena rolled her eyes. "That helmet must be too tight, 'cause you're either blind or clueless."

Kelly glanced back toward the Spirit, checking the aliens' progress. She couldn't let the girl distract her, but it would probably be faster—and quieter—to hear her out than to argue with her about going back. Or so Kelly told herself.

"What are you talking about?"

"You know when someone's following your trail from twenty paces away, but you can't tell when you're the captain's favorite?"

"His *favorite*?"

Kelly was certainly fond of John, and she wanted to believe that the feeling was mutual. After all, they had been living and training together since they were six years old, and if that didn't make them family, then she didn't have one, period.

But his favorite? That could never be true . . . at least, not in the way Lena seemed to think. Spartans weren't just family—they were a fighting force, and anything that interfered with their unit cohesion was apt to get them all killed. Which meant John would never play favorites. He wouldn't be that careless with their lives.

The dropship swept past overhead, on the way back to its mothership, and Kelly realized she was running out of time.

"Don't be daft," she said. "John-117 doesn't have favorites."

"Sure he does," Lena said. "Why do you think he left you with us, and not Linda? He doesn't want you to get hurt, and if we let that happen—"

"We?" Kelly checked her motion tracker and saw nothing, but it only had a range of twenty-five meters—and it only detected moving bodies. "Don't tell me Arne and Oskar are here."

"Not *here*, exactly," Lena said. "Back in the gully. They were too unsteady from the polysumiorphi—"

"Just call it polly-sue," Kelly said. "Polly-sue" was the nickname for the polypseudomorphine she had given the boys to dull their pain. "I'll know what you mean."

"Whatever you call it, I didn't think they were in any shape to be sneaking up on aliens."

"At least you got that right. Sit tight." Kelly started to raise her head to check the Covenant's progress, then decided she needed to be clearer and looked back to Lena. "Don't move a finger."

Lena rolled her eyes, but remained otherwise motionless.

Kelly raised her head to the top of the crystal bushes and found the Covenant troops already starting up the ramps into the two carrier pods. Most were armored in the standard blue harness of common Elites, but about a third wore black armor with a deep-red tinge—a color scheme that was all too familiar. During one of the Spartans' earlier operations, SILENT STORM with Task Force Yama, Blue Team had kept butting heads with an especially deadly Covenant unit wearing the same kind of armor. If Kelly had any lingering doubts that John was right all along about being hunted, they were vanishing fast.

She estimated it would take the platoon about three minutes to stow its equipment and strap into their transport stations. After that, stopping the Umbras would become a suicide mission, and probably an unsuccessful one at that.

She had no idea how old Lena and the other two Castoffs really were. But they definitely were no ordinary children—no more than Kelly and the other Spartans had been growing up on Reach.

And if Kelly hoped to stop an entire platoon of Spartan-hunters, she was going to need help.

Kelly turned back to Lena. "Very well. Consider yourselves conscripted."

"What's conscripted?"

"It means you get to help," she said. "Do Arne and Oskar still have their slings?"

"We always have our slings," Lena said. "But like we've seen, rocks haven't been much good against armor."

"I have some special rocks." Kelly removed a fragmentation grenade from her hip satchel, then showed Lena how to arm the priming switch. She was less than thrilled about trusting the Castoffs to back her up, but she didn't have a lot of choice. "In about four minutes, you're going to see a bunch of aliens chasing me up the gully. Hit them with these as soon as you can be sure of reaching your targets."

"We can do that," Lena said. "Anything else?"

"Yeah. Hurry." Kelly returned the grenade to the satchel, then removed the satchel and her sidearm from their mounts and passed them to Lena. "And if you miss, run."

"No worries." Lena turned and began to scramble back toward the gully. "We don't miss."

Kelly turned back toward the Umbras and began to circle through the brush toward her assault point. At this stage, she put more emphasis on speed than stealth. Even if the Covenant did happen to notice the crystal bushes dissolving into flutter bugs as she approached, the enemy response would only delay the Umbras' departure.

But Kelly had no such luck. She was still twenty paces from her assault point when the Umbras began to raise the carrier pod ramps. Their loads weren't evenly distributed. The first vehicle was nearly full, carrying all ten of the warriors in black armor and eight warriors in the standard blue, with a blue-armored driver and gunner sitting on top. The second Umbra had only a blue-armored driver and gunner and eight warriors in the carrying pod—an indication, most likely, that it was assigned to some sort of support role. She had her onboard computer transmit the emergency message she'd prepared earlier, then opened fire on the driver of the farthest vehicle.

The first burst split the Elite's blue helmet in two. The second one turned his head into a purple spray. Kelly shifted fire to the next vehicle and gave the other driver the same treatment, then launched a grenade toward the gunner's cockpit.

By then, both Covenant gunners were swinging their plasma cannons toward her. She dived away from the gully, opposite the direction she intended to flee, and heard rock cracking behind her as superheated enemy rounds punched into the stony ground.

The cannon fire subsided as Kelly's grenade detonated, taking out the closest gunner. She rolled onto her belly and reversed direction, scrambling back the way she had come. The second gunner's fire swept past, so close she heard her armor sizzle. She loaded another grenade into the M301, then popped up, found the second gunner, and fired again.

The gunner must have glimpsed the incoming grenade, because he hesitated just an instant before swinging his cannon back toward Kelly. That was all the time she needed. She dropped back down, reloaded, then popped up in the last place any decent soldier would expect to find her—exactly where she *had* been.

The grenade detonated in the gunner's cockpit, hurling pieces of his body in three different directions. The ramps beneath the first Umbra continued to rise, sealing the carrier pod up tight. But the ramps under the second, nearer Umbra started to fold down—on both sides.

Kelly fired a grenade into the rapidly widening slot above the nearest ramp, then saw a satisfying sheet of flame flash up through the gap. The ramp continued to descend, and three Elites scrambled out through the forward end of the opening. Their armor was smoking and gouged, but more or less intact, and one of them dropped to the ground and did not rise again.

The other two drew their energy swords and began to stagger forward uncertainly, not seeming to know where their mystery attacker was. Kelly ended their confusion by firing into their torsos until their energy shielding crackled out and their breastplates ruptured.

By the time both operatives had fallen, there was another Elite clambering out of the gap at the back end of the ramp. Kelly knew there would be at least four more dismounting from the other side of the carrier pod—and all of them would be moving to cut off her escape. She launched another grenade toward the rear of the pod, then scrambled up and raced for the gully, firing as she ran.

The Elites were too good to be taken out by a single grenade.

Before it landed, they were already leaping in different directions and tucking into forward rolls. The detonation filled the air with dirt and pebbles, and they came up firing. Kelly felt their bolts pinging off her Mjolnir's outer shell. These guys were good, some of the best blue-armored Elites she had ever traded shots with. She returned fire one-handed, aiming behind her as she ran, dodging their shots and putting a little more distance between them with each step. When her magazine emptied, she ejected it and loaded another.

The gully was only a hundred meters distant, a snaking depression where the crystal bushes gave way to a bed of broken, dusty stone. Smart soldiers like her pursuers would be expecting an ambush as soon as they saw it, so they would slow down and approach cautiously—which meant it would be the ideal place for Kelly to put on some speed. They would never catch her, and she would be gone before they realized they had lost her trail.

Then they would return to their Umbra and set off toward the *Wheatley*. John and the rest of Blue Team would be trapped between them and the hundred-strong force that had departed the *Lucky Break*, and not even Spartans could be assured of victory when they were outnumbered forty-to-one and under attack from two directions.

Kelly reloaded the grenade launcher and fired over her shoulder at a dead run, then repeated her actions once she was empty. The enemy plasma fire was starting to taper off, and she wanted them to think she was getting desperate. They would come after her all the harder if they believed catching her was within reach.

The gully was only twenty paces ahead. She fired one more blind grenade, then reloaded the launcher again, slipped in a fresh magazine, and leaped into a high, arcing dive.

Her pursuers filled the air around her with plasma bolts. As she descended, dropping toward the gully bed headfirst, she fired another grenade back at them—and glimpsed the disheartening sight of two Umbras floating over the crystal brush at full speed.

Only one was coming in her direction.

As she dropped, her attackers—both Umbra and Elites—vanished behind the gully wall. She went into a forward roll and spun up on her knees, then put a long burst into the first helmet that appeared above the rim.

Her motion tracker showed three FRIEND symbols fidgeting about twenty meters up the gully and toward the middle of the bed, where there was no cover to hide behind. She glanced in their direction and saw nothing but dust and small rocks. She checked her motion tracker again and only one symbol remained, still moving about, but not quite as much as before.

She hoped the damned system was not malfunctioning.

Two lines of plasma bolts began to stream toward Kelly from the gully rim, just inside the crystal bushes. Kelly grabbed another grenade and reloaded as she rolled. She had killed only six Elites so far, and these two would be seven and eight. Then there were the two on the Umbra, assuming a new driver and a gunner.

All the rest were on the other Umbra, currently trying to sneak up behind Blue Team. Twenty well-rested, well-equipped Elites, half of them special forces Spartan-hunters, moving fast in a vehicle armed with a plasma cannon.

It was a good thing Kelly had warned them.

She came up on her knees and brought her assault rifle to her shoulder. In two places along the rim, the crystal bushes erupted into flutter bugs as the Elites reacted to her bait and opened fire.

She threw herself into a side roll, then—still rotating—launched her own grenade about two meters ahead of the warrior on the right. On her next revolution, she brought her aim back left and emptied her magazine into the disintegrating crystal bushes.

Whether she scored kills was impossible to tell, and there was no time for confirmation. The Umbra arrived, the bottom of its now-sealed carrier pod scraping on the rim as it dropped into the gully and swung around so the gunner could bring his weapon to bear. The plasma cannon was no longer in the cockpit—no doubt dislodged by Kelly's earlier grenade attack—so now the gunner was holding a long weapon with a tapered muzzle. A particle beam rifle.

Kelly sprang to her feet and sprinted up the gully, once again praying that her motion tracker had not been on the blink when it located Lena and other two Castoffs. The Covenant beam rifle fired twice, and her armor sang out as rock chips flew up and bounced off her outer shell. She changed magazines and returned fire one-handed, hoping to force the gunner to keep his head down—or the driver to fall back a little.

It didn't work. Kelly was fast, but the Umbra was faster. By the time she passed the Castoffs' hiding place, the vehicle was running abreast of her, the driver trying to match her speed and hold a steady course so its gunner could cut her down. She saw no sign of Lena or the others . . . until she was ten paces past, when her motion tracker suddenly showed three FRIEND designators close on her tail.

Kelly dropped into a knee skid and dragged a boot to spin herself around, then saw three small figures rising from the gully floor, throwing off their dusty cloaks and whirling their slings over their heads. Kelly opened fire, more to keep her pursuers' attention fixed on her than because she actually expected to stop the Umbra, and saw the driver flinch as one of her rounds glanced off the energy shielding around his helmet.

The Umbra swerved away, and the Castoffs loosed their grenades. The first struck the hull near the top of the arch, a couple of meters ahead of the driver. The blast took down his energy shield and hurled him against the back of the cockpit, but failed to penetrate his armor. He managed to keep his hands on the controls—until Kelly fired again and put three rounds through the side of his helmet. His body went slack and slid down into the cockpit, and the Umbra drifted to a stop.

The other two grenades hit an instant later, on the far side of the gunner's cockpit. The detonations rocked the entire vehicle and took down the gunner's energy shield—perhaps even stunned him, because he sat motionless and slumped for a couple of seconds.

Then Lena opened fire with the loaner M6D, ricocheting bullets off the side of the Umbra without hitting much of anything. The assault seemed to bring the gunner back to his senses, and he sat up and swung the beam rifle toward her.

Kelly put a burst through the back of his helmet. The beam rifle slipped from his hands, bouncing off the hull and dropping to the gully floor . . . five paces in front of Arne.

Who immediately smiled and limped forward to retrieve it.

"Don't you dare!" Kelly ordered.

Of course, he ignored her and continued to move toward the prize.

Kelly waited until he stooped to retrieve it, then put three shots into the ground in front of him.

Arne yanked his hand back and looked up, slack-jawed, as Kelly approached. "I save your life, and *that*'s how you act?"

"Just returning the favor."

Kelly retrieved the beam rifle, then pointed it at a rock and squeezed the firing handle. A bright purple beam shot from the tip and burned a hole through the center of the rock.

"This is alien stuff," she said. "If you don't know what you're doing, it will kill you just as dead as they will."

Arne studied the smoking hole for a moment, then finally nodded and turned to face Kelly square-on.

"So, you're going to show us how to use it then, right?"

Kelly smiled inside her helmet. "Sure," she said. "When you turn fifteen."

All three Castoffs looked confused, and Lena finally asked, "When will that be?"

"Too soon, probably."

Kelly returned her assault rifle to its magmount, then took the beam rifle and stepped over to the Umbra's carrier pod. She studied the control panel until she identified a luminous square that resembled a touchpad, then pressed it. The wall on her side of the pod began to descend, forming a long boarding ramp that led up into ten empty transport stations.

Kelly waved up the ramp. "Take your pick," she said. "We're going for a ride."

Arne and Oskar both smiled broadly and started up the ramp.

Lena cocked her head. "You know how to drive this thing?"

"Probably."

Lena didn't look thrilled. "And we're going after John?"

"Soon." Kelly took her pistol out of Lena's small hand and returned it to her thigh mount. "But first, we'd better pick up some reinforcements. I think we're going to need them."

CHAPTER 14

Ninth Age of Reclamation
41st Cycle, 151 Units (Covenant Battle Calendar)
Plain of Devout Patience, Mountains of Tremulous Faith
Planet N'ba, Eryya System

A full half-unit after his turbulent descent to N'ba's scorching surface, Nizat's stomach continued to roll. He was leading his warriors across a scrub-covered plateau toward the human salvage ship, and his legs continued to shake. His hearts were pounding in counter-tempo, and he could not draw the parched air through his mandibles quickly enough to disperse his metabolic heat. Even his tympanic membranes were still buzzing with after-roar, a temporary consequence of the friction flames that had enveloped his breaching carapace during its fiery insertion.

The wise thing would have been to stay aboard the *Steadfast Strike*—the "downed" frigate he was using to bait the ONI discovery priests—and spend a few units recovering in its climate-controlled

interior. But Nizat did not have time to be wise. His breaching carapace had barely left orbit before a message had come over the comm
system, warning that the Fleet of Swift Justice was moving fast. Its
assault carrier had launched a single dropship, on a trajectory that
suggested a landing site within striking distance of the *Steadfast
Strike.*

Nizat had not allowed fear to overwhelm him.

A single dropship carried no more than thirty warriors, so in all
likelihood, the insertion was just a scouting band sent to check on
the *Steadfast Strike.* But once the scouts saw a human salvage ship
nearby, and realized what the enemy intended, the Fleet of Swift Justice would act quickly to neutralize the threat. Before that happened,
Nizat needed to plant the Luminal Beacons on the humans—and
motivate them to escape N'ba while they still could.

That motivation would be easy. Despite appearances, the *Steadfast
Strike* remained launch-worthy, and when it departed, the humans
would have no reason to stay.

The challenging part would be making sure they took the Luminal Beacons with them. The first Beacon was still hidden inside
a personal energy shield unit, which Nizat intended to drop aboard
the salvage ship during a feigned capture attempt. As long as his
boarding cadre made it through one of the hatches, he could simply
drop the shield generator and feel confident that the humans would
find it and carry it back to the ONI discovery temple.

The second Beacon was concealed inside a small anti-gravity harness shaped like two small pods linked by an integration cable. Unfortunately, those particular devices were used only to help Yanme'e
fly, and he did not have any Yanme'e in his boarding cadre. It seemed
unlikely that an ONI discovery priest would know of the limitation,
but Nizat still intended to plant it aboard the human ship. It was a
risk, but so was changing plans at the last moment.

"Why have they not opened fire?" 'Lakosee asked. He was at Nizat's side, at the head of the boarding cadre. Like Nizat, he was wearing full combat armor, and the effects of their rough insertion still showed in his unsteady gait. "We have just closed to eight thousand units. We *must* be within the range of their close-defense weapons by now."

Nizat did not reply. The salvage ship's close-defense systems were the greatest threat to his plan. He knew from prisoner interrogations that such weapons typically had a range of ten human kilometers—which was almost thirty-three thousand Covenant units—and they were designed to destroy incoming fighters and missiles, which moved much faster than his warriors. But their effectiveness would be muted in N'ba's thick planetary atmosphere, and he was hoping it would be reduced to fewer than six thousand units, which was when his own forces would be able to return fire.

"I see no hurry to start taking casualties," Nizat finally said. "Our focus rifles are still two thousand units out range."

"That is what concerns me," 'Lakosee said. "Humans are an impatient species. Why would they hold their fire when they have no need? They must be planning a surprise."

"Perhaps."

Nizat looked across the plateau toward the ONI salvage ship. A tall, parabola-shaped vessel standing upright like an arch, it rose just a little higher than the two gray hills flanking it, with its two legs planted in the center of the hollow between. But that was all he could discern. At a distance of eight thousand units, it was wavering in the heat, so blurred by refraction that he barely recognized it as a vessel.

"Or perhaps they are too cunning to fire at targets their weapons cannot see," Nizat said. "With temperatures as they are on a world like N'ba, tracking sensors designed for space will not work properly. They will be confused by background scatter and signal refraction."

"Then this heat may be a blessing," 'Lakosee said. "If we attain focus-rifle range before the enemy opens fire, our casualties will be minimal."

"I am thinking the same," Nizat said. "The gods have favored us."

They continued forward, pushing past brittle, vase-shaped bushes with crystalline leaves that erupted into flitter-nits at the slightest contact. Every ten or twenty steps, they happened across a tall plant with a single leaf that resembled a diamond-shaped sail. Like the vase-shaped bushes, the sail plants reacted to even gentle pressure, folding along a vertical access to enfold anything that touched them.

Nizat had never seen anything like the crystal bushes, which seemed to change from plant to animal at a whim. But the larger sail plants reminded him of carnivorous *g'lul'g* trees, which Sanghelios farmers used to combat agricultural pests. Aside from the flitter-nits, he had not seen anything on N'ba that looked like something a carnivorous plant might eat. But maybe the true fauna came out after dark, in the cool of the night—assuming, of course, that N'ba actually *had* fauna.

Or cool nights.

They traveled a thousand units—about three hundred steps. The human salvage ship no longer appeared to be shimmering in the heat, but it remained too hazy to discern details like gun turrets and missile pods. Presumably, its tracking sensors remained as impaired by refraction blur as did Nizat's own eyes, because it still had not opened fire.

But that could not continue for long.

Nizat passed both Luminal Beacons to 'Lakosee. "Keep the Beacons here until I tell you to come forward," he said. "And contact me when my form grows too heat-blurred to identify."

"As you command."

'Lakosee did not offer to go forward in Nizat's place. To suggest a Sangheili commander could not face the same peril as his warriors was to call him unworthy of his station.

As Nizat advanced, he checked the deployment of his cadre. In the first rank, he had a hundred crew members from the *Steadfast Strike*. Most wore only light shipboard armor, and they were armed with short-range plasma rifles. Only a handful were clearly visible through the heat-shimmer. But those he could see were spread out at intervals of fifty units, advancing in a randomly staggered line that would force the enemy weapons to separately acquire each target.

The first rank's primary assignment was to draw fire, so the focus rifles behind them could identify and eliminate the enemy weapon turrets. Many of them were going to die in the first breaths of the battle. Still, they advanced through the brush at a steady pace, raising plumes of flitter-nits in their wake and showing no fear. Nizat was proud to be among them.

The second rank followed two hundred units behind the first. These were Nizat's Fleet Rangers, dressed in heavy, energy-shielded armor. The original plan had called for the rangers to fight aboard the *Steadfast Strike*, rather than out in the open, so most were armed with short- and medium-range weapons like needle rifles and carbines. But the rangers had managed to secure ten beam rifles and three focus rifles, all of which had enough range to return fire from 'Lakosee's current position.

Barely.

Nizat continued to advance. Fleet Rangers were well-trained warriors, but they were not Silent Shadow. They could only do what was possible.

A thousand units behind the Fleet Rangers followed the *Steadfast Strike*'s complement of five Spectre light assault vehicles. Shaped like a slightly rounded arrowhead and crewed by a gunner and driver, the Spectres were swift, agile vehicles with boosted-gravity propulsion and a heavy plasma cannon fixed to a limited-mobility mount. They were excellent gun platforms, and under most circumstances, they would have been all the support Nizat needed to guarantee success.

Unfortunately, the plateau was divided by a deep, winding chasm that would prevent the Spectres from directly engaging the salvage ship. Nizat had little choice but to hold the vehicles in reserve. As soon as the enemy's weapon turrets were eliminated, he would bring them forward to draw fire and serve as artillery support for his advancing infantry. It was not a very efficient use of such an agile gun platform, but it was the best that the unforgiving terrain would allow.

He led the way for another thousand units.

"I can no longer distinguish your form," 'Lakosee commed. "Shall I come forward now?"

"Not yet," Nizat replied. "Remain where you are until we have destroyed the close-defense weapons."

'Lakosee's tone grew indignant. "Until the danger is *past*?"

"I am sorry to ask so much," Nizat said. "But the Beacons must be kept safe, and when the flesh starts to burn, I can trust no one but you to keep a calm head."

'Lakosee's breath hissed over the comm channel. No Sangheili warrior liked to avoid danger when his cadre faced it, for esteem was won most readily in combat.

"As you command," 'Lakosee said, finally. "But I trust my calm head will not keep me out of future fights."

"When we storm our first ONI base, you will lead the charge. This I promise."

Nizat moved ahead to five thousand units, and the salvage ship loomed even larger. He began to discern the shapes of its larger appurtenances—a band of silvery dots curving along its bow, a line of dark points protruding along the inner edges of its arch, five fan-shaped silhouettes hanging between its landing struts. He could not yet identify the weapon turrets, but he was starting to make out squarish blobs of shadow and light that might have been hangar doors or external bins. When the enemy finally opened fire, Nizat's marksmen would be able to identify the source and attack quickly—as long as they were ready.

Nizat activated his comm unit. "Have the focus rifles advance another two hundred units and set up to counterattack. They are to sustain fire no more than four breaths before changing locations."

"As you command," 'Lakosee said. "What of the beam rifles?"

"They will continue forward with the rest of the Fleet Rangers," Nizat said. Particle beam rifles had almost the same range as focus rifles, but their millisecond pulses were more effective against personnel than hardened targets like turrets and gun bunkers. "And they will limit their fire to counter sniper attacks until further notice."

'Lakosee acknowledged the order and signed off to relay the commands to the appropriate unit masters.

Nizat closed to four thousand units.

The salvage ship began to look more like a vessel than a monumental arch, with an aerodynamic flare as its branched hull descended toward the ground in double sterns. The band of silvery dots that curved along its bow became several rows of viewing ports, and the dark points lining the inner edges of its arch lengthened into the tips of grasping claws. The fan-shaped silhouettes between its landing struts expanded into the collars of huge thrust nozzles, and the squarish blobs of shadow and light assumed the shapes of equipment bunkers and hangar doors. Nizat even saw some splinter-sized lines that were probably quad-cannon barrels, and he began to think it might have been safe to bring the focus rifles a little closer to the target.

Then the splinters began to flash, and forks of overload static danced across his personal energy shield. He threw himself to the ground, already shouting into his helmet comm.

"Focus rifles, open fire! Open fire!"

The bushes around him erupted into clouds of flitter-nits, and fountains of stone chips rose before his faceplate. He rolled across the ground, searching for cover and watching his energy shield power level. There was no reading, only a flashing yellow crescent that meant the generator unit was working hard to raise the shield again.

He continued to roll until he came to a spot where the air was no longer filled with rock shards and shredded plants, then listened to the shriek of focus beams passing overhead, waiting for the sound to fade so he could leap up and resume the charge. He found himself looking at a sloping face of gray-banded stone about half the height of his body. The top had been chewed into a jagged line by enemy cannon rounds, and the surrounding area was littered with plant shards and tooth-sized lumps of soft, gray metal—presumably projectiles from the human weapons.

Seeing no more chip-sprays rising in the immediate vicinity, Nizat pushed his helmet up above the stone and looked toward the salvage ship. There were two plumes of smoke rising from each leg of the hull, and a strobe-like blinking continued to flash from the inner curve of the bow arc. To either side of him were patches of bare stone where the enemy cannons had cleared the ground of all vegetation, and in several places he saw blood sprays and shards of armor and bone—all that remained of the warriors who had died there.

A trio of bright beams shrieked through the air above Nizat's head, converging on the source of the strobe-like flashing. Even beneath the concentrated fire of all three focus rifles, it took a full two breaths for the enemy turret to fall silent.

The beams vanished as suddenly as they had appeared, and a stillness settled over the plateau. Nizat remained where he was, waiting for another turret to open fire.

All that happened was that a fifth plume of smoke rose from the salvage ship. After a few breaths, his restless warriors began to lift their heads, peering over boulders and out of stony hollows, trying to see whether the human turrets had been silenced for good.

'Lakosee's voice sounded inside Nizat's helmet. "Fleetmaster, are you still with us?"

"I am," Nizat said. "Have the first rank resume the advance. All others, hold position."

He rose from behind his cover and began to lead the way. His energy shield status returned to normal. He continued forward, watching for more flashing from the enemy cannons. After fifty steps, he decided it was time to confirm that the focus rifles had eliminated all of the enemy cannon turrets.

" 'Lakosee, have two Spectres come forward," he ordered. "Everyone in the second rank will take cover, and everyone in the first rank will be prepared to take cover."

'Lakosee acknowledged the command. A short time later, a pair of Spectres sped past, reaching the twining darkness that marked the great chasm dividing the plateau. Still, Nizat did not trust that all of the gun turrets had been destroyed. Although humans employed a base-10 counting system similar to the Covenant's, they had a bizarre tendency to cluster things in groups of twelve. His spies had never been able to explain why, but it was so ingrained in the human way of thinking that they even had a special word for twelve items—a *dozen*. And a dozen dozens was called a *gross*.

This strange obsession with twelves extended into their military. Their ships had missile pods that fired twelve or twenty-four. Their fighter craft usually operated in groups of twelve, and their large capital ships often had weapon systems arranged in counts of the same. Nizat had even seen crates of captured weapons that contained items in such multiples.

So Nizat was not ready to believe that the salvage ship had only five weapon turrets on this side of its hull. Six seemed more likely. With six on the other side, the vessel would have a total of twelve turrets. But just ten? That would be suspicious.

" 'Lakosee, send the rest of the Spectres forward," Nizat said. "The focus rifles must be ready."

'Lakosee did as ordered, and the Spectres were barely past Nizat when a single turret near the salvage ship's bow began to strobe. The nearest assault vehicle disintegrated beneath the withering cannon fire, fluttering to the ground in a cloud of metal shards and bloody armor fragments. A second vehicle flipped end over end and erupted into flames.

Then the focus rifles screamed again, and three beams of charged particles converged on the distant turret. The enemy cannons continued to flash for another two breaths, then finally vanished in a flash of white. The last Spectre continued forward to join the remaining two.

After the enemy cannons had fallen silent again, Nizat angled left, toward the mid-advance rally point. He was starting to feel even more confident of being in the gods' favor now. To bring the remainder of their turrets to bear, the humans would have to launch their ship and reverse its facing, and that would take time. More importantly, it would draw the attention of the Fleet of Swift Justice, and the humans did not dare risk *that* until they were ready to move against the *Steadfast Strike*.

Nizat gave the order for 'Lakosee and the Fleet Rangers to join him at the rally point. He would need them close by when the boarding action commenced.

It was not long before 'Lakosee said, "The Spectres report a column of humans sallying from the salvage ship."

"How large is the column?" Nizat did not bother to conceal his irritation. 'Lakosee was an experienced aide. He knew better than to give an improper situation report. "Course and weapons?"

"It is too early to tell. But the enemy is not reacting as predicted. I thought you should know at once."

"Indeed." Nizat looked toward the salvage ship, but it was hopeless. He could make out a long line of shapes moving away from the base of the vessel, but the heat shimmer concealed any detail. "They are humans. Can we *ever* expect them to do the wise thing?"

Nizat switched to the vehicle communications band. The Spectre crews would have better visibility from the firing perches behind their plasma cannons.

"This is Fleetmaster 'Kvarosee. Report what you are seeing."

"Directly?" asked a nervous voice.

"Had I time to follow the Path of Control, you would be speaking to the First Cannon."

"Our First Cannon is dead, Fleetmaster."

"Then you must honor him with your quick obedience," Nizat said. In Sangheili culture, loyalty was always personal: strong for the leader of one's keep, but more tenuous with each step removed. The military's Path of Control was an adaptation of that system, establishing clear lines of authority to reduce conflict and confusion. "If this attack fails because I lack the information I require, the gods will judge the First Cannon by your hesitation."

"As you command." The voice was not one Nizat recognized, probably that of a mere vehicle commander. "A column of at least a hundred humans is departing the salvage ship, advancing on foot behind eight of their four-wheeled vehicles. We see no artillery in the combat vehicles, but all of them have those primitive projectile weapons."

"Destination?"

"It is too early to be certain," the vehicle commander said. "But they may be moving toward the rally point. That would be my suspicion."

It suddenly felt sweltering inside Nizat's armor. He had chosen the rally point because it lay opposite a long ravine offering easy access to the human side of the plateau. His scouts had assured him that once the salvage ship's close-defense weapons were destroyed, it would be a simple matter to climb the ravine and cross the last three thousand units to the vessel.

Nizat studied the line of humans for a moment, trying to divine what surprises they might be carrying. Finally, he decided it didn't matter. Whatever their intentions, the humans were going to complicate his plan.

"You will receive new orders from the Master of Rangers shortly," Nizat said. As much as he wanted to, he did not dare issue the command directly. It was one thing to seek battlefield intelligence in a timely manner, and quite another to subvert the authority of a subcommander. Such affronts were how loyalties were damaged and battles lost. "Be prepared to engage across the canyon."

"As you command."

Nizat switched back to his normal command channel. "You heard?"

"I did," 'Lakosee said. "So, the humans intend to meet us at the ravine?"

"With the right weapons, it would not be a poor strategy," Nizat said. "They can hide behind the rim and fire down on us as we climb. The battle would go hard on us."

"Unless we can drive them back with our cannon fire," 'Lakosee said. "Shall I have the Master of Rangers call the Spectres to the rally point?"

"An excellent thought," Nizat said.

The helmet comm fell silent as 'Lakosee changed comm bands to relay the order. The rally point was still five hundred units ahead, a ragged line of stone outcrops spread along the rim of the dark canyon. On the far side of the chasm rose the dark gash of the ravine through which Nizat's cadre would ascend. Shaped like a spearhead, it was boulder-strewn and brush-filled, broken by sheer faces of stone and long gravel-covered slopes that would make for slow climbing under enemy fire. If he and his boarding cadre could not reach the top of the ravine before the humans did, they might not reach it at all.

And if they failed to reach the top of the ravine, they would fail to make contact with the humans; if they failed to make contact, they would fail to plant the Luminal Beacons.

Which was the only objective that mattered.

Nizat spoke to 'Lakosee again. "Have the beam rifles fire on the column as it advances. The focus rifles are to concentrate on the vehicles."

"As you command," 'Lakosee said.

"And you have spoken to the Master of Rangers?"

"I have," 'Lakosee said. "Our Spectres are coming—"

His answer was interrupted by the roar of enemy rockets crossing the canyon. Nizat heard the *thud-thud-thud*ding of six small detonations, all a few hundred units behind him. With sinking hearts, he turned to assess the damage. His two closest Spectres were lying motionless on the ground, one smoking and on its side, the other in so many pieces it was barely identifiable.

The roar of rockets sounded again, and Nizat saw six smoke trails shoot out of the brush on the human side of the canyon. They crossed the chasm and converged on his last assault vehicle. The Spectre shot upward on a cushion of flame, then tipped onto its side, slid to the ground, and began to launch fragments of itself in a flurry of secondary explosions.

Nizat's beam rifles returned fire, pouring dashes of blue plasma into the brush hiding the rocket launchers. And the human column continued to advance, its wheeled vehicles moving so fast they began to bounce and swerve across the rugged terrain.

" 'Lakosee, the vehicles!"

Nizat began to run toward the rally point, motioning for the rest of the cadre to follow. He could not understand why the humans were forsaking the protection of their ship to fight on open ground, but he had to admit that their tactics were working. So far, they had anticipated each of his maneuvers, holding one close defense weapon in reserve to attack his Spectres, then using that attack to cover a squad of rocket launchers to finish them off. And while they distracted his Fleet Rangers with a now-pointless artillery duel, their wheeled vehicles were rushing forward to claim the top of the ravine. It was clever planning, perhaps even good enough to save their ship—had that been what he was after.

"Ignore their rocket launchers," Nizat said. "Concentrate on slowing the column's advance. If we can meet them on the plateau, it will be even easier to plant the Beacons."

Nizat had barely finished speaking before a trio of beams began to chase the enemy vehicles toward the ravine. It was not easy to destroy a moving target with a focus rifle—the beam had to remain in contact for several breaths before enough energy accumulated—but the three marksmen were the best in Nizat's small fleet. The lead vehicle erupted in flames.

The others raced forward even faster. The second vehicle in line hit something Nizat could not see and went airborne, spinning along its horizontal access and flinging passengers and contents in all directions. The rifle beams converged on a third vehicle, and it veered wildly as the driver tried to escape.

The last five vehicles were already closing on the ravine. Within moments, they would be unloading their passengers along its rim. On the Sangheili side of the canyon, Nizat and the survivors of the first rank were just a hundred units from the rally point. But they carried only plasma rifles and carbines—both medium-range weapons that barely had the capacity to fire across the chasm, much less target the humans waiting at the top of the ravine.

Nizat checked the enemy foot soldiers. His beam rifles had forced the column to disperse, but even through the heat shimmer, he could see that the attacks were having little effect. The humans had simply spread out. Now they were hunched down in the brush, advancing in a broad wave that left the air so clouded with flitter-nits that it looked as though a fog bank was rolling in. The beam rifles were continuing to fire, but there was no way the marksmen could see their targets.

Nizat reached the canyon rim but did not seek cover behind one of the boulders lining it. With the humans racing to seize the good fighting ground, there could be no hesitation in crossing the canyon—and the best way to ensure courage in his followers was to display it himself. He stood on the edge of the chasm, looking across into the ravine, searching for a route that would not leave his cadre exposed to enemy fire for the entire climb.

'Lakosee arrived a few breaths later. Nizat pointed to the ground behind a chest-high block of stone.

"Take cover there. The humans may have some of their snipers moving into position."

"But what about you, Fleetmaster?"

"My faith is my shield," Nizat said.

"I have faith, too."

"You also have the Luminal Beacons," Nizat said. "Take cover."

'Lakosee snapped his mandibles in frustration, but dropped behind the boulder as ordered. "I have ordered the spanning troop to come up at once. The beam and focus rifles, as well."

"Good," Nizat said. "We need to cross as soon as possible."

Even as he spoke, the enemy vehicles reached the ravine. But instead of stopping to unload passengers, they slowed to a crawl and drove over the edge, then began a slow descent down the center.

Nizat was so shocked he did not quite understand what he was seeing. He traced the ravine downward, to where it joined the canyon in a wide, wedge-shaped mouth. And running horizontally across the opening, separating it from the immense depths of the chasm and extending along the canyon wall in both directions, was a narrow strip of horizontal terrain.

The image was dancing crazily with heat refraction—perhaps because the temperature varied so greatly between the canyon's shady interior and its scorching rim—but the strip seemed to run as far as Nizat could see.

" 'Lakosee?" Nizat pointed down toward the horizontal strip. "What does that resemble?"

'Lakosee peered around the edge of the boulder. "A tunnel," he said. "The shape is too consistent to be a cave."

It took Nizat a moment to find anything that resembled either a tunnel or a cave, but finally he saw what 'Lakosee was referring to: a dark area shaped like a flattened diamond, located on the downhill side of the strip he had been asking about.

It was almost certainly the outlet of a culvert.

"I see the tunnel," Nizat said. "But look directly above that. What is that level strip it passes beneath?"

'Lakosee paused for a moment, then said, "That can only be a road."

"Then we are in agreement," Nizat said. "And now we must ask ourselves, why are the humans trying to beat us to it?"

"To deny us a bridgehead," 'Lakosee said. "If we cannot cross the canyon, we cannot board their ship."

"For that to be true, they would have to know we cannot call in air transport and simply *fly* over the canyon. How would they know that?"

"Because we have not done so," 'Lakosee said. "Why would we be doing *this* if we could simply be airborne?"

Nizat was still pondering the question when the Master of Rangers came up behind 'Lakosee. A large, stocky Sangheili in blue, energy-shielded armor, he was missing two fingers and half a mandible—disfigurements that only seemed to make him seem all the more formidable. Seeing that Nizat was standing in the open, he did not kneel behind a boulder as the steward was doing . . . but he stood directly behind 'Lakosee, where at least the lower half of his body would be protected. Nizat expanded his comm net to include the new arrival. "Master 'Zinwasee, we were just discussing infidel tactics." He pointed into the ravine, where five human vehicles were about a quarter of the way down. "Why are the humans trying to reach that road before us?"

"*Why* does not matter, only that they fail." 'Zinwasee gestured toward a line of Sangheili marksmen who were dropping into firing position along the canyon rim. "With your permission."

"By all means," Nizat said. "What of the spanning troop?"

'Zinwasee pointed in the opposite direction, past Nizat up the canyon. "They are already here."

Nizat turned to find twenty members of the *Steadfast Strike*'s crew approaching with their equipment—ten spools of carbolium cable, a bag of transport harnesses, several fusing wands, an anti-gravity launching tube, and twenty nioboron harpoons hastily fabricated in the frigate's metal shop. They stopped about three hundred units away and began working in small teams. Fortunately, they were concealed from the humans by the shoulder of the ravine, but even if that had not been the case, they would still have been out of range.

For now.

An anchoring team loaded a nioboron harpoon into the launching tube, then used the anti-gravity propulsor to drive it deep into the stony ground. At the same time, the line team prepared the cable for launch, removing one spool cap and dumping the coil onto the ground. As all this was happening, the fusers rigged the second harpoon by looping one end of the cable through the threading eye and using their fusing wands to weld it in place.

Once the first harpoon was in the ground, a second team of fusers ran the other end of the cable through the threading eye and tied a large retaining knot in the end to prevent it from being pulled back through. After that task was completed, the anchoring team fired the second harpoon across the canyon, where it sank into the cliff face about two hundred units below the rim. The line team pulled the cable taut and held it in place while the fusers secured it—and the first spanning cable was ready to use, a silvery line the diameter of a finger that descended to the opposite wall of the chasm at a thirty-degree angle.

The entire process took barely ten breaths before the troop was gathering its equipment and moving to the next position. Nizat leaned out over the rim to inspect the cable and saw that the second harpoon had been especially well-placed, burying itself into the cliff just a short distance above the road. It would be a simple matter to slide down the line to the other side of the canyon, then drop off and land ready to engage the enemy.

Nizat rose. "Call your rangers, Master 'Zinwasee. We will cross as soon as possible."

Before Nizat could start for the spanning cables, the beam rifles began to shriek along the rim to his left. He glanced across the canyon into the ravine and saw white flashes coming from the projectile weapons mounted in the back of the enemy vehicles. But they were firing up toward their targets and Nizat's marksmen were protected by the canyon rim, so the infidel attacks did little more than chew at the stone. As the vehicles continued to take damage, blurry shapes began to leap out of the back. Most of the figures quickly vanished behind rocks or into brush, suggesting they had escaped injury.

It did not take long before Nizat began to glimpse heat-blurred shapes descending the narrow ravine on foot. Moving from one boulder to another, they were ducking and dodging, risking death whenever they had to cross a few paces of open ground. Twice he saw a figure drop when a particle beam erupted in its midsection, and once a vehicle overturned when the pilot was hit. But the humans were making difficult targets of themselves, and it seemed clear that at least eight or nine of them would survive to reach the road.

And there were still at least a hundred humans on the plateau above, approaching the head of the ravine. If Nizat allowed even a small force of infidels to take the road before he did, they would quickly reinforce it and deny him the foothold he needed to bring his cadre across the chasm.

Nizat broke into a run. *"Quickly, Master 'Zinwasee!"*

The spanning troop had the second cable set by the time he reached them. He accepted a transport harness from a member of the line team, then slipped the support bar between his legs, secured the bonding tab to his torso armor, and connected it all together with the gravity winch. As he reached over to clip the control ring onto the spanning cable, the cracking rattle of human weapons continued to echo out of the canyon.

Nizat did not bother looking toward the sound. Its muffled quality suggested the humans were firing from inside the ravine, so he likely could not have seen them anyway.

"What is the situation, Master 'Zinwasee?"

There was a brief pause while 'Zinwasee queried his marksmen, then he said, "Under control. The human weapons are starting to have an effect, but we have destroyed another of their vehicles, and they are not yet able to bring their fire to bear on the spanning lines."

"Then we go now." Nizat took his plasma rifle off its carrying mount. "Follow as quickly as you can."

Nizat raced forward. Wondering if he might not be taking the Sangheili lead-from-the-front ethos a little *too* seriously, he reached the rim and stepped into nothingness.

He felt his stomach rise toward his throat, plummeting ten units before the control ring finally caught his weight and began to carry him forward. He descended at an angle for another ten units before the braking field began to bite, slowing his progress to a crawl. Holding his plasma rifle in one hand, he used the other to pull down on the braking control, reducing the friction so he could pick up speed again.

It had been a long time since Nizat's field training, so it took him ten breaths to find a tension that allowed him to slide forward swiftly but still under control. By then, the Master of Rangers was already speeding ahead on the cable to his right, and the third harpoon was pulling its cable past to his left.

Nizat told himself not to look down—but did anyway. A thousand units below lay a shimmering ribbon of blue. Whether it was water or mirage was impossible to say; he knew only that the last thing he wanted was to find out.

He raised his gaze and looked down the canyon to his left, where the bright dashes and rays of his warriors' beam and focus rifles were pouring into the ravine. The orange dashes of contrail bullets—the humans called them tracer rounds—were streaming back in the opposite direction, rising toward the canyon rim. Nizat doubted that the infidels were hitting much of anything yet, but neither were his rangers—and the human attacks were rising from the mouth of the ravine, close to the road.

'Lakosee's voice sounded in Nizat's helmet. "Fleetmaster, please watch your speed. We are already impressed."

Nizat allowed the braking control to rise and bite the spanning cable again. He immediately began to slow, but when he looked forward again, the canyon wall was still coming up too fast. He shoved the brake up and lifted his feet, ready to take the impact in his legs. But the rig did its work, and he decelerated so hard that he pitched forward into a standing position . . . and came to a stop hanging eight units above the center of the road.

'Zinwasee appeared at Nizat's knees. "You have not lost the touch, I see. Can you manage the drop?"

"You have a more important task than helping me." Nizat pointed down the road toward the ravine mouth. It was only three hundred units away, a broad gap in the cliff where the road crossed over the drainage tunnel. "The humans are nearly at the road. If they reach it—"

"I will not allow it," 'Zinwasee said. "Send my rangers forward as they arrive."

Master 'Zinwasee started down the road at a sprint.

Nizat deactivated the bonding tab and dropped the last four units to the ground, then retrieved the support bar from between his legs and quickly hung the entire harness back on the slider ring. The line team had been able to assemble only a limited number of rigs, so midway through the cadre's crossing, a warrior would have to attach a retraction tab so the harnesses could be recalled back up the cable.

Nizat turned to follow 'Zinwasee and found 'Lakosee thirty units down the road, freeing himself from the next spanning cable. Rather than chastise the steward for crossing the canyon before being summoned, Nizat simply ran forward to join him. Initiative and bravery were to be valued in young majors—and if Nizat expected his plan to work, he was going to need the Luminal Beacons that 'Lakosee was carrying.

A fourth harpoon streaked across the canyon and planted itself in the cliff wall. Thinking it might be wise to coordinate with the anchoring team before advancing too far down the road, Nizat stopped at 'Lakosee's side.

"The Beacons are safe?" he asked.

"Indeed." 'Lakosee secured his empty harness to his slider ring, then patted a large equipment pod secured to his armor. "All we need is to make contact and—"

A deafening crack sounded from the ravine mouth, so loud that it overpowered even the clatter of the other human weapons. Nizat looked toward the noise and found the Master of Rangers a hundred units ahead, his energy shield crackling with overload static. A second crack echoed from the ravine mouth, and a jet of purple blood shot from a hole in the master's backplate.

"Sniper!" Nizat grabbed 'Lakosee, then hurled him down beside the cliff and jumped on top of him. "Stay down!"

"But, Fleetmaster—"

"Do *not* move," Nizat ordered. "Protect the Beacons."

'Lakosee stopped struggling to free himself. "As you command."

The sniper rifle continued to crack. Nizat glanced back at the spanning cables to see what kind of support he and 'Lakosee could expect—and found rangers hanging limp on the first two cables, their bodies halfway across the canyon and pouring blood, their braking bars biting hard against the spanning cables.

Another crack sounded, then another, and the ranger on 'Lakosee's cable fell limp. His descent began to slow, his body suddenly dripping violet fluid, and then his braking bar brought him to a halt, leaving him to dangle in the middle of the canyon like his dead fellows. Before those cables could be used again, another warrior would have to slide down and cut the bodies free—and that was not going to happen while there was an infidel sniper covering the canyon.

Weapons continued to clatter from the ravine mouth. When Nizat looked toward the sound, his gaze was drawn to the fourth spanning cable, where another ranger hung dying.

" 'Zinwasee's second blade," Nizat said. "Who is he?"

"Oro 'Gulya'see," 'Lakosee said. "Shall I inform him of his promotion?"

"Do it right away," Nizat said. "And tell him to send no more rangers to die on the cables. They will cover us from the rim. No infidels are to advance up this road."

"As you command."

Nizat remained on top of 'Lakosee for a moment, watching the roadside and searching for the sniper's nest. Most of the tracer bullets seemed to be coming from down in the ravine. But the sniper would have to be higher, almost level with the roadbed, to have killed 'Zinwasee. The most likely place for the nest would be on the near side of the ravine, where the road pressed up against the cliff. Nizat watched the area for ten breaths . . . and saw nothing.

He was no infantry soldier, but it seemed to him that snipers operated on the same principle as stealth vessels: they endeavored to never be where they were expected. Nizat moved his search to the boulder field on the far slope of the ravine. Despite the heat shimmer, he soon spotted a short, undulating rod striped with triangles of black and gray. It was protruding from between two large stones at an angle that encompassed both 'Zinwasee's body and the spanning cables behind Nizat. But the field of fire did not appear to include the area close to the cliff, where Nizat lay with 'Lakosee and the Beacons.

He continued to study the rod and finally discerned the dark circle of a muzzle opening. So, definitely an enemy sniper. Perhaps not a great one, to have been found so easily—but good enough to have killed 'Zinwasee and four Fleet Rangers. Nizat marked the location on his helmet interface, then transmitted it to 'Lakosee.

"Have the cadre lay fire on that location." Confident now that the sniper could not damage the Beacons, Nizat rolled off 'Lakosee. "Kill whatever moves."

'Lakosee relayed the command, and the rangers began to concentrate their fire as directed. The sniper barrel quickly withdrew. A moment later, a blurry figure with a soft, bush-like silhouette began to scramble across the slope—then took a beam strike through its center and tumbled out of sight.

But the sniper's death did not force the humans to retreat. They remained in the ravine, attacking Nizat's cadre on the Sangheili side of the canyon. Their fire continued to build, growing so fierce that when the spanning troop tried to launch the fifth cable, the entire anchoring team was dropped in a single breath.

The launching tube slipped from the hands of a dying warrior, bounced off a boulder, and landed with one end hanging over the rim.

"Cease spanning operations!" Nizat ordered. There was no sense continuing a strategy that, at best, would only result in more Fleet Rangers hanging over the canyon like *chigguts* in a longo sack. "Have the spanning troop withdraw!"

"Withdraw?" 'Lakosee asked. "Perhaps they could relocate farther up—"

"Too late. By the time any reinforcements arrived, we would no longer have need of them." Nizat moved a few units away from 'Lakosee, then reached out. "I will take the anti-gravity harness. You wear the shielding unit."

'Lakosee rolled onto his side, then opened the carrying satchel and passed the harness to Nizat. "You believe we are going to die?"

"There are two of us and a hundred of them." Nizat was surprised to realize that saying the words made him feel almost joyful. They were closer than ever to slipping the Beacons into ONI hands—and as long as they succeeded in that, they would perish among the Worthy. "We would be fools to ignore the possibility."

"Then I am honored to die at the side of a Paragon," 'Lakosee began to affix the personal shielding unit to his armor. "Even if I do not find the prospect quite so cheerful as it seems you do."

"You should." Nizat secured one of the harness pods to his armor, just above his breast. It was not where the pod was normally worn, but he would need 'Lakosee's assistance to secure it to his backplate, and the humans would not know the difference. "We have never been so close to succeeding in our plan."

"But if we die here," 'Lakosee asked, "who will there be to carry it out?"

" 'Weyodosee will take over in my absence."

"Forgive me, Fleetmaster, but I must speak freely. 'Weyodosee is a coward."

"But a *cunning* coward," Nizat said. "And one who will have eight intrusion corvettes at his command. Once he sees that ONI has taken the bait, he will execute my plan—and hope that destroying ONI is enough to win the Hierarchs' forgiveness for following me."

"I fail to see why we should have pleasant thoughts about 'Weyodosee's forgiveness," 'Lakosee said, "if it comes at the price of our death."

"Because with ONI's destruction comes vindication before the gods." Nizat attached the second pod to the other side of his breastplate. "We will be redeemed in *their* eyes and returned to the Path of Divine Transcendence. Have no fear of that."

'Lakosee cocked his helmet in doubt, but gave a smart mandible clack and said, "As you command."

At last, the infidels began to pour out of the ravine. Nizat's Fleet Rangers fired from across the chasm, raining particle and focus beams down on their heads. The humans answered with a sustained rocket volley that left the canyon rim flaking and cloaked in smoke. Nizat and 'Lakosee rose and began to race down the road toward the ravine, firing as they ran.

The rocket fire had barely died away before two of the infidel vehicles climbed out of the ravine and turned down the road away from Nizat and 'Lakosee, their weapons also firing across the canyon at the Fleet Rangers. Behind them followed a hundred humans on foot. Nizat and 'Lakosee continued to pour a steady stream of plasma bolts into their flanks.

Instead of turning to meet them, the entire mass turned after the vehicles and fled down the canyon on foot.

"What is wrong with them?" 'Lakosee demanded, now firing at the infidels' backs.

Before Nizat could answer, a handful of humans at the back of the mob turned and began to spray rounds up the canyon toward him and 'Lakosee. Nizat's energy shield began to crackle with overload static, then one of the infidels slightly elevated his rifle. A much larger round—about the diameter of three fingers—came flying out of the weapon's lower barrel and landed fifteen units in front of Nizat.

Grenade.

There followed a white flash, and Nizat felt himself flying backward.

What happened after, he doubted he would ever recall. But he certainly had not been hurled into the canyon. The next thing he knew, 'Lakosee was kneeling over him, shaking him by the armor. After a few moments, he realized the steward was yelling at him, but with a voice that seemed weak and very far away.

"Fleetmaster, are you well?! Wake up!"

Nizat pushed 'Lakosee away and sat up, then felt something clack against his abdomen armor and looked down to see the shattered remnants of one of the anti-gravity harness pods dangling by the connecting cable. He quietly thanked the gods that at least it was not the pod containing the Luminal Beacon.

"Fleetmaster—"

"I am fine, Tam." Nizat was not entirely sure of that, but there was no pain—and that was good enough. "Help me up."

'Lakosee pulled him up, and Nizat was astonished to see the entire human column fleeing down the canyon—*away* from them. "The infidels are running from us?"

"I could not believe it, either," 'Lakosee said. "Are they cowards?"

"I doubt it," Nizat said. "Mad as *gartls*, perhaps—but not cowards."

He did a quick count of the humans he could still see—and estimated that the mob was about four times that size. That put the number of survivors at no more than eighty. And considering that they were the crew of a salvage ship, only a small percentage would be seasoned warriors. Perhaps the enemy commander had simply decided that with a cadre of Sangheili firing down from the canyon rim, his company could not survive a charge.

Or perhaps he had intended to flee down the road all along.

The infidels had a fondness for turning their vessels into bombs, which they triggered the moment the Covenant captured them. Nizat saw no reason to believe they would treat a salvage ship any differently. The human shipmaster had probably prepared a self-destruct charge when he saw Nizat's cadre crossing the plateau, and now he was simply trying to get his crew to a safe distance before it detonated.

Nizat turned to 'Lakosee and said, "Have the spanning troop resume operations, then come with me." He pulled the mangled anti-gravity harness off his armor and handed the intact pod back to 'Lakosee. "Remove the Beacon from that pod. Before we give chase, we'll need to find another decoy to carry it."

"Give chase?" 'Lakosee said. "Won't the humans find that suspicious?"

"No doubt," Nizat said. He started down the road toward the mass of human corpses. "But what choice do we have?"

CHAPTER 15

Eighteen kilometers into Blue Team's run, the ground started to roll in a series of high, gentle hills that blocked their view of the plateau ahead. The crystal bushes were slowly giving way to tall, diamond-shaped sheet plants that tried to enfold any object that brushed against them. John's legs burned from exertion, and his lungs hurt like he was breathing ammonia. His skinsuit was having trouble bleeding off body heat, and he could hear the accumulating dust rasping in the Mjolnir's joints.

But his HUD showed only a thousand meters to the *Wheatley*. It had been just thirty-three minutes since Captain Dkani's emergency transmission reporting the approach of a large alien force from the *Lucky Break*, and the distant scream-*crump* of Covenant plasma cannons suggested to John that he and Fred and Linda had arrived in time to repel the boarding attempt. He tapped the stock of his BR55 over his forearm to make sure the barrel was not packed with any dust or residue.

"Weapons check," John said over TEAMCOM.

The team was still running in an exaggerated stagger formation, but now Fred was on point, with John about a hundred meters behind him and to the right. Linda was roughly a hundred meters behind John, and also to the right.

John retracted the BR55's charging handle and flicked the fire selector through each position, checking to see that the trigger moved freely. All of the UNSC's battle and assault rifles were designed to function under harsh conditions, but the fine dust kicked up by kilometers of hard running was proving hard on equipment. It slowed fans and clogged filters, and it collected on even a thin film of gun oil to create caked-on layers that cushioned hammer strikes and limited trigger motion.

Once John had confirmed the BR55 was still functional, he exchanged it for the M7 submachine gun and quickly repeated the process. Next he checked the dust seals on the missile tubes he was carrying for Fred's M41 rocket launcher. Then he performed a visual inspection of each of his grenades, paying special attention to the priming slides. He had to bleed a little air through his ventilator to blow some dust out of the slides, but otherwise all of his weapons were in good shape. They should have been. The team had already performed two checks during the long run.

John returned all of his grenades to their satchel, then grabbed the BR55 again and checked Fred's and Linda's status lights. Both green. Weapons ready. His HUD had him at seven hundred meters from the *Wheatley*, with Fred still a hundred meters ahead.

Fred and Linda had to be as exhausted as John was—the Mjolnir's force-multiplying circuits could not do all the work. But everyone's hydration tubes were now delivering a monosaccharide-glycogen solution that would provide energy for the coming fight. Which meant they should be ready to do battle without taking a rest break.

Still, it paid to be sure. A nineteen-kilometer near-sprint was tough, even for Spartans.

"Everybody able to engage?" John asked. "All support equipment operational?"

A pair of status lights winked green inside John's helmet.

"I'm good to go," Fred said. He crested a hill and started down the other side. "But something feels wrong up there."

"Like what?" John didn't doubt Fred's instincts—they were nearly always accurate. But it was hard to prepare for *something*. "Be more specific."

"Okay. It's kind of a stomach flutter—"

"Can it," John ordered. "This is no time for wisecracking."

"Who's wisecracking?" Fred replied. "I'm telling you, something just feels wrong."

"It has to be the artillery," John said. "That's all we have to go on right now—what we're hearing."

"No," Linda said. "I think the trouble is in what we are *not* hearing."

John crested the hill behind Fred. A sliver of dull-gray metal grew visible ahead, barely peeking over the top of another, higher hill. It had to be his first glimpse of the *Wheatley*.

"What aren't we hearing?" he asked.

"Rockets," Linda said. "Point-defense guns."

She was right, of course. The *Wheatley* was just a salvage vessel, but even those carried missile pods and point-defense systems. Unless the missile pods happened to be pointing in the right direction, they would be useless against a surface force.

But at least a couple of the point-defense turrets should have been in position to defend against the alien boarding party. The weapons relied on magnetic linear accelerator technology to launch streams of 50mm high-explosive projectiles at incoming threats, so John and his companions should have been hearing an endless chain of cracking and banging as the supersonic rounds broke the sound barrier on the way to their targets, then detonated on impact.

John heard only the sporadic plasma cannons. No rockets, no grenades, no rifle fire. No defensive sounds at all . . . until a faint crackle he recognized as a striking microwave blast whispered over the hilltop. The crackle was followed by a muffled *boom* and a distant cheer.

A cheer raised by young voices.

Then cut short by the scream-*crump* of plasma cannons. A microwave weapon crackled again, then fell silent and was answered by more frequent Covenant fire. John began to have a sinking feeling.

As Fred approached the crest of the next hill, John said, "Let's stop to reconnoiter. I want to understand the situation before we engage."

"What's to understand?" Fred dropped to his belly and began to crawl toward the hilltop. "A bunch of kids are fighting a bunch of aliens over an ONI ship—and they need help."

As Fred spoke, he was already peering over the hill. He immediately dropped back down and began to prepare the M41 for firing.

"That bad?" John asked, still ascending.

"Not exactly," Fred said. "You'll see."

John stopped twenty meters short of the hill crest, then crawled the rest of the way on his knees and elbows. He was still breathing hard, but it was a relief to finally stop running. He took a sip from his hydration tube, and his legs and arms immediately began to feel stronger as the rejuvenating solution did its work. He detoured around a stand of sheet plants, not wanting to draw attention to himself by triggering their enfolding response. Then he pushed his head up to see what lay beyond the hill.

The *Wheatley* stood wedged into the shallow valley below, a colossal horseshoe-shaped vessel that rose as high as the knolls that flanked it. The two legs of the ship rested on struts as large as main battle tanks, and between the struts hung the collars of thrust nozzles large enough to cover an entire *Razor*-class prowler.

Atop the ship's arch-shaped hull, several bands of viewing ports marked the locations of the bridge and habitation compartments. The inner edge of the arch was lined on either side with the tips of fifty huge claws, which could be extended to grapple the hull of any vessel with a beam less than four hundred meters.

In his mission briefing, John had learned how the *Wheatley* intended to retrieve the target. After Blue Team boarded the *Lucky Break* and killed all of the aliens aboard—presumably *before* any of them detonated a self-destruct charge—the big salvage ship would slip down over the Covenant frigate and grab the vessel in its claws. Then the behemoth would launch them both out of Nethcrop's gravity well, jump into slipspace as soon as possible, make a long series of random follow-up slips, and return to human-controlled space.

Hopefully without a Covenant fleet close behind.

The target of the mission—the *Lucky Break* itself—sat on the opposite side of the plateau, a refraction-blurred disk whose purple hull looked more like a shadow than a frigate. The only hints of detail John could see were its long neck and dovetailed stern. The heat shimmer prevented him from viewing the notch that had been put in its stern by the destroyers of Task Force Pantea, when they jumped it and kicked off this whole mess.

And between the two vessels, roughly a thousand meters from the *Wheatley* and four thousand from the *Lucky Break*, twined the same narrow canyon through which the Forgotten Highway ran—the same deep chasm out of which Blue Team had climbed when they captured Lena and the two boys in their mountain runner.

With its meanders and shadowed depths, the canyon resembled a big black snake sunning itself on the narrow plateau. On the side closest to the *Wheatley*, there were half a dozen wide spots where large ravines dropped out of the mountain range and cut huge notches in the canyon rim.

On the near side of the chasm, four of the indigenous mountain runners were dancing back and forth along the rim, dodging incoming plasma bolts. The farthest runner was so distant it appeared little more than a pinhead of blurred light, while the closest was about the size of John's palm. They were clearly returning fire with their microwave weapons, because across the canyon, crystal bushes were disintegrating into a glitter haze and sheet plants were bursting into dancing columns of flame.

As battles went, it barely qualified as a skirmish. But when John magnified the image, he saw that the fighting had been much heavier earlier. The plateau on the Covenant's side of the chasm was littered with the indistinct forms of equipment and bodies—nineteen of them, to be exact. Another six aliens, all Elites judging by their body shapes and the way they moved, remained in the fight, operating a trio of plasma cannons that remained more or less attached to crippled assault vehicles. Two of the weapons, each manned by a single warrior, were a hundred meters back from the rim, putting them at the limit of their effective range as they fired across the canyon.

The third cannon had been dragged forward onto a promontory, a hundred meters closer to the *Wheatley*, providing the aliens with a 270-degree field of fire that included all four mountain runners. It was being operated by a gunner and a spotter, supported by two Elites armed with long-range beam rifles.

John could see no other forces—dead or alive—anywhere on the plateau, but a quick inspection of the *Wheatley*'s hull revealed why no one had heard the point-defense guns being fired. All six of the canyon-facing turrets had been shredded by some anti-materiel fire.

The evidence was of a quick but deadly engagement between the Covenant forces and the *Wheatley*, but John had no idea what had happened after that. And he didn't understand why the Castoffs were risking their mountain runners and their own lives in a cross-canyon artillery duel. All they had to do was withdraw to a safe distance, then slaughter the Elites as they climbed out of the canyon.

But, of course, they were just kids—and not even trained kids. It would have been more surprising had they *been* using sound tactics.

"Blue Four, take the two gunners in back," John ordered. "Blue Two, take out the cannon on the promontory. I'll make sure we don't take any fire from the Castoffs."

Linda and Fred flashed green status LEDs, which quickly switched to amber as they moved into position. John had the on-board computer assign the promontory cannon as his waypoint—not because he intended to advance toward it, but that he wanted to keep track of its location. Then, knowing he had the greatest distance to travel, John moved forward in a high crawl, going as fast as he could on hands and elbows.

He was carrying his battle rifle in the crooks of his arms. Twice, as the butt brushed a sheet plant, it was torn from his grasp when the leaf enveloped it. He simply tore the plant apart and pulled the weapon free, then crawled into a new lane and continued more carefully for a dozen meters. The only aliens with weapons capable of reaching him were the two Elites with beam rifles, and he was pretty certain they were too busy trying to nail the Castoffs to notice him.

John and his companions were seven minutes into their crawl

when the unmistakable *boom* of a striking plasma round sounded from the chasm. John stuck his head up in time to see a pillar of flame rising from the second most distant mountain runner. Two Castoffs were flying over the front end—no hope of survival for them. And that might have been a mercy. The fire plume was from exploding batteries—and that meant burning acid everywhere.

Linda's status LED went green.

"Blue Four, cleared to fire." John ducked back down and continued crawling. "Blue Two, continue advance."

Normally John would have waited until everyone was in position to engage, but he didn't want any more Castoffs getting wounded. Medical attention ate up resources, and he was already down one Spartan because he had left Kelly behind to help Arne and Oskar.

Besides, he wasn't sure how much time remained. Kelly's last message had warned of an Elite special forces unit coming up behind them, and he needed to have the situation here under control before the next wave arrived.

John heard Linda's SRS99 boom twice. Her LED flashed green three times, indicating target down. He dropped to his belly and slowed his crawl, being more careful now to avoid giving his position away. If the enemy was any good—and it was always smart to assume they were—the two Elites with the beam rifles would have realized the moment Linda fired that the situation had changed. Now they would be searching for real threats to pick off.

The SRS99 boomed three more times, and Linda's LED flashed green again. She rarely missed, but the temperature gradients were taking a toll on her accuracy. She seldom needed three shots to take out a target. John checked his waypoint and saw that it was indicating on his left at a forty-five-degree angle. Time to start closing the distance. He turned toward the waypoint and continued his belly-crawl.

Fred's LED turned green. That would put him just inside the M41's maximum range of four hundred meters, so probably at three-seventy or so. John wasn't aware how close that was to the canyon rim because he didn't know how wide the chasm was at the attack point. But his BR55 had a range of nine hundred meters. That was enough.

John double-checked that the battle rifle's barrel was still clear of dust, then flicked the selector to full automatic.

"Blue Two, engage when ready."

A second passed, then two, then a crackle echoed across the chasm as a microwave weapon struck something on the Covenant side of the canyon. Finally the roar of two rockets sounded to John's left. He brought the BR55 to his shoulder and rose, turning in the direction his waypoint indicated—and found his view blocked by a towering sheet plant. He opened fire anyway.

The sheet plant folded in on itself, revealing a column of greasy gray smoke rising from the promontory across the canyon. The blue flash of a particle beam streaked out from the base of the smoke pillar, traveling in Fred's direction.

"Mine," John said over TEAMCOM.

He linked his HUD with the BR55's scope and swung the barrel toward the source of the particle beam. It took a couple of heartbeats, but finally he spotted an Elite warrior kneeling in the smoke, bracing his beam rifle on a section of broken chassis. John put the crosshairs low on the alien's flank, just under his elbow, and fired a long burst.

The alien's energy shield crackled, and the enemy leaped back and swiveled toward John, trying to bring his beam rifle around to counterattack. Bad mistake. John adjusted to center mass and continued to fire. The Elite tumbled over backward, armor pushed inward and weapon flying free.

John didn't hear the reports of Linda's SRS99 until his magazine was empty. He ejected it without thinking and slipped a fresh one into the receiver, already sweeping his scope back and forth across the promontory, searching the smoke for any surviving Elites.

"All targets down," Linda said. "No sign of reinforcements from *Lucky Break*."

"How about behind us?" As John spoke, he was turning toward the Castoffs and their mountain runners. "Any sign of those Umbras?"

"Nothing yet," Linda said. "I'll maintain watch."

"And stay out of sight," John said. "Blue Two, same for you—but you have the Castoffs. Don't let them fry me."

Both status LEDs flashed green.

John resisted the temptation to walk toward the mountain runners. He couldn't afford a misstep. Those took time to straighten out, and if Kelly was right, the Elite special forces would be arriving in less than an hour. He pointed his BR55 at the ground and raised his free hand in greeting, then turned his voicemitter up to maximum.

"I'm not an alien," he called. "I'm human, and I intend you no harm. But we really need to talk."

The surviving mountain runners scurried toward him, the one in the center approaching dead-on, while the other two spread out to flank him. Not bad tactics . . . but not great either. The Castoffs didn't seem to realize that as long as they remained seated high in their vehicles, they were easy targets for his unseen companions.

The runners stopped twenty meters away, easily inside the range of their microwave weapons, but far enough to make it difficult for John to charge one. There were two Castoffs in each vehicle, a driver and a gunner, all fair-haired and all dressed in dust-colored robes made of the same coarse cloth that Lena and her companions had been wearing. They appeared to be in their late teens or early twenties, which made them quite a bit older than the other Castoffs John had seen so far. But they were all so gaunt and sunken-eyed that it was difficult to be certain.

The gunner of the middle vehicle, a long-faced male with a heavy brow and a blade-thin nose, leaned around the dish of his microwave weapon.

"*You* are human?" He narrowed his blue eyes. "I don't think so."

"Trust me, I'm just wearing special armor, but I am human. Lena and Oskar can confirm it when they arrive."

"Lena and Oskar, they are with you?" It was the driver in the vehicle to John's right who asked this question. A square-jawed woman with broad cheeks and pale-green eyes, she was about the same age as the gunner of the other vehicle. "Anyone else?"

"Arne too," John said. "But they're not with me. They're with another of my people."

"Of course," said the blade-nosed man. "What do you want for them?"

To John's eye, he and the green-eyed woman appeared to be about the same age as marine lieutenants fresh out of OCS—and probably the oldest Castoffs present. Since they were the ones doing the talking—and everyone else was watching in expectant silence—he decided they were probably the two captains Lena had mentioned.

The Mjolnir's onboard computer displayed their names as a reminder on his HUD. Samson and Roselle.

"They're not hostages," John said. "We all just need to work together."

"And Berg and Greta?" asked the woman—Roselle. "If we work together, will you return them as well?"

"We don't have Berg or Greta," John said. "I'm sorry. I think they were probably killed when our ship self-destructed. That was a long distance back, where we crashed."

"The big flash?" Roselle asked.

"That's right," John said. "A member of my team saw two scouts just before the blast. We found a piece of their mountain runner afterward."

Roselle nodded and shot a pained look toward the blade-nosed man—no doubt Samson. They seemed too young to have kids old enough to send on scouting missions—and from what Lena had said, parents did not usually live long enough on Netherop for their offspring to remember them—but the Castoffs' children must have come from somewhere. He could only imagine that Roselle and Samson were old by castaway standards, and the parents of the other kids had already been taken by Netherop's harsh environment.

As John waited for the news of their scouts' deaths to settle in, a line of UNKNOWN designators appeared on his motion detector. Nine contacts were sneaking up behind him, arranged in a quarter circle so they could attack from several directions at once.

Had the contacts been aliens equipped with advanced Covenant weaponry, he figured that in open terrain like the plateau, they would have opened fire before closing to the twenty-five-meter limit of his motion detector. And had they just been a group of people walking up behind him, Fred or Linda would have alerted him via TEAMCOM. So it had to be Castoffs crawling through the brush, trying to position themselves to create an effective distraction for the gunners in the mountain runners.

John jerked a thumb over his shoulder toward the approaching Castoffs. "Don't even try. People will get hurt." To emphasize his point, he switched to TEAMCOM and said, "Blue Two, give them a shout."

A moment later, Fred's voice yelled, "Nice mountain runners you have there! It'd be a shame if something happened to them!"

All six runner occupants glanced toward Fred, and when they

looked back, John was holding his BR55 in one hand and his M7 in the other. The weapons were pointed at two different vehicles.

John turned his faceplate toward the green-eyed woman.

"Call them off, Roselle," he said. "You can't win, and *we* are not your enemies."

Roselle's brow rose at the sound of her name; then she turned to the blade-nosed man and said, "Samson, I think we're not going to pull this off. Let's hear the man out."

Samson scowled, but shifted his gaze past John and said, "Fine. You heard your captain. Back away."

John's motion tracker showed only six contacts leaving the area. He did not turn to look.

"*All* of them," he said to Samson. "I won't ask again."

"Do it . . . everyone," Roselle said. She turned her palm toward the deck and made a quick slicing motion that instantly reduced the tension in her companions' postures, then fixed her gaze on John. "It seems these things have eyes in their backs."

His motion tracker showed six additional contacts departing—for a total of twelve. That meant it had missed three contacts arriving. What the Castoffs lacked in tactics, they made up for in stealth.

"That's a start," John said. "Now, have your gunners step away from their weapons."

"And you will lower *your* weapons?"

"Sure." John lowered the M7. "We're all friends here."

"If we were friends," Roselle said, "you might tell us *your* name."

"It's John."

Roselle looked doubtful. "That is a strange name for a . . . what did you say you are?"

"A soldier," John said. "One who's running out of patience."

Roselle paled, then nodded to her companions. Two of the gunners backed away from the microwave dishes, but Samson remained behind his. John faced him and slowly began to lower the BR55, and Samson simultaneously slid away from his own weapon. When John's battle rifle was finally pointed at the ground, and Samson was standing in the corner of his runner opposite the microwave dish, Roselle glanced up the hill toward Fred.

"Better?" Roselle asked. When John nodded, she tipped her head toward Fred. "Since we're all friends here, you should invite him down."

"Maybe later," John said. "First, let's talk about what happened here."

"What's there to talk about?" Samson asked. "We killed a bunch of aliens."

As John turned to face him, Roselle said, "You shouldn't have a problem with that."

When John looked back to Roselle, Samson said, "Unless *he's* an alien."

"*Are* you an alien, John?" Roselle asked.

"I already told you, no." John stopped swiveling from one to the other, instead fixing his faceplate halfway between them and looking toward whoever was speaking out of the corner of his eye. "And *you* didn't drop all those aliens."

"Okay," Roselle said. "Maybe you killed six—"

"And the crew of the *Wheatley*"— John jerked a thumb toward the salvage ship behind him—"took out the other nineteen. Your weapons don't have the range."

Samson and Roselle glanced at each other; then Roselle sighed and looked back toward John. "It wasn't our fault."

John expected Samson to pipe in next, but he remained silent and merely looked expectant.

"What wasn't your fault?" John asked.

"You tell me," Roselle said. "You seem to know so much."

John thought for a moment, recalling what the *Wheatley*'s communications officer had said over the emergency channel about not being able to hold off the Covenant boarding party, then decided he had a pretty good idea of what had occurred.

"When the aliens started to cross the canyon, the *Wheatley*'s crew exited the ship."

"*Abandoned* it," Samson said. "And we moved in to save it."

"So you're claiming salvage rights?" John asked.

"That's colonial law," Roselle said. "Finders keepers."

"Not for military vessels," John said. "And what would you do with it anyway?"

"You'd be surprised at what we can do," Roselle said.

"I don't doubt it." John turned and pointed at the *Wheatley*. "But that? It's never going to happen. Not even if you *did* know how to fly a starship."

"Don't be so sure we don't," Samson said. "Our ancestors were—"

"Pirates, I know," John said. "That doesn't mean *you* know how to fly a starship—and even if you did, you'd never reach the bridge."

Roselle's eyes narrowed. "Is that a threat?"

"It doesn't need to be," John replied. "Think about what happened to Berg and Greta. Military crews don't just abandon a ship and leave it for the enemy to capture."

"You mean . . ." Samson looked toward the *Wheatley*. "The big flash?"

John tipped his helmet in Samson's direction. "Now you understand. Booby-trapped."

The color drained from Roselle's face, and she turned to the driver of the third runner. "Ebba—"

"I know." Ebba was already reaching for the runner's control globe. "I hope it isn't too late."

John watched the runner bound off toward the *Wheatley,* then looked back to Roselle and Samson. Always one more trick in their bags.

"When we get out of here, you two should apply for Officer Candidate School," he said. "You'd be ONI admirals in no time."

Both Roselle and Samson furrowed their brows in puzzlement, but John didn't explain. The sarcasm had been meant for himself and his fellow Spartans listening over TEAMCOM, so he didn't care whether the two Castoff captains understood. In fact, he was just as glad they didn't, since if they had, their story about being marooned on Netherop for generations would be called into question.

After a moment, Samson said, "*If* we get out of here."

"We will," John said. "That's a military ship. Unless someone has a roll of thermite-carbon cord, they're not getting inside."

Roselle eyed John as though he had just told a very dull joke. "You don't understand, tall man."

"You can't breach a reinforced, triple-locked hatch from outside."

"No need," Samson said. "They are climbing a thrust nozzle into the torus chamber. There will be a service hatch with an internal emergency release."

"An old pirate trick," Roselle explained. "Our ancestors left us hundreds in our learning machines."

"Oh." John looked toward the *Wheatley*, wondering how long they had before a Castoff slipped out of the engineering section and tried to open a trapped hatch. "How long ago did they start?"

"Not long," Samson said. "We had to wait until the aliens left too."

John was starting to feel behind on the intel. "Left . . . ? Where did they go?"

"After the humans," Roselle said. "At first we thought we would have to sneak aboard and kill the aliens in their sleep. But they were just hungry."

Now John was really feeling confused. "Hungry?"

"Yes," Samson said. "Why else would they go after the crew?"

"Maybe they were afraid of the big flash," Roselle said. "And no alien would know about climbing the thrust nozzle, so they might have wanted someone who knew how to open the hatch without blowing everything up."

There were problems with either possibility, but both honestly sounded more reasonable than anything else John could think of. He *had* heard the sordid tales of Covenant Jackals eating human casualties, so Samson's suggestion was not entirely unlikely—even if John hadn't seen any Jackals here on Netherop so far.

Roselle's idea was not crazy either. The enemy commander could easily have anticipated the booby-trapped hatches, given the UNSC's habit of using self-destruct devices to turn doomed vessels into devastating weapons. But it made no sense to leave the *Wheatley* practically unguarded, then take ninety percent of his Covenant force to capture a handful of humans so he could safely open the hatches—not when he *had* to know there was an entire platoon of marines on the way to capture *his* ship.

And there John was again, assuming the enemy commander thought like a human. He shook his head, frustrated with himself, and turned to find the third runner on its way back from the *Wheatley*. There were four heads protruding up behind the driver and gunner; evidently this Ebba had been able to retrieve the boarding crew before anyone made it into the torus chamber.

"Blue Four, keep an eye out for those Umbras that are supposed to be on our back trail," John said over TEAMCOM. "Blue Two, come down and join us."

"*Us?*" Fred asked. "It looks like the Castoffs are getting ready to clear out."

John turned back to see Roselle's and Samson's runners squatting belly-to-the-ground while young Castoffs used the legs to pull themselves up into the passenger compartments.

"Going somewhere?"

"Is that a problem?" Roselle asked, far too innocently.

"Only if you're heading over there." John pointed across the plateau toward the *Lucky Break*. "We wouldn't want any friendly fire."

"With you, everything is a threat," Samson said. "I am growing tired of it."

"It's not a threat." Silently, John added, *Unless it needs to be.* "I just thought we should talk about getting you a ride off this planet."

"In exchange for what?" Samson asked.

"How about not getting in the way?" John said. "Look, this isn't complicated. Nobody wants to see you marooned here for another five generations. I'm offering you a way out. All you have to do is be here when it's time to go."

"How generous." Roselle glanced over at Samson. "It almost sounds too good to be true."

"Almost," Samson said. "The UNSC has always been very free with its help. All it cost our ancestors was their liberty."

"I thought your ancestors were pirates."

"Pirates, Separatists . . ." Roselle shrugged. "Are they not the same to the UNSC?"

"Actually, no," John said. "And especially not when it concerns the Covenant. We're all in this fight together."

"Our ancestors would find that very hard to believe," Roselle said. She nodded to Samson, and both runners, now packed full of Castoffs ranging from toddlers John hadn't seen before—an older companion had probably been hiding them in the brush—to young adults, rose to their legs. "But we will keep that in mind once we are off the planet."

John forced himself to keep his BR55 pointed at the ground. Aware now of their Separatist heritage, he knew he wasn't going to win their trust by trying to intimidate them—and if he didn't win their trust, it would likely end very badly.

"You're smart people," John said. "So think this through. Even if I *were* to let you take the alien ship—"

"Why wouldn't you?" Roselle asked. "I thought we were all on the same side."

"We *are*," John growled. "But you'd never get that ship off the ground. You don't have time."

"There you are with your threats again," Samson said. "It's always the same with the UNSC."

"It's not a threat," John said. "I *really* can't let you have that ship, but that's not the problem. It's the aliens."

"But we killed all the aliens," said Samson.

It hadn't been the Castoffs who took them out, but John let it pass. He glanced back toward the hill and found Fred descending in the open, his battle rifle pointed at the ground, but ready to bring the muzzle up at a moment's notice.

John looked back to Samson. "There's another bunch of aliens coming," he said. "They'll be here in less than an hour, maybe sooner than that."

Roselle's brow furrowed. "What's an hour?"

John had to think for a moment, trying to figure out a measure of time Castoffs would understand, and finally hit upon something all humans had in common. He had his onboard computer display an average person's respiration rate and multiply it out to an hour.

"You take about nine hundred breaths in an hour." John had his HUD do a fifteen-second countdown, and when it reached zero, he said, "You just took four breaths."

"So, not soon," Samson said.

"Not long either," John said. "Do you think you can repair an alien spaceship in nine hundred breaths? And learn to fly it—without any help from your ancestors' learning machines?"

Samson looked over at Roselle, who looked worried.

"How do we know you're telling the truth?" she asked.

"You'll know in nine hundred breaths," John said. Fred arrived and took a position on the Castoffs' right flank, about ten meters from Samson's runner, then turned so he could watch the crest of the hill behind them. "Trust me that long, and the UNSC will relocate the Castoffs to any world you like—even an insurrectionist one."

"Tempting. But our ancestors learned the hard way that UNSC promises always are." Samson continued to look at Roselle. "What if there aren't any more aliens? What if he's just trying to stall us?"

"I'm not," John said. He pointed at Samson's runner. "But unless those things can fly, you're not going to beat us across the canyon anyway. And then *you'll* be the ones left behind when the aliens come."

Roselle swallowed hard, then turned to Samson. "Nine hundred breaths is not so long. Maybe we can trust them that much."

"Smart decision. I'm glad we could come to an agreement," John said.

He turned and scanned the mountain range for a moment, then spotted a sheltered canyon mouth about a kilometer distant. It opened out of the mountains just before the plateau dipped down into a sweeping bowl and fell away into the mirage basin. He pointed toward the canyon mouth.

"You should be safe enough there, as long as you're out of sight when the aliens arrive."

"And we're going to stay here to fight them?" Fred asked, also on voicemitter.

There was a hint of concern in Fred's tone, and John knew why. Blue Team had a mission to complete—one that had nothing to do with protecting a bunch of castaway children.

"Negative," John said. If the *Lucky Break*'s complement was busy chasing down the *Wheatley*'s crew, then the Covenant frigate had to be almost empty—and it would be a dereliction of duty not to take advantage of the situation before a platoon of Elite special forces arrived to spoil the opportunity. "We're going to board the *Lucky Break*."

"That makes sense." There was still a thread of concern in Fred's voice. "What's the rest of the team going to do? Hold off the Covenant in the meantime?"

John nodded. Fred was being careful to conceal their true numbers, but he clearly thought John was missing something—and he had an irritating habit of being right about such things.

"You have a better idea?"

"Not really," Fred said. "But I *am* wondering who's going to handle the *Wheatley* if we let the aliens kill her crew. I mean, *I* don't know how to operate a salvage ship. Do you?"

John let his chin drop. He had inadvertently made a strategic error—he'd stretched Blue Team too thin by leaving Kelly behind with Lena and the other injured Castoffs, and now he didn't have the personnel necessary to get the job done. If he sent Fred to save the *Wheatley*'s crew, and left Linda to watch over the UNSC ship, then John would have to capture an alien frigate of unknown design without any backup—and even for a Spartan, even boarding a ship down to a skeleton crew, that was a recipe for failure.

If he sent Linda to save the *Wheatley*'s crew while he and Fred took the *Lucky Break*, then he would be allowing an enemy special forces platoon to seize control of the salvage ship. They might be smart enough to avoid boarding until they disarmed the booby traps, but if they weren't, it would mean mission failure. Even if John and Fred could figure out how to fly a Covenant starship, they would have to figure out how to repair it first—and if the frigate could be repaired, it wouldn't be sitting on a plateau on Netherop waiting to be captured.

And even if the alien special forces platoon resisted the temptation to board the *Wheatley* and didn't trigger the self-destruct mechanism, Blue Team would still have to eliminate them in order to regain control of the vessel and capture the *Lucky Break*. That wasn't a great option, but at least it was doable.

Especially with Kelly coming up behind the special forces platoon. A Spartan attacking from that angle could do a lot of damage.

"New plan," John said to Samson. "I want you to take Linda and go after the *Wheatley*'s crew."

"Who's Linda?" Roselle asked.

John switched to TEAMCOM and turned toward the hilltop. "Blue Four, show yourself and approach."

Linda rose out of the crystal bushes and started down the hill at a jog. Roselle's mouth fell open, and Samson began to scan the hillside suspiciously.

"How many more of you are hiding up there?" Samson asked.

"You'd be surprised," Fred said. "Trust me."

"Linda may need your support when you make contact with the enemy." John wanted to avoid discussing their true numbers. He had a feeling the Castoffs would be a lot more cooperative if they thought there were dozens of Spartans hidden somewhere in the bushes. "So we'll arm your best fighters with whatever we can recover from the battlefield."

"Sure," Samson said. "What do we get?"

"I told you," John said. "Relocation to any world you like."

"That was for staying out of the way," Roselle said. "Now you are asking us to . . ."

She frowned and looked toward Samson.

"*Support* them," Samson said. He looked back to John. "Support sounds dangerous."

"No more dangerous than what you've already been doing." John didn't mind that they were taking advantage of the situation to negotiate a better deal—he just didn't know what they wanted. "And not as dangerous as wasting time we don't have."

"But what is it that you want?" Fred asked. "How about a nice new swift-cargo transport . . . and proper training in operating it?"

The Castoffs' eyes went wide, and John was pretty sure that, inside his helmet, his own expression was just as surprised. Swift-cargos were enduring civilian transport designs, fast enough to avoid being easy prey, but too lightly armed and armored to be converted to raiding ships themselves.

All in all, it was a perfect suggestion.

But Samson and Roselle were nothing if not tough negotiators. They quickly disguised their delight as disappointment, then looked at each other and simultaneously shook their heads.

"No way," Roselle said. "We want a *Sharpfin*."

Fred whistled through his voicemitter. "A *Sharpfin* is a big ask."

It *was* a big ask, though probably not for the reasons Samson and Roselle believed. A century earlier, *Sharpfin* corvettes had been as popular with pirates as they were with the commercial escort services that used them to guard colonial supply convoys. But by modern standards, the compact vessels were slow, underarmed, and seldom used even for planetary customs patrols.

When Roselle and Samson remained silent and looked expectant, Fred's voice came over TEAMCOM. "Just sigh and say yes," he said. "We'll find one somewhere."

John heaved a sigh. "You drive a hard bargain," he said. "But, okay. If you help us get that Covenant ship off Netherop, we'll get you a *Sharpfin*."

Roselle looked happy, but suspicious. "You don't need to ask a captain? You can make such a trade on your own?"

"Of course he can," Fred said. "He's a Master Chief. In our outfit, that's even better than a captain."

CHAPTER 16

That blur coming down the road was no mirage, Amalea Petrov decided. Despite her cloudy vision and muddied thoughts—*mud*, now wouldn't that be nice? A nice, cool mud bath in the Neos Atlantis Commander's Spa, a little Basumi Peat mixed with Yentog Ash Slurry, a flute of cold zantelle to sip . . .

"Commander, I don't know if ambushing this thing is a good idea."

Right, the ambush. There was an alien transport vehicle coming down the road, and apparently it was real. Amalea looked over at the marine next to her. A round-faced woman with black hair, Sesi Cacyuk lay with one eye pressed to the scope of a BR55 battle rifle. Her cheeks were red and dry, her eyes were glassy, and her brow was furrowed beneath a pounding headache. In short, she looked like Amalea felt.

— 273 —

"Lieutenant," Amalea said, "we *need* that transport."

"Yes, ma'am. I know."

They had lost four crew members and two marines to the heat in the last five hours—and advanced only two kilometers before Amalea realized it would be suicide to continue walking. Exercise only raised their body temperature, and it didn't matter that they still had all the water they could drink.

"It's just . . ." She passed the BR55 to Amalea. "Well, have a look."

Amalea pointed the weapon toward the approaching blur and pressed her eye to the scope. The blur did not resolve into a clearer image, but it doubled in size, revealing itself to be an arch-shaped vehicle floating on an invisible cushion of force. So definitely Covenant—no surprise there.

"What am I looking at?"

"Check the cockpits," Cacyuk said. "Above the carrier pod."

Amalea raised the scope just a touch, centering it on the top of the arch. A pair of heads grew visible, each protruding above the lip of a separate opening. They were still indiscernible and shimmering in the heat, but the last thing they looked was alien.

The one in front wore a familiar blue helmet with a distinctive bubble-shaped faceplate. Almost certainly Kelly-087—Amalea had heard the *Wheatley*'s emergency transmission regarding the Covenant boarding party, and John's reporting that four Spartans were moving to assist. She could only assume that the battle had gone well, and John had sent a captured transport back to pick up what remained of First Platoon and the *Night Watch* crew.

It was the small head in the second cockpit that was confusing. There seemed to be a long mane of stringy blond hair hanging from it, and Amalea thought she could make out the pale oval of a tiny, gaunt, human face.

"What the hell?" During the emergency exchange with the

Wheatley, Amalea had heard John say something about castaways—which had seemed so unlikely that she had begun to think she might be having heat-stroke hallucinations. But even if she had heard correctly, she saw no reason for him to send one back with Kelly. "Is that a *kid?*"

"Okay, good," Cacyuk said. "I thought I was seeing things."

"If so, we both are." Amalea passed the BR55 back to Cacyuk. "Keep everyone behind cover until I give the all-clear."

Amalea climbed out of the gully and descended the slope. By the time she reached the road, the transport was already drawing near. The refraction blur had dwindled to almost nothing, and there could be no doubt that it was Kelly-087 in the driver's cockpit.

But Amalea found her gaze fixed on the figure in the second cockpit. With a face that was almost skeletal, the human girl appeared on the verge of starvation. Yet her blue eyes were bright and alert, her expression just shy of open hostility.

Kelly brought the vehicle to a stop and lowered the parking struts, then ran her gaze across the hill, allowing it to linger an instant on each firing team's hiding place. Her accuracy was uncanny.

Then the Spartan looked back to Amalea and offered a salute. "Good day, Commander." She touched something inside the cockpit, and the boarding ramps on each side of the carrier pod folded down. "I need eighteen marines on the double."

First Platoon had only twenty marines, including their lieutenant, remaining. Still, Amalea nodded and used her helmet mic to comm Cacyuk.

"Bring everyone down." Once Cacyuk had acknowledged, Amalea looked back to Kelly. "Sitrep?"

"I assume you heard the *Wheatley*'s emergency transmission?"

"Affirmative." Amalea checked her chronometer. The transmission had occurred less than an hour earlier, but she had lost two crew members since then, and it felt like ancient history. "I don't understand what the aliens were thinking. Why attack the *Wheatley* instead of waiting us out?"

"My best guess is they're not expecting rescue and hope to capture a means to leave the planet. But who knows?"

"Wait," Amalea said. "You sound like the fight isn't over yet."

"I wouldn't know," Kelly said. "John and the others should be there by now—"

"Then what are you doing *here*?" Amalea glanced at the girl. "With her?"

"Ma'am, that's what I'm trying to explain."

Amalea felt her stomach clench. She was committing a cardinal sin of command, talking when she should be listening. It was a symptom of her half-cooked brain. Had to be.

". . . so we need to bring support forward as fast as we can," Kelly was saying. "I doubt John knows they're behind him."

Damn. Now Amalea was *thinking* instead of listening. "They?"

"The special forces unit, ma'am." Kelly's tone was worried—or perhaps merely impatient. "In the other Umbra."

"Right," Amalea said. Cacyuk had now arrived with the marines and what remained of her crew, so Amalea waved them up the boarding ramps. "Let's move out. Load up."

The marines ascended and started to secure themselves into the transportation pods, but almost immediately, shouting erupted at the top of a ramp. Amalea turned to find a handful of marines arguing with each other and the three remaining members of her crew. Cacyuk stood at the base of the ramp, studying the carrier pod and scowling.

After a moment, she bellowed, "That's enough! Stand down!"

The shouting stopped immediately, but no one descended the ramp. Amalea went to Cacyuk's side and quickly saw the problem. There were ten troop stations on each side of the carrier pod, for a total of twenty slots. Two slots were already occupied by frightened-looking castaway boys. Amalea was livid at this new discovery but did not take the time to ask for an explanation.

That left eighteen slots left for twenty-four men and women, and crowding in was not a possibility. Each station was shaped like a padded coffin, with thick inflatable cushions that expanded to hold the occupant steady while the vehicle moved. From the look of it, even the skinny boys would not be able to ride in the same station without the danger of being crushed.

It was obvious that someone needed to take control of the situation—and that someone had to be her. Amalea stepped to the front of the vehicle, where she would be able to watch both sides.

"This isn't a taxi service!" she called. "If you're not a marine, step off the transport!"

Her crew members glared at her in disbelief and obvious anger, their expressions showing the betrayal they felt. She tried not to care. The important thing was the mission, and at the moment, they weren't important to completing it.

"*Now.* If I have to ask the Spartan to remove you . . ." She pointed out over the mirage basin. "You'll find yourselves learning to fly."

Her crew quickly descended the ramps, leaving only nineteen enlisted marines and the two castaway boys in the carrier pod. If she removed the boys, and the girl in the cockpit behind Kelly, the transport would be able to carry all of the marines, plus their lieutenant and Amalea herself.

Amalea looked up at the girl. "You and your friends, too," she said. "You can wait with the crew until we send the transport back."

"And you can jump off that cliff," the girl shot back. "We were here first."

"I'm sorry," Amalea said. "But this is a military necessity. Being first doesn't matter."

"It does to us. Kelly wouldn't have captured this thing without our help. We're not leaving." She stretched down and patted Kelly on the helmet. "Right?"

"It isn't my decision," Kelly said. As she spoke, she was looking at Amalea. "But they *did* help with the capture. And we would probably be better off bringing them along."

Amalea frowned. She had the feeling Kelly was trying to tell her something, but she wasn't quite sure what. Was the problem due to the heat affecting her mind? Or was the Spartan being too subtle?

No. Spartans didn't do subtle.

Amalea decided to try one more time. She looked to the girl again. "You clearly have the skills to survive here. You'd find the UNSC *very* grateful—"

Kelly's chin dropped toward her chest, and Amalea realized she had made a blunder. She just wished her head was clear enough to figure out what it had been.

"—if you helped my crew until we return."

Kelly didn't even give the girl a chance to reply. "Ma'am, begging your pardon, but we need to move out *now*. We'll be arriving late to the fight as it is."

"Very well," Amalea said.

Whatever Kelly was trying to say, she apparently didn't think it would be wise to leave the children behind. And maybe she was right. As young and malnourished as the castaways appeared, they were in better shape than some of the troops.

Amalea turned to Lieutenant Cacyuk. "Pick your sixteen best marines." She specified that number because both she and Cacyuk would be going along, as well. First Platoon needed its lieutenant, and—judging by Kelly's presence here instead of with her fellow Spartans—Blue Team needed *her*. "Leave the others to be retrieved with my crew."

"Yes, ma'am," Cacyuk said. "If that's what you think is best for the mission."

"I do."

Amalea's decision might look bad on review, but she could always claim that she was acting on Kelly's advice. She could get away with that, as long as the mission succeeded. And the mission *did* come first—even ahead of her career, when necessary.

She looked up at the girl. "Satisfied?"

The girl shrugged. "For now."

"Good enough," Amalea said. "But I'm going to take your seat. Kelly will need to brief me on the way to battle."

The girl stared daggers and looked as though she were going to refuse. Then Kelly growled something Amalea could not make out, and the girl rose and started to climb out of the cockpit.

"Deal," the kid said. "But don't even think about trying to double-cross me. Kelly's on *our* side."

CHAPTER 17

1308 hours, June 7, 2526 (military calendar)
Near UNSC *Phyllis Wheatley* Landing Site, Crystal Bush Plateau
Mountains of Despair, Planet Netherop, Ephyra System

John would have preferred to wait for Kelly to catch up before he sent Linda off to rescue the *Wheatley*'s surviving crew— especially with no support other than a bunch of untrained Castoffs. But if there was a platoon of Elites coming up behind them, waiting was out of the question.

So was activating a long-range comm channel to check Kelly's status. Without an encrypted satellite net in place, the only secure transmissions were low-power, short-range systems like TEAM-COM. John would just have to be patient and trust that no news was good news. It was tough to accept, but had Kelly been taken out, her suit would have sent a static blast over the emergency channel as it self-destructed.

There was nothing to do but carry on, which was why John

and Fred were in the lead runner with Samson and his driver, descending a steep ravine into the deep gorge that divided the plateau. When they reached the road, they would part ways with Linda and the Castoffs, then cross the chasm, sneak across four kilometers of plateau, and somehow capture the *Lucky Break*.

It wasn't much of a plan, but at least it was simple.

As the mountain runner picked its way down the ravine bed, John realized that the *Wheatley*'s crew had defended their vessel more ferociously than he had realized. Every fifty meters or so, a human corpse—the victim of a long-range beam rifle attack—lay sprawled among the boulders. Twice they passed ruined Warthogs. The first looked as though it had simply been traveling too fast for the rugged terrain and flipped forward when both front wheels dropped into a hole. The second had been demolished after a particle beam penetrated its armored hydrogen tank.

Few of the casualties appeared to be trained combat soldiers. They all wore ONI work uniforms of one sort or another, but most of their MOS patches indicated scientific and engineering specialties. Only a few were clad in anything that resembled a weapons belt or ammunition pouch, and just one—an overweight security sergeant who looked as though he hadn't done calisthenics in a year—wore body armor.

That was the price of rushing an operation—it could devolve into a true shitstorm. Proper assets weren't marshaled. People were pushed into roles beyond their skill set, and minor challenges erupted into major disasters. It was the reason military strategists placed so much importance on momentum—skilled attackers moved when they were ready, and defenders fought whether they were ready or not.

And the fact was, all humanity was now on the defensive. The Covenant was pressing the attack at a thousand points along the edge of the Outer Colonies, driving the UNSC into battle half-prepared, pushing it into desperate operations like this one, forcing mistakes that wasted resources and took lives.

As far as John knew, the Spartans were the only hope of breaking that cycle. They were humanity's one weapon that had proven superior to Covenant technology, the one force able to carry the attack to the enemy. The trouble was, the aliens now knew that too—and they had the firepower to do something about it.

The closer John drew to the *Lucky Break*, the more certain he felt that the downed frigate was all a Covenant setup. That was hardly news—Dr. Halsey had said the ship was nothing but a trap in her initial message, and then proceeded to tell him that Blue Team still needed to capture it. And he didn't disagree. It was worth the risk.

But he *did* object to being moved around like some living chess piece, being sent into battle on the basis of someone else's plan. That wasn't the way to win. The attack at Naraka had succeeded because the people executing it—he and Avery Johnson and Marmon Crowther—were the ones who had crafted the strategy. They had taken stock of their resources and designed the assault around what they could feasibly marshal. They were bold, but they hadn't attempted anything they lacked the assets to achieve.

If the UNSC expected the Spartans to turn this war around, then the top brass—Admiral Cole and Michael Stanforth and even Dr. Halsey—needed to understand all of that. And the next time Blue Team was assigned a mission, John would not be shy about making sure his superiors were duly notified of it.

Provided he survived Netherop in one piece.

Finally, up ahead, the ravine entered a culvert and passed under the ancient roadway that had been cut into the gorge wall. As the runner approached, John saw that another Warthog lay on its side on the bank leading up to the roadbed, a meter-wide hole in the floor where the driver's seat had once been. Eight bodies, several of them wearing ship's security armor and clutching sidearms and assault rifles, lay scattered to both sides of the culvert entrance.

John tapped Samson on the shoulder. "Stop here so we can reconnoiter."

Samson relayed the order to the mountain runner's driver with a couple of quick tongue clucks. John and Fred jumped out of the runner on opposite sides. The plan was for Linda and the Castoffs to continue through the gorge in pursuit of the *Wheatley*'s survivors, while John and Fred would cross to the other side of the gorge and carry on with the mission to capture the *Lucky Break*.

It was hard to guess how many aliens they would find waiting for them aboard the frigate, but John didn't see how it could be more than a skeleton crew. The fight in the ravine had been fierce. The enemy couldn't have won it without a fairly large force, and he knew from the *Wheatley*'s emergency transmission that the *Lucky Break* had assigned somewhere between one and two hundred crew members to the task.

As John and Fred started up the road banks, John spoke over TEAMCOM. "Blue Four, there are some weapons here at the culvert that might be worth collecting for your irregulars." *Irregular* was military jargon for civilian soldiers—in this cast, the Castoffs whom John had recruited to serve as Linda's support team. "Just make sure they know what'll happen if they point one in your direction."

"Ricochets?"

"That too," John said. "I think Samson and Roselle are on our side for now. But if they see a chance to get off Netherop without us, their loyalties could easily change."

"That won't happen," Linda said. "I will make sure."

John reached the top of the bank and peered over the edge. Up the canyon, the roadbed was littered with more bodies, and this time many of them were Elites. There were also ten harpoon-like shafts that had been driven into the cliffside, probably by an artillery piece fired from the opposite side of the gorge. Attached to the anchors were the bottom ends of ten thick zip-lines, which ascended across the chasm up to the far rim.

"Well," Fred said over TEAMCOM, "at least we know how we're getting across."

"Maybe," John replied. "If they didn't leave any guards behind."

"Only one way to find out," Fred said. He assembled the M41 and hoisted it onto his shoulder. "Ready?"

John flicked the safety off his BR55. "Go ahead. I have you covered."

Fred checked over his shoulder to be certain no curious Cast-offs had crept up behind him, then fired a rocket toward the top of one of the zip lines. The detonation destroyed the upper anchor and brought the cable whipping down into the gorge, where the far end sank below the edge of the Forgotten Highway and vanished from sight.

When no Covenant soldiers returned fire, Fred climbed onto the road and stood in the open, aiming at the top of the next zip line. The canyon remained silent.

John rose and fired a burst along the rim. Still no return fire.

"Huh," Fred said. "I'm confused."

"Yeah. Me too."

John stepped over to the closest dead Elite and used a foot to roll the corpse onto its back. The alien's armor was even heavier than that of most Elites he had fought, and it had a small hole on the bottom of the backplate where the power pack for a personal energy barrier had self-destructed.

On the alien's hip, there was a carrier for an energy sword, but, of course, the weapon itself had been taken by the warrior's companions. John wasn't sure whether retrieving the swords was a rite of honor or just an attempt to keep the technology out of human hands. He only knew that it was extremely rare to find one on a dead Elite.

"This one looks like heavy infantry," John said. "I think he might even be some sort of assault specialist."

"Okay. Now I'm *really* confused."

Fred returned the M41 to his magmount, then stepped to a zip line. He jerked it several times to test its security, then hoisted himself up and started to pull himself up the line hand over hand.

John covered him as the Castoffs climbed their three surviving runners out of the ravine and began to organize themselves—six to a vehicle—for the chase through the gorge. If the *Lucky Break* truly was "Spartan-bait," he couldn't understand why the enemy commander had abandoned it to go after the *Wheatley*'s crew. On the other hand, if the *Lucky Break* truly was disabled, John couldn't fathom why the Covenant hadn't made more of an effort to drive the Castoffs away from it and preserve their best hope of getting off Netherop.

New situation, same old problem. Aliens thought like aliens.

Fred reached the top of the zip line and disappeared over the rim of the cliff. John waited impatiently, listening with half an ear as Linda explained the basic operation of M6E sidearms and MA5B assault rifles to the Castoffs. They did not seem entirely clueless about firearms, so it seemed likely they had at least read about them in the "learning machines" their ancestors had left for them.

After a couple of minutes, Fred's voice came over TEAMCOM. "All clear."

"On my way," John said. "And stay out of sight. I'm starting to think the *Lucky Break* might actually *be* a lucky break."

"If you say so," Fred said. "But wilco. Being sneaky never hurt anyone."

"And rig some tripwire wands on the anchors." John began to securely stow his weapons. "That Covenant special forces unit is still coming, and we don't need them surprising us."

"You don't think Kelly took them out?"

For once, Fred's question wasn't in jest. He really *did* think Kelly could take out thirty Elite special forces troops alone. And she probably could have, had the equipment she needed not been lost during the *Night Watch*'s disastrous insertion.

"Maybe not all of them," John said. "We have the rocket launcher, remember?"

"Good point," Fred said. "Maybe everyone should carry rocket launchers."

"And give up everything else the team carries?" John asked. "Our sniper rifles and shotguns and submachine guns?"

"Why choose?" Fred asked. "We should just get Dr. Halsey to design a mini-launcher, so everybody can carry their own."

"Sure." John grabbed the same zip line Fred had used—since it had already been tested—and began to pull himself up. "I'll put in a request as soon as we get back."

Four minutes later, he dropped off the line and knelt on the plateau's dark stone. Fred tied a short length of thermite-carbon cord around the anchor, then affixed a tripwire wand to the anchor shaft and inserted both ends of the cord into the wand. The slightest pressure on the zip line would cause the anchor to flex, which would trigger the motion sensor and detonate the thermite-carbon cord.

Now the one thing John and Fred didn't have to worry about was an Elite special forces unit popping up behind them. They turned toward the *Lucky Break*—still four kilometers distant—and poked their heads above the crystal bushes just high enough to get a fix on the frigate's shimmering purple shape. The two Spartans set their waypoints and started forward on their hands and knees.

A high combat crawl—performed on the elbows and knees—would be safer, but a lot slower. Given the heat shimmer, the amount of foliage on the plateau, and the distance they had to cover, John thought they could travel this way for the first three kilometers. After that, they would drop into a proper high crawl to avoid being spotted by any lookouts aboard the *Lucky Break*. But given that there were only the two of them, John thought that he and Fred had an excellent chance of reaching the vessel undetected.

After the first kilometer, John began to feel the strain of stooping, and his skinsuit again started to have trouble shedding heat. He ignored the discomfort and continued forward. The soreness would go away as soon as he dropped into a high crawl, as would the excess heat. Right now they needed to make time, and it had taken them almost fifteen minutes to advance the first kilometer.

At the end of the second kilometer, they spread out, putting a hundred meters between them to avoid being eliminated simultaneously by a single salvo from the ship's point-defense weapons. But the lookouts—if there were any—didn't seem to notice their approach, so he and Fred continued forward another kilometer.

By then, forty-five minutes had passed, and John knew the enemy special forces unit had probably reached the *Wheatley*. The fact that the plateau had not been blasted clear by a Fury detonation suggested that the Covenant commander had been cagey enough not to force the hatches, but that was little comfort. If the alien unit was not attempting to board the salvage ship, then it was closing in on him and Fred—and the Covenant forces would come running once they managed to cross the gorge.

John paused to look back, hoping to see a wisp of rising smoke, or a distant flash of fire, or some other sign that the enemy had triggered Fred's traps. But the heat shimmer above the foliage was too thick. All he could see were the brown mountains silhouetted against a similarly colored sky, and at the base of the mountains the gray arch of the *Wheatley*'s bow, trembling through the haze.

He turned back toward the *Lucky Break* and dropped onto his elbows, then began the long slow crawl across the last kilometer. Every bone in his body ached to stand and run, to race across that last thousand meters so he could slap a breaching charge onto the Covenant frigate's hull. But so far, there was no reason to take such a risk. They had made it this far unseen, and—

The ground shook, a long gentle shudder that came rolling through the stone in waves. The sheet plants surrounding them wrapped in on themselves, and the crystal bushes shattered into flutter bugs. Then a purple form rose into the air ahead—a long-nosed, disk-shaped vessel with a notch in its dovetailed stern. It rode a cushion of blue radiance across the plateau, then floated over the edge and out into the mirage basin.

The *Lucky Break* was leaving.

John rose and stared after the departing frigate, hoping to see it drop like a rock, or erupt in flames, or tip sideways and glide into the ground—anything to indicate it had actually been crippled, that it was simply limping away to avoid being boarded. But the vessel just drifted farther out over the basin and vanished from sight. It might not be capable of climbing into orbit, but it was certainly far from disabled.

Fred's voice came over TEAMCOM. "Jinxed it."

"Not me," John said. "I didn't say anything."

"No, but you *thought* it," Fred said. "*So far, so good*, right?"

John sighed. "Close enough," he admitted. "But how would you know what I was thinking, unless . . ."

"Yeah," Fred said. "Me too."

John turned toward Fred, and found him looking right back, across a hundred meters of wasteland. "You know what this means, right?"

"Well, it's not good," Fred said. "If that ship wasn't disabled—"

"It was bait," John said. "Something we already figured on any-way. Damn. I was hoping to have been wrong about this. Set your self-destruction protocol to tamper-safe."

"You mean *you* haven't?"

Actually, he had. John had barely formulated the order before his onboard computer had activated the protocol. Now if someone tried to open his armor after he was rendered helpless—or killed in action—the onboard computer would initiate a reactor overload. Everything within ten meters would be atomized, and the suit would issue one last static blast over the emergency channel.

So far, the only Spartan who had ever had been forced to use the self-destruction protocol was John's friend Samuel-034—at Chi Ceti IV, on their very first mission wearing Mjolnir. The memory still tore at John inside, like a wound that continued to ache long after it had closed, and he knew it always would. The assault that had com-promised Sam's armor had been John's idea, and not a day went by when he didn't go over the operation in his mind, wishing there had been just a little more time to prepare, that he had had just a little more command experience. But he'd finally come to accept that he could have done nothing to change Sam's fate, that it had just been the nature of combat and Sam's own quick reflexes that had put him in the path of a plasma bolt meant for John.

That was not much comfort. If John could not control every-thing that happened in combat, then he had to admit that sometimes his skills didn't matter, that sometimes he and his team were just at the mercy of random chance and the upper hand of their enemies in the moment. And the burden that such knowledge lifted in guilt was returned in the awareness of his own mortality—and that of his companions. In the end, there was little that John could do but *hope* Sam would be the last Spartan who ever needed his armor's self-destruct protocol. Hope, and stay in control of the things that he could.

And John was okay with that. As a commander, he had to be.

He turned back toward the gorge. "Better run," he said. "Whatever that special forces unit has planned, I'd rather deal with it back in the gorge, not out here in the open."

"And people say you like doing things the hard way." Fred raised his battle rifle in one hand and extended the other over his shoulder, toward the M41 affixed to its magmount. "Bullets or rockets?"

"Rockets," John said. "Whatever happens next, let's be sure they know we came to fight."

Fred exchanged his BR55 for the rocket launcher, then swapped out the half-used tube set for a new one with two rockets. The two Spartans set off at a near sprint, taking care to stay at least a hundred meters apart and to frequently change their position relative to each other. They were moving across open terrain with every reason to believe an enemy with uncontested air superiority knew exactly where they were. As far as John was concerned, the only reason they *wouldn't* get strafed or blasted was that the Covenant planned to take them down some other way.

There was no enemy activity, not in the first kilometer. They covered it in five hot minutes, running zigzag paths with one eye on the sky, ready to dive and roll and come up firing.

And nothing.

The Covenant was letting the Spartans wear themselves out, giving their nerves a chance to work on them, giving Netherop's heat and dust time to foul their equipment. But the aliens understood Spartans no better than John understood the aliens. Fatigue meant nothing to a Spartan. Fear to a Spartan was just motivation. Spartan equipment could be destroyed if you were quick enough and had a large enough weapon. But the process never broke down—Spartans were built to keep going.

And keep going they would.

At the end of the second kilometer, John was starting to sweat heavily. That was fine with him. The skinsuit would collect it and recycle it, use it to keep him cool and hydrated. He sipped from his hydration tube and continued to run. He kept looking just above the horizon, sweeping the sky for incoming Banshees, and he and Fred were eight hundred meters from the gorge when he finally spotted the Umbras.

There was one cresting a hill, about a kilometer away from the *Wheatley*, a tiny sliver of shadow so distant and small he would have missed it, had it not been coming fast and raising a long plume of dust. The second Umbra was closer, a purple half-disk the size of an eyeball. It was standing at the base of the *Wheatley*, its boarding ramps folded open.

John magnified the image and saw a dozen dark-armored forms rippling in the heat. They were spread across the plateau on the far side of the gorge in an evenly spaced line, working their way back toward their transport. Behind them lay the crippled mountain runner that had been destroyed earlier in the Castoffs' artillery duel with the *Lucky Break*'s crew. It appeared the aliens were searching for clues, trying to figure out what the hell was going on.

Welcome to the club.

Fred's voice came over TEAMCOM. "Bandits, eleven o'clock!"

John threw himself into a forward roll and spun onto his back, his BR55 ready to fire. When no cannon bolts came stitching across the plateau, he sat up and looked in the direction Fred had indicated.

Ten cruciform shapes—Banshee silhouettes—were circling over the *Wheatley* and dropping into line for a head-on strafing run.

Beneath them, the Elite special forces unit was now running for its Umbra—no doubt alerted to John and Fred's presence by their air cover. The Banshees were coming fast, but they were still too distant to strafe.

That would change soon.

"Set up for head-on shot?" John asked.

When Fred's status LED flashed green, John sprang up and ran for the gorge rim, circling around so that he would be directly in front of Fred. The best way to engage a strafing aircraft with a rocket launcher was head-on, because the M41 lacked the range to catch a fast-moving craft from behind. But it took time to shoulder the weapon and align the sights. And alien or human, incoming pilots were usually reluctant to make an easy target of themselves by making a long, straight approach.

The Spartans had developed a technique to remedy that problem.

John grabbed a grenade from his satchel and put his thumb on the priming slider. The enemy squadron crossed the gorge and spread out in a ten-Banshee line, making sure John would not be able to avoid their fire by dodging to one side. He raised his BR55 in one hand and pulled the trigger, more because he knew the muzzle flash would prove a distraction than because of any damage the weapon might do.

Streams of plasma bolts began to fly from the lead Banshee's nose, blasting up the ground across the plateau. He thumbed the priming slider and hurled the grenade into the air, putting all of his speed and strength into the throw. He doubted he was going to hit anything, but it would give the pilot something else to think about— and if John happened to get lucky, it would make the other pilots think twice when they came in for their next runs.

The grenade was still climbing when John's HUD flashed green—the onboard computer alerting him that now was his best chance to dive between bolts without taking a hit. He hurled himself forward, drawing his legs up tight and curling himself into a ball, making as small a target as possible. He hit the ground on the brow of his helmet and on his elbows and knees all at once.

He rolled onto his back and saw a chevron-shaped line of Banshees overhead—then Fred's rocket came streaking toward the middle one. The rest of the squadron split even before the fireball erupted, turning away in two separate directions.

John never saw the results of his grenade launch.

He was already on his feet and zigzagging for the gorge at a full sprint. Fred would be following fifty meters behind, moving perpendicular to John's vector, as always taking care to avoid offering two targets in a straight line. John looked left, watching as the five Banshees that had split in that direction circled back toward the *Wheatley*, preparing for another full-squadron run. He knew that Fred, being second in line, would be watching on the right. Blue Team had drilled the procedure a thousand times, because a squad that knew what to do reacted faster, and a squad that reacted faster survived more often.

"They're sure taking their time," Fred remarked.

"Probably didn't like the results on the first pass." John watched as the four Banshees from Fred's side joined the five from his side, then fell into single file, circling over the *Wheatley*—likely while their commander outlined a new attack strategy. "But since they're giving us the time, maybe a tube switch—"

"On it," Fred said. "But next time, I'll need your tubes. I'm down to single loads."

"Affirmative."

With no reason to maintain comm silence any longer—the enemy already knew where they were—John activated the emergency channel.

"Blue Leader with Blue Two, requesting any available support at *Wheatley* landing site," he said. "We have an enemy squadron, nine Banshees on strafing runs, plus two Umbras on the surface moving to engage. Our location five hundred meters across gorge from *Wheatley*."

John was not *entirely* surprised to hear a chain of sonic booms echoing down from above the clouds. After all, Task Force Pantea *had* promised to send support as soon as it arrived.

"*Pantea Nandao squadron Echo One arriving two minutes,*" a female voice said over the emergency channel. "*Repeat: minutes two.*"

"Acknowledged: minutes two," John said. "And thanks."

"*Our pleasure, Blue Leader,*" Echo One replied. "*And sorry about the Banshees. They must have slipped in below the clouds.*"

"Appreciate it," John said. "You're here now."

The Banshees pulled out of their circle and started toward the gorge in single file.

Then Amalea Petrov's voice came over the emergency channel. "*Night Watch Actual, Echo One?*"

"*Go ahead, Actual.*"

"Only lead Umbra hostile," Petrov said. "Repeat: only lead Umbra hostile. Second Umbra captured and friendly. Location fifteen hundred meters from *Wheatley*, inbound with Blue Three and seventeen marines."

John could not help smiling inside his helmet. Not only had Kelly survived, she had arranged transport for First Platoon.

"*Blue Leader, verify* Night Watch *Actual?*" Echo One requested. It was a standard field precaution. Just two months earlier, the Covenant had used a communications link to attempt a software infiltration of Battle Group X-Ray's ship AIs during the Second Battle of Harvest, and signals espionage was a favorite trick of the insurrectionists, when they could get their hands on UNSC comm equipment. So the precaution was one that most careful pilots would undertake, given the situation. *"Second Umbra friendly?"*

"Blue Leader confirms," John said.

As they crossed the gorge, the Banshees were spreading out into a diamond formation that would saturate the area with cannon fire. Fred might be able to mow another one down with the M41, but the enemy fighters were going to put a plasma strike on every square meter of ground. The good news was that if the two Spartans could avoid being hit more than once, they would probably survive.

"And hurry," John said. "Please."

"Mach twelve, baby," came the reply. *"We'll be gone before you know we're there."*

And they were. In one breath, the Banshees were starting to spit plasma, chewing up everything between the two Spartans and the gorge rim. Fred launched both rockets, and the enemy formation loosened just a bit as nervous pilots jerked their controls.

Then a dozen holes swirled open in the cloud canopy behind the Covenant squadron, and the Banshees erupted into a diamond-shaped veil of flame and shrapnel. A compression wave banged the air so hard that John felt it in his boot soles, then a cone of friction smoke stretched across the sky. John spun around, looking toward the far end of the curtain, expecting to find a flight of Nandaos waggling their wings as they departed.

Instead, he saw only another set of holes in the clouds.

"Blue Leader, confirming nine kills," he commed. "Zero Banshee escapes. And thanks for saving our behinds."

"Our pleasure," Echo One said. *"But that attack run sapped us, and we still have to climb out of this gravity well. We can give you air cover for another twenty minutes, a quarter that if you need us to try for the Umbra."*

"Negative on the Umbra," John said. He motioned to Fred, and they resumed their run toward the rim of the gorge. "But we really appreciate the air cover. Out."

"*Negative Umbra, air cover for twenty,*" Echo One confirmed. "*Be advised, there's something strange going on between the Covenant stealth flotilla and its incoming fleet. They actually exchanged fire, but—*"

Petrov's voice broke in. "Confirm . . . did you just say fire exchange between Covenant elements?"

"*Confirm exchange of fire, Covenant fleet firing on Covenant stealth vessels.*" Echo One's tone sounded annoyed. "*But that's not the important part.*"

"Continue important part," Petrov said, as though it were perfectly acceptable for a prowler commander to break into someone else's transmission. "Hard to believe there's bigger news than that, but continue."

"*Not bigger,*" Echo One snapped. "*More important. Situation in orbit deteriorating rapidly. Pantea holding to best of its ability, but outgunned and outnumbered. One way or another, Pantea will be gone inside four hours.*"

"Four hours," Petrov replied. "Acknowledged."

"*Four hours max,*" Echo One replied. "*Echo One out.*"

"Maximum hours four," John said. "Acknowledged. And thanks again."

A click sounded as Echo One signed off, but Petrov remained on the channel. "What's the situation with the *Lucky Break*, Blue Leader?"

"Not so lucky." John looked back toward the mirage basin and saw no sign of the enemy frigate—not that he had expected to. Without a decent-sized crew to man it, even a Covenant frigate would have headed for cover at the first sign of the Nandao squadron. "It's out of reach."

"It self-destructed?"

"Negative," John said. He and Fred were only fifty meters from the gorge now, and he could see the enemy Umbra on the opposite side, approaching the ravine that the Castoffs—and the *Wheatley*'s crew—had used to descend to the Forgotten Highway. "It flew off without warning."

"And you *let* it?"

This was too much for Fred. "Excuse me, ma'am," he said. "We weren't close enough for the grappling hooks."

Petrov fell silent, then said, "This is no time for your insubordination, One-Oh-Four."

"There's no insubordination, ma'am," John said. "It's true. We *weren't* close enough for grappling hooks."

The two Spartans reached the rim of the gorge and dropped to their stomachs, taking care to stay far enough from the zip-line anchors to avoid being hit by flying shafts if the booby traps detonated. Across the way, the enemy Umbra was descending the steep ravine, far more easily than had the *Wheatley*'s Warthogs—or even the Castoffs' mountain runners. As ungainly as the transport looked, it simply glided over the boulders and uneven ground on its cushion of force, with its nose riding high.

Now that John knew Kelly and First Platoon were coming up behind the enemy unit, he had no worries about being able to eliminate it. He and Fred would simply disarm the booby-trapped zip lines until the first wave of Elites was halfway across, then rearm them. Their Mjolnir armor might take a few whacks from snapping anchors—but that would be nothing compared to what happened to the Elites.

After a moment, Petrov came back on the channel. "I probably deserved that."

"Confirmed," John said.

She pretended not to hear him. "But we need to agree on what comes next. Is there any hope we can still capture the *Lucky Break*?"

"There's always hope."

It was a Spartan thing to say, but as John spoke, a fireball appeared in the sky far behind the *Wheatley*, plummeting toward an impact somewhere beyond the mountains. The flaming sphere was far too big to be a Nandao or Baselard—it was at least destroyer-size, maybe larger. John hoped larger, because then it would have to be a Covenant vessel instead of UNSC.

"But that hope is getting pretty slim," John added.

"Then it's time to call for extraction," Petrov said. "You heard Echo One. The situation in orbit is deteriorating fast."

"Understood," John said. "But not yet. We have personnel to retrieve."

"Who?"

"You've met Lena and her two companions?"

"Affirmative." Petrov did not sound happy about the experience, and based on his own interactions with the Castoffs, John couldn't really blame her. "Blue Three brought them along when she picked us up in the Umbra."

"There are eighteen more Castoffs just like her in the gorge with Linda," John said. "She went after *Wheatley*'s crew, and they volunteered to support her."

"Can't Spartan-058 extract alone?"

John couldn't quite believe what he was hearing. Was Petrov really suggesting that Linda abandon a band of castaways—*and* the crew of a UNSC salvage vessel—to be slaughtered by the Covenant? That was even more ruthless than the orders Commander Yao had given on Alpha Corvi II, and not something John intended to allow—not as long as they were on the surface and he was still in command of the mission.

As he struggled with the suggestion, down in the gorge the alien Umbra climbed out of the ravine and turned its nose down the Forgotten Highway. John could see the gunner's oblong helmet swiveling as he ran his gaze up each zip line and peered over the transport's sides at dead Elites.

But the driver seemed more concerned with the route ahead than with the corpses. He simply steered the Umbra close to the road edge, then carefully eased forward, traveling in the same direction the *Wheatley*'s crew had gone—as well as Linda and the Castoffs.

"What the hell?" Fred asked over TEAMCOM. "I thought they were after *us*?"

John was about to suggest that maybe the Covenant had decided it would be a lot easier to capture one Spartan than two—then realized the enemy had no way of knowing where Linda was. No aliens had been in the gorge when John and Fred parted ways with her, and it was unlikely that a reconnaissance pilot could have spotted her riding in a mountain runner located half a kilometer down in a shady, winding gorge.

But the aliens were definitely after something, and whatever that was, it was probably smart to deny it to them.

"Take them out," John said over TEAMCOM.

He put a BR55 burst into the gunner's head and saw the energy shield go down a fraction of a second before the helmet shattered. The driver instantly overcame his surprise and accelerated hard, the boarding ramps beneath him already starting to come down so the troops inside could evacuate.

They never had a chance. Fred's first rocket blew through the near-side ramp and filled the transport bays with flame. The second rocket entered through the same hole, and fire shot from seams John didn't realize the transport had.

The driver leapt free, flames billowing from the cockpit behind him, and John shot him dead before he hit the roadbed. The Umbra veered off the edge of the highway, then plummeted toward the bottom of the gorge, a long tail of smoke trailing behind it.

"John?" Petrov asked over the emergency channel.

Not being privy to TEAMCOM transmissions, she hadn't heard the exchange between John and Fred, and probably had no idea what had just happened.

Typical officer.

"Are you going to answer me?" she asked.

"Sorry, ma'am," John said. "I'm just trying to understand. Are you ordering me to abandon a band of castaways *and* the crew of an ONI salvage vessel?"

"Of course not," Petrov said a little too quickly. "We're on the surface, so you're in command."

"Yes, ma'am, I am," John said.

"But be sure you're thinking clearly," Petrov said. "If you start risking Spartans on low-value missions, you're not going to be in command for very long."

"That's a fair point, ma'am." John paused, grinding his teeth and fighting to retain his composure. "But I'll take my chances."

"You're making a mistake, son."

Petrov paused, giving him a chance to change his mind, but she was only making him angrier.

When John remained silent, Petrov sighed and continued, "But it's your call."

"I'm glad we agree on that," John said. "And, ma'am?"

"Yes?"

"Don't *ever* call me 'son.'"

CHAPTER 18

Nizat 'Kvarosee's quarry had emerged from the gorge and followed the ancient roadway across a thousand paces of talus-covered slope. There the road, so buried in shards of dark stone that it was barely discernible, reached the base of a cliff and turned back on itself in a tight switchback. The infidel column had just rounded the switchback and started to descend back along the road's second traverse.

At least, Nizat *assumed* the column was his quarry. Through the haze of heat refraction, all he could truly see was a line of about fifty dark-uniformed ghosts fluttering along behind a pair of self-propelled gun carts.

He had once heard a reconnaissance operative refer to the gun carts by their human name, *Warthogs*, and perhaps that was a better term. No worthy commander would allow his combat equipment to be encumbered with casualties, yet a scout had reported earlier that both gun carts were so burdened with disabled humans that the gunners barely had room to stand.

It was a problem Nizat hoped to soon eliminate for them.

He belly-crawled back into the gorge, where Tam 'Lakosee waited with what remained of the *Steadfast Strike*'s security cadre.

The steward took his arm and pulled him to his feet. Normally Nizat would not have allowed such a familiar gesture, but Nizat had run as far as anyone in the blistering heat, and he was grateful for the help.

He brushed the dust from his armor, then said to the steward, "Call the marksmen forward."

'Lakosee turned to relay the order, and Nizat took the opportunity to appraise his unit. Between heat deaths and the enemy's preemptive counterattack, he had already lost half his force. Judging by their slumped shoulders and unsteady posture, he would soon lose another quarter.

Had there been a cadre of Ground Swords available to him, the attrition would not have been so high. But surface warriors were usually more loyal to their clan *kaidon* than to the fleetmaster who ferried them to battle, and there had been no time to recruit one to his cause.

Ten Fleet Rangers armed with beam rifles and dressed in active-camouflage armor pushed forward through the mass. Nizat could tell by how their helmets sagged and their weapons dangled that they were suffering as much as he was. But there was little Nizat could do to give them rest—and nothing at all to cool them.

Distressingly, humans were even more vulnerable to heat than his Sangheili. Their red-faced bodies had lain curled along the roadside every few hundred paces through the gorge, and Nizat knew that if he did not catch up to the column soon, the entire complement from the ONI salvage ship would die from the elements.

And Nizat needed his quarry alive, because nothing would be gained by planting Luminal Beacons on dead bodies. He did not know much about ONI, but he was fairly certain that they would not go to much trouble to retrieve corpses.

Once his marksmen had gathered around, Nizat pointed toward the switchback on the far side of the slope.

"The time has come to corner these *igzuks*."

"How many shall we kill?" asked the tallest, a young blade named Bel 'Tuosee.

"Take out the gun carts first," Nizat said. "After you have accomplished that, continue firing. But confine your kills to their most efficient soldiers. Our attack must look real . . . but so should their victory."

'Tuosee tipped his helmet. "As it is commanded, so it shall be."

He and the other nine marksmen engaged their active camouflage, then dropped to their bellies and began to creep out onto the road. The light-bending technology made them almost invisible even from a few paces away, so crawling into position was probably an unnecessary precaution—especially given the image-blurring caused by N'ba's incessant heat. But beam rifle marksmen had cautious natures—it was an important survival trait—and they were taking no chances.

Still, Nizat could not help feeling nervous. With the Silent Shadow closing in on him—their scouts had certainly discovered the infidel salvage ship by now—the success of his plan, his only hope of redeeming himself with the gods, as well as the Prophets, rested on the abilities of the marksmen. It was all he could do to refrain from reminding them to watch for tripwires and pressure plates. This group of humans liked to lay traps even more than most, and so far the cadre had lost sixteen warriors to grenade blasts and fire mines.

Knowing that his admonitions would only prove a distraction, he turned back to 'Lakosee. "The Beacons are ready?" he asked. "The volunteers are clear on their assignments?"

"We are."

'Lakosee pulled an infidel emergency locator from his equipment pouch and handed it to Nizat. About half the size of a plasma grenade, the device had been captured from one of the humans who had died ambushing them back near the salvage ship, at the bottom of the slider-lines they had used to cross the gorge.

Nizat was not certain that the locator signal still worked properly—he had no way to confirm its function, even had he wished to risk testing it—but it now contained the Luminal Beacon that had originally been concealed inside the anti-gravity harness he had once hoped to trick the enemy into stealing.

He had been forced to rapidly change plans when the harness was damaged during the gorge crossing. While there was every reason to believe the humans would take a fully functional device back to their discovery temple, it seemed less likely that their attention would be captured by a piece of non-functional equipment. And it had occurred to him that while the humans would be cautious about examining any Covenant technology they captured, they would be more careless with their own equipment. So he had decided to improvise by planting the Beacon in a piece of equipment that an ONI infidel would carry home without thinking about it.

Nizat had never favored improvising in combat. But it seemed to be a technique that served the demon Spartans well, and the surest way to defeat one's enemy was to make their strengths your own.

He studied the captured locator long enough to confirm that the infidel device still looked somewhat natural, then asked 'Lakosee, "You intend to plant it yourself?"

"If you will allow me the honor."

"And you know who to look for?"

'Lakosee's helmet swung up and to the right, a sign of confirmation. "A specimen without fighting prowess, preferably without armor or weapons," he said. "A discovery priest who will be unlikely to recognize an insincere attack."

"Good." Nizat returned the device to 'Lakosee. "You will make me proud, there can be no doubt."

'Lakosee held his helmet a little higher, then turned and waved forward a huge warrior in the blue energy-shielded armor of a First Blade Fleet Ranger.

"You know Gri 'Waqilsee, Fleetmaster?"

"Of course."

To be precise, Nizat actually did not. While the Fleet of Unsung Piety was small, it still had three thousand crewmen—and he couldn't possibly remember all of their names. But this Gri 'Waqilsee was evidently the one who had volunteered to wear a faulty energy shield into battle and deliver the second Luminal Beacon. So it was only fitting to honor his courage by pretending to know his name.

"Tam 'Lakosee has spoken of your devotion."

"I am honored that you would say so." 'Waqilsee did not appear susceptible to flattery, but he seemed to appreciate the effort. "I will endeavor to be worthy."

"I have no doubt that you will."

What Nizat left unspoken was that he would be nearby to make certain 'Waqilsee had no second thoughts.

"The shield will last just long enough to draw the infidels' interest, and it will not self-destruct when you fall," 'Lakosee said. "Your death will be our signal to retreat. It will look as though your loss has demoralized us." Nizat looked 'Waqilsee up and down, then added, "Even so, if *I* were an infidel, I would be trembling in fear already."

Realizing that he had not yet heard the beam rifles attack, Nizat turned back toward the mouth of the gorge and peered out at the long, barely discernible terrace that marked the road's traverse across the talus slope. He knew the marksmen were there, but the only sign of their presence was a few blurs amid the rocks—and those could have been nothing but refraction ripples caused by rising heat.

He knelt on the roadbed, trying to peer out at the area near the switchback without presenting a silhouette that might draw the enemy's attention. The humans had stopped a quarter of the way along the lower traverse. The gun carts were idling at the head of the column. Behind the two vehicles, the humans sat on the slope with cloaks and other covers pulled over their heads to provide shade.

Thinking the drivers must be contemplating some hazard not visible from his vantage point, Nizat cautiously moved forward, working his way closer to the road edge so that he would have a clear view down the near side of the slope, where the plateau ended and the gorge spilled into the talus field.

The gorge bottom lay only a hundred paces below, a jumbled band of rounded boulders that turned sharply downhill and descended along the edge of the plateau in a dry riverbed that had probably once been a long, beautiful cataract.

Where the road reached the dry cataract, there stood the abutment of a fallen bridge that had spanned the river to enter the mouth of a large, dark tunnel.

The humans were contemplating the tunnel, Nizat realized. They were thinking about the cool relief they would find inside, planning a way to cross the dry cataract and haul everyone down a sheer cliff into the tunnel mouth.

And if they figured it out, Nizat's plan was ruined. They would have an excellent, defensible position where they could wait in comfort and pick off his force at leisure.

Nizat activated the communications unit inside his helmet. " 'Tuosee, why are you not yet attacking?"

"Because the angle is poor and the range is long," 'Tuosee said. "If we attack now, you will have a thousand paces of steep, graveled terrain to cross, and our ability to cover you will be limited. If we wait—"

"There is no time."

It was voice of Ob 'Nathisee, shipmaster of the *Steadfast Strike*, cutting into the transmission. "The Silent Shadow has arrived. Their first transport reached the infidel ship a full unit ago, and as we departed, we saw it entering—"

"You have taken the *Steadfast Strike* and *departed*?" Nizat was in complete disbelief. Truly, fate was playing the cruelest of tricks in what had become an utter folly here on this godsforsaken planet.

"Only the plateau, Fleetmaster," 'Nathisee said. "We are still on N'ba, but we had to move. The Silent Shadow sent a Banshee flight after us as well."

Nizat took a breath, then said, "You did well. But if the Silent Shadow arrived a *unit* ago, why am I only hearing about it now?"

"We have been trying to raise you since we saw the first transport," 'Nathisee said. "We had almost lost hope."

Of course. Nizat had been deep inside the gorge, and the *Steadfast Strike* had been . . . where, exactly?

"What is your present location?"

"We await your will out in the mirage lands."

"You are in the *open*?" Nizat began to wonder if it was really 'Nathisee to whom he was speaking. The voice sounded like the shipmaster's . . . but the assassins of the Silent Shadow had their tricks. "What of the Banshees the Silent Shadow sent?"

"Destroyed by the humans. I am hearing from Shipmaster 'Weyo-dosee that your plan is working. The humans have engaged the Fleet of Swift Justice, and they are keeping it well occupied."

"Welcome news," Nizat replied. If 'Weyodosee was in contact, that meant Nizat's flagship, the *Quiet Faith*, still survived. "And what action is the Flotilla of Unsung Piety taking?"

"Awaiting your return, Fleetmaster."

"I see." Nizat did not really understand why he felt so disappointed. He would have done the same thing in their place. "My loyal shipmasters are waiting to see if I survive down here."

"They are reluctant to engage Covenant vessels, worthy Fleetmaster. And the humans are buying us time to escape. If the *Steadfast Strike* launches soon, the battle will serve as a distraction."

"A wise thought," Nizat said. "You have read our location?"

"We have."

"Then await us at the foot of the plateau, where a dry cataract tumbles alongside the cliff. We will join you once we are finished here."

'Nathisee did not acknowledge the order.

"We will not be long," Nizat said. "The humans are in sight now."

"I understand that. I heard the marksman's report." 'Nathisee hesitated, then finally said, "But you *cannot* wait, wise Fleetmaster. There are demons behind you too."

"Spartans." *Of course* there were Spartans. They had been sent by the gods to be his personal tormentors. "How many?"

"It is impossible to say," 'Nathisee said. "We observed just two, but only because the Silent Shadow was upon us. Had we not left at that moment, the demons would have boarded us before we knew they were coming."

"How could that be?" Nizat demanded. "Did you not post a guard?"

"Of course, Fleetmaster," 'Nathisee said. "But you know how the demons are—they appear when they wish, then vanish before you realize they have destroyed you. We only saw these two because they had to show themselves when they fought off the Banshee attack."

"Wait," Nizat said. "You are telling me they saved you from a Banshee attack?"

"Exactly," 'Nathisee said. "The Banshees arrived as soon as we launched. They were coming in from our flank, and then two demons rose out of the brush and surprised them. They destroyed one and drove the others off."

"And then what?"

"Then we were gone," 'Nathisee said. "But our sensors . . . what we saw made no sense. The surviving Banshees returned to take their vengeance . . . and then they vanished."

"Vanished."

"There were some stray signals above the clouds," 'Nathisee said. "Perhaps some demon fighter craft—"

"Now the Spartans have fighter craft?"

"Possibly, Fleetmaster," 'Nathisee said. "I cannot say. The only thing I know is that there could have been a hundred demons on the plateau, and we would not have realized it until they killed us and captured the ship. And they must have entered the gorge behind you."

"Never assume what a Spartan must do. You will regret it every time." Nizat grew thoughtful, then said, "But that would put them behind the Silent Shadow's transports as well, would it not?"

"Certainly so," 'Nathisee said. "Both vehicles were traveling toward the same place where the human gun carts entered the gorge. Where else could the transports have gone?"

Nizat thought for a moment, then clacked his mandibles in satisfaction. "Nowhere else. The transports *have* to be behind us."

'Lakosee, who had been standing in front of Nizat, listening to the entire exchange, tipped his helmet to the left.

"Forgive me, Fleetmaster," he said. "But does that make you *glad*?"

"Oh yes. Very glad indeed."

"Why?"

"Because *now* I understand. The Spartans are not my curse." Nizat turned and looked back up the canyon—an area he now thought of as the Gorge of Deep Resolve. "They are my salvation."

'Lakosee glanced away, nervously seeking the gaze of Gri 'Waqil-see, then slowly looked back to Nizat.

"Fleetmaster, perhaps the heat has grown too much—"

"I am well, Tam. . . . I *am*."

'Lakosee looked back to 'Waqilsee.

Nizat slapped both hands on 'Lakosee's shoulders. "In fact, I am better than I have been in a long, long time." He turned the steward so they were facing each other. "The Spartans are a gift from the gods. Do you not see? They were sent to save us from the Silent Shadow."

CHAPTER 19

1438 hours, June 7, 2526 (military calendar)
Serpentine Canyon, Crystal Bush Plateau
Mountains of Despair, Planet Netherop, Ephyra System

Linda had constructed the sniper's nest—a big slab of slate laid over two rows of low stones—more for the Castoff Roselle's sake than her own. In her climate-controlled Mjolnir armor, Linda could lie out all day and remain operational. But no human, not even someone born into this brutal environment, could endure the blare of Netherop's sun for more than twenty minutes and be fully ready to fight.

"Why do they wait?" Roselle's words were little more than a whisper, though it was unlikely anyone would hear. There was a hot, blistering wind coming upslope that would prevent her voice from carrying to anyone below. "It's been fifty breaths since anyone moved."

Their nest—properly called a *hide*—was atop the plateau's edge, half a kilometer above an almost indiscernible road that left the mouth of the canyon and descended across a thousand-meter talus field to a tight switchback turn. There, about fifty meters down the road past the switchback, the human crew of the *Wheatley* sat behind two idling Warthogs, trying to shade themselves with cloaks and tarps.

Linda and Roselle had been in position for thirteen minutes, having climbed out of the gorge after Linda scouted ahead and realized the Covenant column had reached the gorge's mouth and stopped to reconnoiter. Seven minutes ago, Linda had noticed the telltale refraction of active camouflage—and pointed out to Roselle the spectral blurs of three Elite marksmen crawling down the first leg of the talus-buried road. A trio of snipers was overkill in an area as small as the talus field, and Linda suspected the aliens were preparing to launch a shock attack against the *Wheatley* crew.

If she was right, there were probably several more of them out there. She just hadn't spotted them yet.

"Well?" Roselle asked. "What are they waiting for?"

Linda wasn't sure whether Roselle was referring to the marksmen or to the *Wheatley*'s crew—but it really didn't matter. As soon as *someone* moved, it was game on.

"We are in no hurry," Linda said. "The longer they wait, the longer we have to find our targets."

"You're not getting anxious?"

"There is no reason to be anxious." Linda saw a stone wobble just below the road's edge and had her computer mark the location as TARGET FOUR. "The fight will start when it is time. Until then, I prepare."

"You must get bored," Roselle said. "I wish they would do *something*."

"Stop wishing." Whatever occupation Roselle might choose to

pursue after leaving Netherop, Linda hoped it would not be as a sniper. "The time will then go faster. You must be in the moment."

"I've never heard anything so stupid," Roselle whispered. "What does that mean, *be in the moment*? We're always *in* the moment, and then we're in the next one."

"But do you always pay attention?" Linda asked. "Look at the way images shimmer in the heat. At the white patch the sun makes in the clouds. Listen to how the wind rasps across the stones. One way or another, you will not have many more of these moments on Netherop."

"And you think that'll be a bad thing?"

"There must be something about Netherop you will miss."

"Would that be the heat . . . or the disease?" Roselle asked. "Or being hungry and thirsty all the time, or getting cooked before your children are old enough to know your name?"

"I suppose I would not miss those things either," Linda said. "But I hope you won't be disappointed in your new world, wherever that is. Every planet has its own kind of beauty—and its own kind of hell."

"You have visited many planets?"

"*Visited* is not a word I would use . . ." In the distance, a fireball punched through the cloud canopy and dropped toward the far horizon. Then another appeared, closer at hand, and Linda recognized the narrow nose of a *Halberd*-class destroyer protruding from the front of the flames. She began to wonder if any of them would ever reach another planet at this rate. "But I have been on many worlds, yes."

"To fight?"

"Sometimes only to train."

"But more often to fight the aliens," Roselle surmised. "What is this war about anyway?"

"The aliens are trying to destroy us," Linda said. "Every last one of us, everywhere, it seems."

"But why?"

"They believe it is the will of their gods," Linda said. Roselle was asking questions Linda had meditated on many times. So far the answer had eluded her. "I don't know why they would believe such a thing. Nobody does. Maybe killing us is just in their nature."

"Or maybe your generals are afraid to tell you the real reason," Roselle said. "Maybe the UNSC did something so terrible to the aliens that its commanders can't even let its own soldiers know what that was."

Linda actually looked away from the field of combat and found Roselle staring at her, scowling in complete seriousness.

"No." Linda gazed back down the slope. "That is not it."

"So . . . you're in on it, then?"

"Negative," Linda said. "There is nothing for me to be *in* on."

"Then why do you want to kill all the aliens?"

"I don't *want* to kill them," Linda said. "I just want to stop them from killing *us*."

"Good luck with that. You do realize that as long as you keep killing them, they're going to keep killing you—and the rest of us along with you." Roselle pulled the charging handle of the MA5B that Linda had entrusted to her. "And it doesn't sound like things are going very well for our side."

"They are not," Linda admitted. "But there is nothing to do about it. Such things are above me. *Far* above me."

"So that's it?" Roselle asked. "You just fight and die?"

"I try to take the long view. Then there is not so much to worry about."

"I'd say dying is a lot to worry about," Roselle said.

Linda shrugged. "We all die. You, me, all living things. Life is a temporary state."

She saw a plume of dust rising near the switchback, then scanned the area with her sniper sight until she spotted the rippling blur of active camouflage. An Elite marksman was working his way into position behind the *Wheatley* crew.

"And the end of life, that is just timing," Linda said. She checked the range to her target—eleven hundred meters. "Ear protection."

"What?"

"*Now.*"

Without even waiting to see if Roselle had complied, Linda fired. Two heartbeats later, the Elite's armor flickered into view as her sniper rifle's large round blew the front out of the alien's torso armor.

Linda followed the priority arrow toward her next target and set the aiming reticle just to the right of a dodging blur. The range was only eight hundred meters this time, and it took the round only one heartbeat to arrive.

She had hoped to catch the target in the flank as he spun around, but her aim had been a little high. When the alien's active camouflage failed, she saw his helmet tumbling away from his torso.

The priority arrow directed her to the next preselected target, but Linda could not find the blur of refracted light that she expected. She wondered if the marksman had followed the contrails of her first two bullets back to their hide and simultaneously spun around, his beam rifle ready to fire. If so, her next shot would be her last, because a particle beam was every bit as deadly as the 14.5x114mm high-velocity, armor-piercing round her own weapon fired.

But it had only been four heartbeats since Linda opened fire from above and behind the aliens. Nobody was that fast, not even an Elite.

She switched to her next target and glimpsed a blur diving behind a low outcropping of shale. She put a round in four centimeters from the edge, drawing a spray of stone flakes. An Elite with a fist-size hole in his backplate rose and staggered away. A few centimeters of brittle shale was not much protection from firepower that could punch through a meter-thick concrete wall.

Linda followed the priority arrow to her last target. He was motionless, so she could not see his camouflage-blur—even when she looked directly at him.

But then she noticed the forks of a beam rifle emitter nozzle protruding from the uphill side of a talus heap. It was not pointed quite in her direction, so she set her targeting reticle about a meter back from the muzzle and fired. It was always good to know the specs of the enemy's weapons.

The range was only five hundred meters, almost point-blank for an SRS99, but this time Linda could only assume that her attack was fatal. No sooner had she pulled the trigger than particle beams began to drill through stone all around her. Roselle's MA5B chattered endlessly as she returned fire on full auto. The roof of their hide began to rain shards.

Then Linda felt a sudden shudder in the surrounding stone. It was much too large and deep to be caused by the collapse of the roof over their little hide. But there wasn't a lot of time to wonder about it either. She retreated toward the back exit.

Roselle's assault rifle clicked empty. Instead of following Linda, she reached for a fresh magazine. Linda grabbed her by the leg and forcibly dragged her out.

"You need to fire and *move!*" Linda ejected her magazine and inserted a fresh one into the SRS99's receiver slot.

Roselle looked confused. *"What?"*

For a moment, Linda thought Roselle had just failed to insert her ear protection and been temporarily deafened by the sniper rifle's boom inside the hide.

Then she realized that the ground was not only still shudder-ing, but the tremor was actually growing more powerful. And Linda hadn't truly heard Roselle's reply, either. There was a roar in the air so loud that Linda had only recognized the shape of Roselle's lips as she mouthed the response.

Linda rose, then looked toward the talus field and saw a wall of dust billowing up. She crept to the edge of the outcropping and peered into a rumbling black cloud so thick she could not see fifty meters into it. The entire slope had let loose, and now it was crashing down toward the mountainside in an immense rockslide.

Roselle stepped to Linda's side, watching openmouthed until the roar began to subside, then finally tapped her on the arm and shouted, "How did you *do* that?"

Even now, the rumble was so deafening that Linda barely heard the question. She raised the volume of her voicemitter to maximum before replying.

"It was not me," Linda said. She continued to peer toward the switchback on the far side of the bowl, waiting for the dust to set-tle so she could see what had become of the *Wheatley*'s crew. "But now you understand about waiting. The crew was trying to draw the aliens into the slide area. Many of them are engineers, and that is what military engineers do: build ways to kill the enemy."

Roselle's lips wormed into a look of disgust, and she mouthed, "Nice."

"Yes. It is better than dying." Linda glanced back toward the cleft they had used to climb up from the gorge, then asked, "Can you climb down alone?"

Roselle nodded. The roar had diminished to a growl, and Linda could understand her without much trouble when she yelled her an-swer. "On Netherop, you don't live to be an old woman if you don't know how to climb!"

Linda studied Roselle more carefully. Though her skin was weathered, she did not look that much older than Linda herself—certainly no more than her midtwenties.

"How old *are* you, really?"

"Old enough," Roselle said. "I've carried six kids."

"Six?" Linda did some math and decided her assumptions were probably not far off—Roselle could easily be in her midtwenties. "And your children—they are with the others back in the runners?"

"The two that are still alive, yes."

"Ah." Linda suddenly felt sad for Roselle, though she wasn't quite sure why. Children were dying by the millions on a dozen different worlds. Maybe it was because Linda had a shot at saving the ones in this particular place. "Then I will try to be sure those two grow old."

"That'd be nice," Roselle said. "But what about your 'life is a temporary state' speech?"

"Temporary does not always mean short." Linda pointed her toward the cleft, then said, "There is no telling what the aliens will do now. Make sure Samson is ready. And tell him not to be brave."

"Trust me, Samson knows how to run an ambush." Roselle pushed the fresh magazine into her MA5B. "He's old too."

Roselle started toward the cleft, and Linda watched her go. She had *no* idea what the Elites were trying to do, so she had left Samson down in the gorge, ready to launch an ambush in case the Covenant decided to turn around and go back for some reason. It didn't seem likely, but John was right—when it came to the aliens, you needed to be ready for anything.

After Roselle had taken a few steps, Linda called out, "Roselle?"

The young woman stopped and turned, frowning. *"What?"*

"The charging handle." Linda made a pulling motion with her free hand. "You must load the first cartridge manually."

"Sure." Roselle pointed the rifle at the ground and fumbled around beneath the rear sight, then found the handle and pulled it back. "I remember that."

Linda shook her head and returned to their ruined hide. The Castoffs were far from trained soldiers, but they did have good survival sense. She would just have to trust that, if the need arose, they would stay calm—and keep their weapons pointed at the enemy.

After two full minutes, the rockslide was finally diminishing. The growl had faded to a steady clattering, and the dust had dissipated enough to allow glimpses of bare stone. In light of recent events, there no longer seemed much sense in maintaining comm silence. Linda opened the emergency channel.

"Blue Four, any *Wheatley* crewman. Sitrep."

"*Wheatley* Actual," replied a deep male voice. It would be Dkani himself, unless the captain had been killed and replaced by a subordinate. "First, if that was you on the '99, thanks. We failed to see that infiltration attempt coming."

"And the Covenant did not see your rockslide coming," Linda said. "You won this fight."

"Maybe we didn't lose," Dkani said. "But winning is a stretch. We have two Warthogs, and fifty crewmembers in no condition to walk."

"What is your weapons status?" Linda asked.

"I'm not sure that matters right now," Dkani said. "Without transport, we're going to die of heat exhaustion anyway. And from what I've seen, so will the Covenant."

"First we survive." Linda put a note of censure in her voice. Half of surviving *anything* was holding on to the belief and the will to keep on. "Then we transport."

"Of course," Dkani said. "We have the light antiaircraft guns on the two Warthogs, with four thousand rounds of ammunition each. Probably thirty assault rifles with two or three magazines apiece."

"Grenades? Launchers?"

"We're not an assault company," Dkani said. "We had some thermite paste and C7, but that's long gone."

"It's no problem," Linda said. She stood and scanned the area. Everywhere she looked, the terrain was rugged, broken, and steep—a nightmare extraction zone at best, especially for a unit of half-dead scientists and engineers. "Your situation is very good."

"You think so?"

"Oh yes," Linda said. "Piece of pie, trust me."

As she spoke, the clatter of boots began to rise from the depths of the gorge. The rim was thirty meters down a craggy slope from her current position, so Linda could not tell which way the aliens were heading. But she didn't think it was back into the gorge, toward the Castoffs—if the aliens had decided to withdraw, they wouldn't be running.

The dust from the rockslide had thinned to a hazy veil, and she could see that most of the slope ahead had been swept clean of talus. All that remained between her and the *Wheatley*'s crew was eight hundred meters of steep bare slate. The slope was divided into an upper and lower section by a long swath of loose talus, which had accumulated on and buried the roadbed as the rockslide swept over.

But the engineers had carefully picked the column's stopping place. The lead Warthog sat atop a small vertical ridge, which had served to direct the rockslide away from the *Wheatley*'s survivors and back toward the middle of the slope.

"Now the aliens are coming to charge you." Linda didn't want the captain to panic, so she added, "That is a good thing, really."

"Sure it is," Dkani said. "Now we don't have to wait for the heat to kill us. The Covenant will do it faster."

"How you die does not matter," Linda said. "Only that you don't. There is no sense arranging transport if you get killed."

"You believe it's possible *not* to?"

"It is, if you listen to me," Linda said. "The Covenant will be worried about the Warthogs and your LAAGs first, so you must use them as soon as the fighting starts. Do not hold back. Open fire as soon as you see the enemy. If your gunners can see the mouth of the gorge, open fire now."

"But we have only four thousand rounds for each gun," Dkani said. "And LAAGs fire five hundred rounds a minute. We'll be out of ammunition in eight minutes."

"Open fire *now*," Linda said. "You are not going to run out of ammunition."

"Oh." Dkani paused a moment, then said, "I see."

Dkani's voice grew muffled as he issued an order, and the LAAGs opened up an instant later. Alien voices began to scream near the mouth of the gorge.

"Good," Linda said. "Now have everyone dig belly scrapes in the talus. Pile the refuse on the uphill side, but leave a firing port."

"You mean dig foxholes?!" He had to shout to make himself heard, because he was apparently standing close behind the two Warthogs. "We don't have many shovels!"

"Not foxholes. You do not have time for that." Linda was starting to grow impatient. Did ship captains not attend basic infantry school? "Just scrape a hole with your helmets or your hands and pile the talus up around it."

"Yes. I think we can do that!"

Again, Dkani's voice grew muffled as he relayed the order. The screech and thump of Covenant weapons sounded from the gorge mouth as the aliens began to return fire.

"Have everyone in the belly scrapes hold their fire until the aliens are only fifty paces away."

"That's terribly close!" Dkani said, still shouting. "The MA5B's range is almost ten times that!"

"Your people have only three magazines each," Linda said. "And they do not know how to shoot. If they open fire at five hundred meters, they will kill no one."

"I'll try!" Dkani's voice was barely audible over the LAAG fire.

"You must do better than try, Captain, if you want to stay alive." Linda dropped into her old hide without bothering to cover it. Any alien countersnipers were long gone—along with most of the talus on the mountain. "And, Captain?"

"Yes?"

"Move away from the Warthogs," Linda said. "You are the commander. You should not be so close to such high-priority targets."

The enemy began to emerge from the gorge and cross the slope toward the *Wheatley*'s crew. The aliens who tried to race across the bare stone started to slip and slide within the first few steps, and they quickly gave up and returned to the talus-covered road. This made it easier for the LAAG gunners on the Warthogs to cut them down. A dozen Elite bodies simply came apart as the big rounds tore into them.

Then a trio of purple beams shot from the mouth of the gorge, burning three holes through the first LAAG's feed assembly. Ammunition began to cook off, and before Linda knew it, the gunner and primary weapon were flying from the Warthog in separate directions.

Three beams, so three marksmen. Leaving the SRS99 behind, Linda pulled her MA5C off its magmount, confirmed there was a grenade in the underslung launcher, then raced down the craggy slope to the rim of the gorge and peered over.

The three Elite marksmen were kneeling two hundred meters below, on the far side of the road. Their rifles were of a kind she had not seen before, and they were braced atop stacks of stone, waiting to recharge as the marksmen lined up their shots on the second Warthog. Twenty meters behind them, and half-hidden by the lip of the rim, stood a cluster of Elites in more elaborate armor. Linda was not sure whether they were officers or special warriors, but they were clearly waiting for the first waves of the attack to deplete their quarry's ammunition.

Even Linda couldn't kill everyone at once. She fired the grenade down into the midst of the rifle marksmen, then watched as the detonation hurled them forward into their weapon braces. In the next half-second, she put a three-shot burst through the head of each marksman to finish him off, and in the half-second after that, another three-shot burst into each rifle to make certain the weapons could not be used by anyone else.

By then the warriors in the fancy armor had turned in her direction and were firing their plasma rifles up along the gorge wall. Their angle was just as terrible as hers, so no one had a chance of hitting anybody. Still, she needed to keep them guessing. Linda stepped back from the line of fire, reloaded her grenade launcher, grabbed a hand grenade out of her satchel, then fired the 40mm and dropped the M9 into their midst.

Grenades were really not all that deadly in the open—especially against well-armored opponents—but they did attract a target's attention. After they picked themselves up, the Elites stumbled away from the attack zone and turned to fire up at her. Linda emptied the last of her magazine into the nearest one, then backed away from the gorge to consider her next move.

One more alien warrior down—who knew how many to go? But the second LAAG was still firing, more than three minutes into the battle. The engineers were doing better than she had expected.

Over TEAMCOM, she called, "Blue Four, requesting sitrep any Blue member."

When the channel remained quiet, she tried one more time, then decided she was still on her own . . . at least for a while. Without a satellite relay, TEAMCOM did not have much range, and the sharp curves and high walls of the meandering gorge would play havoc with its limited signal bounce capabilities. The rest of the team would be coming just as soon as they finished with the *Lucky Break*. She was sure of that. But it was anyone's guess as to how long it would take them to the secure the frigate first.

She lobbed another M9 into the gorge just to keep the Elites on their toes, then returned to her old hide and took up the SRS99 again. In theory, her attacks would make the aliens reluctant to continue their advance, since it was now clear that they would be attacked from the rear. They would pause their own assault until someone could flank her and eliminate the threat. That would mean retreating a half kilometer to the cleft she and Roselle had used—the same cleft where Samson and a handful of adolescent Castoffs were waiting to ambush the Covenant with assault rifles and sling-thrown hand grenades.

But aliens weren't much on human tactical theory. Instead, they just poured out of the gorge en masse, scrambling across the bare stone and the talus-covered road in clusters of two and three that were easy targets for the second Warthog's LAAG. Linda saw a trio of warriors cut in half as a burst swept across their midsections, and another pair that erupted in a purple spray when the Warthog's un-disciplined gunner lingered too long.

Still the aliens charged. Ten clusters, and in each one, a single

Elite carried a long-range carbine, which he shouldered and began to fire as the clusters drew to within five hundred meters of the Warthog.

Linda held her fire. She was a special asset, and her job here was to leverage her attacks by identifying and eliminating the elements crucial to the enemy's strategy.

So far, she had no idea what that strategy was.

Linda's motion detector would alert her if anyone approached to within twenty-five meters, but that would still allow a top-notch scout enough room to creep over the rim and launch a flank attack while she was distracted. She made a five second scan to check and saw . . . nothing.

Whatever the Covenant was up to, it didn't make sense.

She returned her attention to the battle. Now that the aliens were within carbine range of the second Warthog, they had dropped to their bellies and were continuing to crawl forward. Every couple of seconds, a rifleman would pause to return fire. They were close enough that the carbines' radioactive rounds were starting to dimple the Warthog's body. Worse, they were distracting the LAAG gunner—and he still had plenty of ammuntion left. The battle was only five minutes old.

Linda opened fire on the rifleman farthest from her, targeting not his head but the carbine itself. The weapon blew apart in his hands, taking one appendage with it. She did not bother to finish him. He was no longer a threat, and there were plenty of aliens who were.

She moved on to the next rifleman and fired again. This time the carbine broke in two, the butt slamming into the Elite's helmet so hard it sent him sliding down the slope headfirst. She risked two more attacks, taking out another carbine and a warrior when he lifted his helmet at the last instant, then crawled back from the edge to change the SRS99's four-round magazine—and to check for any hostiles creeping into position behind her.

Still no sign of any countersniper efforts.

A chain of crackling detonations indicated a change in alien tactics. She moved a few meters upslope and crept onto an outcropping she had identified earlier as an alternate firing position.

The Elites had resumed their charge, this time behind a barrage of plasma grenades. They were still out of range and blasting only bare moutainside. But sheets of flame and smoke were erupting ever closer to the *Wheatley* survivors, and the LAAG gunner seemed uncertain of how to respond. Sometimes he fired into the flames, and sometimes streamed rounds to either side. No matter what, the Covenant used the concealment to good effect, rushing forward in half a dozen different areas at once.

But the Elites in the elaborate armor remained near the back of the charge, still using those in front to screen their approach, and that was not normal. Elite commanders usually took the lead, inspiring their followers through their own ferocity. Whatever the enemy was planning, the guys in the elaborate armor were the key.

Linda identified eight targets, two groups of three and one group of two, who seemed to be hanging back. Seeing no clear way to determine who was the most important, she put a round through the middle figure of the rearmost trio.

The warrior pitched forward at an angle, tripping the companion on his downhill side, and the pair began a swift slide down a bare face of rock. The Elite on the uphill side stopped and turned to extend a hand toward the one who had stumbled over the casualty. The uphill alien was unusually large, with a stocky frame and a generator pack on his backplate, so Linda assumed he was probably just a bodyguard for one of the others.

Linda quickly moved to the next trio. Taking a cue from the bodyguard's automatic reach in the first group, she shot the Elite on the second group's downhill side. As his chest erupted in a purple spray, his companions' only reaction was to break into an evasive dodge and continue their charge.

So, not too important.

She moved to the last group on her list of targets, the pair running together, close behind the main body of warriors. She blew a hole through both of their torsos in a pair of quick shots, then backed away from the outcropping's edge to avoid being targeted while reloading. It was probably an unnecessary precaution, given the Covenant's unwavering focus on their charge, but . . . better safe than dead.

Linda had barely slipped the fresh magazine into the receiver when the second Warthog's LAAG finally stopped firing. Seven minutes into the battle—he had lasted a lot longer than she expected. She rolled into the third firing position she had selected—a small hollow at the base of the outcropping she had just been atop—then crept forward until she had a clear view down onto the slope.

The second Warthog was in flames, and now the Elites were charging the *Wheatley*'s survivors at a full sprint. The aliens were still two hundred meters away, but the crew's assault rifles began to rattle off panicked, magazine-emptying bursts that managed to drop only three enemies.

The time for tactical leverage was gone. Linda traded the SRS99 for her MA5C and leaped out onto the smooth shale. Her boots immediately slipped out from beneath her, but she spun onto her butt, picked up her feet, and began to descend the steep slope in a half-controlled slide. All she really needed to worry about was catching on something and launching herself into a tumble, and in her Mjolnir, even that would not be disastrous.

Leaning back and controlling her descent with her elbows, she watched the battle with growing concern. The aliens had only closed to within a hundred meters, and already the *Wheatley*'s assault weapon fire was dropping off due to ammunition depletion.

Linda was five meters from the road when her motion tracker showed a bunch of FRIEND designators approaching fast. She turned to find a pair of Castoff mountain runners scurrying across the talus, with Samson standing behind the microwave weapon in the lead vehicle. There were six adolescent Castoffs kneeling in the passenger compartment behind him, armed with assault rifles, submachine guns, and shotguns—all pale with fear, but brows furrowed in determination. Roselle was not among them.

Linda checked the next vehicle—and did not see Roselle in that one either. She was glad. Whatever Samson thought he was doing was a bad idea, and the Castoffs were going to need someone left alive to lead them. She reached behind her and scratched her fingers against the stone until she began to slow, then planted her heels and launched herself on an interception trajectory.

"Incoming!" she yelled. "Make a hole!"

The Castoffs swung their heads around, then dived for the corners of the passenger compartment as Linda began the downward leg of her arc. She tucked and spun into a forward flip, then landed on the deck in a lunge position, trying to absorb the impact in the bend of her forward leg.

Linda had no trouble keeping her balance, but the runner tipped onto its downhill legs and started to go over—until she hurled herself against the uphill side and rocked it back down.

Samson looked back over his shoulder, his brow arched and his mouth hanging. "Next time, just *ask*. We'll stop."

Linda ignored the complaint. "What are you doing here?"

"The aliens did not come to the ambush," Samson said. "So we're bringing the ambush to the aliens."

"That is not how ambushes work."

"You want us to go back?" Samson looked back toward the gorge. "I don't think it will work. The aliens don't seem to like your plan."

"No. They seem to have a different plan. Whatever it is." Linda tried again to raise John on TEAMCOM, but there was still too much signal interference. She sighed and said, "We will keep going."

"I agree." Samson turned to the driver, a broad-cheeked woman with a long mane of dusty red hair, and said, "Keep going."

The driver had not shown the slightest sign of slowing down.

Linda stood. "What would you have done if I said to turn around?"

Samson flashed a broken-toothed grin. "Keep going," he said. "We talked about it, and we decided we are going to help you save your friends. There will be no excuse for you to go back on your word."

"We won't."

"So you say." Samson looked forward again. "But you *are* UNSC."

Linda shook her head in exasperation. "Just do as I order," she said, pointing skyward, "and I'll try to get you up there alive."

Samson nodded. "I will hold you to that. And there is something you should know." He jerked his chin behind them. "We saw your friends rounding a bend in a tall floating thing. It's five hundred breaths behind us."

"You're sure it was my friends?" Linda asked. Five hundred breaths converted to a little over half an hour—not soon enough to swing the battle—and "tall floating thing" sounded like a Covenant troop carrier. "I have been trying to contact them and gotten nothing."

"I am sure," Samson said. "They were too far back to signal, but the driver's helmet didn't look long like one of the aliens'. It was more like yours and John's, except that it had a big round face."

"Okay," Linda said. He was definitely referring to Kelly's helmet. "It's good to know somebody will be here to pick up the pieces."

She stepped into the front of the runner and saw the nearest clusters of aliens about three hundred meters ahead. The most distant clusters were already approaching the switchback and stepping off the road, pouring plasma bolts down the slope toward the *Wheatley*'s crew, who lay sheltered in their hastily dug belly scrapes. There wasn't a lot of return fire coming from the humans.

"How far can you sling those grenades I gave you?"

"Not far," Samson said. "Maybe half this distance."

"Okay, when we close to a third of this distance, launch everything you have," Linda said. "Don't wait for my order."

"I wasn't planning to."

Firing from a moving vehicle was going to be difficult, but Linda found the Elite in the ornate armor who'd stumbled over her earlier kill, then set the targeting reticle in the center of his back.

The reticle kept bouncing, and not in a predictable pattern. The runner's spiderlike legs kept slipping in the talus, and its sporadic gait made a poor firing platform.

She fired a three-round burst and saw a spray of stone chips rise two paces ahead of her target.

The Elite reacted instantly, diving headlong down the slope and starting an uncontrolled slide toward the smoking wreckage of a Warthog. Linda could never hit him now, so she shifted fire to the huge warrior who had been running alongside him. When a fountain of stone chips shot up beside him, he and several other aliens began to return fire over their shoulders. But they were shooting on the run with plasma weapons that lacked enough range and did not pose much of a threat . . . yet.

She fired again, emptying her magazine and watching her rounds skip off his torso as his heavy energy shield deflected her attack. Too bad. If not for the extra protection, she might have taken him down.

As she changed her magazine and lined up her next shot, a half dozen grenades dropped into the midst of the Covenant advance and detonated—hurling her target to the ground and taking his shields down. She managed to hold her attack until he came to a rest, then put three rounds through his flank, just under the rib cage.

Somehow, even mortally wounded, he managed to push himself up and turn toward her. Linda put another long burst into him, and he finally dropped and stopped moving.

The other Elites in the cadre were in full melee mode now, rushing the belly scrapes with little fear of being shot by their ammo-depleted quarry. Linda did a quick count and thought there might be twenty to thirty aliens still fighting. Taking them down would be a challenge, since they seemed determined to battle to the death. But she would be attacking from behind, so she could dispatch ten before the others realized what was happening. She just hoped the cadre didn't have any more warriors lurking around in active camouflage.

Or utilizing those heavy energy shields.

No more thinking. She was starting to sound like Dkani. Linda grabbed an M7 from a Castoff and checked to be sure it was fully loaded, then braced a foot on the edge of the runner.

"Take your runners around the switchback," she ordered Samson. "And shoot over the aliens' heads. *Not* into the fight. Over their heads."

"What good will that do?"

"You won't kill me, to start," Linda said. "And if you want John to keep his word . . ."

"Okay, then," Samson said.

Linda was already jumping. She landed just beneath the edge of the road, where the talus was still thick, so she didn't tumble to the ground. She started downslope, using the MA5C to fire three-round bursts into the aliens' backs, putting down four Elites in six tries. It felt too easy—like the Covenant didn't even care they were being mowed down from behind.

She killed another one, and then she was in the middle of the *Wheatley* survivors, where the aliens were firing down into the belly scrapes and slashing around with energy swords. Linda went to work with the M7, jamming the barrel down on an Elite clavicle, then against a neck, then firing six-round bursts, dropping three more warriors before a squad of five looked up from the carnage they were dealing.

Finally, they seemed to realize *they* were the ones in trouble.

The squad was arranged in a semicircle around three belly scrapes, where two pudgy men wearing engineering badges were trying to pull a slender Elite in ornate armor off a gray-haired woman. The Elite was kneeling astride her, trying to free his arms to attack, while his four companions stood around him facing outward, using their plasma rifles to cut down anyone attempting to fire into the melee. When they saw Linda coming in their direction, the four aliens stepped around and closed ranks, putting themselves between her and their companion, and swung their plasma rifles around.

"Take cover!" Linda shouted.

The two engineers looked confused, and one started to open his mouth.

Linda fired the grenade launcher at the aliens' feet and felt a blast of heat and shrapnel as the detonation flattened her targets. Not waiting for the fireball to contract, she stepped into their midst and alternated between the M7 and the MA5C, putting a burst through each helmet. The submachine gun clicked empty as the third helmet shattered, and so did the assault rifle as the fourth one puckered and split.

Linda turned toward the gray-haired woman, expecting to find a bloody mass. But the woman was on her side, curled into a fetal position, covering her head and screaming.

So far, so good.

Luckily, the Covenant had taken the brunt of the grenade blast, and the two engineers were staggering back to their feet. Both were peppered with superficial shrapnel cuts, and one was bleeding from the ear and the nose—a result of having his jaw clamped tight when the grenade detonated. The other had some shallow nicks in his scalp that were pouring blood like a waterfall. Head wounds were like that—they looked scary, and sometimes they were.

Linda tossed her M7 along with a couple of magazines to the one bleeding from his ear and nose, and pointed him toward his injured friend. Then she ejected the magazine from her assault rifle, inserted a fresh one into the receiver, and began to look for her next target.

There weren't any.

The Castoffs had rounded the switchback in their mountain runners and were racing back down the road at full speed. They were whooping and yelling, firing their weapons in long inefficient bursts over the heads of the surviving Elites—who had evidently realized they were being flanked and decided to withdraw down the slope.

At a full sprint.

So much for fighting to the death.

There were only about twenty of them left, and Linda would have loved to finish the job. But a damage chime was sounding inside her Mjolnir, and there was going to be no shortage of wounded among the *Wheatley* survivors. She checked to confirm the Mjolnir problem was nothing important—just a small tear where a piece of shrapnel had slipped through a joint to her inner skinsuit—then turned back to the three lucky survivors.

"Everyone okay?"

One of the men pointed to his ears. That was what happened when you didn't cover up before a grenade detonation. Their hearing would recover—mostly—in a few hours.

The woman seemed in better shape. Her face was bruised and swollen, either from the Elite or maybe just from landing on a rock, but she stood and seemed relatively steady on her feet. Her MOS patch indicated she was a research scientist. It probably also indicated what kind, but Linda didn't recognize what an eye with a star-shaped pupil stood for.

Linda checked the woman's rank and the nameplate above her pocket, then asked, "You're okay, Captain Stocken?"

"Oh, yes," Stocken replied. "Thanks to you."

"Glad to be of service, ma'am." Linda noticed an emergency locator lying in the belly scrape behind the captain and retrieved it, then held it out to her. "You must have dropped this, ma'am."

"Thank you." Stocken took the device and started to slip it into its belt holder, then stopped and passed it back. "Hold on. This must be someone else's. I still seem to have mine."

Linda looked down at the captain's equipment belt and saw that there was indeed a locator in the proper pocket.

"So you do." She slipped the extra locator into an empty pouch on her cartridge belt, then said, "Ma'am, I noticed a Section Three patch on your uniform."

Stocken nodded. "That shouldn't be a surprise, given what we were here to collect."

"It isn't." Linda took the captain by the arm and started to lead her up the slope. "But fighting Elites hand-to-hand is hardly a Section Three MOS. Let's find a medic and get you checked out."

"I'm fine." Stocken jerked her arm free. "I was watching you fire from the . . . well, whatever that many-legged vehicle is."

"It was nothing, ma'am," Linda said. "We're trained to—"

"I know what you're capable of, Spartan," Stocken said. "I'm interested in the last alien you killed from the vehicle. It looked like he had a fairly heavy personal shield."

"Yes, ma'am. That is how it seemed to me."

"I saw an external generator," Stocken said. "Is it still intact?"

"It seems likely," Linda said. "The grenades only took his shields down. I had to kill him with a rifle burst."

Stocken's eyes grew so wide that the wrinkles vanished around them. "Then what are we waiting for?" She started up the hill. "Let's go find the son of a bitch."

CHAPTER 20

A pall of black smoke appeared above the gorge, and images began to flash through John's mind of what he had seen beneath such clouds before. Tank-sized pools of molten metal, roofless bunkers ringed by fifty-meter soot stars. Stray arms hanging from splintered tree limbs. Heads smashed flat against pavement.

A hundred bodies plasma-fused into a single corpse.

John did not try to force the images from his mind. He had witnessed atrocities, and any attempt to deny those memories would only bring them back later, and in a stronger, more insidious way. That was what Dr. Halsey had said, and she was usually right about such matters.

Instead, John focused on the task at hand. He was riding in the gunner's cockpit atop Kelly's captured Umbra, so he was on ambush-watch while she drove them through the gorge at breakneck speed. With her attention fixed solely on the road and its hairpin curves, she would see any obstacles blocking their way long before he did. So John kept his attention on the gorge walls, scanning side ravines for fresh rockfalls and scrape marks, and searching along the rims for alien silhouettes and suspicious-looking boulder piles.

He saw nothing.

The black smoke continued to thicken overhead, and John grew ever more concerned about the *Wheatley* crew. At first he had bought the idea that the Covenant was chasing them in an effort to capture someone who could disarm the ship's self-destruct devices. Then a squadron of Banshees had shown up, and the *Lucky Break* had flown off. The enemy didn't need to steal a ship to escape Netherop.

So why had the aliens continued to chase the *Wheatley* crew?

There *had* to be more to it than a simple desire to kill every human in sight. A quarter of the heat casualties that the Umbra passed along the road were Elite, and sport-hunters didn't run themselves to death for the fun of it.

A little earlier, John had caught a few broken syllables of an emergency message from the *Wheatley* crew. The transmission had been unintelligible, which meant there was no longer a UNSC vessel overhead to amplify the signal and relay it down into the gorge. But at least there had been a message, and that meant someone in the crew was still alive.

Right?

John had tried TEAMCOM a dozen times since then and received no response due to distance or terrain or both. But the distance was decreasing, and the terrain configuration shifted every time Kelly powered the Umbra around a corner. He spoke over TEAMCOM again.

"Blue Leader, Blue Four, sitrep?" John waited five seconds for a reply, then said, "Blue Leader, Blue Four, status check."

Linda's status LED remained dark. That just meant she was out of range. She could be alive, dead, in trouble . . . or sitting by a pool somewhere, sipping an ice-cold *gooro*. He had no way to know.

After ten seconds, John signed off the same way he had every time before. "Blue Four, be advised—we're coming." There was always the possibility she could hear them. "We're coming as fast as we can. Out."

"Blue Leader, will you stop worrying already?" It was Fred's voice, relayed into the gunner's cockpit by the Umbra's intravehicle communications system. John had no idea how the thing worked—he couldn't even find the speakers—but it was so efficient that had he wanted to, he could have eavesdropped on every word spoken inside the transport bays. "We'll get there in time."

"No wisecracks?" John asked. "Maybe I should be telling *you* not to worry."

"Just being careful," Fred replied. "If I make you laugh too hard, you might fall out and get run over."

The effort was there, but John could tell that Fred's heart wasn't in it. He was as concerned for Linda as John was.

"Thanks, but right now you're not as funny as you think you are," John said. "How are the passengers hanging in down there?"

"Not bad," Fred said, "considering the driving."

"I *heard* that," Kelly said. "Would you rather I jumped us from bend to bend?"

"No offense," Fred said. "But Petrov and First Platoon aren't used to these kinds of maneuvers. It smells like a drop bay full of newboots down here. Even Lena and the boys are losing their lunches."

Fred would not be too affected by the stench, of course. His

Mjolnir had an integrated toxin-control system that would filter out most of the odor-carrying particles to prevent him from growing nauseated. Still, John was glad to be riding in the gunner's station.

The Umbra swung around two more tight curves, and then John spotted some fresh scrape marks running up a near-vertical flume. The flume was adjacent to one of the tightest inward curves on the entire road, and that made it the ideal spot for an ambush.

There were only three ways to deal with an ambush against a vehicle. The best method was to call in an airstrike or artillery bombardment to clear the ambushers from their position. Unfortunately, that just wasn't an option—even if John could get a signal inside the gorge.

The second-best method was to stop, dismount, and flank the ambushers. That's what John would have done—had he not been so worried about Linda and the ever-growing pall of black smoke above the gorge.

The third method was to race through the kill zone so fast that the enemy had no chance to launch a successful attack. John checked the road ahead for loose ground or carefully placed corpses that might hide a concealed explosive. Seeing none, he braced himself in the gunner's cockpit, pointed his BR55 toward the canyon wall, and began to yell over TEAMCOM: "Go go go!" He grabbed a grenade with one hand and with the other fired a short suppression burst toward the flume. "Go fast!"

Kelly did not need to be told why. They had drilled such maneuvers hundreds of times in training, so she just pulled the throttles back and took the Umbra as fast as she dared—perhaps even a little faster.

For such an ungainly-looking vehicle, the transport handled well, its force-cushions working like sway bars to keep the body from tipping too far outward, its rocket-like acceleration carrying it through the turn before the back end had a chance to drift. Nothing exploded as they rounded the corner, and as John glanced up the flume on the way past, he saw that it quickly narrowed into a chimney-like cleft.

And three meters up the cleft was a Castoff mountain runner. It was hanging in the wide part of the chimney with all ten legs splayed out, bracing itself against opposite walls. Four small blond heads were peering over the side of the passenger compartment, each one staring down the barrel of a UNSC assault rifle.

John lowered his grenade and his BR55. Then, in a breath, the Umbra was safely past the flume.

"Stop." This time, John spoke over the Umbra's communication system so Fred and First Platoon would not come out guns blazing. "It's the Castoffs."

Kelly decelerated as quickly as she safely could, and John tried TEAMCOM again.

"Blue Leader, Blue Four, sitrep?" If the Umbra was starting to catch up to Castoffs, it *had* to be getting close to Linda. "Blue Leader, Blue Four, status."

Still nothing.

Once the Umbra had slowed to static hover, John stowed his weapons and slid down the hull. "Hang tight, everyone. We'll be under way as soon as I can get a sitrep from these kids."

Kelly's and Fred's status LEDs flashed green, and he could hear the voices of Lena and Arne rising from the gunner's cockpit as he walked away. He couldn't make out what they were saying, but he was pretty sure they were demanding to be released so they could rejoin their camp. Maybe later.

John had walked about twenty paces when the mountain runner clattered out of the flume and started down the road toward him. Roselle was standing at the front of the passenger compartment, manning the microwave weapon, and a blond boy barely tall enough to see over the front deck was standing at the driver's orb. Protruding up behind them were the barrels of several assault rifles, along with the heads of four children even younger and smaller than the driver.

John raised his empty hands. "I'm friendly."

"I already know that." Roselle leaned around the microwave dish. "If I didn't, your floating thing would be splattered all over the bottom of the gorge right now."

John eyed the microwave weapon. Given the Covenant's typically poor EMP shielding, she might have been right—had she been quick enough to hit her target as it raced past. He stopped fifty paces from the Umbra and waited for the mountain runner to get closer to him.

"Is anyone injured?" John had been taught that it was always smart to show concern over the condition of one's native allies. In this case, he truly wanted to know. "Do you need anything?"

"To know if the road between us and Samson is safe." Roselle tapped her earlobe. "What do you hear in your helmet?"

"Not much. There's no signal, but it could just be terrain-blocking." John didn't want to give her false hope. He glanced skyward and added, "But *that* doesn't look good."

Roselle followed his gaze. "You mean all that smoke?"

"Right," John said. "When it's that dark—"

Roselle made a shooing motion. "Get back in your floating thing, John. There may still be aliens in the gorge, so we'll follow a hundred paces behind." She leveled a finger at him. "*Don't* let anything shoot us."

"I'm not sure you should follow yet." John didn't like the idea of Roselle and the children seeing the carnage the smoke suggested. It was not something they would ever be able to forget—especially if they happened across the body of Samson or a relative. "The battle might not be over, and even if it is, we don't know who won."

"The battle *is* over." Roselle looked at John as though he were an inattentive child. "The smoke is from our steamers."

John looked skyward again. Of course—the coal boilers in the mountain runners. "The runners are recharging their batteries?"

"Yes," Roselle said. "So I'm pretty sure we won. Dead people have no need of charged batteries."

"Fair point." John started to turn around, then thought better of it and paused. "When we reach the battlefield, you might want to keep the younger ones back. It's going to be ugly, no matter who won."

Roselle's face softened. "Good advice, John," she said. "If you aren't a father already, you'll make a good one someday."

"Thank you, ma'am," John said. He had no plans to become a father any time soon—and probably not ever—but he was glad to see he was starting to win Roselle over. "I appreciate the vote of confidence."

He returned to the Umbra and climbed back into the gunner's cockpit. While Kelly drove, he used the intravehicle comm system to inform the others of what he had learned.

Lena was the first to comment. "So, Roselle is behind us, and you're making me and Arne and Oskar ride with everyone throwing up? Nice."

John ignored her and tried TEAMCOM again. "Blue Leader, Blue Four, sitrep? Blue Leader, Blue Four, status."

This time, Linda's reply came immediately. "Enemy has withdrawn." Fred and Kelly's status lights strobed green inside John's helmet, and he felt his own stomach turning somersaults of joy.

Then Linda continued her report. "Twenty-eight *Wheatley* survivors secure, five immobile due to injuries."

John's elation faded. He was still thrilled to hear Linda's voice, but the *Wheatley* crew had suffered a seventy-percent casualty rate, and he *still* had no idea why the aliens had placed such a premium on attacking them.

"First, glad to hear your voice," John said. Kelly and Fred filled his helmet with more green blinking, though the strobing was not quite as fast now. "Second, what about the Castoffs?"

"No casualties," Linda replied. "All twelve in good condition."

At least that was something. Roselle and Lena would be happy with the outcome, even if Dr. Halsey and Admiral Cole were not.

Assuming Blue Team could even get back to Halsey and Cole.

"Status vehicles?" John asked.

"Two mountain runners good condition," Linda replied. "Everything else . . . I guess there *is* nothing else."

That meant they had a total of three mountain runners and one Umbra available to transport. As John started to do the math, his onboard computer displayed the answers on his HUD.

VEHICLE CAPACITY: 40. PERSONNEL IN NEED OF TRANSPORT: 69.

The onboard computer was assuming a capacity of six individuals per mountain runner. John knew he could probably squeeze ten kids and smaller adults into each runner, even leaving room for casualties. But the transport stations in the Umbra were fixed—a driver, a gunner, ten slots on each side, and the only way to double up was to have one kid stand on another kid's shoulders, which wasn't very practical. So that left him seventeen slots short—and only the four Spartans of Blue Team were capable of reaching a landing zone on foot.

Assuming they were even going to *need* a landing zone. There had been no recent contact with Task Force Pantea, so their only hope of escaping Netherop might lie in returning to the *Wheatley* and taking their chances in a lumbering salvage ship whose point-defense systems now lacked the capacity to swat away a fletterbug. When John and Fred climbed aboard the Umbra, First Platoon had been forced to leave two marines at the *Wheatley*, and maybe that had been a blessing in disguise. At least there would be someone there guarding it until everyone else returned.

The Umbra finally emerged from the gorge onto a peculiar kilometer-wide slope of dark bare stone, traversed only by the broad band of the talus-buried road upon which the vehicle was traveling. The two mountain runners were located on the far side of the slope, about eight hundred meters away, and John found his gaze immediately drawn to the two columns of black smoke rising from their boiler chimneys. Unbelievable. He could not have thought of a better way to signal their location to the Covenant air cover had he tried.

As Kelly eased the transport along the road toward the far side of the slope, John kept up a constant scan of the horizon, expecting to see the tiny specks of inbound Banshees at any moment. But Task Force Pantea must have been having some success in orbit, because the only thing he saw was a trio of disk-bodied Covenant spacecraft trailing flame tails as they plunged to their destruction.

By the time the Umbra had closed to within a hundred meters of the smoke-spewing mountain runners, he was beginning to feel that a true "lucky break" was on their side, and maybe a squadron of enemy fighters wasn't going to drop out of the clouds and destroy the last vehicles available to his makeshift company.

He didn't stop looking though.

Kelly brought the Umbra to a stop fifty meters behind the two mountain runners, where four Castoff adolescents were hanging close, paying more attention to the coal boilers than was likely necessary. John didn't blame them. They were young—almost the age of Blue Team itself, come to think of it—and yet completely unprepared for the savage fruit of interspecies warfare.

Samson and the seven other Castoffs were on the slope below. They all looked a bit frightened and nauseated, but they were following instructions and doing their best to help prepare the wounded for transport. Linda stood in the center of the battlefield, watching for incoming fighter craft and leaving it to the *Wheatley*'s officers to organize the evacuation, and John felt the tension drain from his entire body. He couldn't help it, even though she was surrounded by the charred and mangled corpses of ONI personnel. She was still standing, and there were more than two dozen Elite warriors who weren't.

He glanced behind them to make certain that Roselle's runner had made it across the slope behind them. Then, as the Umbra's boarding ramps began to descend, he spoke over the transport's comm system.

"Lena, take Arne and Oskar and check in with Roselle for your assignments," he said. "Don't go anywhere near the battlefield. There could still be live ordnance down there that you wouldn't recognize. Is that clear?"

"Affirmative," Lena said. "What's ordnance?"

John tried not to chuckle. "Stuff that blows up when you look at it wrong. First Platoon, I want a twelve-marine perimeter with eight people watching the sky and four watching the ground. Everyone else assist with the evacuation. Clear?"

"Affirmative." The voice belonged to Sesi Cacyuk, their lieutenant. "And what's our action if we *do* see incoming craft?"

Cacyuk was pointing out, not so subtly, that they didn't have the equipment to defend themselves against an airborne attack. But it had become a familiar situation on Netherop, and she seemed to be getting used to it.

"Announce direction and height," John said. "And hope for good luck."

The ramps were down far enough that the marines were beginning to dismount. Most appeared rejuvenated by the long ride in the vehicle's climate-controlled compartments, despite their motion sickness.

Fred and Petrov emerged together from near the front. Fred stepped away instantly, automatically moving away from the transport in case it was hit by enemy fire. Petrov stood on the edge of the ramp, surveying the scene below and making herself an obvious target for enemy snipers.

Someone had never spent a day in infantry school.

John jumped out of the gunner's cockpit on the uphill side of the Umbra and then—as Kelly settled it onto its parking struts—cautiously stepped around the back end. No battlefield was truly secure until you were off it, but all he saw coming toward him was a thin, gray-haired woman in a Section Three captain's uniform. She had taken a beating during the battle, but her bruised jaw was set and her blackened eyes were fixed on the designation number over the breast of John's torso armor.

Linda's voice came over TEAMCOM. "Incoming, John. Captain Stocken, Section Three xeno-technology scientist. Tougher than she looks."

"She looks pretty tough right now."

"She went hand-to-hand with an Elite and managed to hold her own until help arrived. She claims today is the UNSC's lucky day."

"Right," John said. "Seems like we've heard *that* before."

Linda's LED flashed green, and John turned to greet the arriving scientist.

"Captain Stocken—"

"Sierra-058 tells me you're in charge while we're on the ground," Stocken interrupted. "Is that correct?"

"Yes, ma'am, it is," John said. "What can I do for you?"

"Not for me, Spartan. For Section Three. For the entire UNSC." Stocken pointed down the slope toward the corpse of a well-armored Elite, who looked to be half again the size of most of their warriors. "*That* is a suit of armor with an intact personal energy shield."

"I see." John didn't need to ask what she wanted. A functional personal energy shield was near the top of the Covenant equipment capture list. He started down the hill toward the body. "Let's see what kind of tools we'll need to secure it."

"Tools?" Stocken's tone was alarmed. "What do you need with tools?"

"To properly remove the shielding unit, ma'am," John said. On his motion tracker, he noticed a FRIEND designator leave the Umbra and start after him—Petrov, no doubt. "Isn't that what you want?"

"I don't want it removed!" Stocken reached up and grabbed John by the forearm. "Are you insane?"

John stopped and stared down at her hand. "Negative. My last psych eval was almost normal."

If he had hoped to ease the captain into a more subdued approach, it didn't work. She latched on to his forearm with her other hand as well.

"You don't understand. The shielding may be incorporated into the armor. If you remove it, the entire unit could be inoperable. We might *never* figure out how it works!"

A knot began to form in John's stomach. "Ma'am, we don't have the transport space to take the entire body," he said. "We're already seventeen people over capacity."

Stocken's expression only grew more resolute, but before she could object, Petrov caught up to them.

"That's not quite accurate, John." She gently removed Stocken's hands from John's forearm, then turned to face him full-on. "We have all the capacity we need for UNSC personnel."

John understood Petrov's implication, but he was going to make her say it. "Ma'am, I don't understand."

"Sure you do." Petrov looked up the hill toward the Umbra, where Roselle was collecting Lena and the two boys. "There are twenty-one Castoffs, and they aren't UNSC personnel."

"Are you suggesting we leave them behind?"

"I'm pointing out they already know how to survive here on Netherop." Petrov continued to look toward Roselle and Lena as she spoke. "And that personal energy shield? It's number five on the equipment capture list."

Lena must have felt the weight of Petrov's gaze, because she glanced back, then turned and said something to Roselle. Realizing that he was studying the pair just as hard as Petrov was, John turned his faceplate back to Petrov.

"I'm aware of the energy shield's importance," John said. "We'll find a way to transport it."

"The entire suit?" Stocken asked. "It can't be just the shield unit."

"Yes, ma'am," John said. "The entire suit."

"I'm glad to hear that," Petrov said. "If we can deliver an intact shield unit, we just might turn this mess into a successful mission."

And save your career, John thought. Petrov's decision to rush the insertion protocol had been a poor judgment call. She had been forced to scuttle the *Night Watch*, and the *Lucky Break* had slipped through Blue Team's fingers because of the delay in reaching it. She probably wouldn't end up being court-martialed because their primary mission had come up empty—but it would be a long time before she received another promotion. Or even a decent assignment.

But if Petrov could deliver something like a personal shielding unit, all would be forgiven. Her career would shoot right back on track, and despite losing the *Night Watch*, she might even come out with a promotion.

John sighed. So be it. The mission came first.

John spoke over TEAMCOM. "Blue Three, once you have the Umbra secured, I need you to help Captain Stocken with a suit of Covenant armor. She'll be waiting for you at my current location."

When Kelly's status LED flashed green, John turned back to Stocken. "Wait here. Sierra-087 will help you secure the armor appropriately. But please be reasonable. There will be soldiers walking so that alien corpse can ride."

Stocken's face blanched. "I'll certainly keep that in mind. Thank you."

John started across the battlefield toward Linda. He was not happy to see Petrov fall in beside him.

"I thought we agreed you were going to leave the Castoffs here?"

"I agreed to get the armor to the LZ. Abandoning castaways on a hostile planet isn't an acceptable way to achieve that. It would violate the Uniform Code of Military Justice." John waited a second for his onboard computer to display the appropriate section number so he could quote it to her. When it did not, he continued, "Either that, or the Colonial Administration Authority Laws of Deep Space."

Again, the appropriate reference did not appear on his HUD.

"Or something."

The HUD continued to remain blank, and he began to wonder if Petrov had a legitimate point. Certainly he had a moral imperative to help the Castoffs. But maybe it wasn't a legal imperative during time of war.

John didn't care. Petrov was not in charge on the surface, and he intended to honor the deal he had made with Samson and Roselle.

But what if that meant someone in the UNSC had to die?

"There's more to this situation than legalities, Master Chief," Petrov said. "We're at war, and Netherop would be the perfect place to establish a deep-operations support base. We'd simply ask these people to hold it for us until the UNSC could send a force to relieve them. It probably wouldn't even be a year."

John shook his head. "They'd never volunteer."

"They might," Petrov said. "Depending on the alternatives."

John's motion tracker showed a FRIEND coming up behind them fast, and it wasn't a Spartan.

"Let's talk about it later," he said. "We have company."

They stopped walking and turned to find Roselle approaching. Petrov put on a broad smile and held out her hand.

"You must be Roselle."

Roselle stared at the hand in open contempt. "How do you know who I am?"

"I came here with your companions—Lena, Arne, and Oskar." Petrov continued to hold out her hand, then finally gave up and lowered it. "I asked a few questions about who you all are and how your group has survived here for so long."

"They used the word *interrogate*." Roselle made a point of turning toward John. "So, we've helped you rescue your crew. Now you'll keep *your* promise?"

"Yes." John forced himself not to look at Petrov as he spoke. "I'm working on that now."

"How?" Roselle demanded. "You'll call a ship?"

"First we need to identify our landing zone." John was deliberately dodging her question until he knew what his options were. "There's no sense calling for extraction until we know where we want them to meet us."

"Extraction?" Roselle asked.

"Our ride," John said. It was hard to get used to the Castoffs' spotty knowledge of what was everyday terminology to him. But that was to be expected, given that their only formal education came from the "learning machines" passed down from their radical Separatist ancestors. He couldn't even guess what they probably imagined the outside galaxy to be. "We can't land a spacecraft on the side of this mountain—not if we expect it to launch again."

John started toward Linda, this time with Petrov and Roselle trailing close behind. He realized he was going to need to stay one step ahead of both of them until he found a solution to the extraction problem.

John opened TEAMCOM. "When was the last time anybody heard from Pantea?"

"Right after the *Lucky Break* took off, when those Nandaos saved us from that Banshee squadron," Fred said. "Nothing since."

Linda and Kelly flashed green status LEDs.

Then Linda added, "I was on the emergency channel with the *Wheatley* crew before this battle. I think Pantea would have clicked in if they had a vessel overhead."

"Not necessarily," Kelly said. "Remember, we're at the bottom of the battle cone. There's a pretty fierce fight raging above us, all the way into orbit."

That was true. Given the situation on the ground, Pantea would be doing everything they could to keep the enemy from winning air and orbital superiority. And despite the two columns of coal smoke rising from the mountain runners, the battlefield hadn't been strafed or bombed yet. That suggested that Pantea was still up there—and having at least a *little* success. Or maybe that was just wishful thinking. There was no way to tell.

"You think they're just maintaining comm silence?" John asked.

"That's precisely what I would do," Kelly said, still speaking over TEAMCOM. "I'd put out a few low-profile listening posts, then fight the edges until I heard a solid extraction call."

"Makes sense," Fred said. "Only one problem."

"We cannot know if they are actually there," Linda said.

John reached Linda's side and stopped. "So we'll just have to designate a landing zone—and then hope they show up."

"Well, we *might* pad the odds," Kelly said.

John turned toward the dead Elite with the personal energy-shield generator. Kelly was standing over the alien's corpse, pretending to listen as Captain Stocken lectured her on the intricacies of moving a scientific specimen.

"What are you thinking?" John asked.

"That there aren't any good landing zones around here anyway." Kelly raised her chin and made a show of surveying the rugged terrain. "So we may as well tell them to extract at the *Wheatley*."

John thought for a moment. Unless he could find a way to squeeze everyone into the available vehicles, they would have to make two runs back to the salvage vessel—and that would mean delaying their extraction by a couple of hours. On the other hand, Kelly was right—there definitely weren't any good landing zones nearby. He could send someone up onto the plateau to scout for a good spot, but that would take time too. Nor was a special-purpose extraction an option. Blue Team and even the marines could probably rope up into a hovering Pelican, or jump off a cliff into an open drop bay. But what about the *Wheatley* survivors? Or the Castoffs?

No way.

John felt a rock clang against his backplate.

"Hey, are you *in* there?" Roselle demanded. "What's the plan?"

John looked down at the rock until she finally dropped it, then said through his voicemitter, "We're going back to the *Wheatley*."

"I thought we might," Petrov said. "Good choice."

Her approval wasn't reassuring. "Am I that predictable?"

"It's not hard to predict the best alternative," Petrov said. "Launching the *Wheatley* may not be much of a backup plan, but it's better than nothing."

"What does she mean?" Roselle asked. "Why do we need a backup plan?"

"Because we haven't heard from our task force in a while," John said. "They're our ride, and we can't be sure they're still up there."

"And even if they *are*," Petrov added, "they're fighting a battle they can't win, and we have no idea how long they can last. We might be forced to attempt our escape in the *Wheatley*."

Roselle scowled at John. "And you didn't think to tell us this?"

"The last time I saw you was *at* the *Wheatley*." John was growing irritated, but not at Roselle. Petrov was deliberately trying to frighten the younger woman, and John thought he knew why. "And we *were* in contact with Pantea. Their Nandaos had just destroyed a Banshee squadron."

"Unfortunately, conditions have deteriorated since then," Petrov said. "Attempting to escape in the *Wheatley* would be a long shot, but—"

"We don't know that it will come to that, Commander." John's tone was sharp. They were still on the surface, which meant he was still in charge here. Petrov needed to remember that. "There are a lot of reasons we might be temporarily out of contact with the task force."

He kept his faceplate turned toward Petrov and was not unhappy to see Roselle's brow rise at the exchange.

After a moment, Petrov said, "My apologies, Master Chief. I didn't mean to worry anyone." Her tone was conciliatory, and she turned to address Roselle directly. "I just thought you should understand the risks . . . in case you'd rather stay here on Netherop."

"Yes, I understand." Roselle had gone pale, but she managed a smile and reached out to squeeze Petrov's forearm. "If it comes to launching in the *Wheatley*, we will certainly keep the risks in mind."

The light drained from Petrov's smile. "I'm very glad to hear it."

She turned to John. "All that remains now is to decide *how* we're going to get everyone to the landing zone. Making two trips through the gorge will delay the extraction rendezvous by at least two hours, and even if Pantea isn't gone already—"

"Two trips?" Roselle asked. "Why?"

"Vehicle capacity," John said. "Between the Umbra and your mountain runners, we can carry fifty-two people at the most. But we have sixty-nine, plus some equipment, to transport."

"So we need to carry an extra seventeen people in the runners?" Roselle shrugged. "It's no problem."

Petrov's jaw fell. "It isn't?"

"Not at all. We'll just unload the coal bins." Roselle took Petrov by the arm and started to pull her up the slope toward her own runner. "Come, you can take my runner. It wasn't in the battle, so the batteries will be fresher."

As the two women departed, Linda tipped her helmet, then spoke over TEAMCOM. "Something is wrong," she said. "Roselle is not that nice."

"And Petrov is?" Still troubled that he did not understand the reason for the Covenant's relentless—and costly—pursuit of the *Wheatley* survivors, John began to survey the small battlefield. "Let them sort it out. Linda, we need an action report. Everybody, listen up."

All status LEDs flashed green, then Linda continued over TEAMCOM.

"It will be a very simple report. After leaving the gorge, Captain Dkani had his engineers set a landslide trap on the talus slope." Linda pointed down the slope to a pair of burned-out Warthogs. "He tried to lure the aliens into the kill zone by resting the column where you see the two Warthogs."

"And that worked?" John asked.

"No. The Covenant sent marksmen in active camouflage to launch a surprise attack, and when I opened fire, Captain Dkani sprang his trap prematurely." Linda shrugged. "He was not infantry."

"Was?" John asked.

"I told him to move away from the Warthogs," Linda said. "He was too slow."

John nodded. The captain knew the risks; in any battle, officers were high-priority targets. "Then what?"

"Then the Elites charged across the slope," Linda said. "I joined Samson with two runners full of Castoffs in a rear attack, and we routed them."

"*Wait.*" John felt his chest clench. "The Covenant chased their target through thirty kilometers of gorge, then just hit the *Wheatley* survivors once—and *ran?*"

"I would say withdrew." Linda pointed down the slope toward the basin in the distance. "But yes, twenty or thirty of them fled down into the mirage basin."

"That's where the *Lucky Break* went," Fred said. "The aliens weren't withdrawing. They were extracting."

"That can't be good," Kelly said. "Especially since *we're* still here."

"Perhaps they are coming back for us?" Linda asked. "Perhaps they were waiting until all four Spartans are together?"

"If so, they're sure taking their time," Fred said. "If they wait any longer, I'm going to break out a cot."

"Affirmative," John said. "But if they weren't after us, then what were they after?"

John thought for a moment, trying to imagine what the *Wheatley* survivors could have been carrying that would be worth the long pursuit the Elites had undertaken to capture it. No ideas came to mind. The only thing that made any sense at all was the same thing

Blue Team had decided back near the *Wheatley*—that the Covenant was pursuing the crew because they wanted a way to disarm the ship's self-destruct device. It still seemed remotely possible, especially considering Pantea's reports earlier of the two Covenant task forces firing on each other. Maybe the price of failing a mission in the Covenant was death, and the *Lucky Break*'s crew had been trying to escape their own kind. Or something . . . it made as much sense as anything, and he wasn't about to make the mistake of assuming he knew what the aliens were thinking.

John started down the slope toward the ruined Warthogs, then activated his voicemitter, raising the volume to maximum.

"Where's Captain Dkani?" he called out. "I need to find the captain's body."

A young woman looked up from the casualty she was bandaging, then gestured toward the slope.

"You'll find some of him over there." She pointed a little farther down the slope, then a little farther across it. "And over there, and there."

"What about his commpad?" he replied. "Have you seen that?"

"You're kidding, right?"

The woman returned to her casualty, and John deactivated his voicemitter, pausing to consider what he should do next. Even if the aliens had captured Dkani's commpad, they would have to crack the encryption code before they had any chance of locating the disarming codes for the *Wheatley*'s self-destruct devices. And that was assuming Dkani had actually stored the information on the device. Being both ONI and the commander of a scientific unit, he was far more likely to have committed those codes to memory.

The same was true of most of the other senior officers who might have been entrusted with the information. It was possible they would have stored the disarming codes on their own commpads. But how would the aliens know who had stored them and who had them memorized? And would they even be capable of accessing a human commpad?

Probably not, but John couldn't be sure. He would have to identify every officer who knew the code, then verify that he or she had *not* been captured by the aliens. Wondering where to begin, he turned to survey the battlefield—and saw Fred and Linda hustling toward him.

"You know it doesn't matter, right?" Fred asked.

"What doesn't matter?" John asked.

"What the Covenant was after," Fred said. "Whatever it was, they got it."

"And that means we can't let them keep it," Linda said. "We have to chase them down."

CHAPTER 21

1548 hours, June 7, 2526 (military calendar)
Last Hope Escarpment
Mountains of Despair, Planet Netherop, Ephyra System

John was back in the gunner's cockpit atop the Umbra, peering over a rising dust cloud as the transport plunged down the outrun at the bottom of the landslide chute. Petrov and the Castoffs were in the three mountain runners, on their way back to the *Wheatley* with what remained of the salvage ship's crew. Blue Team and First Platoon had mounted up to pursue the enemy down the mountain and recover whatever it was that they had captured. The aliens had a twenty-minute head start—but they were hot, tired, and on foot. The Umbra would catch them.

Probably.

John had to make a conscious effort to look over the dust curtain instead of into it. But when he did, he had a decent view of the searing landscape below, where there was an ever-broadening band of jade-green refraction shimmer at the bottom of the chute. Beyond it stretched the vast blue blur of the mirage basin. At the near edge rested a long, unidentifiable gray smudge. Magnifying the image only blurred the object beyond recognition, but there could be little doubt that it was the *Lucky Break*, waiting to extract the alien raiding party.

Could it still be boarded and captured?

That was a fantasy. There was no hope of taking the Covenant frigate's crew by surprise, and even if John did manage to capture the vessel intact, what would he do with it? He had no idea how to fly a Covenant starship. And he could no longer count on the *Wheatley* to transport it. The lumbering salvage ship had lost all of its point-defense systems on one side, and it would be swarmed by enemy fighter craft the instant it began the surface hop. But before it could even attempt that, the recovery operations and launch preparations would take hours. By the time the *Wheatley* was ready to lift the captured frigate out of Netherop's gravity well, the Covenant would have complete orbital superiority. Both ships would be destroyed long before the *Wheatley* could carry them into slipspace.

John had to face it. Blue Team's attempt to capture the *Lucky Break* was a complete bust, and any effort to save the operation now would only push the mission from bad to disaster. Success now meant one thing: denying the Covenant *their* success. With a little good fortune, he might even figure out exactly what that meant.

Far out over the basin, streaks of color began to flash through the canopy of brown clouds in both directions. The sounds arrived a few seconds later, the shrieks and rolling booms of an air battle erupting into a real snarl. This, he assumed, was Task Force Pantea's response to the extraction request that Lieutenant Commander Petrov had put out as Blue Team and First Platoon departed. Pantea—or what remained of the task force—was beginning its run. And that meant John's operation now had an even tighter timetable.

He checked the chronometer on his HUD. Assuming Pantea intended to follow Petrov's schedule, the extraction vessels—probably four Pelicans—would arrive at the *Wheatley* in exactly thirty minutes, and the salvage ship's self-destruct charge would be detonated as soon as everyone was clear.

John didn't dare risk drawing an airstrike by breaking comm silence now. But he would have to do it soon. Pantea would need at least a little time to divert one of the Pelicans to his location and rig for a special-purpose extraction. He recorded an emergency message outlining what he wanted and where he thought he would need it, then set it to transmit automatically in fifteen minutes.

The flashing in the clouds grew brighter and steadier, and trails of flame spiraled groundward as fighter craft began to plunge to their destruction. John kept watch for incoming surface attacks, swinging the gunner's stool around every thirty seconds to check the horizon behind them. So far the Umbra's dust cloud was not drawing the attention of ground-attack craft, but that was bound to change as the air battle drew nearer.

John addressed Lieutenant Cacyuk and her marines over the transport's intravehicle comm system. "We have enemy fighter craft in the area. If I give the order to evacuate, blow the ramps and move away fast."

"We know the drill," Cacyuk said. "We're not *that* green."

"Yes, ma'am." John understood her subtext. The passengers of most vehicles destroyed by air assault never even saw the attack coming, so most officers chose not to remind them how vulnerable they were. But most vehicles weren't crewed by Spartans. "Just be ready. I have a good field of view, so we should have a few seconds to clear the Umbra if we need to."

"Good to know," Cacyuk said. "Thanks, Master Chief."

As the Umbra continued to descend, the green band of refraction shimmer appeared to rise above the dust curtain, growing more solid and deeper in color. Soon the heat distortion vanished entirely, and John found himself looking at a virtual barricade of very tall, spiny succulents. They were growing atop the alluvial fan that spilled out of the landslide chute into the mirage basin, and the thorny tangle appeared to be as impenetrable as it was massive, with flat, intertwined stems rimmed in needle-sharp hooks.

Kelly slowed the Umbra as they approached the barricade, veering away from an obvious ambush possibility where the landslide outrun had pushed into the thicket.

"What do you think?" Kelly asked over the Umbra's comm system. "Plow through, or dismount and advance on foot?"

John magnified the image and ran his gaze along the edge of the thicket. In their Mjolnir armor, he and the other Spartans would be able to bull through without any problem. But for the marines, it would be an entanglement hazard of the first order, akin to a hundred-meter barrier of double-stacked concertina coils.

Of course, the Covenant had also been confronted by the thicket, and John could see four recently cut tunnels where they were attempting to penetrate it. The passages were spaced about five meters apart, two each to either side of where the landslide outrun had pushed into the tangle. He shook his head.

Alien logic.

Had *he* been trying to rush a company of hot, exhausted troops through such a massive entanglement barrier, he would have conserved energy by cutting only one or two passages.

"Dismount and advance on foot," John said. "They're setting up an ambush."

Kelly stopped the Umbra and dropped the ramps. First Platoon raced out and established a fifty-meter perimeter, while John took Blue Team and Lieutenant Cacyuk forward to inspect the passages the aliens had cut. However carefully they moved, they kept brushing against the stems.

After a dozen paces, Fred said, "Whoa." He spoke over SQUAD-COM, so that both Blue Team and First Platoon would hear. "I think these plants are reaching for us."

John stopped and moved a forearm closer to one of the stems. It might have fluttered a little, but there was a strong, hot wind coming out of the basin, and it was making the whole thicket tremble.

"You're imagining things," John replied over SQUADCOM.

"No, he's right," Cacyuk said. "Look."

John turned to see the sleeve and pant leg on one side of her battle uniform hooked in a dozen places.

"It'll take forever to cut through this stuff." She drew her combat knife and hacked the stems away. "It's like concertina wire that reaches and grabs you."

"Good," John said. "It'll slow the Covenant down."

They reached the first two passages and quickly peered down each. Both were about two meters high and a little over a meter wide—just large enough for a single-file line. The light inside the tunnels was dappled and shadowy, dim enough to help conceal someone hiding a meter or two off the trail. And, of course, each passage made a turn about three meters in, which concealed the rest of its length from view.

Given the situation, there were only two things the enemy could do here—and both called for the same response from Blue Team and First Platoon. He summoned the marines forward and explained what he wanted.

And that was the moment when his recorded message transmitted over the emergency band: "Blue Leader, any Pantea extraction craft. Request SPIE line extraction twenty personnel this location fifteen minutes. Over."

The response came immediately. *"Pantea Extraction Coordination, Blue Leader. SPIE line extraction fifteen minutes your location confirmed. Don't be late. Hot line likely."*

"Acknowledged," John said. The aliens would probably detect the transmission, but with the air battle already raging over the basin, they would be far too busy with decoy messages to track it down and do anything about it. "Hot line likely. Out."

"Hot line?" a young marine whispered over SQUADCOM. "What's a hot line?"

"Don't worry about it," said a husky-voiced woman. "We'll never make it back in time anyway."

"Enough bellyaching, Sawyer," Cacyuk said. "Did you join the Marines to take joyrides or kill aliens?"

"Who's bellyaching?" Sawyer replied. "I'd rather die than hot line any day."

"If those are *really* the choices," the young marine said, "I'd kinda like to try the hot line. Whatever it is."

"You'll love it," Fred said. "Trust me."

"Is that an order?" the young marine asked.

"Can the chatter," John said. "First we kill, *then* we hot line. Got it?"

John almost added *all of us*, but didn't. He was not going to improve anyone's morale by lying to them.

SQUADCOM fell silent. They entered the thicket moving fast, with each member of Blue Team leading the way down a different passage. Fifteen meters behind each Spartan followed a marine fire team, spacing themselves at four-meter intervals. Since the passages ran along serpentine courses, that spacing generally kept the entire line in the Spartans' motion tracker range. Occasionally the rearmost designator would fall temporarily offscreen. When that happened, the marine would be asked for a status check, just to be sure he or she hadn't been taken from behind by an Elite in active camouflage.

John watched for tripwires and areas of disturbed ground that might suggest buried explosives, but he didn't expect to find many. Given the long run down the gorge and the hand-to-hand charge against the *Wheatley* survivors, he doubted the Covenant could be carrying much in the way of mines or remotely detonated explosives. But it was wise never to assume. For all he knew, Covenant land mines were invisible, thumb-size stickers.

Three minutes into the thicket, John's motion detector showed a line of five UNKNOWN designators fidgeting a few meters to the right side of the trail. One designator was about three meters behind the middle trio, serving as a rear stop, and another was three meters ahead, serving as the front stop.

The five ambushers were so well camouflaged that as John passed by, he could not see any of them with nonenhanced vision—though he was careful not to take an obvious look. He simply continued forward until he saw the first marine draw even with the rear stop. Then John shouldered his BR55, spun toward the alien in the front-stop position, and spoke over SQUADCOM.

"Column One, to your right."

He fired a long burst into the thicket, running it from ground level up to waist height. A form rose from the shadows, shedding armor-deflected rounds and succulent-stem camouflage, and managed to loose off a couple of wild plasma bolts before John's second burst put him down.

Automatic-weapons fire was sounding from the trail behind him as Sawyer attacked the rear stop. Behind her, Lieutenant Cacyuk was leading the other two marines into the thicket, one hand using the barrel of her assault rifle to bat aside the hooked plant stems and her other hand chopping at them with her combat knife—charging forward to flank the main body of ambushers, who had just realized their peril and were starting to rise from their hides to redeploy.

John rushed them, his armor shedding hooked succulent stems as he plowed through the thicket. All three Elites turned to face him—and were cut down when Cacyuk and her fireteam opened up from their rear.

It was over just that fast, six seconds from start to finish. John paused long enough to finish off the aliens that weren't quite dead yet and check their armor styles. Finding nothing to suggest that these were anything more than ship's crew armed with antiboarding weapons, he led the marines back to the main trail and continued the advance.

Five minutes gone. Which meant he had only ten minutes to finish the job and return to the extraction site.

Three times he heard nearby gunfire as the other Spartan-led teams defeated their would-be attackers. Twice he found short passages that had been pushed through the thicket, suggesting he was passing another dogleg ambush like the first one. Equipped with his motion detector, he needed only a few blind shots to confirm there was nobody lurking. The enemy was just laying decoys in an effort to lull him into complacency.

Finally, eight minutes into the advance, the tangle of hook plants began to thin, and John realized he was approaching the mirage basin. There were no more side passages pushed into the thicket. And the *Lucky Break* sat two hundred meters ahead, shimmering in the heat on a rock-and-sand surface. He could see a line of tracks leading straight toward the ship, but they disappeared into the heat diffraction about thirty meters distant. John worked his magnification up and down the scale, but could not see a single figure—even a blurry one—moving toward the vessel.

But the sky above was not as quiet. It was filled with missile trails and flame plumes, and the fork-hulled shape of a Covenant dropship was swooping in to land.

"Well, that's great timing," Fred said over TEAMCOM. "I was afraid this might be getting too easy."

Nizat 'Kvarosee tried to feel honored that the gods continued to test his worthiness with obstacles such as the thorn tangle, but in truth he was growing hot and weary of proving himself. He lay in ambush with his last twenty warriors, hidden on the blazing ground three paces back from the edge of the thicket. Their carbines and plasma rifles were tucked tight against their shoulders, ready to cut down the demon Spartans and their servant soldiers the moment they started across the basin toward the *Steadfast Strike*.

That is, if they started across the basin.

With a Silent Shadow dropship coming in to land, the humans might think better of their pursuit and quietly withdraw. Or they might choose a less obvious plan and try to circle around, or call in an airstrike. Nizat hoped not, but he simply did not know what the gods had planned.

He had been trying to understand, without success, why the Spartans continued to pursue him ever since the cadre rearguard had reported that the demons were loading a band of their servant soldiers into a captured Covenant transport. He did not have the faintest idea, for even at Borodan's third moon and Zhoist, when they had destroyed so much, the demons had shown themselves to be focused and dangerous foes who attacked with purpose and clarity. But now? They seemed to be acting out of simple vengeance.

Nizat's greatest fear was that the humans had somehow discovered the Luminal Beacons he had planted, and now they wished to recover the receiver units. But that was a truly baseless worry. Even if the demons *had* stumbled upon the Beacons and miraculously guessed their function, the receiver units were still aboard the *Quiet Faith*—assuming that vessel had escaped destruction, of course.

Nizat believed it had. Qoo 'Weyodosee was a competent captain, but he also would not linger when he saw certain death coming his way. By now, the fool was probably hiding at the edge of the system, waiting to see whether Nizat would survive.

And survive he would . . . so long as the demons did not withdraw. The crew of the *Steadfast Strike* remained loyal to Nizat, and so would the craven 'Weyodosee, once Nizat returned to space and demanded it of the errant Sangheili.

"We should go to the sword and kill the humans now," 'Lakosee whispered. He did not dare use their armor communications for fear of betraying their location to the arriving troop carrier. "At least then we would only need to fight one enemy at a time."

"Have faith," Nizat said. "The gods have sent the Spartans to save us from the Silent Shadow. We must trust in their wisdom."

"I would rather place my trust in my sword," 'Lakosee said.

But he remained motionless at Nizat's side, and they watched as the Silent Shadow's troop carrier positioned itself to land halfway between the *Steadfast Strike* and the thicket of hook plants. The reason Nizat's frigate did not attack the dropship was obvious. With only a skeleton crew, it could man either its weapons or its flight stations. And the *Steadfast Strike* would have no hope of escaping if it was not ready to leave the instant Nizat boarded.

It took a moment for Nizat to understand why the Silent Shadow wasn't firing on the *Steadfast Strike*. First, they would want to confirm his death, and that would be impossible if they used their fleet to obliterate the frigate from orbit. Second, with the fierce battle raging overhead between the humans and the Fleet of Swift Justice, they might not have assets available for a plasma bombardment. But, most importantly, they would be afraid of destroying the Luminal Beacons and facing the wrath of the Prophets. Until they recovered the sacred artifacts, they would do nothing to risk their demolition.

And therein lay Nizat's salvation.

"How long must we wait?" 'Lakosee hissed, this time so loudly that Nizat feared the Spartans had surely heard him. "I refuse to die on my belly like—"

The last part of 'Lakosee's sentence was drowned out by the roar of infidel rockets streaking away from the thicket. They hit the Silent Shadow troop carrier barely a second later—four quick, stomach-banging detonations that blew both forks off and sent the craft crashing to the ground in three flame-trailing sections.

'Lakosee turned to Nizat, his mandibles splayed wide. "Have we been saved?" He started to rise. "By our enemies?"

"By our *gods*," Nizat corrected. He put a hand on 'Lakosee's shoulder and held him down. "But not yet. Wait."

This time, 'Lakosee dropped to his belly without objection.

They watched quietly for a few breaths. Nizat prayed that the warriors of the Silent Shadow were as resilient as he had always believed they were, that they would rise from the ashes to avenge themselves . . . and they surely did.

There were at least eleven of them, rushing out of the flames with their carbines and fuel rod guns booming, shredding the hook plants where the Spartans and their servant soldiers lay hiding. More infidel rockets shrieked from the thicket, and the clatter of their weapons filled the air. The energy shields of the Silent Shadow attackers began to crackle and flash with overload static, and the brave warriors began to stagger as infidel bullets punched through their armor.

"Now!" Nizat yelled, using both his voice and the communications system. "Now we go with the grace of the gods!"

Nizat leaped to his feet and charged, looping wide around the Silent Shadow to avoid becoming entangled in the battle between them and his savior Spartans. Still, four of the dark-armored Sangheili saw his tactic and turned to face him—and were quickly cut down by enemy flanking fire.

Nizat and his band of pious survivors drew even with the still-flaming wreckage of the downed troop carrier, all of them panting and staggering in the heat after only a hundred paces, so hot that he could feel the ground burning beneath his boot soles and his brain sweltering in his skull.

But they were going to make it. All that remained was to duck behind the downed troop carrier, where they would be protected from the infidel weapons, then cross another hundred paces to the *Steadfast Strike*.

Nizat turned to angle past the wreckage . . . and the last of the Silent Shadow fell, freeing the Spartans to shift in his direction. He saw the orange dashes of contrail bullets streaking past, heard his energy shield crackle as the first rounds hit, but then he was behind the troop carrier, and safe. He stopped and looked back. 'Lakosee and six others were close behind him, but the rest of his cadre fell, tumbling sideways to the ground as they were knocked from their feet, bouncing and jerking among the rocks as enemy fire continued to riddle their bodies.

Such loyal followers, such pious warriors. Surely they would be remembered when the Worthy were called to join the Forerunners in divine transcendence.

Nizat would see to it personally.

He felt a hand on his elbow, and realized 'Lakosee was pulling him forward.

"Fleetmaster, come!"

Seventy paces ahead, the boarding ramp of the *Steadfast Strike* was already halfway down, and Nizat could see the arm of an eager crewman waving them forward.

Then Nizat glimpsed the crescent-winged silhouette of a Gigas fighter-bomber descending out of the low brown clouds beyond the frigate, and an instant later, there was nothing but the crewman's arm tumbling through the air toward them, silhouetted against the blinding bright ball of an erupting plasma bomb. An eternity later, Nizat's armor clanged against stone and he began to tumble, having dropped back to the ground after being hurled who knew how far by the pressure wave. Then he bounced across fist-size rocks until he finally ran out of momentum, coming to rest with his back pressed against a boulder, the startled cries and pained wails of 'Lakosee and the rest of his cadre ringing inside his helmet.

Wary of demon snipers and infidel attack craft—though a small voice in the back of his mind asked what it mattered if they killed him now—Nizat rolled to his belly and flattened himself against the ground, struggling to orient himself to the battlefield.

For a few moments, he could see nothing but dazzling flashes of light in every direction, and he feared he had been blinded. But then he began to make out tiny cruciform shapes chasing flashes of orange and red across the horizon, wheeling against the brown clouds and skimming low across the ground, and he realized he was witnessing a fierce air battle.

He spotted the smoldering wreckage of the demon-downed Silent Shadow troop carrier a little to his right. Beyond it lay a flaming wall of foliage that had once been the hook-plant thicket. Something was still pouring plasma bolts into it, so he turned and followed the stream . . . back to the crescent-winged Gigas fighter-bomber he had glimpsed earlier, hovering now over a glassy crater where the *Steadfast Strike* had rested.

The sky above the Gigas was filled with looping, swirling contrails, the air so full of missiles and cannon fire and disintegrating fighter craft that the brown clouds seemed to be raining flame and shrapnel. And in front of the Gigas, striding across the rocky plain toward him, was a trio of Sangheili warriors in brightly colored armor. Two wore red trimmed in yellow. They flanked the third, a Helios Ultra in ivory armor trimmed in orange, the color so deep and rich it seemed almost to be gold.

Honor guards from High Charity itself.

Determined not to die on his knees, Nizat struggled to his feet and reached for his energy sword—only to discover that it had been knocked free during the destruction of the *Steadfast Strike*. He pulled his plasma pistol instead . . . and found himself holding a twisted wreck of a weapon that would have taken his hand off the moment he squeezed the activator.

The honor guards reached him, the two underlings stepping to Nizat's flanks, and the Ultra stopping a pace in front of him. They did not even bother to palm their energy swords, a gesture of contempt so insulting that Nizat would have attacked them with his bare hands, had he not been so weak and reeling from blast sickness that he would have tripped over his own feet.

The Ultra glared down at Nizat for a moment, then said simply, "You know why we have come. Return the sacred Beacons, and your death shall be swift."

"I understand." To his dismay, Nizat found himself trembling as he answered. He had expected to die more bravely. "First, do me the honor of answering one question."

"I will do you no such honor," the Ultra replied. "Return the Beacons and seek your forgiveness from the gods, or make us search for them—and suffer the consequences."

"It is not that simple. The receivers were aboard two vessels in the Flotilla of Unsung Piety." Nizat was lying, of course. Both receivers had been aboard his flagship, the *Quiet Faith*. "If the receiver is destroyed, the Beacons are worthless."

The Ultra nodded. "This I know."

"Then you will also know that my answer means nothing until I am told the fate of my ships."

The Ultra was quiet for five breaths, then said, "Only the *Silent Truth* and the *Quiet Faith* have escaped . . . for now."

"Then I cannot do as you ask." Nizat dropped his head, trying to hide his relief. The coward Qoo 'Weyodosee was unlikely to go hunting ONI with only two vessels . . . but as long as the *Quiet Faith* survived, there was hope that Nizat's plan might live on without him. "The receivers were aboard the *Still Devotion* and *Worthy Silence*."

"You are certain?"

"Do as you have been commanded." Nizat extended his hands, offering them for the first amputations. "It will not change the truth."

The Ultra's posture sagged almost imperceptibly, but instead of reaching for his energy sword, he looked to his escorts.

"Remove the armor."

Nizat's mandibles fell open. "I am to die *unarmored*?"

"I fear it is worse for you than that, Fleetmaster." The Ultra made a show of glancing around the basin, then gave a soft clack of his mandibles. "Far worse."

"You intend to maroon me here?"

"You and all those you command, yes." The Ultra nodded to his escorts, who stepped forward and began to strip Nizat of his armor.

"A pity you were unable to return the Beacons. At least then you would have died with your helmet on."

John had barely registered Fred's wisecrack—*I was afraid this might be getting too easy*—before the Covenant dropship moved into position and began to descend between their thicket and the *Lucky Break.*

"Rocket launchers!" he called over SQUADCOM. "Everyone who's ready!"

A fan of smoke trails shot from the thicket, and barely a breath later, four rockets hit the dropship—four quick, stomach-banging detonations. The craft lost both carrier forks and crashed to the ground in three flaming sections.

Good.

Now he needed a plan. John checked time until extraction—6:29 appeared on his HUD—and realized simplicity was best. *Kill all the aliens, then get the hell out of here.*

John belly-crawled to the edge of the thicket and pushed his head out, searching for the Elites he had been chasing. A force of twenty or thirty aliens did not simply vanish. It had to have circled back, hiding inside the brake, waiting for a chance to make a run for the frigate.

John's contemplations came to an abrupt end as a volley of plasma bolts and cannon rounds came streaming out of the dropship's smoking wreckage, shredding the thicket around him. It seemed impossible that anyone had survived the crash, yet there they were, eleven Elites in dark-red armor, emerging from the flames with their weapons blazing.

Rockets and M301-launched grenades began to scream back at

the enemy even before John gave the order. He opened fire with his BR55 and saw their energy shields begin to crackle beneath the withering fire from Blue Team and First Platoon. The Elites had to be from that same special unit he had seen several times before—the one that had come hunting Spartans on Seoba and above Naraka. The very unit that had poured out of the Umbra he and Fred had destroyed back in the gorge.

Alarm bells went off in John's head, as deep-rooted fears of a trap being sprung came to the fore. Maybe the point of this whole bizarre, complicated Covenant operation here on Netherop had been to lure Blue Team into this thicket, to trap them here in the bottom of a landslide chute, where they would be unsupported and easy to capture.

Then his motion tracker went wild. Twenty hostile contacts appeared out of nowhere, just fifteen meters to his right. John did not turn to look. The worst thing to do when you were stupid enough to let yourself get drawn into a crossfire was to panic and lose focus.

But he *did* check his HUD for time to extraction: 4:14.

The Spartans could make it through the thicket easily, but First Platoon . . . those marines had to leave *now*.

John made his decision.

"Hostile contacts right flank." He finished the Elite he'd been attacking—kept firing until he saw the alien fall—then hunkered down and changed magazines. "First Platoon disengage and withdraw to extraction point."

"Affirm—"

"Go!" This was no time to confirm orders, no time to do anything but act. "Blue Leader and Blue Two will engage the flank attack! Blue Three and Four, maintain fire!"

Three status LEDs flashed green. John pulled the BR55's charging handle and turned to meet the flank attack.

Except it wasn't an attack at all—just twenty exhausted Elites running for cover behind the downed dropship. He opened fire on full automatic and heard Fred doing the same, and between them they dropped twelve targets before their magazines clicked empty.

The survivors disappeared behind the wreckage.

John checked his HUD. Exactly two minutes until extraction. The skies over the *Lucky Break* had become a flaming web of missiles and cannon bolts, and there was something big and ugly coming their way—something with crescent-shaped wings and cannon mounts the size of Nandao fighters. If the Spartans didn't leave now, they were either going to be dead or be living on Netherop for a long, long time.

"Blue Team, withdraw." Whatever the aliens had taken from the *Wheatley* crew, it was theirs now. Sacrificing a team of Spartans would do nothing to solve the mystery. "And ammo up. We may be shooting our way into orbit."

A line of LEDs flashed green. John turned and began to power through the tangle of hooked thorns, following the waypoint on his HUD, ripping a new passage straight through—

The air went white. The sky went white. *Everything* went white. The thicket vanished in a flash and the pressure wave hit him from behind, blowing him forward and sending his battle rifle flying.

John tucked into a flip, brought his feet around and stuck the landing, then sprinted over the alluvial fan's still-molten gravel. Far ahead of him, he saw a tiny, delta-winged shadow swooping down over the landslide chute. It was a Pelican, heading for a line of seven marines. Just seven survivors. Damn, that was bad.

The marines were standing two meters apart, their left hands pointing their weapons at the ground, their right hands raised high and holding oversize carabiners.

A squadron of dart-shaped Nandaos was flying close escort above the Pelican, crossing back and forth in a tight diamond-weave pattern, launching air-to-air missiles and cannon fire at anything that so much as turned its nose in the dropship's direction.

Kelly, fast as always, appeared from John's right and raced ahead to take her position at the end of the extraction line. She then simply raised her arm and curled her hand down to form a hook. A Spartan's grasp was stronger than any carabiner.

Fred took the next spot, then Linda, and John last. The Pelican deployed its SPIE line—a long, elastic cable that dangled sixty meters beneath the belly of the craft—and began the retrieval run.

With stiff, half-meter loops every two meters, the SPIE line had its own integrated sensors and AI-controlled fiber-tensioning strands that kept it extended parallel to the ground, just shy of two meters above the surface. As it passed over the waiting marines, it swung down one loop at a time to catch their upraised carabiners, then took the slack out of their harness rigs and jerked them into the air. John saw the first marine rise, followed by the second and the third.

Then the Pelican passed overhead, its thrust nacelles turned downward to hold it in a semi-hover while it was traveling so slowly. John heard the big nose cannon chugging as it opened fire on something behind him, but he didn't dare turn to look. The SPIE line would do its best to adjust to any inadvertent movements on his part, but the loops only had so much play. If he pulled his hand out of the way, the Pelican would either have to leave him behind or make a very risky second run to retrieve him.

The seventh and last marine was lifted into the air, and John was glad to recognize Sesi Cacyuk as she sailed by overhead. Then the line caught Kelly and Fred, sagging ever so slightly beneath the weight of their Mjolnir. Linda rose next. Finally John heard the loop chime against the armor on the inside of his wrist.

He brought his hand down to his breast and felt the loop slip into place in the crook of his elbow; then the ground vanished from beneath his boots, and he felt the SPIE line starting to swing as the Pelican accelerated and turned away from the combat zone.

Being at the end of the line, he was in for a wild ride. About sixty meters below and behind the Pelican, he swung out over the basin in a wide, sweeping arc. The dropship's greatest vulnerability at this point was to a surface-to-air attack, so John kept a careful watch on the ground. And he did not understand at all what he was seeing.

Where the *Lucky Break* had sat parked a short time before, there was now only the shallow, glass-bottomed crater typical of a big plasma strike. Next to the crater stood eight unarmored Elites, staring up at the departing Pelican trailing its long line of dangling soldiers. The aliens' mandibles were splayed wide in rage . . . or maybe it was laughter. Given what little John knew of their species, it could have been anything.

As the Pelican straightened its course and turned toward the mountains, John swung around again. He found himself looking toward the long plateau that he and his fellow humans had traversed in their futile attempt to capture a Covenant frigate.

From this vantage, it did not look like a plateau at all. The face on this side was lined by hundreds of cave openings, all cut in geometric shapes such as trapezoids and diamonds, hexagons and triangles and even an occasional daring crescent, all arranged in neat, diagonal rows that ran from the base of the cliff to the top.

John was looking at a vast, primordial city built by a society that had perished a hundred—or a thousand—or possibly a million—centuries before. Whoever was here had lived and died and never reached the stars, then vanished so completely that no memory of them remained—even on their own planet.

It was the same future the Covenant wished for humanity, John knew—total oblivion, an eradication so complete that any knowledge they ever existed would be wiped from the history of the galaxy. And he had no idea why, could not imagine the cause of such brutal hostility from a civilization that humanity had not even known existed two years ago.

Then the Pelican passed over the cliff and began to climb. With the dropship now safely out of the combat zone, the pilot could fly a steady course, and the crew chief began to retract the SPIE line. John rose in fits and jerks as each soldier above him was drawn into the troop bay and freed from the recovery loops. Far to his left, he saw the bare slope and wrecked Warthogs where the aliens had attacked the *Wheatley* survivors. For a time they flew over the serpentine gorge through which the ancient road ran, a harsh environment Blue Team was fortunate to have traversed in one piece, but which had claimed so many others. The chasm was too deep and dark to see much of anything, but for some reason the pilot slowed and waggled his wings.

Finally they passed over the immense crater and pressure-swept blast plain where the *Wheatley* had stood on its struts only a few hours earlier. There was nothing here anymore, save for a cluster of supply pods that one of the Pelicans must have dropped to lighten its load. Apparently, the salvage ship's self-destruct charge had been detonated as planned—*after* the Castoffs and other survivors had been recovered, John hoped.

Then John was pulled into the troop bay with the rest of Blue Team and First Platoon. The crew chief was a broad-faced woman with rosy cheeks and sparkling green eyes. She closed the belly hatches, then tapped John's helmet and pointed him to one of the seats that lined the cargo bay.

"Take your seat, Master Chief," she said. "It's going to be a rough ride."

John took the assigned seat and waited while the automatic crash harness came down. The Pelican accelerated hard, climbing for orbit. It was only then that he saw the alien corpse, still fully armored, lying in the center of the deck, strapped to the D-rings normally used to secure Mongoose ATVs. The huge Elite that Captain Stocken of Section Three had insisted on recovering looked as though its personal energy shield generator was still attached to its armor and intact.

At least *that* much had gone right.

John felt a pair of eyes on him and looked up. Captain Stocken was smiling at him across the bay.

"You did it, Master Chief." The gray-haired woman jabbed a wrinkled finger at the armored form. "With the technology in that shield generator, ONI finally has a chance to turn this war around. Even though the namesake of this mission didn't make it, *this* could just be the lucky break we've been looking for."

"I hope so, ma'am," John said. "We sure need one."

John didn't add what he was thinking—that if Section Three's lucky break didn't pan out soon, humanity could be done.

Instead, he turned toward the front of the troop bay, where the crew chief sat in her jump seat flanked by—he couldn't quite believe it—Roselle on one side and Samson on the other. Near them sat Lena, Arne, Oskar, and three more Castoffs he didn't recognize.

Lena raised a hand and waved. "Hey, John. I was getting worried about you."

"You were?" John tried not to sound doubtful. "Well, there was no need to. Spartans never die."

"Sure, John." Lena rolled her eyes. "Whatever you say."

John smiled inside his helmet, where no one could see, then turned to the crew chief.

"Chief, I don't mean to tell you your job, but what were you thinking?" He pointed at the alien corpse strapped to the center of the deck. "Bringing an asset like *that* back into a combat zone?"

The crew chief shrugged, as unconcerned as crew chiefs always were by any criticism that didn't come from their pilots.

"No choice," she said. "We lost a bird on the way in, and the other two left the extraction point as soon as they were full."

"The extraction point?" Kelly said. "What about the people I left behind on the road?"

"Back toward the *Night Watch* crash site?" the crew chief asked. "We checked. That's why we were the last bird to the *Wheatley*."

"And?"

"Sorry." The crew chief allowed her gaze to linger on Kelly just long enough to suggest she meant it, then looked back to John. "But that's why the hot line had to be us. We were the only ones that still had seats."

Even packed to the gills, with no equipment or vehicles, a Pelican could hold no more than twenty people. John did the math and quickly realized that at least nine people had been left behind somewhere along the way—and given that their own Pelican still had three empty seats, it was more than that. And the capacity problem couldn't have been at the first extraction point, or there wouldn't be *any* empty seats.

The problem had to have come before the *Wheatley*, somewhere in the gorge. John looked back across the troop bay to Captain Stocken.

"One of the runners didn't make it back to the *Wheatley*," he said. "Why not?"

Stocken shook her head. "I don't know." She looked toward the front of the troop bay, then added, "I was in the first of those mountain runners."

John turned to find Roselle looking apologetic. "Commander Petrov's runner didn't have as much battery power as I thought." She shrugged, then made a dismissive wave toward the dead Elite.

"But there was no way to recharge. We had to dump all of the coal to carry *that* thing."

"But it's okay," Lena said. "She volunteered."

"That's right," Roselle agreed. "I believe I heard her say something about Netherop being a great place for a deep-support operations base."

John looked back to Roselle. "Tell me you *didn't*."

"Didn't what?" Roselle raised her brows and did a decent job of looking innocent. "I am only telling the truth. Ask *her*."

She pointed to the crew chief, who scowled and gave a reluctant nod. "I have no idea what happened in that gorge," she said. "But I managed to contact Commander Petrov on the way to get you."

"And?"

"The commander made it very clear you were the priority," the crew chief said. "In fact, her exact order was, 'Get the Spartans and get the hell out.' "

EPILOGUE

Wearing full dress whites, John-117 stepped into the interior compartment of the Chester W. Nimitz Secure Conference Suite aboard the Battle Group X-Ray flagship, the *Valiant*-class cruiser *Everest*. For once, the overhead was high enough that he had no need to duck, and the bulkheads were lined with holographic images of great military aviators from World War II on Earth. John recognized the portraits of Jimmy Doolittle, who launched a B-25 off an aircraft carrier to bomb Tokyo, and Lilya Litvyak, who was the Soviet Air Force's first female ace. He made a point of standing a little straighter in their presence, rising to his full height as he moved to the end of a conference table surrounded by FLEETCOM brass.

"Master Chief Sierra-117 reporting as ordered."

"At ease, Master Chief."

Vice Admiral Preston J. Cole was seated at the far end of the table, which felt as long as an M512 cannon. To his left sat Dr. Catherine Halsey and to his right was Vice Admiral Michael Stanforth, a hollow-cheeked man who commanded ONI Section Three. All were dressed far less formally than John—Cole in a blue-camouflage working uniform, Stanforth in black ONI utilities with no name or insignia other than the triple stars of a vice admiral on his collar tips. Halsey wore her customary lab coat over gray utilities. They watched him with relaxed expressions, which made John think he had overestimated the gravity of the proceedings when he received a summons to provide "clarification" for a Court of Inquiry.

To Stanforth's right sat a puffy-cheeked lieutenant from the UNSC's Judge Advocate General Corps in blue service dress bearing the nameplate J. STONE on its breast. Across from him was a hazel-eyed woman with red hair and a thin nose, also in blue service dress. Her nameplate read B. NETT, and on her collar tips she wore the golden oak leaves of a lieutenant commander. Seated between her and Dr. Halsey, wearing plain blue working uniforms without insignia or rank, were the Castoffs Samson and Roselle. They were slouched in their chairs, looking out of place and uncomfortable, doing their best to seem bored. But John could tell by the couple's pale complexions that the proceedings were scaring them to death. They glanced at John without seeming to recognize him. It was the first time they'd seen him without his armor, so maybe they thought he was just one more UNSC giant.

Cole gave John an understanding nod, then said, "Thanks for making the trip over from the *Kayenta*, Master Chief. I'm advising you that this *is* a formal proceeding, but nobody's career is at stake here." He shot a reassuring smile toward Samson and Roselle. "And nobody is at risk of confinement."

Roselle rolled her eyes, and Samson glared.

Cole pretended not to notice. Whether or not the pair realized it, the inequality in the ranks of the two JAG officers sitting across from each other suggested that the admiral had seriously stacked the deck in favor of the two castaways—and John liked him even better for that.

Cole continued, "We're just trying to establish what went wrong with the operation—"

"Pardon me, Admiral, but that's an unfair characterization," Dr. Halsey interrupted. "There may have been a lot that didn't go as planned for us, but clearly this was a Covenant trap—perhaps to capture some of my Spartans—and we denied them their objective. Morever, we still recovered a vital piece of Covenant technology. That personal shield generator is of a type we've never even seen before."

"Which I'm sure will yield some useful battlefield technology in a few years," Cole said. "If we can last that long."

Stanforth spread his palms. "We have to start somewhere, Preston."

"I know." Cole sighed and nodded to Halsey. "My apologies, Doctor. It's just hard not to be in a hurry. Worlds are falling like dominoes."

"Oh, I *am* in a hurry, Admiral," Halsey replied. "Be assured of that."

"I've no doubt, but that has nothing to do with this inquiry." Cole turned back to John. "The reason *you're* here, Master Chief, is that we need to confirm—"

"You said *establish*," Stanforth interrupted.

"*Ask* you about some events that occurred—"

"That *may* have occurred," Stanforth corrected.

Cole exhaled in exasperation, then finished, "On Netherop."

Stanforth's gaze shifted to John and remained there. As the

not-so-secret commander of ONI's Section Three, he was more or less the man who controlled the fate of the entire SPARTAN-II program. If he decided to pull the plug, that was it. The same if he decided to replace John as the squad leader or declare that his armor should be battlefield pink.

And he was making his expectations pretty damn clear.

Stanforth gestured to the JAG lieutenant. "Lieutenant Stone is here to represent the interests of the marooned."

"Excuse me, Admiral," said the thin-nosed JAG woman, Lieutenant Commander Nett. "That hasn't been established. From what Samson and Roselle tell me, Commander Petrov *volunteered* to remain on Netherop."

Stanforth glared at her and she gave it right back to him. John liked her already.

"Lieutenant Stone, we'll start with you." Cole gestured toward John. "Proceed."

Stone turned toward John. "Spartan, uh, One-One-Seven, I guess . . . did Commander Petrov ever suggest to you at any time that it might be better for the mission to leave the castaways on Netherop so you and the other UNSC personnel could escape with the personal shield generator recovered by Captain Stocken?"

"She did."

As soon as John spoke, Samson's eyes bulged and Roselle's jaw dropped.

"Wait! *You're* John?" Roselle might not have known him without his helmet on, but she certainly recognized his voice. "You're just a kid!"

John smiled. "Don't let the smooth skin fool you," he said. "I'm older than I look."

It wasn't a lie—not really.

"Are we done with the reunion?" Stone asked. "Because I'd like my question answered: Did Commander Petrov ever suggest to you that it might be better to leave—"

"My apologies, sir," John said. He wasn't going to let the lieutenant ask the question twice. "That's correct, sir. She did."

"And what was your response?"

"That I thought it probably violated the Uniform Code of Military Justice or the Colonial Administration Authority Laws of Deep Space."

" 'Or something,' you also said?' " Stone asked. "Do I have that quote correct?"

"That's right."

John wondered if Stone had been given access to his Mjolnir's onboard computer data, because the guy knew things he shouldn't . . . unless, of course, Stanforth had arranged for a temporary security clearance. It didn't matter, because John had no intention of lying— but he would need to be careful about shading the truth.

"I felt certain that *some* law would apply under the circumstances," John continued. "I just didn't know which one."

"I see." Stone turned to Cole. "Let the record show that in time of war, no such law *would* apply. Commander Petrov's suggestion was completely in line with all applicable standards of conduct."

"So noted," Cole said.

Stone turned back to John. "Now, Master Chief, is it possible that one of the castaways, perhaps Ms. Roselle here or a minor in her care, overheard this discussion?"

The guy was smarter than he looked.

"I have no way of knowing what they overheard."

"I asked if it was possible," Stone said.

"As I said, I don't know, sir," John answered. He saw Stanforth watching him, but it didn't matter. He wasn't going to lie for anybody. "We were in the middle of a battlefield. People were dying and calling for help. Roselle was a long way uphill, and I was concerned about being strafed by Covenant attack craft. So, sir, that's what I mean when I say, *I don't know.*"

Stone's face reddened. "Would it surprise you to hear—"

"The Master Chief has answered the question," Nett said. "There's no reason to badger him."

"I quite agree," Cole said. "You may proceed, Commander Nett."

"Thank you, Admiral." Nett turned to John. "Now, Master Chief, was there a time when you asked the castaways to assist—"

"Wait," Stone said. "I wasn't finished. We need to establish whether Commander Petrov was deliberately marooned."

"She *volunteered*," Cole said. "That was established when the Pelican's crew chief told us about her order to collect the Spartans and—I quote—'get the hell out.'"

"Sir," Stone said, "Respectfully, Commander Petrov wasn't aware at the time that her marooning would be permanent."

"*Permanent?*" John thought he might have some trouble picking up his jaw from the floor thanks to this bombshell news. "I thought she wanted to establish a deep-support base on Netherop."

"She may have *wanted* to," Stanforth said, "but the Covenant rendered that idea moot. They've seeded the entire planet with orbital mines. We can't even get a drop pod through now."

John's gut sank. That was definitely the last thing he had expected. "How about messages? She needs to know that we saw Covenant operatives being left behind as we extracted. They could still be active on the planet."

"We've tried," Stanforth said. "There's no way to know whether she's received any of our transmissions. But if she has, rest assured that she's going after them. Petrov is as tough as it gets. The Covenant is in for one hell of a fight."

"I agree, sir," John said, still reeling from the surprise. "This is the last thing I expected to hear."

"So you can see how this changes her circumstances," Stone said, seizing his opening. "If Commander Petrov was tricked into being marooned—"

"Lieutenant—*enough*. She volunteered," Cole said. "I *said* that was established, and all the unforeseen circumstances in the galaxy won't change that fact." He nodded to Nett. "Please continue, Commander."

Stone sank back in his chair, fuming. Stanforth glared at John, and John wished more than anything right now to be wearing his helmet and reflective faceplate.

Nett asked, "Master Chief . . . was there a time when you asked the castaways to support Linda-058 during a combat operation?"

"The details are classified, ma'am," John said. "But, yes, I can confirm the request."

"And the request was honored?"

"Yes, ma'am."

"At great personal peril?"

"I would assume so, ma'am," John said. "I wasn't there, but the evidence suggests that was the case."

"I understand." Nett turned to Cole. "And what did you promise in return?"

Stanforth leaned forward. "It doesn't matter what he promised. A Master Chief is still an enlisted rank, and enlisted ranks don't have any authority to make promises on behalf of the UNSC."

Roselle turned to glare at John, and John began to understand why Stanforth was trying to pressure him. The Castoffs had clear insurrectionist sympathies, and given what they had learned about Spartan capabilities, Stanforth would not be eager to let them out of ONI's control.

Understandable, but it didn't matter.

Cole nodded to John. "Go ahead and answer the question, son."

Son. But finally, from someone who was worthy of saying it. "Yes, sir." John turned back to Nett. "I promised them a *Sharpfin* escort corvette—"

"A *Sharpfin*?" Stanforth gasped. "Are you out of your mind?"

"I'm sure we can find one somewhere," Cole said. "What else, Master Chief?"

"That the UNSC would take them to any planet they wanted to live on," John said. "Even if it was insurrectionist-controlled."

Stanforth turned to Cole. "You see the problem, right?"

"Settle down," Cole said. "We don't even know that there's a problem yet."

Stanforth turned to Samson. "Tell us where you want to live."

It was Roselle who answered. "We want to live on Gao," she said. "We have heard that Gao is a free world."

Cole winced, and John knew why. Gao was practically in full rebellion—even *with* the Covenant invasion starting to turn toward its sector of space.

"I'd say we have a problem now, wouldn't you?" Stanforth asked Cole. "Gao is Hector Nyeto's home planet."

John's teeth clenched at the mere mention of the man's name. The former commander of a prowler wing, Hector Nyeto was a traitor and insurrectionist mole. Just a few months earlier, he had done his best to get John and eleven other Spartans killed during the Spartans' first big operation against the Covenant. After being exposed, Nyeto had escaped with three *Razor*-class prowlers, and he was now believed to be hiding in the Gao jungles, beyond ONI's immediate reach.

Still, John couldn't conceal his astonishment, and Dr. Halsey actually slapped her brow. Only Lieutenant Commander Nett seemed unfazed.

"So what?" Nett said. "Assume that Nyeto *is* on Gao. All that really means is that the Gao insurrectionists *already* know about the

SPARTAN-II program. What harm can come of letting Samson and Roselle settle their people there? Whatever Netherop's castaways know about Spartans, surely it pales in comparison to Nyeto's intel."

"In comparison to what Nyeto *did* know." Stanforth's tone was mild, but he did not sound like a man on the verge of yielding. "There have been advances since then."

"Really?" Nett asked. "You're suggesting that people who've been cooking over open fires and digging for water for three generations are going to understand those advances? After spending less than a day with the Spartans? Are you serious?"

Stanforth shook his head. "We can't know what they understand."

"I think we can. But, if it makes you feel better, I'm sure Samson and Roselle would promise not to reveal anything they've learned about the Spartans." She turned to Roselle. "Right?"

"Sure." Roselle nodded enthusiastically. "If John keeps his promise, we'll keep ours. No one will ever hear anything from us about John and his giant friends. You have our word."

Stanforth looked at the ceiling, but Cole was not so quick to dismiss the offer.

"Well, John?" he asked. "Can we trust them?"

John didn't even have to think about it. The Castoffs were as shifty as a valley breeze, but once they'd made a deal with him, they had risked their lives to honor it. And if he couldn't behave just as honorably after giving his word . . . well, then, what was he even fighting for?

He turned his gaze toward Samson and Roselle and held their eyes until he received a subtle nod from each of them, confirming that this was a deal between just the three of them and not the UNSC, and then he looked back to Cole.

"On this, you can trust them," John said. "If they say they won't talk about me or the Spartans, then they won't. I'm sure of it."

"Very well. It's decided then." Cole turned to Samson and Roselle. "We'll get you to Gao as soon as we can find a way to do it that won't cause another war."

"With our *Sharpfin*?" Samson asked.

"Absolutely," Cole said. "Just as soon as we can locate one."

"Not so fast." Stanforth raised a finger. "There's one thing I want to make clear."

"Clear is good," Samson said. "We like clear."

"We have assets on Gao," Stanforth said. "We hear things. And if we hear so much as a whisper about *anything* that happened on Netherop, we'll hunt you down and put a stop to those rumors. Permanently."

Roselle was unfazed. "You won't hear any whispers from us. We won't betray John." She braced her arms on the table and leaned forward. "But for a man in your job, you're a very bad liar. If you could reach someone on Gao, this Nyeto fellow you all seem so concerned about would already be dead."

Stanforth's eyes flashed, and John thought for a moment that Roselle had just blown the deal. Then the admiral chuckled, leaned back in his chair, and let out a full-throated laugh.

"Fair enough, Ms. Roselle." He stood and reached across the table, offering her his hand. "We have a deal."

Roselle stared at his hand for a moment, then reluctantly accepted it. "*Don't* make us regret this, Admiral. You wouldn't enjoy it if we had to hunt *you* down."

Stanforth's smile broadened. "I appreciate the warning, Ms. Roselle." They shook, then he turned to Nett. "I think we're done here, Commander. Dismissed."

Nett smiled, then rose and touched Roselle and Samson on the arms. "If you'll come with me, I'll escort you back to your compartments."

Samson seemed bewildered. "We won?" he asked, rising. "In a *UNSC* court?"

"Court of Inquiry," Cole corrected. "There's a difference. But, yes . . . you won. You can thank the Master Chief."

Nett was already escorting the pair around John's end of the table.

When they stopped, Roselle said, "Thank you, John." She took both of his hands in hers, then said, "You will come and see us, yes?"

"Count on it," John said. "But maybe not on Gao. The last thing anyone needs right now is another war."

**Ninth Age of Reclamation
47th Cycle, 110 Units (Covenant Battle Calendar)
Cave of Eternal Reflection, City of Darkness
Planet N'ba, Eryya System**

In the wadi below, a woman sat alone in N'ba's long night, roasting plant pads over an open fire. Her thin face was framed by a tangled mat of blood-brown hair, and her weary eyes never seemed to leave the skewers she occasionally turned over the low flames.

How long the woman had been sitting there, Nizat 'Kvarosee could not say. He knew only that she had come in the darkness and built her fire, and in the time he had been watching her, she had filled ten large bags with the roasted plant pads. The process might have taken her two units or twenty—Nizat could not tell, and he no longer cared. Time on N'ba had become eternal, day followed by night in endless repetition, light and darkness and light again with no meaning and no escape.

And how could there be?

To escape was to flee, and it would be folly to do so when it came to the will of the gods. They had taken Nizat from his beloved Sanghelios, from his clan and his hereditary keep, and placed him here on N'ba for a purpose. If he could no longer see that, then it was he who had been blinded, not they.

The one thing that Nizat *did* know about the woman was that she had arrived with the humans who had come to capture the *Steadfast Strike*. She could not have arrived after that. To prevent Nizat from being rescued by the return of a loyal captain, the Silent Shadow would have placed a shell of self-directing plasma torpedoes in orbit around the planet. This was what Nizat himself would have done, and he had good reason to believe it was what they had done. Since the Fleet of Swift Justice's departure, he had seen five fireballs plunge from the sky.

Nizat knew with certainty that none of those fireballs had been the *Quiet Faith*. The vessel's shipmaster, Qoo 'Weyodosee, was too timorous to mount a rescue operation beneath the watchful eyes of the Silent Shadow. Instead, he would gather more vessels to his cause, then activate the Luminal Beacons and attempt to win the forgiveness of the Hierarchs by destroying ONI.

And in his success lay Nizat's sole hope of redemption. If 'Weyodosee prevailed, the gods would see that it was only through Nizat's planning and inspiration, and surely they would absolve him of his past mistakes and welcome their loyal servant back onto the Path of Divine Transcendence. Given 'Weyodosee's habitual timidity and customary lack of boldness, that was a small hope indeed, but it was better than none at all. In his current circumstances, hope was all that remained to Nizat.

Hope and faith.

Nizat's contemplations were interrupted by the arrival of Tam 'Lakosee. Like all the Sangheili marooned on N'ba, the faithful steward had grown as gaunt as a skeleton, and his skin had turned ashen and scaly. 'Lakosee dropped to his haunches next to Nizat and stared down into the wadi where the woman had made her fire.

"We must make our move, Worldmaster," 'Lakosee whispered. "It will be light soon, and we will lose our advantage."

Nizat continued to watch the woman. She wore a sidearm on her hip, and a long gun leaning against a nearby boulder was never far from her reach.

After a moment, Nizat whispered, "How do you know?"

"That we will lose our advantage?"

"That it will be light soon."

"Because it has been dark for a long time."

"*How* long?" Nizat pressed. "Here the darkness is interminable, and we have no way to count units. So, I ask again—how do you *know*?"

'Lakosee's tone grew harsh. "We know because we are hungry. Do you not feel it?"

"Ah." Nizat continued to watch the woman. If she had heard 'Lakosee's outburst, she showed no sign and continued to turn her spits. "So the gods have sent us this human because you are hungry?"

"The gods or fate, I do not care," 'Lakosee said. "We are hungry, and we need weapons and water bladders. She can provide for all of those needs."

"Perhaps," Nizat said. "But I cannot help wondering what *she* needs in return."

"Why do you care?"

"Because if she was truly sent to us by the gods, the last thing we should do is misuse their gift."

"And if she was sent to us by fate?"

"Never trust in fate," Nizat said. "It is an excuse for poor thinking."

'Lakosee clacked his mandibles in frustration. Still the woman did not look up.

"We are hungry, Worldmaster. There is not much meat on her bones, but there is some. If you will not join us, we will—"

"Tell me, Tam: How many plant pads can one woman eat?"

"Those are teardrop pads," 'Lakosee said quickly. "If you roast them, they will keep for a long time."

"True." Nizat paused, then asked, "And how many bags of teardrop pads can one woman carry?"

"Not . . . ten." 'Lakosee fell silent, then finally said, "Perhaps we should watch her for a while longer. She may have companions hiding in the dark."

"A worthy thought," Nizat said. "And while we wait, perhaps we will see the gods' true purpose in sending us this gift."

"It pains me to say it . . ." 'Lakosee sank to his knees. "But I often worry that our gods have forsaken us."

"As do I, Tam." Nizat laid a hand on his steward's shoulder. "And so . . . I pray."

ACKNOWLEDGMENTS

I would like to thank everyone who contributed to this book, especially: my first reader, Andria Hayday; my editor, Ed Schlesinger; our copyeditor, Joal Hetherington; our proofreader, Susan Rella; Jeremy Patenaude, Tiffany O'Brien, Jeff Easterling, and all of the great people at 343; and cover artist Christopher McGrath. It's been a blast!